ALSO BY SENA JETER NASLUND

Adam & Eve

Abundance, A Novel of Marie Antoinette

Four Spirits

Ahab's Wife; or, The Star-Gazer

The Disobedience of Water

Sherlock in Love

The Animal Way to Love

Ice Skating at the North Pole

THE FOUNTAIN OF ST. JAMES COURT

or, Portrait of the Artist as an Old Woman

THE FOUNTAIN OF ST. JAMES COURT

or, Portrait of the Artist as an Old Woman

SENA JETER NASLUND

WILLIAM MORROW

An Imprint of HarperCollins*Publishers*

THE FOUNTAIN OF ST. JAMES COURT; OR, PORTRAIT OF THE ARTIST AS AN OLD WOMAN. Copyright © 2013 by Sena LLC. All rights reserved. Printed in the United States of America. No part of this book may be used or reproduced in any manner whatsoever without written permission except in the case of brief quotations embodied in critical articles and reviews. For information address HarperCollins Publishers, 10 East 53rd Street, New York, NY 10022.

HarperCollins books may be purchased for educational, business, or sales promotional use. For information please e-mail the Special Markets Department at SPsales@harpercollins.com.

FIRST EDITION

Designed by Lisa Stokes

Library of Congress Cataloging-in-Publication Data has been applied for.

ISBN 978-0-06-157932-5

13 14 15 16 17   OV/RRD   10 9 8 7 6 5 4 3 2 1

For *Lucinda Dixon Sullivan*, friend

"I could tell you my adventures—beginning from this morning," said Alice a little timidly: "but it's no use going back to yesterday, because I was a different person then."

—*Alice's Adventures in Wonderland,* chapter 10, "The Lobster Quadrille"

The passion for painting was innate in me. This passion has never failed, perhaps because it has always increased with time; even today, I experience all its charm, and I hope that this divine passion ends only with my life.

—Élisabeth Vigée-Le Brun,
Souvenirs de Madame Louise-Élisabeth Vigée-Le Brun, tome 1, lettre 1

CONTENTS

THE FOUNTAIN OF ST. JAMES COURT
or, Portrait of the Artist as an Old Woman

I
MIDNIGHT
Crossing the Court

FOUNTAIN

NO MATTER IT WAS ALMOST MIDNIGHT, she would deliver her manuscript herself. (A lopsided moon hunched high overhead.) She hesitated between the fluted columns of her porch—it was dark, it was late, it was chilly—and prepared to make her way carefully down the semicircular steps toward the fountain.

In the crook of her arm, she cradled the printout of her new book, swaddled in a large white envelope. Warmth from the just-minted pages passed through the envelope and through the gray sleeve of her sweater to her forearm. The envelope's flap stood open and the manuscript murmured to its author, *Alive, a-live, O!*

Her manuscript's small, assuring voice might have provided a descant to the cascade rushing over the brim of the fountain's high chalice, but the falling water brooked no song but its own. By night, by day, the fountain—surmounted by a sculpture of Venus rising from the sea—was preeminent on St. James Court. A bronze scarf billowed around the figure's back and modestly covered her loins in front. Whether the fountain waters sang of dark midnight or of its own well-illumined being, Kathryn was unsure.

A waist-high wrought-iron fence bounded the fountain's wide receiving pool and around that encircled a collar of vivid, fine-bladed grass. Like the manuscript she held in her arm, the grass aspired to assert its right to live, though October 2012 was moving fast toward the colder weather of November with its discouraging frost.

Under the gibbous moon, a few bright windows shone among the Victorian houses of St. James Court, along with a scattering of dim porch lights. Old-fashioned gas lamps—set at a height that a man on a short ladder might have reached—flickered around the edges of a two-block swath of wide, grassy median. In a circular break in the green, the illumined fountain and its falling waters suggested a lantern emanating a golden haze. *If I were a moth,* Kathryn thought . . . *But the fountain is not a lantern, and I am not a moth.*

She began the descent from her porch, her eyes fixed on the figure of Venus. Moonlight from above and beams from underwater spotlights wove a cocoon of light around the goddess. Yes, at night the emblem of love and beauty shone like a bright candle.

Not a moth, not a moth, yet Kathryn had written something about moths in her book, and they had escaped to flutter about her head. Perhaps she *was* a moth, or had been a moth, to the bright ideal of marriage—or was it to the purifying ritual of divorce?

Kathryn glanced down at the warm bundle she carried in the crook of her arm. While her manuscript, titled *Portrait of the Artist as an Old Woman,* was based on the eighteenth-century French portrait painter Élisabeth Vigée-Le Brun, the book had promised its author to be a looking glass— albeit streaked, clouded, and freckled by imagination—in which the author might glimpse revelatory images of herself. Though almost old, Kathryn Callaghan still hoped to learn from her mistakes.

She paused behind the fountain to regard the backside of Venus: the rush of water falling in a perfect circle from the rim of the chalice, the high spurting jets, and the swaying of the dimpled surface of the pool. Her novel was done; there was no need for Kathryn to rush as she crossed the Court; she could linger to reassure herself with the fountain's achievement of beauty and to partake of its endless energy.

What did it signify, after all, this historical novel she was calling *Portrait of the Artist as an Old Woman*? Perhaps something about *loss* and the self-serving mirror image of loss named *gain*?

But did anyone want to read about an old woman? About an artist, living or dead? Of course Ernest Hemingway had managed very well with his short tale *The Old Man and the Sea*. And then, James Joyce's portrait of an artist—admittedly male, and young to boot—had dominated creative imaginations for a hundred years.

Recently divorced, this, the third time, Kathryn felt vulnerable, a creature emerging from the snug walls of her library into damp, autumnal realities. Tonight, especially, her skin felt raw, abraded by the backwash of divorce. She pulled her sweater a little closer to her body. At midnight, October air in Louisville was predictably damp and chilly, she told herself—not an omen. Was it possible Élisabeth Vigée-Le Brun's sustaining knowledge— she had lived, mostly happily, to age eighty-five—had been about neither loss nor gain but about some other nebulous abstraction? Something about *love*? Or *art*? Like dimly lit windows in the distance, ideas caught the edge of her attention for a moment, then winked out.

Her discontinuous thoughts were displaced by a long-wished-for fact, a flare of joy from the center of herself: Kathryn's nearly lifelong friend, soon to be the manuscript's first and most astute reader, had recently moved onto St. James Court. Yes, this midnight mission was to deliver her manuscript to Leslie. For the first time since Kathryn's Alabama childhood, friendship could be accessed just across the street.

In that fact was cause to remember the warmth of bonfires of autumn leaves, such as people used to burn in Montgomery in the street gutters running in front of their homes. Kathryn relished a remembered whiff of their bitter, smoldering aroma. Now Leslie, born in Montgomery (as Kathryn had been) but lately of New York City, had moved to this neighbor-hood, Old Louisville. Leslie! who often called her Ryn. Even at midnight a person could cross safely over St. James Court, could relish the light of a waxing moon, the golden nimbus of a beautiful fountain. This crossing was not in order to visit—too late for that—but just to leave her manu-script at Leslie's door.

As Kathryn considered the cascading waters of the fountain, she fin-gered the thick edge of the stack of pages within the yet-open envelope and made a wish, not for herself but for her newborn novel: *be accessible.*

Accessible. It was a word that needed to stand in the middle of the street and pant ecstatically for its own breath.

Be as accessible (as *beautiful?* as variously *meaningful?*—how much did she dare wish?) *as this fountain,* giving pleasure in myriad ways to anyone who might regard it. Be accessible, my *Portrait,* she breathed.

PORTRAIT

MY DAUGHTER, LITTLE JULIE, and I stand amazed on our own Rue du Gros-Chenet, for we have been accused of happiness by a Paris fishwife. Years later, standing in the spring woods of my country retreat at Louveciennes, I am remembering not only the season and year that fall of 1789 but also the street clatter and the iron odor of revolution hanging in the Parisian air. The resemblance of this old woman's accusing finger to her nose terrifies Julie. Her young eyes dart back and forth between those reddish, twin grotesqueries, from knobby nose to joint-swollen finger, and back to nose. Then my little girl turns from the angry woman, closes her eyes, and burrows her own sweet nose and face into the folds of my skirt. My small daughter hides herself in me.

The Parisian fishwife points at me, smacks her toothless gums, and accuses, *"C'est l'artiste!*

"She's the artist, the painter," she rants on, accusing me. "The queen's favorite. Her favorite, night and day."

With shielding hand, I press my daughter's head closer against my thigh, and Julie, with the thumb and forefinger of each hand, pinches up the ample fabric of my green baize skirt and draws it around the back of her head, the better to hide. Her small, vulnerable back and the waterfall of her little skirt are clear evidence of her presence.

In that moment, I embrace again not only my daughter but the idea that she and I must abandon Paris—soon. Hiding will not suffice. Tomorrow perhaps, during October of this most dreadful year 1789, or soon, we must try to escape while it is still possible to escape. But exactly which day and how soon? We have tickets for the next day on the common stagecoach, but I am not yet convinced we will be on it. I ask myself again, *Must I leave my studio, my home, my friends, my country; life, as I have lived it? This home, this neighborhood, has defined me.* And my resolution to escape with Julie hitches and stumbles.

Close to where we stand, the rumble of carriage wheels over cobblestones covers the old fishwife's other curses, but a taller, younger woman, pitifully thin, has brought her similar long nose—perhaps *they* are mother and grown daughter—and stinking breath to my face. Perhaps she is drawing near to bite my cheek. The emaciated younger mother hisses, "I'd like to eat your rosy little girl. Feed her to my brood. Limb by limb."

I feel her desperation, and I feel again the shudder of Julie's little body pressed against mine, in Paris, on Rue du Gros-Chenet. Remembering, I shudder now, many decades later, standing alone in the beautiful wood of Louveciennes. Through the fabric of my thin spring dress, I press the flat of my hand against my aged thigh. Not the tender cheek of little Julie but only my old hand. I am eighty-five, and it is only my own hand that keeps company with my thigh.

Perhaps that starving mother did not say this. Perhaps, being so very old now, in Louveciennes (for it is spring 1841), I only *remember* October 1789 that way. Even now I am haunted by the Revolution.

Fifty-two years have passed, and I, in my mid-eighties, stand still, a living statue, here in the center of gentle nature, her green folds falling softly away from me, wherever I gaze, and spring is a lime-green dress, woven of myriad fine threads. *No harm, no harm, no harm* is the song hummed in the woods of Louveciennes by every leaf, bud, and grass blade surrounding me. *We only live.* Is it a crime to live? To create a happiness for yourself, through your own work?

When I return to Paris, wrapped in furs for the winter, there will be no time for such questions. No leisurely lingering among trees, my body caressed by ever-warming air. When I have reclaimed my cozy apartment, that majestic city will glow and shudder around me, forgetting as best she can that blood and fear have swirled about her ankles. My own feet move quickly whenever they address Parisian pavements, and I lift my eyes for consolation to the soaring columns and domes, to the classical and the Gothic, to the tall unfinished twin towers of Notre Dame, and I speed my body to the inner sanctum of the salons of my friends.

In Paris, alarmed, all those many years ago, I told the starving mother and daughter, *"We've* done no harm."

It was a statement I repeated many times in those revolutionary days: wonderingly among my friends, pleadingly to God on my knees at the altar, and reassuringly to myself when I lay rigid with fear in my bed. I say it again, aloud, now, pausing in my morning walk among the trees of Louveciennes, as I believe I did then at the beginning of the Revolution.

"We've done no harm. Not here. Not anywhere. Not in the whole broad world."

With spring-clean ears, the leaves listen, here in the pleasant shade of Louveciennes, where I stand alone, small as a child among tall trees. But my mind visits again that distant moment with Julie, my little daughter, pressed close to my body.

"We love the king, who never did us harm," the ragged old woman self-righteously declares.

Not the king (not till later) but only my friend the queen was the target of their venom. *It is all the queen queen queen the bitch the foreigner . . .*

So long ago. Did I but dream their ugly hatred? Perhaps those haggard women never blew the stench of rotting teeth into my face while my little girl hid in my skirts. When an image is vivid enough, who can question its reality? A portrait, a dream, a fantasy is not the same as a face of flesh, but each may tell a truth that would otherwise be hidden. Perhaps the populace never roared with glee when yet another victim was fed to the guillotine.

They went by the hundreds, my own beautiful friends, lying face-down on that awful sled, relieved of their powdered wigs, like moths to the candle. Some in closed carriages like the king of France, some in an open tumbrel: peasants, tinsmiths, shopkeepers, seamstresses, myriad aristo-crats, the king, the queen of France. Whatever their conveyance from the prisons—from the Tower of the Knights Templar, as came the king, or from the Conciergerie, as came the queen nine months later, or from la Force—they progressed toward a distant flickering of sunlight reflected from a high steel blade.

But do we not all stand in the shadow of a high blade waiting in its scaffolding, so like a doorcase, if we think of it as the image and metaphor for death? Looking up, we know that polished blade is the mirror of our inevitable mortality. That is something we must all face, our mortality, the vulnerability of our ridiculous, once lovable, bodies.

Our bodies are drawn toward death, biologically, as surely as the moth is drawn to the lantern. But during the Revolution, the guillotine was not a lantern, and I was not a moth . . .

FOUNTAIN

I N OLD LOUISVILLE, a puff of air blew a new veil from the cascading water through the railing. The world of Élisabeth Vigée-Le Brun dissipated. Where did it go? Where had it been? In the memory of the author? In pages yet to be read? Absorbed by the froth of the fountain? Into the scarf of air enveloping the globe?

Placing a hand on the iron railing, Kathryn Callaghan lingered behind the figure of Venus and sucked damp October through her nostrils. Then she looked up at the night sky and began (not at all compulsively, she was sure of that, but *necessarily*) to practice the art of revision on the moment she was inhabiting. For the sheer practice of it, she gathered the moment with words, and revised them. *Just before midnight, beneath a wad of moon* (actually, it was just after midnight, not before, but she liked the repeated *b* sounds of *before* and *beneath*). And what shape was this amorphous, in-between-phases, undefined moon? Neither crescent, nor half, nor full. Like a warped egg. Kathryn remembered how Humphrey, her little boy, had loved to hold a wobbly hard-boiled egg in his hand.

Just before midnight beneath a wedge of moon, an author of a certain age scurried across the street encircling the fountain of St. James Court.

Of a certain age, but not of a great age. Nor was Leslie, of Alabama and New York, who would read her book in the morning, of a great age. *No matter it was almost midnight, a writer of a certain age . . . a waxing moon . . .* Less than two weeks ago, Leslie had moved to St. James Court to write and to reclaim her skill as a musician. To reclaim her life. Like Kathryn, she, too, was divorced again. Sad, again. Free, again.

Across the decades, across a street not in Louisville, but in Montgomery, Alabama, Kathryn had seen Leslie for the first memorable time, dressed in a high-waisted green velvet jumper, with soft tucks across the bodice, with starched and ironed short, puffed sleeves, two stiff white balloons, upstanding like little wings. Kathryn would have painted her portrait, if she had had that skill, but Leslie was moving among a group of grown women, maids, all dressed in gray uniforms with their own touches of bright white, symbol and assurance of immaculate cleanliness despite their dusky skins. Leslie's mother and her neighbors were on the move, walking great distances in small groups toward the big white homes where most of them worked, for they were part of the Montgomery bus boycott. They were changing history, that peacefully walking group of gray-clad Negro women, with one vivid young spruce tree, the young girl Leslie, daughter of her mother and of them all, in their center.

From the curb across the street, watching the group in uniform gray but with Christmas green at its center, Kathryn knew she had never seen any child, black or white, so beautifully dressed—like a storybook doll—and later she would learn that Leslie's mother was a seamstress, an alterations lady in one of the department stores, not a domestic, but someone who had her foot in the big world of business, run by men. Leslie's mother sewed in a cubicle beside Rosa Parks, her friend, also a seamstress, known to history as a point person in the peaceful pursuit of civil rights.

The Montgomery street might as well have been the Amazon River that day, full of piranhas, but Kathryn's and Leslie's eyes met, and they would remember, both of them, because it was a momentous day, and when enough legs had walked enough Montgomery miles, to the moon and back, when laws were changed and access became an easier possibility, the girls would meet each other halfway, rebellion in their eyes, dead set against the strictures of the South both as to race and to the national and international subservience of their gender. When Rosa Parks, a woman, had refused to give up her bus seat to a white man, a nonviolent, highly effective revolution had begun.

Later Leslie and Kathryn would see each other across a study table; each would know they were the mirror of the other, eyes lifted from their books for only a moment in recognition, and their long friendship would begin.

Of a certain age but not of a great age, they were now, Leslie and Kathryn. Their own postmodern generation considered over eighty to be a great age! Maybe over eighty-five. Kathryn held as dear friends two other women, Ellen and Letitia, who had seen their ninety-second birthdays, and they were not done. Not done with living and enjoying it. And she remembered another friend, now dead, Ann, whose life was vital till a week before her death at age ninety-five. Approaching mere seventy, yes, Kathryn and Leslie could start over again, both of them, if they needed to. Each held two handfuls of future. They would live their ten greatest years. Maybe fifteen.

Was it only yesterday, just before her diligent plowing ahead to the end of the book, her ninth, that Kathryn had heard her third husband was getting married again? Their fifteen-year marriage not yet cold in its grave? She had determined to postpone thinking about it till she had finished her novel. Thinking of Mark would have been immobilizing. When Mark and she married, Kathryn had only been in her mid-fifties—so young that seemed now. And was his next wedding truly imminent, to be celebrated far away, overlooking Casco Bay, in Maine? What a twinge that marriage news had given her. An arrow to the heart.

Or to the vulnerable heel? (She had thought she was glad to show Mark her heels.)

Last book, #8, thanks to his defection, she had been left struggling not just to write her book but merely to finish sentences, one by one. *Just let me reach the period,* she had prayed to herself. *First this sentence; then another.*

Mark had never finished reading her big, breakthrough novel, published a decade ago and dedicated to him. She had struggled twice through his magnum opus, a treatise on the neurological communication among the corpus callosum, the cerebellum, the medulla oblongata, and all their Latinate subdivisions. (Fortunately, she had taught high school Latin, very young, in Alabama, before her first flight from the South to San Francisco.)

She would not think about his lack of interest in her writing. There was the moon in the midnight sky. Here was another book in her arms. She sought a few bright specks of stars, visible at a distance from the moon. She would name them: Ellen, Letitia, and that faint, more distant one, Ann. *Here's to the brilliance and kindness of old women!*

And one of the stars, visible only to the peripheral vision, yes, let it memorialize Kathryn's mother, dearest of all, whose artistry lay in the musical arts, in the violin and piano. Lila, victim finally of dementia, despite all her brightness, dead at eighty-nine. *Some of our family live a long long time,* she had said to child Kathryn on their open front porch, the new moon hanging in the west, *way on up in the eighties, and even into the nineties.* Was this a fearful prophecy or a reassurance?

Let that most distant, faintest, dearest star be named Lila, she who inhabited vacancies and sailed toward infinities far beyond the midnight sky of Louisville. Ah, that potent word, *let,* the gateway to all possibility— not merely to geometric proofs—to the fluidity of imagination.

October already! And the moon bloated past clean-edged half but not yet full. Vacancies, what were they to bronze Venus? She had surveyed the endless seas. Nestled in water, she indifferently continued her business of being beautiful. With knees slightly bent for balance, she rode her clam-shell. Glistening and wet, sleek as a seal, she stood.

Admire her while you can, Kathryn told herself, for the fountain waters would be turned off in November, usually the drab Monday morning after Thanksgiving. For a moment Kathryn dreaded that day. In the moonlit court, clutching her book, she dreaded even the next day.

What did it mean to live even one day happily?

She felt muted, obscured. She saw the fountain but no one saw her, and so loneliness set in, and she imagined her being was invisible, an evaporation, nothing.

Nothing: long ago she had felt like nothing when Peter had left her and little Humphrey. Strange how the defining envelope of self had melted away. Peter loved someone else, and so she had melted into the air. Being a professor, a mother, a fledgling author had not sustained her. Panic and pain. The bell of her head had rung only those two notes back then. She felt ashamed of herself now for her disintegration; her face flushed.

But shouldn't an author silently evaporate from her own warm pages? The world she had created in *Portrait* had no place for her within it. Kathryn had written the novel using the first person, using the word *I* as though the author had assumed the painter's identity and narrative. Shouldn't an author be subsumed by the voice of the narrative she had created?

Élisabeth Vigée-Le Brun had been a real person, one who also crossed streets—perhaps dodging elegant, horse-drawn carriages and filthy beggars—who heard cries of shopkeepers and vendors, smelling sewage and longing for the scent of roses and jasmine. Like Kathryn, Élisabeth had also feared the loss of a beloved only child—the loss of the child's affections, or, far worse, the loss of the child's life. Kathryn thought of her own son in Sweden, Humphrey, now grown but forever vulnerable.

While Kathryn was writing the book, she became Élisabeth. Standing near carts with heavy, turning wheels, had not Élisabeth thought, *There, let me throw myself there to the god of death, only let my child live safe and happy?*

PORTRAIT

*J*ULIE! I WOULD CALL OUT in the greenwood of Louveciennes and have you, here and now, by my side. If I could. If I called out, I believe you would come, now, if you could. I clasp my old hands together. Sometimes you and I held hands as we walked the streets of Paris, when you were quite small, vulnerable. If I felt color drain from my face, I saw your countenance overcome with blank wonder.

Once you came here to Louveciennes with me when I was to paint a portrait of Madame du Barry. I had painted her twice before but always as though she were an innocent child, with a circlet of pink rosebuds, because she demanded it. She spoke with a childish lisp to endear herself to the old king, the lascivious old Louis XV. It was not becoming. When they carried her to the guillotine, she fought the whole way, screaming, flailing with arms and feet, her whole body resisting with every ounce of strength. Like a furious child being carried off to her bedroom. I do not judge her for that.

They did take children to the guillotine. The children and even grandchildren of Malesherbes. But I took you away to Italy. I saved you that time.

The Académie classifies me appropriately as a portrait painter, not as a history painter. In my paintings I do not net the rush of events, for in a portrait, one makes time stand still. However, there are scenes from history that should be painted and made to hang in the Louvre, for a country needs to look at its shame, to acknowledge and salute it. Gazing at some of the terrible realities of the Revolution, the face of France should be bathed in tears.

Someone should have painted a row of lampposts where bodies dangled by their necks.

And the narrative of Malesherbes—that should have been depicted visually for history. When ancient Malesherbes placed himself before that mockery of justice referred to as the trial of the king of France, Louis XVI, the revolutionary tribunal asked the old attorney how he dared to defend the king. In their monstrous minds, the anointed of God was already tried and found guilty. *How dare Malesherbes defend the king?*

Old Malesherbes thrust his wrinkled face into the judge's face and answered, "Contempt for death, sir, and contempt for you."

Yes, I could almost paint that moment, for it consists of faces, but that is not the bloody scene the Louvre needs most to hang in its stately halls, though his words will surely resound with the last trumpet of Judgment Day. The loyal old statesman, unjustly exiled by Louis XV but volunteering, nonetheless, to serve as adviser to Louis XVI, underestimated the barbarity of the French revolutionaries. Executing the king would not satisfy. Nor would the death of Malesherbes.

The tribunal arrested every member of the family of Malesherbes to be found in France, children and grandchildren, Malesherbes himself, and took them all to the scaffold. Faces, surely not of humans but a vast throng of snarling brutes, assembled to witness the justice of Paris. One by one, children and grandchildren, Malesherbes's entire family mounted the high platform and were fed to the guillotine, saving the old man for last so that he would see the decapitated bodies of every person he loved. Justice! Their heads, young and old, caught in a basket! All? All. Surely he was glad, at the end, to join their number.

The Reign of Terror. For all its horrible, ineradicable vividness, I could paint none of it.

Not even the king and queen in their imprisonment. I could not bear to vivify those moments dishonoring those whom I served and loved.

Those history paintings could only be rendered in shades of blood.

FOUNTAIN

FAINTLY ECHOING FROM THE RECESSES of memory, faintly mingling with the moving waters of the fountain, Kathryn, lingering at midnight, heard—what?—a poet's words (Gerard Manley Hopkins's), about a sky-high bird, a falconlike bird of prey, a windhover. As Kathryn recalled Hopkins's windhover, both the poem and the bird riding the wimpling air, she felt diminished. What had Hopkins admired about the bird?

The achieve of, the mastery of the thing—

Her book was finished, but its achievement was in doubt. She would move on now, cross the Court, deliver the manuscript.

Hesitant step by dreamy pause— What was that glittering on the pavement? It was a broken jar, and it looked dangerous. Very unusual, here in the domain of Venus, for broken glass to be about. Hugging the book pages against her side, Kathryn determined that she loved what she had finished and where she was that moment in time and space. Divorced (and for the third time; her latest ex-husband about to be remarried) though she might be! Let it lie.

"Let it be forgotten . . ." She perversely remembered from high school days a piece of a Sara Teasdale poem. "Let it be forgotten, as a flower is forgotten, / . . . as a hushed footfall / in a half-forgotten snow." But everything in her novel and in her brain rejected the idea of forgetting: let it be remembered. Let it all be remembered. *Portrait of the Artist as an Old Woman,* cradled in the crook of her arm. What does a portrait do but fix a moment in time, for memory's sake?

Even as a child, growing up in Alabama, Kathryn had resisted the vacuum pull of forgetting. Riding in the back of the family car, after a visit to Howard Johnson's Ice Cream 28 Flavors (she knew her father was slowly dying of lung cancer even as he drove the car), she looked back at a crumpled piece of paper they passed, mere trash in the gutter, and vowed to remember. *I will remember even this, forever.*

But she knew, as she aged, that she was forgetting, forgetting nearly everything. Not Alzheimer's. Not that, though the monster, or its kin, had claimed both her mother and her mother's mother. Hers was a less precipitous forgetting—natural, surely, whatever that was. But so much lost. Not that particular emblematic Alabama moment gripped by a desperate girl, daughter of a dying father: a crumpled piece of paper, white, in the streetside gutter, left behind as their car passed on.

With more years than her father had been allowed to accrue, she felt herself a shadow, like a thief in the night, though she could not say what she had stolen. She looked ahead at the condo building where Leslie lived. The *flats,* residents of St. James Court sometimes said, to evoke the British flavor. Mist came like breath of ghosts over the ornate wrought-iron fence encircling the pool.

Boundaries, boundaries, her therapist had taught her after the failure of her second marriage, but she had had to say many times *Explain it again,* so foreign was the concept to her. She had thought morality, goodness itself, lay in having no self-serving boundaries. She regarded the six flats that faced the Court, two stacks of three each, each with its own wrought-iron balcony. What was imagination for except to transcend boundaries?

Now the damp mist placed kisses on the back of her neck, while she stood in its drift. *Bises,* the French would say. She pulled up the hood of her sweater. A block away, the headlights of a car turned off Magnolia to drive slowly south into the Court. And why did Kathryn shudder? What instinct sounded an alarm, unheeded though it was, during that moment devoted to the delivery of her fresh-printed manuscript? Who, the embodiment of menace, might drive back into her life? Who or what did her bones remember? Woolf had written that it was dangerous to live even a single day.

JUST BEFORE MIDNIGHT, safe at home on Belgravia Court, lying on his back, asleep, Daniel Shepard suddenly lifted both arms and slapped them down, hard, on the mattress, as though to break a fall. And he cried out, for he had dreamed he was in the highlands of Vietnam, shot and falling, years and years ago. Of course the force of his movement woke Daisy, fortunately not lying close to him just then.

"Dreaming?" she asked. She had no need to ask about what. "Let's take the dogs out." She sat up. "They'll like it. Just up to the rondelle." A change of scene would break the spell. Actually it was *returning,* coming home with his dogs after being away, that would reassure her husband in a deeply somatic way.

And so they dressed at midnight, casually and quietly—Daisy insisted on light jackets against the night chill. If they didn't walk, Daniel might not sleep till dawn.

The dogs did like the unexpected outing; it made them feel important, sniffing the concrete edges of the sidewalk. Daniel chuckled at their alertness and said they were pretending to be on patrol.

Daisy said, "I want to see what our ginkgo looks like in the streetlight." At both ends of St. James Court, there was a grassy rondelle in the street, each sporting a single ginkgo tree, now uniformly dressed in autumnal gold. And Daisy was right: the golden glow of the streetlight made the golden leaves look thicker, richer. "Like an opera set," she said.

Just then a lone car came too rapidly down St. James; Daniel could hear its urgency. Instead of exiting to Hill Street, the vehicle leaned into a curve to circle the rondelle and return back up St. James. It was an old car and its rattling and wheezing called immediate attention to it; the front passenger door was mismatched. Daniel glanced at the driver and took Daisy's hand. The driver, the back of his head, resembled someone dead, a friend killed in Vietnam, but really, no (that wasn't true), it was the car itself, too heavy, too big, too insistent, that Daniel didn't like. He shuddered.

"It's all right," Daisy said, for she recognized the shudder, very rare now, an unexpected, thorough shuddering. She squeezed his hand, felt the sudden moisture in his palm.

Daniel didn't want to worry Daisy so he tried to say nothing. This was Louisville, not the war. But the shudder had never been wrong. It had fore-warned him during the war, when he was in close proximity to danger, but he wasn't superstitious. Hadn't been, not for decades.

So he said it; he articulated the warning: "That driver is the enemy." When Daisy did not reply, Daniel tried again. "He's up to no good."

They turned back down Belgravia. Even the dogs were satisfied. It was good to be walking home. Daisy glanced back over her shoulder at the ruby taillights of the car. Then, like a stringed instrument sensitive to sympathetic vibrations, she shuddered.

PORTRAIT

OH WHAT A LOVELY DAY . . . here is a woodsy day, wherein I shall pause to paint again the gentle landscape of Louveciennes, in watercolors. And gather mushrooms for the table, for my visitors this evening who are coming out from Paris. My kin. Till nightfall, *what a lovely day,* to wander, gather, paint, enjoy.

But what of Mlle Sombreuil? Unless a history painter seizes the subject, the courage of the daughter of M. Sombreuil, Parisian governor of Les Invalides, will be lost. How might not I but a history painter depict Mlle Sombreuil? If I were painting her within the conventions of portrait painting she would appear as she had at dinner, for in the early days of revolution I was invited to her parents' table so that my nerves might be soothed. *Mlle Sombreuil at Dinner:* a young lady with perfect composure amidst lighted candles and crystal compotes holding oranges and grapes. I see her in profile, and then her head turns to look at me, and she speaks softly.

In those days the atrocities of the Revolution had so invaded my psyche that I became unable to paint. I had also become unable to eat. Kind friends invited little Julie and me to stay with them in apartments near that great bulwark of a building, Les Invalides. Within its substantial domain, I began to feel better.

I could take broth again, and burgundy wine had been given to fortify me. To strengthen my body as well as my spirit, I took walks with my friends beyond the gates and grounds of Les Invalides; I saw that the pavements of Paris had been torn up to form barricades. I heard rough men speak of being paid to threaten the social order. But here among friends, that evening I felt safe. Gates and heavy doors had been locked; the damask cloth was laden with silver and Sèvres porcelain, and candlelight bathed all of us in serene beauty. Those pearls, woven in the hair of the young gentlewoman Mlle Sombreuil, I would have painted so that they gleamed like a row of little moons.

But the subsequent events of history do not allow this portrait to represent the truth. Could not a history artist record the cruelty that the Revolution later dealt her? Artists paint the Crucifixion and their work is displayed with pride; should we not picture and honor mere humans in *their* agony—victims of quieter, less visible acts of horror?

We must see her father, the governor, arrested and thrown in a jail cell, a holding pen for the doomed. He is not alone. His distraught daughter clings to him and covers him with kisses; she pleads with the revolutionaries for her father's life and tears apart her psyche with the passions of anxiety and grief.

Through the hall just outside the door of her father's cell runs a stream of the blood of those already murdered. Waves of blood pulse down the corridor. To block the exit, Mlle Sombreuil braces her own body in the door. Her slender hands curl around the doorposts as though she is hanging on a cross, and she implores heaven for the life of her father. The jailers hesitate and confer among themselves. They have an idea.

One of them dips a cup into the stream of blood, fills the cup to the brim, and says, "Drink it."

She would be painted thus, by a truthful history painter: She stands beside the stream of blood flowing down the corridor of the prison. Her head is tilted up, the communion cup is at her lips, her eyes are closed. With her other hand, she holds the hand of her father, who has averted his eyes. She is drinking human blood. She is saving her father's life. Paint her gown a ghastly white splotched with blood. Paint the crouching darkness and red terror, the human wolves surrounding them. She drinks to the Revolution.

Her father is freed.

Two years later he is arrested again and executed.

FOUNTAIN

A FRENCHMAN, A FRIEND—one to become more than a friend, Kathryn hoped—had mentioned, in one of their lively conversations, that many more had died in the American Revolution than in the French one. She had not said to him, But include the aftermath: Napoleon, war all over Europe, the bitter march into the Russian winter. When she tuned in to his French voice—thoughtful, energetic, pleasantly accented—instead of her own, Yves (pronounced like the name Eve) was going on to say—*unless you're a complete pacifist*. Immediately, she had said, *I am*. She liked the way he excavated an opinion to the bedrock of its worldview. His mind had the tough edge of a scraping device.

Tomorrow evening, Yves was coming to see her, up from Montgomery, the first capital of the Confederacy. About pacifism, she knew she had accidentally lied; she was not *une pacifiste complète* but an incomplete one. If someone violent entered her home, posed a threat to herself or anyone she loved, she would not hesitate to shoot, she knew. But that would not and could not be, not now, not ever again: now grown up, her son was living happily happily far far away. *Love love love . . .*

In her jeans pocket, Kathryn fingered the key that Leslie had lent her when Kathryn had spoken of printing out and delivering her novel that night. She thought, as she fingered the metal of the key, of the trigger of the gun given her months ago by her friend, the long-retired professor Ellen, age ninety-two. The snub-nosed .38-caliber Colt revolver was in its soft gray bag, protected from dust, in a drawer at home. Would she ever feel a need to carry it? Her friend had carried it, at a much younger age, in another city, because, she said, it gave her the freedom to be out at any time. For herself, Ellen had repudiated the culture of fear.

Because Yves was coming for a few days, his first visit, she had labored long to complete the draft. He was a scholar, had written books on Flaubert's *Madame Bovary* and Proust's *Remembrance of Things Past*. That girlish feeling; was that why she had experienced a frisson of fear out alone by herself, had experienced the chill of furtiveness, danger, had remembered she owned a gun, while crossing St. James Court at midnight?

No, it was because the capacity for cruelty, one human to another, existed just as much now as it had during the time of the French Revolution. A marriage could break, a book could fail. The pavement could open and a flame like a dragon's tongue could drag anyone into the underworld.

With *Venus Rising from the Sea* behind her now, Kathryn hurried up the gentle easement between street and sidewalk, across the public sidewalk, up the walkway to the St. James condos. Turning the key Leslie had given her in the front-door lock, she thought, *Strange how the back feels unguarded, if it's night, when one inserts a key in the lock.*

As she climbed up the inner staircase, her imagination ran ahead and tiptoed into Leslie's unit: the beautiful furniture inside, the cocoa-colored walls, the puffy cream chairs, the contemporary ebony-black coffee table sculpted like an arrested wave of lava, slightly menacing—created by an aging woman designer. A silk and wool rug, the wool so fine that it came only from the necks of baby lambs. Spirits would be lounging about, one of

Leslie's characters, her half-real, half-imagined great-grandfather, a share-cropper on a farm in Crenshaw County, Alabama, at Helicon. Wearing worn bib overalls, Leslie's soft great-grandfather, hair like frost on his dark head, would be taking his ease. And there, a three-part Chinese cabinet, standing head high and open like a giant book, with so many drawers and compartments no one could ever remember what was stored here or there. An *analog for memory*, Leslie had explained.

So as to disturb no one real or imagined inside the condo, Kathryn leaned the large white envelope, its flap standing up like a pennant, against her friend's door, and considered what she saw: blue scrawl of writing on a white, rectangular envelope resting against a door: *Read at your leisure.* All of her labor, hours, days, years of writing, had shrunk to this. She placed the envelope near the leading edge of the door. The unsealed white envelope looked comically surreal, an upright fish, open-mouthed, gasping for air.

She bent forward, dropped the shiny borrowed key into the envelope with her pages, pulled the covering strip away from the band of sticky, and pressed closed the seal.

She moved the envelope from near the door's leading edge so that the white packet stood in the exact center of the door—as though its position mattered—and then she turned away.

AS KATHRYN WOUND DOWN the building's interior stairs, a train sounded its long call in the distance. Elongation, a stretching out without letting go. A liminal sound: inside or out? Between. In transition. As she stepped back into the night, her hand trailed behind, her fingertips lingering a moment on the smooth knob. It was hard to leave her manuscript behind—even with Leslie. Again, the distant train exhaled its whistle. Was that the same sound the world over, the sound of a train calling its own name? How its whistle elongated and became part of the night. *Lonesome,* that was the word she wanted—a common, two-syllable word, but none better. A word blown here from the American West by a westerly wind. The train whistle's long yawning was an opening of the unconscious. Without her manuscript, she felt more lonesome.

Quiet city (she quickly recrossed the paved circle), quiet except for the fountain's artificial, ever-rushing rain shower. She glanced south at the lopsided moon, located now over the tops of the oaks. It was autumn and come daylight the Court would blaze with October colors. Hunching her shoulders, she felt a stranger to herself, a distant cousin to the exiled moon.

A leaded, softly illumined fanlight spread wide above her door, and she thought of fanlights over doors in Dublin, left over from the eighteenth century, and of James Joyce. In college, Leslie and Kathryn had loved Joyce's *A Portrait of the Artist as a Young Man,* Leslie more than Kathryn. It had been reported that young Joyce had said to the great poet Yeats, "I regret that you are too old to be influenced by me." Well, here was Kathryn's answer to Joyce, a century later: *Portrait of the Artist as an Old Woman.* Let the world digest that lump, a bronze truth.

Who was the quintessential artist? A rebellious and restless young man egotistically sure of his unforged destiny, or an old woman, Élisabeth, a person whose granary was overflowing with the harvest of her actual achievements? Who loved her life with every breath because it was true to her essence. A woman like Ellen, like Letitia, like Ann, like Lila, her mother. People to be honored and treasured. That was why Kathryn had written a book about a woman who loved her art more than herself, whose life was her art.

She'd left the lights blazing up there in her second-floor library. When Kathryn had hesitated, in the wake of the surprising success of her breakthrough book, about buying this Victorian house on St. James Court, it had been Leslie who said, from a distance, from New York, "You can cradle the little house in the Highlands in your heart, always, if you want, but the house on St. James Court will cradle you."

Perspicacious Leslie had been exactly right.

Above the library, the dormer windows in the mansard roof of the third floor were dark, as always, unless the tenant was entertaining a sighted guest. Janie, the third-floor tenant, was blind. Her separate entrance on the north side of Kathryn's house was originally used as the servants' entrance. It provided Janie with autonomy. Her staircase led all the way to the third floor, though doors on the landings at the first and second levels could and would have accessed the main house when it had been full of late-Victorian bustle: family, visitors, servants; the sounds of horses' hooves and carriage wheels in the Court. Janie and Kathryn were friends.

Before mounting the porch stairs, the fountain behind her now, Kathryn paused to listen to its voice. Perhaps she need not hurry to the silence inside. What was it the rushing water of the fountain wanted to say, about time?

More, more, there is always more.

Kathryn framed her reply: At least till winter comes, and the water is shut off.

But she smiled, pleased to think of the amount of time left. Surely at least ten more good years, maybe fifteen. She spread her ten fingers in front of her, admired the backs of her hands and her fringy fingers. Kathryn was sixty-nine. One of her former creative writing students, now the Kentucky poet laureate, had written a book titled with a relevant but more graceful phrase: *A Sense of Time Left.*

And who are those who leave time altogether? Those with Alzheimer's. Already Kathryn sometimes simply fell into a daze, exiting the moment to enter a timeless place, unaware that mentally she was no longer present. At first it happened only when she was alone in the house, alone after Mark had left. Now, sometimes, if a conversation or a meeting was too prolonged, once even at a movie, her attention had wandered away to an emptiness, a zone lacking even time. This vacancy was not the rich moment embraced and fully lived by Woolf's Mrs. Dalloway or Mrs. Ramsay. Their moments contained everything, were inclusive and consciously realized; they connected everything. Such a moment was the fulsome point from which a universe might expand. Kathryn Callaghan's moments of daze were empty, unconscious, vacuous, isolating, a disconnect, a rabbit hole.

Automatically, at least for now, such a moment would pass; it would resolve itself, and she would quietly return to the present. But suppose someday automatic failed, and there was no return?

Just before she reached her hand out to the door, Kathryn recalled she'd not bothered to lock it, just crossing the Court and coming right back as she was. If Kathryn fell down the rabbit hole, would Humphrey come home to care for her? No. Nor would she ask it. But would she be allowed to stay in this beloved house, the fulfillment and crown of her life of writing and teaching? She doubted that could be arranged either, though sometimes the Victorians had managed to keep a madwoman in the attic.

Her third floor had a lovely view. Enough rooftops to keep a Cézanne busy, and the park treetops, to the north, seemed as pretty as a small woods.

The front door squeaked, and Kathryn began to set the security alarm, but there was something wrong with it. Tired, she slowly climbed the lovely carved staircase, whose spiraling spindles suggested harp strings arrested in a moment of vibration.

Up the heavily padded maroon carpet, so very satisfyingly thick. In the library the chandelier, a circlet of twelve lights festooned with crystals, still blared the brightness she had needed for her work. She slid the rheostat till it dimmed the light to an orange glow, then down to nothing. Lights out, at last, in the library.

Next she passed through a simple open archway from the library into her bedroom and pulled the chain ending in its clear glass marble that hung over the foot of the bed. The ceiling lights went dark. Across the front of the house, the library with its bay and her bedroom with its Palladian window became rooms holding hands in the dark, facing east together, content, ready to rest till morning.

By fountain light shining through the pleated paper window shades, Kathryn removed her sweater and her jeans and her underwear, then quickly pulled a flannel nightgown sprinkled with ruby flowers over her head. After turning back the covers on the king-size bed, she separated the pillows and settled her head into the flat trough between them. She liked to lie perfectly flat, perfectly still, but on each side she pulled the pillows close so that their ends cradled her ears and cheeks. How she had loved, at night, before or after love, to lie with her cheek on Mark's hospitable shoulder. Neither husband #1 (James) nor #2 (Peter, Humphrey's father) had permitted that.

Long ago, until she was sixteen, she had slept with her mother, her head pillowed on her mother's arm. Probably both James and Peter had sensed that fact, resented being asked to play the mother's role. Mark was neither so finely tuned nor so insecure as to notice or mind. He had said he was glad she liked to cuddle. But for her the posture amplified the best of childhood: trust, comfort, the gateway to the realm of unending love.

Gradually, she drifted downward toward sleep, remembering parts of her novel (left leaning patiently against Leslie's condo door) that had seemed good and perhaps beautiful. She smiled. Accessible?

Bed, the homeplace whether shared or not. Home safe. Fatigue was the gateway to rest. Tonight her mind was full of gates, one thing opening into another. After the excitement of completing the draft, it was hard to relinquish her hold on consciousness. Why not think and think: it was such a pleasure, when traveling in the right direction.

Only slightly awake, she imagined a letter she might write to Humphrey, far away in Sweden. *Humphrey.* Or had she imagined herself inside the mind of Humphrey and the letter he would write to her? Some of both. Wasn't imagination a revolving door between the outer and the inner, the other and the self?

How splendid it would be to receive a congenial e-mail from Humphrey.

> *Sometimes I think we are surrounded by the shadows of other selves.*
> *Shadowed, perhaps, by the potential of other, unrealized parts of either*
> *our brighter psyches or our darker parts (usually well repressed and*
> *made obscure so that we can live with—tolerate—whom we appear*

to be, both to ourselves and other people), we are truly never single or singular. Hovering brightly in our periphery, there is the shadow self of hope and of our belief in who we will be tomorrow. Not a belief in what we may accomplish but of some definition of our quintessence. Action, accomplishments, exist or they do not exist in the world, but essence? Well, it can be whiffed, at best, and then it's gone. It evaporates into the air; it may step out of our bodies to run ahead of us, waiting, perhaps around the sharp corner of a skyscraper, or it stumbles down a rabbit hole and leaves us to plod on. Shadow selves may be forever young while we age. I am speaking not of past selves but of something more nebulous, of the potential selves that live within us unborn till we die.

The dual sense of *I*, sometimes herself, sometimes Humphrey, dissipated. Humphrey was in Göteborg and Kathryn in Louisville.

ABOUT THREE IN THE MORNING, Kathryn got up sleepily to use the toilet. She had trained herself to move slowly and carefully. No need to take a fall, break a hip. To ensure balance, her hands automatically met the habitual handholds; her left hand found the rounded corner, cheek high, of the maple chest of drawers; the fingers of the right hand recognized the frame of the door leading to the bathroom; her left hand located the stamped-metal doorknob; then her right hand touched the smooth basin of the pedestal sink. She seated herself. (Outside, out of sight, to the north and to the south along the green of St. James Court, gas lamps flickered in their glass-sided rooms.)

With eyes half-closed, Kathryn remembered or re-created in half dream a scene from summer on the Court's green lozenge to the north: a grassy carpet for an outdoor, afternoon wedding. Empty rows of gleaming plastic chairs waited for the guests, facing Venus and the front of the fountain. Not unusual, a wedding on the grass, a flurry of white dress against green. Before long, she had gone again to the window. Of course the ceremony was over—weddings were always too brief, she believed, for their momentousness—but the shiny white plastic chairs had not yet been removed.

Shockingly like a fleet of gravestones, the empty chairs stretched between the wide-spaced double colonnade of large trees. The shadows of summer leaves flitted over the chairs.

Humphrey and Edmund's wedding had been on the green.

Seated on the commode, Kathryn opened one eye to look out the clear top of the long vertical window beside her. Visible from no other vantage point, the very tall chimney of her neighbor's house thrust itself up into the sky. Often at this time of night the entire sky was weirdly pink, not a natural rosy hue but a surreal shade, though it was several hours before sunrise. *Tall Chimney, Pink Sky,* she would name the view, if she were a painter.

Very carefully, she groped her way back to bed—the wrought-metal doorknob reminded *I am Victorian* and the smooth rounded edges of the maple chest of drawers *I came from Alabama with a banjo*—and went promptly to sleep. (Her father, a physician, had purchased only furniture with benign, rounded corners, having seen too many children with the light of their eyes put out.)

Inside the white envelope, its shoulders leaning against Leslie's condo door, unseen by human eye, several chapters well within *Portrait of the Artist as an Old Woman,* the more confident (less fraught?) pages of Kathryn's novel continued to hum to themselves. *Childhood,* they agreed. Let us have that tune again.

II
MORNING MURMURS

PORTRAIT

THE MORNING IS A MURMUR OF RAIN above where I am sleeping, our white beds in rows, among other little girls sent as I have been sent to the convent for early education. *Not far from Paris,* my mother reassured. Some of the big girls *are* far from home, from Rheims and Rouen and even Normandie. The sleeping girls make little sounds as they rest, like little pigs, soft grunts, small sighs through their noses. Sometimes I hear a short syllable from one of their throats, though their lips stay pressed together. Each of their faces is a picture, and this time is the best time to draw them because they are mostly still.

I am very quick with my charcoal stick in the margins of Jeanette's notebook. The margins make rows, like the beds, and I draw only their heads, in *profile,* a word that Jeanette taught me. *Élisabeth, when you draw the side of the face, you are drawing the profile,* she explained. She is twelve and I am six, which means, she says, that she is twice as old as I am.

Every forehead is different, the shape of each nose and how it joins with the forehead, the distance from the base of the nose to the lip, and the slope from the lower lip to the chin. I like the chins and the jawbones especially because that means I am almost done and I will soon get to begin a new forehead.

We are interspersed in our row of beds: big girl and little girl, for this is a mostly kind convent and the nuns know the little girls, only six like myself, miss their families, but I will not stay here when I am a big girl but go back to live all the time with Maman and Papa in Paris, not in the country. The big girls' faces seem more distinct. It is more difficult to capture both the softness of the little faces and how they are special. But I can almost guess which ones will grow up pretty.

Very quietly so the straw in my mattress doesn't creak, I leave my bed and go toward the cabinet to see myself. Will I grow up pretty? I tiptoe to the bookcase, which is a cabinet on the bottom and glass doors above. There is black cloth behind the glass, and I have seen the big girls look into it as though it is a mirror. But I am too short.

When I return to my bed, Jeanette has propped her head up on her elbow, and she is looking at me.

"Am I going to be pretty?" I ask her.

"I can't tell," she whispers back. Her voice is quiet as rain and blends with it. "Am I pretty?" she asks, and smiles at me. I look at her and survey all the other faces for comparison. All the morning faces look almost holy.

"The most beautiful of all," I answer, but I realize I do not mean the way she looks but the way she *is*. And by *all* I mean only of all the girls who are here, for I know my own mother is the most beautiful in Paris. Maman's hair and how she arranges it make her a goddess. The nuns do not like us to mention the goddesses, but they walk the streets of Paris, and my father likes to say when we go out together to the park, "What a goddess!" and smack his lips and wink at me.

When the nuns find Jeanette's notebook is full of faces, they are disapproving, but one giggles and says, "Look, it's Marthe!" Then they make Jeanette hold out her hand and they bring the ruler *whack whack whack* down on her palm for wasting paper and time, but she still does not tell that it is I who have made the drawings of sleeping girls.

They do not notice that one sketch is better than all the others, but I do: Emma, who is breathing while she sleeps with her lips open. The way I drew Emma and her lips makes you imagine air moving in and out.

After that I draw on the smooth gray stones on the back of the well house where no one ever goes, and Jeanette stands watch while I draw, but, hidden behind the slate house, I am alone, except for Jeanette whose back is turned. Because I have no models to look at, I have to try to memorize the faces I have seen, but I miss looking at a person while I draw. Every glance up and back sees the person a little differently. But here behind the well house something else is interesting: the black marks against the gray of the wall are . . . *moody* and special in another way. How black looks against gray.

In the night, I like to listen to the rain drone, like black on gray, and it is not a sad sound because it is raining everywhere when it rains, and on the roof at home over the bed where Maman and Papa are sleeping, in Paris. But I am hot with fever, and I wish the rain could fall on me. I hear Jeanette speaking to me, and then I hear her moving over in her bed to make room for me. She opens her arm, and I put my bare foot on the cool floor, and then my head inside her shoulder, my cheek against her chest in the place she has made for me. She wraps her long arm around me on the outside so I won't fall off the edge. No one ever knows, and in the morning I am well.

When I am six and seven and eight, I am often unwell, and for this reason I am sent home more often than the other girls, and I am glad. Whenever I leave the convent under the flag of illness, Jeanette always smiles at me when she says good-bye, and adds, "I shall be very glad when you return to your second home." On one of the occasions, just before I leave, Jeanette whispers to me, "I have placed in your satchel one of your drawings. Be sure to show it to your papa, after you are home." I have noticed that she always shows the greatest respect to Papa when he comes to fetch me, and that he likes her as well. I know it must be the drawing of a bearded man who delivers vegetables and has a soft donkey, for that is the best of all my drawings, and I have taken care to hide and save it.

Once I am home, I stay in bed all the next day, and Maman sits by my bedside. She cuts an apple in half and with the tip of a dull knife, she scrapes the apple and presents a bit of it on the end of the dull blade to my mouth. "Like a little bird," she says to me, about her method of feeding me, and I open my mouth. With her thumb, she scoots the pulp onto my tongue. Always the apple presented in this way loosens my digestion, and my health improves. My little brother Étienne, who lives at home all the time while I am away and is only five to my eight years, watches this procedure with awe: the laden knife enters my mouth and returns empty, after I close my lips on it, with no injury to me.

That evening, when our beloved Papa is home, I show him the drawing of the bearded man. As soon as he sees it, he cries out with piercing joy, "You will be a painter, dear child, if ever there was one!"

One morning soon after my return to the convent, it rains very loudly in the night. I awaken early and go to the door. Just outside the doorstep—I am alone—I find the place that is usually smooth and hard as stone is very smooth, but now it is soft and wet. Before anybody can step on it and leave a footprint, I take a stick and draw ducks on it, like ducks on a pond. Their bills, like noses on faces, are the most fun to draw, with no chins at all, and then the beautiful curves of their necks and breasts. When the girls see, they all squeal with joy, and each one jumps over the slick mud where I have drawn with the stick so as not to mar what I've made.

Then they all know I can draw.

And Jeanette asks one nun if she can have little pieces of paper for me to draw on, and now I am much better at drawing. Some girls look straight at me and don't even blink so that I can get their faces right. Two silly girls make faces at me for fun while I stare and draw. I don't care. It's all such fun. Their funny faces are fun. There is a rhythm: you look, then draw, you look again, over and over. Sometimes two or three girls stand behind me, and when I look at the girl being drawn, they do, and when I look back at my work, they do. All our heads move in unison. We are a spectacle.

Sometimes the big girls fold their arms and stand at the side and watch all of us, till they get bored, and unfold their arms, and walk back to their sewing. Jeanette is natural about everything, and I like it that she's always there. After I've finished the portraits, some girls stare and stare at themselves on paper and turn the page at different angles.

Finally one day Jeanette, almost as tall as one of the sisters, gives me the best piece of paper yet, almost as big as a whole page in a book; the grain is close and smooth. She tells me that she has heard soon I am going home to stay. I nod. I know. I am happy. One edge of the paper sheet has been pulled away from binding stitches, and I am shocked because I know that Jeanette has stolen it away from an actual book. Amazed, I look into her clear brown eyes. "I won't tell," I promise, barely moving my mouth.

"Would you please draw me," she asks, "for me to keep, and I *will* keep it always and you will always be my little girl even when I have become a nun?"

I realize I need the charcoal to be sharp for this paper, and I have Jeanette sharpen it with a keen knife before I begin, and again whenever it starts to blunt as I work. I am glad to learn that I am going home to stay with Maman and Papa, and I say, "At home, when I visit, Papa gives me crayons to draw with. I wish I could draw you in colors." I would very much like to render not only the color of her eyes but their clarity and also the texture of her hair, which in color almost matches her eyes.

But Jeanette assures me that she loves the charcoal and she points out that the paper has a creamy tint to it, a hint of yellow, and that provides some color, and I see in a flash that she is right, "like the skin of a ripe cantaloupe," I say. And I add, "I want to draw more of you, not just to the neck but farther down, too."

It is early in the morning and the other girls are still sleeping in rows— it will be like this forever—but the whole room is full of morning light, and it is pleasantly warm and even smells a little like a ripe cantaloupe.

Jeanette pushes the sleeve of her nightgown off one shoulder, and I draw the beautiful round of the outside of her shoulder and Jeanette's round chin looking over the soft shoulder, and a suggestion of her upper arm as she looks at me. Right into my eyes, she is looking, whenever I look up. But I change her eyes to give her happy eyes instead of sad ones.

FOUNTAIN

B EFORE THE FIRST LIGHT OF DAWN, Kathryn half awoke to a bird's zigzag chatter, five perfect notes descending the scale, a rickrack of sound, and then she fell rapidly into dream. Down six decades through the rabbit hole of self she sped, till she bottomed into her self six years old, twirling in the center of her green circle skirt, red rickrack zinging like lightning around its hem as she swirled. What dizzy pleasure to be the center of red lightning riding undulations of green! And she the generator!

How many years had wrapped her round since Kathryn Callaghan had caused her green skirt trimmed in red to rise and ripple, the green and red rising and falling, rising and falling in waves of obedient fabric! Her short blond hair whipped her eyes as she twirled, till she squinted them shut for protection. The dream disappeared.

Here was predawn, too-early morning in Louisville, where, in the perfect comfort of her soft bed warmed by the heat of her own body (approaching seventy), she felt no weight of years (though she desired sleep). She thought of Woolf's Clarissa Dalloway, who had only been slightly past fifty that June day in London, and Kathryn's own nearly seventy years. Kathryn, too, had loved walking in Bloomsbury—the size of the blossoms of those pink English roses; lavender wisteria, long and full as a healthy male forearm—with her son. That trip had been for Humphrey, who had broken up with his long-term boyfriend. Kathryn had wanted Humphrey to be out of the reach of Jerry, who had a bad temper and a streak of violence in him.

But here in Middle America, a rickrack of childhood red had laid itself down in the convolutions of her brain. She courted a blacker darkness, the black of Yves's French hair. Did he color it? Probably. So what. So did she, though hers was chestnut artfully highlighted with gold.

Not heavy, not tired? After so many years lived? Not even after a double handful of lovers and three husbands, each of whom sooner or later wanted someone else? Someone younger?

Well, yes, of course these husbands would woo someone younger behind her back (she turned over restlessly), even when she herself had been only in her twenties. This last husband, when both she and he were in their fifties and sixties, had been the worst. Wooing other women before her very gaze—herself, taken for granted like a hat rack—he, like his predecessors, had denied his intent when Kathryn made gentle inquiry. Really, for the most part, Kathryn had made herself blind to their new interests.

At least when #1 had proclaimed his need for others, Kathryn, too, had been young; she had been fairly shocked. But . . . but . . . but, her mind had stuttered in disbelief, no one understood him or would appreciate him as well as she; she had been sure of that. James was making a mistake! And she loved his promising brilliant mind as well as his body. They were graduate students; she was twenty-nine. (He was tired of sneaking around, he declared. Monogamy was philosophically and biologically unnatural.)

The second, #2 (she enjoyed envisioning the crosshatch before the number; it was like a little screen, a slant of burglar bars, separating herself from the ex's numeral), had surprised her, too, not through proclamation but by confession. Because he needed to grow, Peter had had to spread his wings. Good-bye, Kathryn; good-bye, Humphrey, my lad!

Left to her own awareness, her trusting blindness, she would never have known the misdeeds of #1 and #2.

But #3, a giant of a man with a head full of natural curls only beginning to turn gray, wanted her to be in the wrong; he claimed innocence and believed his intentions had been misconstrued, his lies and secrecy nothing more than a mistake. Her mistake. No need for blunt and righteous openness, like #1, or for unfettered personal growth, like #2; for #3, no residue of guilt and certainly no remorse, not even an admission of the needs of his insatiable ego: she had failed to understand that he could do no wrong. No need for reformation on his part: his goodness was intact, inviolable; there had been no mutation or evolution of his nature.

When, after months of fruitless marital counseling, she suggested he move out and she acquire the house, he was gone within a week, not a murmur of attempting reconciliation. She understood: Mark had wanted to be caught; he was glad to go. Despite being a neurosurgeon, Mark was greedy for affirmation: so many other women (new ones) needed to admire his gentle goodness before it was too late. He needed to feel new; after all, he was well into his sixties. And she was the one who had introduced him to the girl from Guatemala, a new neighbor, and had asked him to consider her credentials as a surgical nurse.

Was that where she had gone wrong?

She remembered their early lovemaking, his beautiful eyes; yes, she would willfully remember their early lovemaking. He could be passionate and gentle. (Except when angry. Then a barrage of scalding insults spewed from his mouth, his face purple with rage.)

Kathryn rotated in bed as though skewered on a spit and roasting in the flames of hell; she extended a foot to a still-cool region. Much more could be thought about *The Husbands*, categorized, crosslisted as *The Exes*, shelved in the memory library, but she wanted to stop. It had been a year since the divorce from #3. A busy, productive year. Time enough to heal.

But he was getting married again. Perhaps today. Blithely going on. She was sure he would not think of her or even remember her, not for one second. (Partly she blamed not him but the all too often untenable institution of marriage.)

Maybe the title of her next novel, after *Portrait*, would be *The Husbands*. A bitter title. She would prefer to write a novel that hinted of satisfaction, eternal renewal, something optimistic if not triumphant. One of her friends had published a book titled *The Sisters*. It had held both the bitter and the sweet. Hope.

Kathryn wished that uncanny predawn bird would sing again in rickrack steps, a well-tempered, even scale. But it did not.

Instead, knowing, gleeful voices chorused, *One, two, three strikes, you're out, at the old ball game.* #1, #2, #3.

PORTRAIT

W HEN PAPA STEPS OUT OF THE DARKNESS and through the convent door and goes down on one knee to receive me, I run into his arms with all speed, force, and eagerness. Once inside the carriage, he tucks me against his body, and I sleep, sitting up against him all the way to Paris. For a while I notice the sound of iron circles turning on cobblestones and then I awake with the cessation of motion.

Now my mother is standing in the doorway with the soft light behind her, shining around the loose curls of hair touching her shoulders. She is holding a finger to her lips, for I am not to awaken my little brother. I reach my arms to hug her waist and plant the top of my head just under her chin. *There now, there now,* she loosens my grip and leans forward so that her face is almost level with mine, but looking down a bit at me.

"You can peek at him on his couch, but you must not wake him."

When I see him I step back because now, by the light of a single candle, he resembles a painting of an angel. How can he have been so transformed?

I am almost afraid. His lips are parted, and there is enough light so that I can see they are pink and tender, and perhaps the same hue tints his cheek.

Thus I fall in love with my little brother, for he is beauty incarnate.

My father is explaining the lateness of our arrival to my mother— before he fetched me, he tells, a wheel came away from the axle. She does not reply. I remember my fatigue, sitting all day in the visitor's chair beside the convent door to the world. I see Jeanette down the distance of the long hall, passing from one door and through the opposite door. She assumes I am gone and does not look at me, waiting long and long. In a way, I am already gone forever. *It's true,* I hear my father say to my mother.

At the breakfast table, in his animation, my little brother is even more enchanting. When he sits down beside my mother and she hugs him, I see a lamp flare up behind her eyes, and I think, *Happiness: this is what they mean by happiness.* And I know that I have no skill in my fingers or in my knowledge of forms and shading to render the charm of my mother's expression with my art. But I myself am a little mirror, catching her light and reflecting it about me.

When my father joins us, he looks at me, jumps back as though in surprise, says, *Good morning, Brightness,* and kisses me on the forehead. He draws me onto his lap, big girl that I am, leans over and pecks the near cheek of my mother, and says, "Now we are complete."

"One would think so," she replies in a merry way.

"How is Pussy Cat?" he asks, and I look around for kitty, for I have forgotten we possess a cat. But he is looking over my head, not on the floor where kitty would be.

With her free hand, my mother tosses a red apple into the air, and then catches it with the same hand. "Ready to pounce," she replies, and so I learn his pet name for her.

Confused, I ask, "Where is our kitty?" and I look around for the interesting tabby with her brown and black blended streaks. From under a rocking chair comes the face of a new white kitty with a black ear, but she streaks out the door upon seeing me. I observe that she also has a black spot on her side and a long black tail. I know she will be back, for all the cats at the convent came to like me, and everyone said I had a way with cats.

"Can you draw the new kitty, Élisabeth?" my father asks me. "I have some new crayons for you."

"May I try now?" I slide off his lap so that he may fetch my present. "May I name her Angel?"

"Is there a difference between an angel and a goddess?" my father asks.

"I don't know," I answer truthfully, but I like the question. He does not supply the answer, and I am not surprised. He likes to leave things for me to decide about on my own.

Soon I am trying to draw the white kitty, but I am puzzled about separating her whiteness from that of the page, though I know I can do it with a black line. I am pleased that my father's gift to me includes a very thick pad of pages, gummed together at the top. For a moment I think of Jeanette and miss her.

That night—I am full of happiness—I watch my mother combing and curling her hair around her finger as she sits at her dressing table. When I ask her if I may look in the glass, she stops her twirling and says with some surprise, "Of course you may. As often as you like." Then she asks, with a bit of caution in her voice, if we were not allowed to look in the mirrors at the convent.

"We had no mirrors," I reply. I remember the convent's pretty neatness and rows of beds, the shades of gray and white.

Then she draws me to her so that my cheek touches hers and we are reflected together. I gasp at the intimacy of our faces. I like the feel of my cheek against hers.

"One can learn a great deal from mirrors," she says. "Do we look alike?"

I see that her hair and skin and eyes are darker than mine. I see that she is truly beautiful in a *burning* way. After a moment, I murmur, "No," but I hardly hear myself for my eyes are already roaming around the mirror to see what else it frames and reflects, and I see a stack of pretty round boxes, the color of honey, each different, rising in graduated sizes from the dark blue carpet, and beside the boxes is a tall coatrack with a brass hook, where hangs a beautiful dressing gown with silver threads and rows of dark roses, golden marigolds, and green apples. "I am very happy to be home," I say sincerely into the mirror.

With the many things around us, the mirror presents a picture full of colors, and if I move my head a little, the contents of the picture shift, and the colors change, and so the picture changes its mood.

FOUNTAIN

WITH HER EYES STILL CLOSED, Kathryn let one foot caress the top of the other as she lay in bed waiting for dawn. She needed full sleep—everyone did—to maintain mental health. These last two years she had consoled herself with her work, but now it was done. Delivered. She would keep her eyes shut and feel her way back to sleep. Bony feet, slender feet, if overly long. Well-cared-for feet.

Let. Let me luxuriate. In the dark morning, in the spacious comfort of her king-size bed, Kathryn let her feet explore the microclimates of the realm between the sheets and recalled her cool night journey across St. James Court. The printout in her arm. The autumnal lopsided moon high above and the damp kisses blown from the fountain to her flesh. *Bises.* French kisses, but not in the American sense of French kisses. Lightly, on the cheeks: a greeting friend to friend. What she wanted was to dwell in her own skin, peaceful and joyful. That was her ambition for her life. And also for Leslie and her new life in Louisville. But how does one deep rooted in the mores of the twentieth century live the single life in the twenty-first century?

While consciousness waxed and waned in the predawn, Kathryn held a goose-down bed pillow close to her body as though it were that so-dear baby, Humphrey, now grown, moved away, happily married to another man; a son considerate, loyal, and loving to his mother. Not that there had been an absence of difficulties between Humphrey and Kathryn, who, suddenly restless, rolled over. She was thirsty. Her eyelids fluttered.

When morning would come full and bright, Kathryn resolved to rejoice in it. Can't one *choose* to be happy, to some extent? To the extent of one's independence of others? Now she sat up, dazed, wanting to sleep again, her eyelids scratchy. This was the day that Yves would come. Sometimes she could set her mood like resetting a watch (who wore those anymore?). Sometimes the black cap of depression settled over her head and face and enveloped her body. Only the kindness of another person could lift it.

Could there not be, during Kathryn's lifespan, a pleasant autumnal period, a drowsy time of rich fulfillment, a harvesting, Keats's full granary, with only hints of sadness?

If she was to create a satisfying autumn for herself and a cozy winter, then of course she must begin with this new day. She thought again of Woolf's Clarissa Dalloway beginning her day in June, not long after the end of World War I. Kathryn lay down again.

Didn't she, Ms. Callaghan, have an advantage over Mrs. Dalloway? After all, Kathryn was a writer, unlike Clarissa Dalloway, who, for all her insight and ready response to life, could only make an art of party giving and of living, that slippery and insubstantial substance. But Kathryn respected Mrs. Dalloway, a quintessential human, and respected her party giving, too; Kathryn retracted her sense of superiority and revised her idea. Mrs. D. was a practitioner of the art of living. (Mrs. Dalloway had been correct in *her* marital choosing.)

As a writer, Kathryn knew how to make something out of nothing, or at least out of very little, out of the scraps of life that would otherwise dissolve back into the earth. *Not scraps. Life itself. Woolf knew.* The slightest gesture, the lifting of an eyebrow, the opening of a pocketknife, had meaning.

And Clarissa's marriage, frowned upon by her closest friends, Sally Seton and Peter Walsh, was a success, had been nothing like Kathryn's failures. Clarissa's marriage had let her breathe, and it had given her an anchor.

Through all her years of young womanhood and middle age, Kathryn had struggled to make a nest of life and failed. Yes, she could look at her own accumulation of years squarely: she had failed in one aspect of life (marriage) but succeeded, perhaps, in another, in friendship, though friendship had its own fragility. Surely it was time for Kathryn to overhaul the ideal of marriage. She would need to gather strength to want something else. *Singleness.* Could she make that idea stand up straight like the numeral 1?

One must not get up too quickly. She remembered her strategy: make it a habit now to rise slowly; alone as she was in the house (except for Janie on the third floor, who was her friend and would come if called, if called loudly enough); the day might come when standing up too soon could trigger a fall. Not now. Though danger was in the distant future, best to get in training.

She scooted down into the bedcovers.

Let myself Kathryn equal Ryn, she began: a wren, a domestic little bird. A creature rather sparrowlike, a bit larger, perhaps, at least more rounded, with a distinctly speckled breast? No, a breast of soft dun and buff—disappearing colors.

Ryn; through the years Leslie had named her. Not a dignified writer—Kathryn—but a small bird shuffling in the roof gutter for seeds; merely a wren.

Let. Let what happen? Let me feel renewed in this day.

Let me live again. Fully alive, independent as a small bird scavenging for myself, happy and complete in myself, my friends, my work, my home, my claimed territory: Old Louisville. (Immediately she thought of the vastness of the world and of the many places she had lived or visited: England and France, of course, but also Sweden when Humphrey was a little boy. Perhaps he too was looking for renewal, in Sweden, now with Edmund. She remembered the miracle of crocuses, colorful in the spring snow after the long, dark winter. Russia, Egypt, India. *Argentina to Zanzibar,* literally.) But she was as domestic as a wren at heart. *Let* . . . Let me have it all: the wide world and the pleasure of my beloved home—so much more beautiful than I ever deserved—near the fountain of Venus rising from the sea. And next? In a moment, Ryn knew, identity wavered, evaporated, never hardened into a line dividing the self from possibilities.

When she saw Leslie, perhaps even today, perhaps Leslie would call her Ryn.

The predawn bird, that *Outsider,* the *Other,* the feathered *Singer* of St. James Court, who had stepped down chromatically a well-tempered scale—like *rickrack*—like the progeny of J. S. Bach, now took flight; the soft whirr of wings-engaging-air geared it away; or was that sound the whirring of her own mind? Had she not heard the slight rasp of bird feet leaving the stone windowsill? She imagined the unseen bird to be black, a chip of night, with a gold circle around its eye, a well-worn yellow beak. Not a wren, something more mysterious and confident.

PORTRAIT

PAPA BRINGS ME HANDFULS OF COLORS. They are pastel sticks, such as he himself uses in his paintings, and they roll out of his hands onto the table. We look at them together and sometimes he asks, *What does this color have to say to that color?* The first time he asks I look at him in surprise. Most adults do not seem to know that everything speaks to everything else. Not in words exactly, but now he is asking for words. Slowly, watching his face, for I do not want to disappoint him, I answer.

"This blue says to this green 'I like you, for there is some of me in you.'"

My father puts both his arms around my head and squeezes my head against his heart. While he holds me there he says, "Tonight you will stay up late, until you are truly sleepy, because special friends of mine are coming over—"

I mumble into his sleeve, and the moisture comes out of my mouth and wets the cloth of his sleeve, "Are they women or men?"

He releases me and says, "Men, little daughter soon to be grown up." I am almost twelve. He holds me by my shoulders at arm's length and looks into my eyes, quite seriously. "But they are special men with heads full of knowledge. They are making a compendium of what we know. Everything humans know at this point in history. It will take many separate books to hold it all, but it will be very simply organized, by the alphabet. I want you to hear them talk."

"Are they painters? I would like some paints so I can make pictures like the ones at the Church of Saint Eustache."

"Do you like it at Saint Eustache?"

All the colored light floods my mind and a piece of my mind flies like a swallow into the vaulted ceiling and I am unsure of whether that space is depth or height, but I say what I love most. "I like to stand next to Maman and sing." Sometimes my mother cups her hand around my shoulder and squeezes me close when we sing together or when I hit the high notes exactly in the center of the pitch.

"So you have an ear as well as an eye, my gifted one?"

I do not know what to say. What is a gifted one? I hope I am not to be given away. My father reads my silence, or is it my face he reads, the way my cheeks have loosened, for I felt them do it.

"To be gifted," he says, "is to have special talents, gifts, that are part of your soul, for God has placed them within you and they will always be there."

Suddenly I know that I am my father's treasure; that he treasures me though I am not pretty, and in fact that does not matter in the least to him, though it matters very much to the world. Even though he reminds himself I am about to grow up, he still speaks to me as though I am a little child.

"Enjoy all your gifts," he tells me. "They bring pleasure to others, but what is most important is that it makes you yourself happy to have these gifts: first, even before you use them; second, while you use them; and third, after you have used them. Let your gifts fill you up with happiness."

I nod in agreement. I already know what he has told me; I have always known it but even his words are not splendid enough to match the feeling that comes before, during, and after I have done what I love to do.

"Sometimes," he says, "if you work hard and finish your work and share it, there is a fourth time of happiness."

I feel around inside my mind but I cannot find the fourth happiness, so I ask him.

"It comes when other people praise what you have done; it is the least important pleasure but there is no reason not to open yourself to it. It is untrue to yourself not to open yourself in a humble and happy way to praise. Take it in, if it comes, and let it give you confidence and strength for future work."

I know that soon I will ask for oil paints.

"Which stick speaks to your hand this morning? Which one says, 'Choose me'?"

When he says these words, the tone of his voice makes me think of Samuel in the Holy Bible, when he hears the voice of God calling his own name, and he replies, "Here am I. Send me." And the voice of God is exactly the same as Samuel's own inner voice.

FOUNTAIN

KATHRYN FLUNG THE COVERS AWAY as though they were a cape and, still lying in bed, propped her head up with a bent elbow and her open hand. There was the morning sunlight, bright and strong, the color of sauterne streaming through the horizontal slats of her plantation shutters. The dear clear light of morning! Never again would she take a home anywhere that did not face east. She sat up in bed and opened her arms. Already after nine o'clock.

"Come, let's go at break of day," her mother used to sing and spritely play on the piano, "to the hills and far away." As she played effortlessly, she would turn from the keyboard to face her little girl flanked by two slightly older brothers, tilt her head toward imaginary hills, and lift her eyebrows encouragingly.

Kathryn would go walk in the park; in fact, she had promised to do so, with Peter, Humphrey's father, once her second husband, now her friend.

What else might one do with the day after, the day after you've finished a novel? She almost felt like a stranger to herself, for having written a new book, wasn't she a different person? What did you do on such a day?

You made the day ordinary by cooking oatmeal and stirring in blueberries and walnuts, you made the day dear with memories of other completions and with small, current satisfactions (you waited for feedback, all day); you kept the momentum of living going onward (a guest—the raven-haired Frenchman would drive up from Montgomery—and plans). You thought forward—if it's a book and not a baby that you've birthed, then you thought, at least Kathryn did, of the next one.

Two or three ideas for future books were always knocking at the door, like so many waggle-tail puppies trying to be appealing (so lighthearted she felt, she would indulge a rare bit of metaphoric silliness) with their titles clamped in their teeth, heads bowed respectfully, lifted eyes, large and endearing. She might pretend to want to stamp her foot, pretend she wanted to say, "Shoo, let me alone, let me rest," but really Kathryn was pleased. Nonetheless, she did plan to rest some; she *would* let her mind go on idle; she was *pleased* to have finished the writing, to rest, to congratulate herself a little: *I did it.* She told the puppies to hold their horses and shut the door in their faces.

Yves was coming up from Alabama, and though he was thoroughly French, Parisian in fact, he would bring with him a hint of jasmine or magnolia, though it was autumn and the time of the large white fragrant blossoms, big as cereal bowls, had passed. Perhaps he was the progeny, on his mother's side, of the French Revolution she had written about.

Still, he also brought a whiff of the American South, for he had chosen to live there. And he lived in the old Deep South—in Montgomery, not Birmingham, which did not even exist till after the Civil War. Authentic Montgomery, heavy with primary sin. Why had not the tablets of Moses carried the injunction *Thou shalt not enslave one another?*

Through the Palladian window at the foot of her bed, she savored the broad, glossy leaves and the tall straight trunk of the older and bigger of two magnolias growing in the front yard. *Don't you hate the mess,* one of her fastidious neighbors to her north (Mrs. Bishop) once asked, but Ryn had said nothing. No, she did not hate the mess. Magnolias shed in late spring when new strong leaves pushed aside the golden tan ones. Bushels of the ripened brown-and-gold leaves, large and rigid, carpeted her walk well into June. If you picked up one mottled leaf from the clutter, you saw it was shiny as though lightly lacquered on one side and a lovely soft matte finish on the obverse. Each stiff leaf was unique in its honey-and-brown mottling. Élisabeth Vigée-Le Brun would have enjoyed their hues.

How little she knew Yves, but was not everything implied by the way he practiced the art of conversation, even in English? Learning French had been, for Ryn, even more elusive than staying married; at least she'd gotten a passing score for years at a time in marriage.

As ready as a barrel, Kathryn rolled out of bed. Woolfian! Yes, she would live a Woolfian day. As she dressed and readied herself for breakfast, anticipating her French visitor from Montgomery, she whiffed a still older South, an earlier time, an entire century earlier and more: summer moonlight, jasmine, roses, magnolia, honeysuckle, all suffused by the stench of bloody civil war.

She wandered into her library to stand in the bow window. Jefferson Davis and Robert E. Lee had loved their libraries. A too-bushy magnolia was blocking the view of the fountain, but she could hear the rush of falling water. Outside trees would be preening like giant roosters, red and gold.

But it was morning of the first day after finishing *Portrait of the Artist as an Old Woman*. When she wrote a novel, she liked at least to try to nudge the great wobbly balloon of public consciousness; she liked at least to dent some spot on its enormous side with her elbow. But this morning she didn't want another idea, another project. *Portrait* was *not* finished: revision, revision, revision. And she would love the revising, her hands falling in love with the grain of the words as surely as a wood-carver loved to touch again what he had carved.

Dressed in soft, loose jeans and an equally soft and loose corduroy shirt, Ryn descended the stairs, wide and more thickly carpeted than any moss on forest floor. For a moment she felt herself both a creature of the woods and a denizen of deep civilization. She must go closer, be in the air and light of outdoors, with the fountain. As though entering a grove of trees, she stepped onto her front porch into the semicircle of columns.

The glory of the fountain on bright mornings was the way the ascending sun, at a short moment in its arc, caught every drop of water. That moment was now.

Light, dressed in water, displayed itself as bright globules, as parallel lines and broken dashes, as continuous streamers, as spurts and gushes and splashes. Sunlight inhabited every orb or flake of water. Every drop of moving water packaged light as though it were palpable cargo.

For Kathryn Callaghan every cell sang with the joy, the thrill, and the fulfillment that Beauty offered. Light, invisible and elusive but here given form, stood for the miracle of art. How water made light visible; that was how the art of writing must capture and irradiate life. On a sunny morning for a quarter of an hour, the fountain of St. James Court became a ceremony of light.

PORTRAIT

THE STAINED-GLASS GLORY of the Church of Saint Eustache draws close around me, while Maman approaches the communion altar and I sit in the hard chair, because we have not had time for me to go to confession before Mass. When Maman asks if I have sinned since last confession, I answer truthfully that I cannot remember, but also I like sitting quietly by myself in church. I am pretending to be grown up, for I am twelve.

A splotch of red falls from a high window onto one of my shoulders, like a little red cape, but the redness is made of light and if I place my hand on my shoulder then the back of my hand becomes a large rose petal. Thus I play with the light and listen to the reedy sighs of the organ, a sound that makes me think of stiff reeds growing in water such as those at the convent beyond the well house. I remember the gray slate wall but I cannot remember any particular thing I drew there. I think of Jeanette's kind face and especially her sad eyes. *Amber,* now I know the name of their color, almost the same as the color of a cake of rosin glued to soft leather. One of my father's friends rubs rosin on his bow before he plays the violin. Sometimes I play, too, on a little guitar, with my fingers. When painters and poets and philosophers come to our house in the evening, we all sit very close together because the room is small. I like it that way.

Within the Church of Saint Eustache the space above our heads lifts and lifts, and it is hard to fathom its volume. I like it very much. Colored patches of sunlight, hovering high, are like angels. I would like to see a real angel. *It is not impossible,* my mother said once, looking at me hopefully as though she would very much like to be the mother of a little girl who saw angels. She showed me an engraving of Bernini's statue of Saint Teresa of Avila and also told me the name of the sculpture. *Ecstasy.* I hear myself say the word out loud now, as it is part of the name of Bernini's work. I know that I do not understand this puzzling word, neither then nor now. I was not and am not sure what my mother wanted me to learn as we stared at the engraving.

That sculpture it depicted is powerful, and the memory of it frightens me, even while I sit in church. Saint Teresa is a grown woman *reclining* when the angel visits her. He points a spear at her, and she is afraid. And they are all so very white as though they are all really the same thing, like a big monster.

I glance at my mother as she prays and notice the two vertical lines gathered between her eyes. She seems in pain. I think it is about my father. I think she wishes he were with us. With two fingers, she pinches the place of the two lines between her eyes and brings them closer together.

Maman has also shown me an engraving of a sculpture, also all one piece, of men battling monstrous snakes; its title is *Laocoön and His Sons.* Maman says it was originally carved in Greece before the birth of Christ, but now the Vatican has acquired it, or a copy of it. *Thus men ever battle their own nature,* she said to me, and I asked her what she meant. She did not really explain; she said, *Virility is ever a powerful force.*

"Almost every Sunday," I hear a man say behind me in the great cave of the Church of Saint Eustache. Why has he not gone to the altar? Here and there, a chair is occupied by a lone child, who has been brought to Mass but is not yet old enough to take communion. I keep an eye on them. Though I made my first communion at the convent, sometimes I wish that event had occurred here, but Maman wanted to secure me to the church before I left the safety of the countryside. A young Louis XIV took his first communion here at the Church of Saint Eustache. The thought of royalty overwhelms me.

"Every Sunday?" another man inquires, behind me.

"Gorgeous," the first man replies. "Worth seeing, yes?" And suddenly, though I don't know how I know, I *do* know that they are speaking of my mother. I know I must guard her, that I *do* guard her, and I turn in my seat and scowl at them and make a face like a very ugly fish monster in one of the paintings here.

Both men look down and avoid my eyes. One of them scratches his eyebrow and mutters, "Gargoyles abound." I whip my head around and point my nose at the very high ceiling, still frowning. I don't care what they call me. I have always liked gargoyles. They are useful. They keep evil spirits out. The low foot pedals of the organ croak like frogs in the country, and there is the reedy sound, too, and I turn to look at the painting of John the Baptist because the blue color behind his head has as much brightness as any of the stained glass, though light does not shine through it. This painted sky is my favorite patch of color in the entirety of Saint Eustache. Down by the foot of Saint John there is a little puddle, and it is so expertly painted that it really is like water, and a few green weeds grow out of it.

Quickly I look up again at the face of the saint because I realize that like the painted water in the puddle, the face seems *mobile*. It cannot *be* mobile, but the painter has suggested that it might be. I stare hard to memorize it, and when I am home, I shall paint it myself, from memory. When I look until I think I understand, I hear myself make a little gasp. The effect comes from the shading, from the way definite and indefinite shapes have been worked together.

Perhaps I will paint the ugly fish face, too, and tell my father it is a self-portrait (but that would worry him about me), or perhaps I will tell my mother, "My name for this fish is 'Guard Dog.'"

When we leave Saint Eustache, my mother looks fresh, as though she has just washed her face. I ask her not to walk so fast, but she takes my hand and says she is eager to get back home to my father.

"And Étienne," I say.

She tells me that I am a very good big sister, that I must be tired from so much sitting, and would I like to take Étienne and Nurse for a long walk, perhaps to see my friend. I agree, but when we get home, my father has already gone out.

I see the pucker between her eyes. I start to ask where my father is now, but I change my mind and do not ask.

FOUNTAIN

NEARLY TEN O'CLOCK and still no breakfast. Without a glance, Kathryn passed the enormous blue oil painting of high-flying trapeze artists above her mother's aged upright piano: *Oatmeal was on the agenda.* With blueberries and walnuts, the usual, but today being a special day, she would also prepare thick hot chocolate. She would use the special, expensive mixture given her by elegant white-haired Ralph Raby, her friend, once a distinguished St. James Court resident, before he moved to Mexico.

She measured the heavy-grained powder, added stevia and whole organic milk into one pot, then measured water for oatmeal into another. She stirred both pots. Now she would be vigilant. Neither oatmeal nor chocolate must be allowed to boil over on her new glass-topped stove, so difficult to clean. A mistake of a stove for someone of Kathryn's habits. Absentminded, untalented in culinary art, she had bought it for its two ovens, to warm food for Humphrey and Edmund's wedding. (A wedding on the court, with Venus of the fountain rustling her blessing in the background. With a policeman in plain clothes, should Jerry come, unwelcome and disruptive.)

If Humphrey's old boyfriend suddenly should appear even today—it would be terribly upsetting—Kathryn would shout, *Iceland! He's moved to Iceland, I mean Sweden, with his partner, six foot seven, an Olympic athlete. Weight lifter! Heavyweight boxer! Slingshot deadeye.* Ryn pictured Michelangelo's seventeen-foot-tall David, young but with a slingshot in his hand and a deadly gleam in his carved eye. Humphrey's old boyfriend, Jerry, would study the floor, sneer, and turn away, if she yelled all those epithets. He was shrewd enough not to endanger himself. He'd already experienced the horror of jail—as a car thief—before he came into Humphrey's tender life.

Edmund would laugh about being described as a heroic warrior in Kathryn's fantasy. He *liked* looking scholarly. He was slight, with humor in his eyes.

In five minutes the oatmeal was cooked and the chocolate low-heated to just short of boiling. From their everyday wedding dishes, Mark had dealt her a bowl and a plate, a cup with no saucer, incomplete but cheerful: a sunburst design with indigo and pink flowers. One place setting. She decided against it and selected a pure white bowl and plate which she was sure he had left behind as a simple discard. No. Having fed his dog from the dishes, he had spurned them. She didn't mind eating after dogs occasionally. Didn't the dishwasher sanitize everything?

Kathryn served herself and sat down alone at the large kitchen table.

Her fingertips caressed the green-painted tabletop her brother had antiqued, years ago. Bubba had not been out of his teens then; how had he known to update the old table, to make that gift to his family, to find the time, generosity, and skill to hatch the plan and execute it for the sake of the rest of them: that was why Ryn touched the table; she wanted to understand that part of her brother's nature. To feel less alone.

At home in Montgomery, there had been a double-barreled shotgun left over from Civil War days. Held together by a broad rubber band, it had stood in the corner for a long time. Then it was gone. Only after she turned fifty had Kathryn realized that her mother had probably pawned it after her father's death.

When Ryn had been a small girl, before he died, her father had wanted to teach his boys and girl how to fire a gun; he had taken her and her brothers even farther south, to his old homeplace forty miles below Montgomery (an ancient woman, born into slavery, was allowed to live in the weathered brown house, two rooms, one with a fireplace, and there had been a dogtrot between the two rooms to admit any summer breezes that might enter)—so that his children could learn how to protect themselves, if necessary. She had been five years old. At age five, under her father's tutelage, she had fired a pistol into the piney woods at Helicon, Alabama.

Her father's pistol, like the antique rifle, was gone, no doubt also pawned by her mother trying to meet domestic necessities. How easily she could imagine her mother riding downtown on the bus, her heart beating fast because she concealed a gun in her purse or in a wrinkled paper bag beside her foot. Well, Ellen, her ninety-two-year-old friend, had somehow sensed a deficit and given Kathryn a handgun.

A .32 was lighter than a .38, Ellen had explained as they sat in velvet Victorian chairs. A .32 was a nice gun, but not powerful enough, necessarily, to stop an assailant. Ellen wanted Kathryn to have the .38. *Think of it as a friendly tool. It may help to craft your sense of safety when you're back home.*

IT WAS LESLIE, a gourmet of food as well as of literature, who had said, "Ryn, walnuts and fresh blueberries are oatmeal's ticket to heaven." (Not the way her mother fixed hot cereal—with butter and brown sugar. She could still feel its titillatingly incongruous texture in her mouth: damp sand.) Though Leslie had published only one book, she was both a more savvy reader and passionate writer than Kathryn. Kathryn sighed. More up-to-date in all intellectual matters.

Leslie was a person of focused courage, Ryn felt, while she herself just blundered from one hope to another. Because Leslie was African American, Kathryn wanted her to write about the civil rights days, but Leslie wanted to write fiction about the invisible power of music, not about race. What Leslie wanted to write about: how music traveled like veins of silver and gold through the earthiness of life. Besides, it had been the sexism of the time, not the racism, that had chained Leslie.

Kathryn recalled the anger of #2, Peter, when, on the way to the hospital to deliver the baby who turned out to be Humphrey, she had insisted on going by the post office to meet a contest deadline for fiction. At the time, she had still been trying to publish a first book; Humphrey would be nearly nine years old before a small press finally took Kathryn's first collection of short stories. Oh, the time it took! Kathryn had paid her dues, as some people in the trade liked to say, but she did not believe in the concept.

It was Kathryn's unhealthy habit to groan under the weight of failure—another divorce—but hardly to recognize as real any success—another book finished. Not really finished, but finished for now. For today, it was done. Tomorrow she would consider Leslie's suggestions. Sufficient unto the day is the hot chocolate thereof.

A single sip of the hot, rich chocolate, and life was good. She touched the antiqued tabletop with the tips of her fingers. The day was hers. *I loafe and invite my soul*, the good gray poet Walt Whitman had written. Surely she deserved to linger and loaf, solitary, impinging on no one else's schedule, over oatmeal, while the morning ticked away. Before walking in the park with Peter, before Yves came to visit, she would be satisfied without either of them, *full of herself*. Hadn't her mother used that phrase? But always it was as a coconspirator that Lila had used the phrase.

Home, St. James Court, was the heart of the city—the heart, the heart; how she longed for the heart of things; she didn't care if some considered the term tarnished by sentimentality—at least the Court was the residential heart of the city, beloved by its inhabitants.

She knew most of them, her friendly neighbors, a diversity of races, ages, sexual orientations, and economic conditions: babies, children, teens, up through the decades to people quite a bit older than Kathryn herself.

Everyone had a nod or a greeting for those they met. Her community—as delicious as another sip of breakfast hot chocolate—Old Louisville.

Ryn heard the feet of Janie and those of Tide coming down their stairs, past her kitchen door, and out the side of the house, to take their morning walk. Ryn did not need to see them to know they were creating their own breeze, so rapidly they moved, and Janie's softly waving black hair was floating back over her shoulders. There, in Janie, was independence incarnate, and trust, too, between her and her dog. Another sip of chocolate, smooth and thick. *Goodness,* the chocolate said, coating her tongue, you can have goodness in your life, thick and rich: satisfaction, delight.

Sometimes she believed that hopeful idea; other times chocolate had vanished from the cosmos, swallowed by some black hole in herself.

Back then, at home in Montgomery, the table had been lord of the dining room; here it was the generous kitchen table in the double-size kitchen. Where would Yves and she eat? She hadn't decided yet. Did he want to give anything to her life? Doubtful. But still, with his French upbringing, he was extremely interesting, made her feel fully alive and hopeful.

SHE PICKED UP THE CHOCOLATE and strolled aimlessly into the living room, just her and the chocolate, to savor its message. Except for her mother's piano and her father's clock, all the furnishings in the red living room were contemporary. It was the center of the house, with five doors, leading like arteries to the rest of the house. Humphrey's taste was evident here: an allegiance to the now, but with treasures and selected influences revered from the past.

Kathryn and Humphrey had bought the trapeze painting the day Kathryn signed a huge book contract. What a conspiracy, what a self-indulgence it had been, what a celebration of the contemporary Louisville painter Joyce Garner. Full of themselves, of shared glee, Kathryn and Humphrey had celebrated the contract at Proof on Main Street, drank a bottle of champagne to the twenty-first century, and plotted the joyful spending to come, on art, on travel, on beauty. She had wanted to say to every creative soul in the city: *Celebrate!* Celebrate with me: to art, to life!

Kathryn glanced down at what would have been called a Turkey carpet in the Old South, a palette of red and blue, swirled together, a flower riot of strong colors, and floating above it, on the mantel a touch of yellow in the small, soft sculptured horse (signed *g. schulz*), bought at the Unitarian auction. Back then, at the auction, Humphrey had been a child, but even then there had been an unuttered pact between mother and son, how they would spend money like joy, without stint, and when they recognized what they must have from life, how they would spend themselves. (Not always wisely. Usually with passion, grit, and even a measure of courage.)

Even when Humphrey was a child, they would aid and abet and conspire to get for themselves, for each other, that which they wanted. That day, at the auction at the First Unitarian Universalist Church, Kathryn and her child had looked at each other and known exactly how the other felt. They would have it: the soft yellow horse with gray spots; the antique Japanese kimono; the small sphere of glass holding inside its sway not only a world but also that world's cloud-swirled atmosphere and a hint of outer space.

On a long car trip—after Peter had left them—listening to the Ninth Symphony blossom into its climactic "Ode to Joy," Humphrey had wanted to possess for his own *that* celebration of human achievement: "Teach me," little Humphrey demanded. "Teach me the German words." Fearlessly, never mind the size of the audience, Humphrey would grip his pint-size cello between his knees and play and sing in confident German what Beethoven and Schiller had made for the world.

Maybe, *she* herself had made, Ryn thought, not a work of those proportions, but still a work of art in her new novel, something for those for whom language and literature enhanced life. Human achievement: it was almost the same act to celebrate it fully as it was to create it in the first place.

PORTRAIT

BECAUSE PAPA HAS GONE OUT, I timidly say to Maman that perhaps I will not take my brother for a walk, after our luncheon—that I would like to stay home to paint. And so she leaves Nurse with me (who always goes to sleep in the rocking chair very quickly), and she and Étienne kiss me good-bye on both of my cheeks, one on each side. They are so happy that I almost wish I were going to be part of that happiness. But inside me is the happiness of preparing to paint, like a golden plum but warm.

I watch them walk away, her long arm in saffron reaching down, his hand in hers, and his arm clad in emerald green. In a blink, they are gone.

Carefully and slowly, I get out all the things that I will need, and I arrange them exactly so. I want the light to be similar to the one in Saint Eustache, the natural light, not the stained-glass phantoms. I will not paint Nurse this afternoon, but because she is still, I study her. Nurse's face is turned away, her head resting on the back of the rocker, her breathing quiet. Her cap bunches prettily on her head.

I cannot raise my table easel very high, but I want the angle to be as it was at Saint Eustache. The painting of Saint John glows like an ember in my imagination, but I want to fan that ember into a new flame. My own vision. I am excited because I do not know exactly what my rendering of Saint John will become. I raise the easel by putting each of its legs on a stack of Papa's books. I put cushions on the floor and kneel down lower, lifting my arm up. It is awkward.

After I chalk in the outline, I rest a bit. To refresh my eyes, I study the sleeping head of Nurse, the very slight change that is made in her features as she breathes in and out, regularly. Part of me is idle, gathering energy, almost dozing. Then I assemble my brushes, a bouquet of flats and rounds, but now I must close my eyes to what is present and remember, even before I begin the mixing process. The absolute quiet in the house is delicious to my ears. I realize I have forgotten to put my smock on over my dress, but I do not want to risk forgetting, and I decide to proceed.

I start with the saint's eyes, for the center of the eyes were painted with the greatest precision; but now I only position and suggest them, and I work as rapidly as I can, using my favorite round. Because the hairs of my favorite have a bit of snap to them, they return to place after use, and I feel pleasure about the competence of my tool. I am doing only the face, a pure portrait with no world about it. It is almost frightening how stroke by stroke a companion comes to life at the tip of my brush, out of the sized linen. The word *blasphème* comes to mind, though I have never thought it before when I have created faces, in any medium. Like a ball, the word rolls around in my head.

I suck in my breath, as I did in church, for an idea has occurred at the back of my mind. My hand has almost become my brain, and it knows more and dares more than I can think. But the idea is this: that the word *blasphème* has come to me indicates the degree of my success. I have almost fooled the eye: this is not art, but life that I have quickened on my little canvas, and that, perhaps, is blasphemy. I want to make the face *live,* and it almost does, and I am half afraid of the saint and what he must think of me. There cannot be a face without some affect, some expression, nor can there be expression without thought.

I know what to do. I will give him a modern collar: he will seem like an ordinary man, a Parisian. Now he is mine and no longer belongs to the Church of Saint Eustache. The collar is very easy; I have looked at those of Papa and his friends dozens of times to understand how they're constructed. But this new face floating up from the woven threads, covering the threads, still has something of a holy glow to it. And then I know something shocking that no one has ever said to me. It is life itself that is holy.

I remember drawing in the mud with a stick. The Bible says we are made of clay, but it does not say we are holy. But how can it be otherwise?

Life is the holy glow. I feel very frightened. I look at my hand that knows so much and moves so surely, almost without my will. My hand is full of life, and what I am doing is holy because it lives. I put down my brush and cover my eyes. I am trembling.

I am sublimely happy.

I have no idea how long I have worked, but Nurse is starting to stir, and the face of a new man is looking at me. He is young and pink and cream. His face is made of new skin. I have created him, entirely new. It seems strange to do something so ordinary as to walk across the familiar room. I do not want anyone to see my painting before Papa, so I carry it on the easel to the buffet and turn the easel so it faces the wall.

Papa has told me many artists do this. It would be rude for anyone, even Étienne, to peek around, and of course he would not grasp the easel to move it. He is not allowed. Maman and Étienne will notice the turned easel when they come in, but they will not ask me about my work. If I like, I may speak of it, and they will be all interest and courtesy. Étienne is good at this sort of conversation, even though he is very young. He is always happy for me, and he will say, "What was the best part?" meaning when did I most enjoy my work? And I will point and explain everything.

But not this time. I will ask him what he saw and did on his walk with Maman, and what flavor was his fruit tart.

AFTER WE HAVE HAD OUR LIGHT SUPPER, Papa returns with three friends, and one of them is the painter Doyen. They are all very light-hearted, and Maman sits close, listening and sometimes commenting. I like all of Papa's friends. Each of them interests me in his speaking and posture. While each has an interesting face, there are always certain expressions for each man that I like best to see and I watch for those moments and for what topic or feeling brings their features together in the way that I consider most harmonious or curious. Everything changes at the same time: the eyes, the corners of the mouth, the angle of the head and tilt of the chin, certain lines around the eyes and mouth.

At last there is a little silence, but Papa has not yet brought out his pipe, though he is reaching for it when I say, "Papa, would you like to see what I painted today?"

Immediately he is all attention. His eyes and skin and *alertness* tell me he cares more about what I have said than anything else he has heard. He takes his time in replying. Nothing is hasty. He looks directly at me, already proud, and the light comes into his eyes. The slow smile of invitation and delight begin together.

"What do you have for us, Louise-Élisabeth?"

All of the men have stopped moving; they are inspired by the quality of Papa's attention, and also I think of them as my friends even though they are grown up and I am just a girl. It would be difficult to paint them as a group, but for a moment they are completely still, waiting, as though they could be painted. Maman puts her hand most kindly on my back and says, close to my ear, "Please do show us, Élisabeth."

I lift the wooden stretcher and its canvas off the easel and carry it by the edges in such a way that Papa will be the first to see it. He stands up, waiting for me to present my work. My painting is not very big. I tilt it up for him to see. And he gasps, just the same quick little gasp that I have!

"My child," he says, and both his hands are gently on my shoulders, "I have said it, and it is true. You are and ever will be a painter." He looks straight into my eyes and back to the painting and back and forth.

I watch his eyes fill with tears of amazement, but he *knows*. He does not doubt anything. Rays of joy seem to emanate from his fatherly face, and pleasure pierces me, like a spear to the heart, like *ecstasy*.

His words calling me a painter are a spear, a wreath, a crown, settling on my head. I feel both its lightness and its weight.

His friends all jump up and crowd around. They shake my father's hand and touch his shoulders in congratulations; they exclaim. Speechless, Doyen embraces my father. The philosophical ones completely agree and go on and on. When Doyen, the painter, finally speaks, he says, "She has the gift," and all of them become silent. They do not touch me.

My father sits back into his old leather chair; he gathers me into his lap and puts his arms around me. Still holding the rigid square of canvas, I turn the painting so that my mother can see it, too, but Étienne has already gone to bed.

I know the face is not really the face of Saint John because after I changed his collar, there were some other touches to make him more like my father's friends. What pleases me most is the shade of blue I put behind his head, though the face, and the way it seems like a real face, is what seems important to everyone. In the morning I will talk to Étienne about how I made that glowing blue.

FOUNTAIN

W ITH HER CUP OF CHOCOLATE, Ryn sat in the quiet gray chair, a skewed parenthetic nest itself, to remember her journey since the last divorce.

More than two years ago, here she had sat after Mark had left the house; this place, at the heart of the house, this soft chair had called to her: *Sit here. Be.*

Having wandered here to the center of the house and taken this seat, she had felt the clouds shifting inside her being. She had begun to swell, to expand, to fill every lovely room and corner of the house; her unfettered self rubbed against mirrors and windowpanes, it rose to the chandeliers and slid along the faceted crystal; spirit rose like a vapor up the stairs. In outward rush, all, all space had been filled and fulfilled. *Joy!* Freedom.

She had gasped, astonished, and the expansion had reversed itself. Consciousness contracted, came back to her close as a cocoon, and traveled still closer to a depth inside herself. There was an inward rushing, then she came to a still pool. Recognizing the place, she knew its name for the first time. *Peace.*

Here alone, in this house, single, she had traveled outward and she had journeyed inward and she had known them both: joy and peace. Now a memory, but those moments had been real, that mystic journey inside her house on St. James Court.

WHEN MARK HAD MOVED OUT, she wrestled with the question whether she, alone again, should return to the little house in the Highlands, which she still owned, or stay grandly on St. James Court.

Her beloved aging mother had lived there in the small house in the Highlands with her, and baby Humphrey, and Humphrey's father, Peter. Sitting in her mother's rocking chair in her mother's upstairs bedroom under the eaves, one day in that long-ago time with windows and light coming in from three directions, Kathryn's mother had said, "This is the nicest room I've ever had." Knowing that her mother had loved their old home in Montgomery, Kathryn had felt honored. It had been very hard for her mother to leave that familiar, jasmine-scented city, the home in which her own three children had grown up. But she had adjusted. Kathryn had succeeded in providing for her mother, just as she'd always planned that she would do. When the dementia had set in and when Kathryn woke herself in the morning sobbing because she had taken her mother to a nursing home, finally, Peter had said, "Bring her back, Ryn, if you want to. We'll manage."

But Kathryn had doubted they could. And hadn't her mother, Lila (a name with the scent of lilac and lavender), said, "The day may come when you need to take me to a nursing home, and if it does, then you just do it. And don't feel bad about it. It's not as though we won't see each other anymore"? And Kathryn had seen her mother, every day, while her mother's mind slipped away. But always they had been glad to see each other, whatever and regardless of recognized identities and labels. They had transcended that: *loved one* she was to her mother, and her mother to her: completely, absolutely, unreservedly loved.

That awful day in the parking lot, after a visit, automatically the car radio had presented the Busoni piano transcription of the Bach Chaconne for unaccompanied violin. Before her marriage, Lila had played the piece on the violin; after marriage and four children (three of whom lived), she had played the piano transcription (*Easier to play the piano, when you're pregnant, than the violin,* she had said), and here it was full throttle on the car radio, thanks to WUOL-FM, but played on a big Bösendorfer—it had to be—because the low notes were lower than any ordinary piano could have reached reached reached all the way down to the gut string of Kathryn's being, strung from the base of her skull to her tailbone, plucked, and the deep resonance caused Kathryn to scream out loud, safely inside the rolled-up windows of the car. All she could do in the midst of such beauty was to scream for her inability to save her mother, for her mother's loss of herself.

The music had caught Kathryn off guard. It had not been a matter of letting herself scream. The scream had roared out of her. Through the radio, when Bach and the Bösendorfer had reached into her and unleashed her sorrow, the gush of Kathryn's grief had filled the car. That was the way it was with music, when you suddenly, unexpectedly heard music that hooked an essential component of your identity.

KATHRYN REMEMBERED HOW IT HAD BEEN on the ocean liner, the first trip to Europe, when on the return, the ship orchestra had struck up "Dixie," a song that stood for so much that was wrong in the South that Kathryn had actively opposed, and yet, still, it was the song of her childhood home. And there was the convulsion of the heart and the warm tears in her eyes at the unexpected resurrection of "Dixie" in the middle of the ocean. That moment she had felt obliged to label pure sentimentality.

When she had taken the teaching job in Louisville, Kathryn had thought *If the South is too much for me, I can just cross over the Ohio River into Indiana; I can cross on the frozen ice if I need to, like Eliza in* Uncle Tom's Cabin. *Yes,* Kathryn had thought after Mark had moved out: *I could go home to the little house in the Highlands,* the house where she had lived when she wrote her earlier books. Because she still owned it, she could go back to the dear little house she had bought for Peter and her mother and herself, where Humphrey was conceived and took his first steps. How bravely he had descended the small staircase to declare at the bottom in an articulated, idiomatic sentence, "I made it." She could go back there.

No, she couldn't. Humphrey had demanded and begged that his mother not move back. After Peter had left them for another woman and her boy and girl, after Mark had come into their lives, and during Humphrey's teen years, terrible things had happened to Humphrey in that house. The boyfriend, Jerry, had treated Humphrey in ways that Kathryn could not face. Better never to go back. (And she, in her liberal, permissive way, had let those terrible things happen. *No!* The word barked out of her into the present moment on this distant day of triumph, this day, which she now inhabited.) No. She had not "let" it happen. She had believed Humphrey was safer and happier than he would have been without his companion.

When Mark came courting, he had been the courageous neurosurgeon, one who wanted to travel the world with her, come to stay (they thought) for the rest of their lives. Mark had been like a new father for Humphrey, someone who cared about his feelings, Humphrey had proclaimed. Mark had a cousin who was gay; he understood.

That house in the Highlands was small; it would have been just right for her now, a family of one. However, having failed to keep Humphrey safe within those walls, now she did not deserve to live there.

Always her own past (though not Humphrey's), even if full of pain, seemed precious, worthy to Kathryn of being preserved. The past was like a big soft person, both baby and old woman, needing her protection and tender care. But wouldn't she feel in touch with the precious past if she went back to that little one-and-a-half-story house, charming Bavarian, with wood paneling and a real fireplace, the whole back full of windows facing the south and the cloistered garden, and a wild black cherry tree in one corner sheltering the clubhouse Peter had built, before he left, for little boy Humphrey?

How could a thing, even a house, be precious? *Life* was what mattered. Every individual life to be treasured, and none, none should ever be wasted. She rubbed the palm of her hand on the chair's gray suede cloth. It was the theme of all her books, and the thread that ran so true through her life. There was no one she wished ill, not even those whose infidelity had broken her. Had not they come to her full of their own brokenness?

Still, how to live? Where should she live? Again she remembered Leslie's balanced phrase, insightful and true: "You can always hold the Highlands house in your heart," Leslie had told her, "but the St. James house cradles you." Such were the powers of Leslie's mind, incisive and precise. Kathryn brought the thick-edged mug to her lips again: still delicious, but cooling. Was Leslie reading now *Portrait of the Artist as an Old Woman*? How did its sentences sing, with Leslie's musical ear hovering over them?

Kathryn decided she would reheat the chocolate, bring in the newspaper, and dawdle. To the stove: her fingers hesitated—because practical things were difficult for her during intense times—then turned the controls. If dementia came to Ryn, would she live in a continuous moment of other worlds?

Her mother, never very sure of how mechanical or electric things worked, eventually had sat baffled before the task of turning on a new radio. But she could still play the piano up to a week before her death, with her right hand, while Kathryn played the left hand. Bach, an easy Bach piece, had been the last; an easy piece because Kathryn had never been up to much more on the piano, despite loving it.

Reheated, the warm chocolate filled Kathryn's mouth and throat, pleased her tongue, as she stood looking over her kitchen sink into the large back garden. The heated swimming pool mirrored the October blue sky. Golden leaves, wider than a hand, fallen from the giant cottonwood, floated on its surface.

ACROSS THE COURT, on the other side of the fountain, graceful Leslie, slender, healthy, skin with a hint of lavender like hot cocoa, sat down in one of a pair of matching chairs, big puffs like giant white-leather marshmallows. *Portrait of the Artist as an Old Woman.* But wasn't it *"A" Portrait of the Artist . . .* that James Joyce had written? Leslie removed the large rubber band from Ryn's printout and, without looking at it, placed the loop on a circular side table, where the elastic promptly curled up on itself like something alive. *Old woman?* Leslie thought. She didn't feel old. Leslie felt *new.* Young is not the only other side of old. *New, as opposed to old.* And Kathryn, divorced, seemed renewed, too, Leslie thought. They were both slender and supple, could walk miles, never mind the number seventy.

PORTRAIT

NEW YEAR'S DAY," Papa says over and over, briskly rubbing his hands together. There is mischief in his eye, and I know why. In the mirror, he settles and resettles his hat, looking for the most jaunty effect. He is full of vigor because when he goes walking on New Year's Day, he knows he may kiss any pretty woman of his acquaintance whom he meets.

"Put on your coat," Maman tells me merrily, and to him she adds, "Élisabeth is old enough to walk with us this year."

"Really?" Papa says, hesitating. He winks at me. "Then you will see your father enjoying himself. Once a year!" He pulls my ear, quite gently, and adds, "And suppose someone wishes to kiss you?"

I look down and murmur, "But I am only twelve." The truth is no one would want to kiss me because I am not pretty. My eye falls on my little brother. At almost nine, he also has Papa's charming, merry manner, but Étienne is not so boisterous. When he talks with anyone, despite his young age, Étienne is a radiant person, one of both light and warmth, equally full of ease and natural goodwill. It is very easy to love Étienne because he is very loving, and I love him very much.

But not in quite the same way as I love Maman and Papa. Because he is my little brother, he needs me to take care of him, and he is a delight in his little person. I look at them, so much bigger, and think I will always take care of Étienne because he will always be my little brother.

How quickly Papa walks when he sees a pretty woman of his acquaintance coming toward us, with her escort. We all emanate clouds of frost around our heads. He leaves Maman and me and runs ahead. Maman doesn't mind at all. "Oh, here comes so-and-so!" she says cheerfully. "Do you remember meeting Yolande, Élisabeth?" One time, Papa comes back and says appreciatively, "That Bette is a real beauty," but Bette is not the name Maman has given this lady.

Maman herself is kissed several times, with quiet courtesy, and it is easy to see that no other lady compares to her either in figure or face. One of the gentlemen even says, "Mme Vigée, you are the star of the avenue!"

After he goes on, and he is very handsome, I explain to Maman, to be sure she understands, "He means you shine brighter than anyone, Maman, in your beauty." I surprise myself by adding authoritatively, "And he is a man who tells the truth."

Maman hugs me. "What else is true of a star, my daughter?"

I puzzle a moment and then I answer. "Stars hang high in the sky, and no one can touch them." I feel a little troubled. "But he kissed you, Maman."

"So he did, and it was a very nice kiss, indeed, but that is because this is the first day of the new year."

I think of the word *gorgeous* when I look at my mother's rosy cheeks, her dark abundant hair, and the sparkle of her expression. I know she truly loves me, though she loves my brother more, but she loves our father most of all. She knows she is beautiful, but she is more than that: she is attractive. How are she and my father different? I do not have the sentences for that comparison. *Comparison* is a way of thinking.

Often I have heard my father saying to the men who are writing the encyclopedia, *Compare and contrast, that is the basis of all categories.* And sometimes when we look at paintings created by the same artist in the Louvre, or by different artists, Papa says to me, *Compare and contrast, my daughter, for that is the way to sound judgment.*

I have found this to be true, but first my eyes tell me the truth, immediately, and then by thinking about how the paintings or even sculptures are alike and different I find words for what I already know. And then I see with even more delight. My eye is more sure than Papa's eye, and sometimes he changes his mind. I am very very tactful when we disagree, for that is something I have learned from Étienne. Maman says he was born with winning ways. Winning ways are tactful, considerate ways that win one affection.

It is cold this New Year's Day, but we go into a café and drink hot mulled wine; even I have a demitasse half full into which my mother pours water to cool down the drink. We sip it slowly and open our coats to let in the warmth of the café. Everyone is merry and talks loudly with excitement. My father has removed his hat and it sits in the fourth chair, looking rather wise for a hat, but then out the window he sees a woman whose hair bubbles in golden ringlets.

"Marie!" he exclaims. Quickly he gulps down all the mulled wine, then he grabs up his hat and runs out to kiss her. Because his hat blocks our view, we do not really see the kiss, but we know from the way his arm encircles her that he *is* kissing her, and then her face comes away, and she is smiling at him with her lips pressed together and her eyes dancing.

"There is a woman with wanton ways," my mother says. She is not upset, but there is disapproval in her voice.

"What are wanton ways?"

"She is not true to her own dignity. She gives the men too much encouragement."

I am trying to understand the import of what my mother has said and so I ask her what being true means.

"Women must be true to their husbands and they must always be true to their own natures, as well, regardless of how the husbands act."

I think of how my mother has received the kisses of her men friends today. She has been friendly; her face glows. But her eyes do not dance. She does not pull her head back while she holds the man's eyes and pout her lips, as though she would like to be kissed again. *Once a year,* my papa said, and I think also that only one kiss is allowed.

After we come home, Étienne and I are sitting together by the fire. He asks me, "Was there lots of kissing?"

"Yes," I answer and smile at him. "And hot mulled wine, too."

"I love kissing," he says happily, but I do not feel entirely cheerful, though I take care to hide the dark streak in my mood from my little brother.

Before it becomes dark, Maman says that we will celebrate New Year's Mass at Saint Eustache, and she holds out her hands to Étienne and me. I feel happy thinking of the beauty of the church, and how I like it when Étienne and I sit quietly together while Maman takes communion. I keep my brother company and watch over him. The church seems to swell up and become bigger and more grand and mysterious when the two of us sit together waiting, sometimes whispering to each other a little.

Because it is a special day, I think perhaps Papa will join us, but he says that it is his turn to sit by the fire, and he would like the pleasure of a nap in the quiet house. I understand, for I too love quietness and because Nurse and Cook have been given the day through the kindness of my parents it will be especially quiet by the fire. The logs will burn down, and when we come home there will be the red glow of embers in front of my father's crossed feet. As soon as his eyes are fully open and looking at us, he will say quietly, without moving, *How nice it is to have you home, my dears.* We will be gone a long time, for today there will be the organ and the choir, and I will be in ecstasy.

IT IS EXACTLY AS I HAD HOPED. Of course we leave our coats on. Before Maman goes forward for communion, she tells me that if my feet feel at all numb that I should take Étienne to one of the braziers to warm his feet.

There are many children today among the chairs with woven backs and seats, and I like seeing them, and how the big children take care of the little ones, sometimes holding handkerchiefs to their noses, but Maman does not take us outside at all if we have drippy noses.

The music of the organ and the choir completely fills up all the space inside the church. The space is so full that the sound presses hard into our ears, for it has no other place to go. The late-afternoon light has a heaviness, and there is darkness in some places already inside the church, but the candles glow beautifully though they are not strong enough to keep the gloom back very far. Still I can see quite well.

Maman returns and asks, "Warm enough?" and I nod, for the organ swells and blooms like a flower that presses against my heart, and then the choir sings Latin words, and I see there are tears in my mother's eyes at the beauty of the music and because we three are here together, and suddenly there are tears in my eyes, as well. Now we sing together, my mother and I, and we enter the music at exactly the same moment together on exactly the same pitch, with just the same fullness of spirit. From my mother, my eyes have learned how to feel more powerfully and how to express my happiness, and suddenly the tears spill down my cheeks.

She sees this and hugs me very tightly and closely to her side and puts her other hand on the top of my brother's head, but he doesn't notice us. My mother kisses the top of my forehead, and she whispers, "You are my true daughter."

I know what she says is true, and that my heart is true to her, and I will obey her and try always to add to her happiness.

When we come home, Papa is not dozing by the fire as I had imagined, but he has left us a note saying that he has gone out to talk politics for the first night of the New Year. As I drift to sleep, I hear Maman sniffling, and I fear she has caught a cold. It happens that Papa makes some noise, perhaps a stumble, when he comes in, loud enough to wake me, and I hear him say ominously, *From what I have heard tonight, it will probably be only a short time till our world is turned upside down.*

FOUNTAIN

N OT HAVING READ A WORD, Leslie stood up and left the printout in her chair all in one gesture. She was restless. Here in her new condo, she could go outside without really going out. It was a convenient arrangement to live in the air, a level above the street. Safe.

For a moment she remembered her husband—stout, built close to the ground—and then she dissolved the image.

She thought of her second marriage as a silk scarf, paisley, lying in the gutter, with the muddy, brutal footprint of her husband upon it. Forget the disappointing or shocking particulars; she had reduced them to metaphor. The fineness of her fiber was what she had offered him, and he had trod upon it.

Though the apartment was not large and her bed was still surrounded by boxes to be unpacked, it affirmed the spaciousness of her new world to walk through the front room, open the French doors, and stand outside on the balcony. *Gotta get me some air,* her grandmother would have said.

Yes, when restlessness came to her, when the urge was strong "to get some air," why there were the French doors and the balcony and her own fresh air. Just below, in a tumult of waters, stood dark green Venus, like a waterspout having just twisted her way free of the sea.

With what quick rushing the water cascaded into the pool below! *Why rush to be or do anything?* She smiled because she knew only an aging woman such as herself, who had freed herself from living too busily for the sake of others, would have the leisure to ask such a question. Here was retirement and one of her best friends across the street. Of course it meant a great deal that they had known each other when they were young. Ryn could remember Leslie's grandmother and her mother, how she had almost ruined her sight with the endless work of a seamstress in Montgomery.

Leslie thought of the long hours her mother had sat in the alterations department, sewing, beside Rosa Parks. A few times, Leslie had ventured to visit them there, and it had been a great pleasure to come upon them, unexpectedly, at their work. They wore identical glasses, bifocals, each lens with a little window set in the bottom, glass in glass, for close work. Their work was very fine, precise. Always their glasses were polished, spotless, and gleaming. Leslie recalled a contemporary quilt she had seen in Chicago, in the DuSable Museum. The quilt artist included not only the iconic image of Rosa Parks, seated alone at the front of the bus, but also, on the seat just behind her, the image of President Obama. The truth of the quilt had brought a lump to Leslie's throat and glazed her eyes with tears. Yes, more than half a century later, he had ridden to victory on Rosa Parks's bus.

Leslie pinched herself: *Wait too long, my lady of leisure, and you'll never get your second book written, let alone published.*

More than a week ago, perhaps the second morning after moving into the condo, Leslie's late sleep had been interrupted by Ryn on the telephone, inviting her to come over to her house, to view the fountain looking east so that she might see it as a fountain of silvery light. Now in plain daylight, in its greenness, the sculpture and pool seemed almost as natural as the ocean.

Evenings, when the west-sinking sun touched the waters, sometimes Leslie had noted a hint of gold or faint tints of pink or mauve reflected in the wide receiving pool. Now, off her right shoulder, above and across, beginning to sense the presence of another person, Leslie glanced up.

And there was Shirley on her own balcony, the neighbor whose flat was on the third level on the north side of the flats. Leslie and Shirley and all the tenants facing St. James Court shared the central entrance and the main staircase, which also divided the condos into those with windows on either the north or the south side of the building. Standing on her balcony, Shirley hovered like a long gray shadow. Leslie thought of the Shaker village at Pleasant Hill, near Lexington, where two individuals—one male, one female—appointed by the community lived at its center in a high apartment, isolated, watching the behavior of all the others. "The Eyes of God," the Shakers called the rotating, community-appointed overseers. Rather like the church deacons back in Montgomery.

From her third-floor flat, Shirley might feel she had quite the over-view of St. James Court, Leslie speculated. Because those who lived in the St. James flats rarely engaged in conversation from balcony to bal-cony, especially not across different levels, Leslie need not call out a hello at this moment. Decorum, respect for privacy, was part of the Court friendliness. It was relaxing to be here on the northern cusp of the South; the pace was slower than New York's had been, complacent. Familiar. That was all right with Leslie now. Back in her youth, she could never have lived here on St. James Court. Nor were neighborhoods integrated racially in Montgomery. Now nobody blinked.

Leslie scarcely knew Shirley, and she wouldn't take time to chat now. She needed to settle into reading, but she glanced at her cello case, standing like a sarcophagus in one corner. Because Ryn had been working so long and steadily on her book, she'd introduced Leslie to only a few neighbors. But Leslie wanted to be a part of things; it would bring her pleasure to feel a part of Old Louisville. In New York, Leslie had been a part of her neigh-borhood, and it had been easy enough to divide the sheep from the goats.

Didn't Ryn say there was classical music (and tea) in the second-floor lobby of the Brown Hotel, on Sunday afternoons? Only a mile to the north from St. James Court. What about the Old Louisville Holiday House Tour? Yes, that event coming next, in early December, invited the public into the decorated interiors of the Victorian homes. And she'd certainly attend the gala fund-raiser for charity in a huge tent on the green held the weekend before the St. James Art Fair. The first weekend in October, Ryn said more people strolled the artists' booths than attended the Kentucky Derby. Community, community!

Intending to begin immediately to read Kathryn's novel, Leslie had pulled on jeans and a loose cashmere sweater, without having had breakfast. But she hadn't felt ready. The book deserved a particular kind of focus, and she needed to settle herself. Now she was hungry. It was nearly eleven o'clock. Were most writers practicing procrastinators? Devotees of guilt and drama? She stepped into the hall and glanced at herself: the jeans fit as though they had been tailored, and the loose sweater was a fine foil for them. It was an innocuous outfit; one that would offend no one, but later she'd put on something more considered. Being well dressed was important; Ryn would think Leslie was depressed if she weren't nicely put together. Well, dressing with care was, for Leslie, a way to ward off depression. It was amazing how little she had aged. Most white people thought she was barely fifty.

This morning and every morning in the future, it had been and would be good to wake up purposefully, Leslie thought. With *significant* purpose. Not merely an effort to make the best of an unsuitable relationship. What folly to have supposed her last husband was any more congenial or trustworthy than the one before. Twenty-five years of tempestuous, bad-tempered marriage. A waste.

No more.

When they left the South, she'd had a chance for freedom and he stole it—with no notion that he didn't have the right. He took what had been won, and oppressed her.

FROM HER BALCONY three stories above the fountain, Shirley zipped up a soft gray cocoon of a robe as she saw her neighbor Kathryn Callaghan emerge on her front porch. Shirley had lost her job, so why not wear a robe all morning if she wanted to. She wasn't going out. She'd watch Ryn, or whomever she pleased. Dressed in sloppy wine-colored corduroy jeans and a loose dark blue corduroy shirt, wearing sneakers, it was obvious Ryn had taken no care of her appearance. There was something distasteful about a published author in love with such old clothes, purple and blue. What was she trying to prove? Shirley watched Kathryn stop on her walkway to survey her yard; a hodgepodge of chrysanthemums in many colors flanked the walkway.

Kathryn would probably be feeling some kind of silly *gratitude* or affection toward those old clothes, Shirley thought, for making her body comfortable. For having acquired a big shirt a shade of midnight blue that matched her eyes? Simply because these clothes had been hers for a long time? For one reason or another, Shirley knew Ryn would find not just contentment but undue satisfaction in her outfit. If a neighbor spoke to her, Ryn would feel not the least embarrassment about looking sloppy, even down-at-the-heels as though she couldn't afford a better outfit. It must be nice to work at home. Shirley felt a wave of resentment, but she made herself ride the wave and let it go.

Kathryn was a friend, or at least unfailingly friendly, and then, of course, despite being a published writer, Kathryn had experienced her own disappointments. Three husbands. Not one good and faithful man whose happiness lay in making his wife happy. This, Shirley had for herself (though they had lost the house on Belgravia and found it necessary to move into the St. James flats). St. James Court was an upstart compared with Belgravia, where most of the houses dated back to the 1880s. Shirley zipped her robe a little higher to the top of its mandarin collar, so that the robe was neat and fashionable as well as comfortable.

Still, the view here on the Court was interesting to her—St. James and its fountain. But what a din it made, all that rushing water calling attention to itself! Belgravia maintained a quiet elegance.

It doesn't beat, it gushes, Shirley thought suddenly, of the heart, remembering the home she'd left on Belgravia Court. She grieved, too, for the bank where she'd worked, the other women, but losing her home! It was as though a vital organ had been taken from her own body. She thought of her former fireplace, not a mere Victorian mantel of natural wood, a few spindles and a dull, oblong mirror, but a work of art, glazed tiles, a rich, black-hued blue, not a one cracked or missing. Cobalt blue. The tiles were from the same famous Cincinnati manufacturer who had tiled the Rathskeller in the basement of the Seelbach Hotel downtown.

Whenever Kathryn had visited Shirley and Trevor on Belgravia and a real fire burned briskly (Shirley's husband knew exactly how to build and tend it), Kathryn always said, "Why, that's the most gorgeous fireplace I know, the blue surrounding the orange-red!" She said it with real joy, a generosity of admiration, which was one of the reasons Shirley liked her. Kathryn could take pleasure in what belonged to others.

She and Kathryn recognized what was truly unique and admirable in each other, never mind the warts. Theirs was a realistic neighborliness, Shirley thought. She clenched her fist and then spread her fingers. That was where the strength and beauty of a good neighbor lay—in being realistic, honest. Each knew and forgave the other's shortcomings. Forgiveness like smooth vanilla pudding, they offered each other. Shirley smiled.

But Kathryn had never shared a deep trouble with Shirley, as she had with Daisy, who still lived on Belgravia. Shirley thought of a time when Shirley and Kathryn and a few of Daisy's other women friends had accepted an invitation to tea at Daisy's house, and Kathryn had suddenly talked about desperate times. Not the economy. She had told about her personal traumas in an offhand way, at first, then she had become overwhelmed with emotion.

Kathryn, in the presence of Shirley and the guests, had said how when she was really overwhelmed, back when both Kathryn and Daisy lived in the Highlands before they moved to Old Louisville, how Kathryn, desperate, had simply found herself, twice, on Daisy's doorstep, knocking at the door. *Both times, Daisy just took one look at me—she hadn't been expecting me—and she said, "Why, Kathryn, won't you come in and have a cup of tea."*

Shirley knew Kathryn was telling the stories to honor Daisy and not because she trusted Shirley or the other guests with privileged information. They scarcely mattered; Kathryn just wanted them to understand that Daisy was a special person. It was an honor to be invited to the home Daisy and her husband, Daniel, shared on Belgravia. A bitterness came into Shirley's mouth.

The tale of how Kathryn had turned to Daisy was about how Kathryn had finally taken her mother to the nursing home. A late bloomer, Kathryn had been on the cusp of publishing her first book with a small university press; it was long ago. As soon as she left her mother at the nursing home, Kathryn had come to Daisy for succor. *It was the only place I knew to go,* Kathryn told the neighbors over tea. And ah, yes, five years before that, Kathryn had broken down over enrolling her darling young son in day care.

Life's turning points were things people just had to get around, like corners, Shirley had remarked sagely, before she bit into one of the delicious tea-cake cookies Daisy had provided. In response, all the other guests, but neither Kathryn nor Daisy, had silently nodded in agreement.

What an excess of feeling had gushed out of Kathryn, despite Shirley's wise, objective tone! Holding one of Daisy's nicest teacups with the fingertips of both hands, Kathryn had allowed twin rivulets of tears to course down her cheeks and fall from her jawline. *Her mother, so old and defenseless; her son, still a toddler*—probably that was what she was recollecting.

Not the least worried about causing the tea to be spilled, Daisy had reached over and touched Kathryn's hand. *You did what you had to do,* Daisy had said in a firm, even voice. But the writer still felt guilty though the event was long ago. What did ordinary readers of Kathryn's novels know about her instability? Her confusion? Or was it grief? Yes, it was grief, not guilt, Shirley was sure. An excess of grief.

Shirley had felt that unwanted surge too, sometimes. Not that she had let on. When they had to leave their home on Belgravia for the St. James condo, for instance.

Kathryn was behaving as though she had *killed* her child or her mother, or killed something in herself, when she took him to day care and her to the nursing home to live. Those were just natural things to do; it fell to most people to have to do one or the other, if not both.

Shirley regarded the two square planters that fitted into the corners of her balcony. The plump little yellow chrysanthemums nudged each other in a way that suggested a cup of Lemon Zinger tea. Given air, sun, and water—and she had plenty of all of those elements on her balcony—her chrysanthemums should flourish till hard frost. From one planter, Shirley plucked out unwelcome yellow leaves and tossed them over the railing. It was a rather grand gesture, her flinging of leaves off the third-floor balcony.

As she turned her attention from the concrete planters to her narrow flower boxes hanging from the iron railing, Shirley realized that Kathryn's mistake, based on vanity as well as good intentions, was that she thought she could and should have *any and all* of the goodness of life; Kathryn didn't like feeling she was incapable of achieving whatever she wished. That was it: Kathryn believed she was entitled to *any and all* of the goodness of life.

But sometimes—no one knew this truth better than Shirley—you couldn't take care of others the way you'd wish to do. Maybe people who had enough money could, but most people couldn't. Not with Alzheimer's. Shirley had had to take her own father to a home, and it wasn't very nice either, though it was the best they could afford. It stank.

Across the Court, Kathryn, in her sloppy clothes, had descended the semicircular steps of her house and was studying a few pink blossoms on the autumn sedum (or live-forever, as Shirley's father would have called it; he had loved plants). Now Kathryn proceeded toward the sidewalk, down her double-wide walkway between her magnolia trees, which from Shirley's high angle were towering piles of still-shiny green leaves while all other foliage was turning colors. Kathryn stepped lightly down three more steps to the public sidewalk. She lifted her head to look at the fountain, then turned right, scuffing her feet through the brilliant red leaves the maple tree had dropped. *Acting like she's a schoolgirl again,* Shirley thought. Kathryn's head was bowed as if she were interested in the pavement or the fallen leaves.

Perhaps this was a moment when the past was all too present for Kathryn, just as it was for Shirley sometimes. Juggling all those balls from the past, the present, and the future exhausts the mind, causes you to look down to avoid the world hanging all around you. You want to think, to focus, to sort it all out, what's happened and why. Headed south toward Belgravia Court, Kathryn kept her eyes on her laced-up walking shoes. She hadn't looked across the Court to see who might be out on her balcony; she hadn't waved.

It wasn't usual for Kathryn to walk like this in the morning; early in the day was when she did her writing; dusk was the time for absentminded walking. It was in the evening when Shirley and Trevor were walking the little dogs that they encountered Kathryn, exchanged pleasantries. Because Trevor thought she was famous, he didn't want to stare at her and embarrass her, but then he would go and address her by a nickname! Just one quick glance, then Trevor would say in a friendly voice, "Good evening, Ryn."

Why would her husband make up an ugly nickname just as though he understood her in some special way! Kathryn was a lovely name. Ryn sounded like part of *rent,* not what you pay for lodging but rent like a tear in a piece of cloth, like in the Bible when a person rent his clothes to show his grief.

Maybe Shirley's slightly famous neighbor had finished her novel and didn't need her best brain, as she called it, this morning. She could waste it on a walk. Shirley hoped so (she sighed); she knew how hard Kathryn worked at the writing. Hours and hours. Sometimes, like last night, even burning the midnight oil. Thank God, they had had regular hours at the bank. People *needed* regular hours or life fell apart. On the other hand,

Shirley knew that sometimes a writer got stalled. What would that feel like to Kathryn?

Kathryn's library light had been burning last night when Shirley went to bed at eleven. Since the plantation shutters had been left open, Shirley had noticed Ryn seated at her large white desk, in front of the computer. Stalled, probably.

Shirley heard a car coming too fast rushing down the west lane of St. James Court. She welcomed the diversion. It was tough just being home all day. When the driver passed Kathryn's house, she saw him swivel his head quickly to look at the house, not the fountain. He had bright red hair. Kathryn was already halfway to Belgravia Court, and she paid no attention when the speeding car passed her. Rather recklessly, the car looped around the south end of the court and sped up the east lane, right under Shirley's balcony. She couldn't see the driver much now, just a glimpse before the car was too directly below, but the way he had dashed past Kathryn's house reminded Shirley of somebody. Not in a real hurry to get where he was going after all, this too-fast driver, since he had turned around at the south end and come back. Or lost and confused.

It was an old car, pea green, long and heavy, with some sort of mod orange drawing painted on the passenger door. Probably a substitute door that hadn't been on the original car. Not a bad-looking fellow, red hair and all. Then she remembered Humphrey's old boyfriend. That was who he'd reminded Shirley of. The way he drove had a sort of contempt in it. She hoped it wasn't him. In the end he had made Humphrey miserable, and Kathryn had gone to Atlanta to help her son move out.

Shirley imagined Kathryn standing like a peace totem between the two young men in Atlanta. Packed boxes and suitcases or satchels were scattered around. The other guy had gotten the cat, pure white, a glamorous powder-puff cat, and the big dog.

Probably not Humphrey's old partner. But what about the way the driver just wheeled into St. James Court and then turned around at the south end and raced back north again, fast? He hadn't paid any attention to the fountain. It was the main thing to look at. Most people slowed down at least a little, and hardly anyone ever drove fast; the west lane and the east lane were single lanes, too narrow for fast driving even if they were one-way passages. The lone driver could have exited at the south end, turning either left or right into Hill Street, though turning left was rather hazardous as visibility was limited. Shirley knew she was a careful observer. That was the way to make sense of things. And to make very few mistakes at the bank.

Why had they let her go? No chance now of a trip to England for her and Trevor. Kathryn and Humphrey had gone to England that spring when he broke up with the bad boyfriend. Humphrey and his mother were awfully close—always celebrating this or that together. Traveling at the drop of a hat.

From the flower box hanging on the iron railing, Shirley plucked out a baby oak tree. Planted by a squirrel probably. All her hanging flowers were blue. Plumbago, which had done well, lasting well into autumn. They were bright blue, restful and spritely all at once, like chips of the October sky. Nothing but blue plumbago in her narrow boxes, like a blue horizon hanging along the railings in front of the balcony; the bright blue flowers had a unifying, elegant effect that way. What with the sturdy yellow chrysanthemums in the concrete planters, the colors reminded Shirley of the way French painters sometimes liked to pair the colors blue and yellow.

Kathryn's yard always had a huge mixture of colors; her chrysanthemums now were an autumnal medley: rust, gold, bronze, yellow, snowy white, dark red. The statement they made was too complex. Confused, actually, or greedy, this trying to have *any and all*. Kathryn was out of sight now, around the corner walking west on Belgravia.

KATHRYN HALF HOPED she would run into her friends Daisy or Daniel on Belgravia. She was beginning to feel that this morning was a morning to reconnect with the world. Daisy and Daniel never held her writing hibernations against her. And there was the ginkgo tree at the south end of the Court: completely, uniformly gold. It lacked variety and complexity, but it was a tree that excelled in consistency. Pure, bushy gold every fall.

III
RITES OF AUTUMN

FOUNTAIN

YES, THIS IS AUTUMN, *at the height of her splendor,* Kathryn thought as morning yawned and elongated itself, *and I'm glad I'm free to enjoy it, whether Yves visits or not.* She lifted her arms over her head, laced her fingers, and stretched. Autumn. *Oh wild west wind, thou breath of autumn's being!*—Percy Bysshe Shelley. But that would come later. Now it was blue sky and colors galore; she admired the five-pointed yellow leaves, like a star or a hand, of a sweet gum tree against the sky. The prickly sweet gum balls swayed like balls on a jester's costume. Her muscles were warmed up, and now she would walk more quickly; she would get twenty minutes of good exercise before she met Peter in the park at eleven thirty.

Some two weeks earlier, when the St. James Art Fair weekend was in full swing, the sidewalks of St. James Court and Belgravia and the walks of Fourth Street and even Third Street had been full of people browsing the rows of tents: pottery, furniture, jewelry, clothing, photographs, rugs, sculptures, woodcuts, yard ornaments, stained glass, oil paintings, purses, watercolors, and hats—the whole array. For more than fifty years, artist-vendors from all over the country had converged every October on Old Louisville; Kathryn loved the medieval feel of it. A harvest homage to beauty, handmade, individualized, worthy. This autumn weather had been sunny and mild. Perfect.

And the trodden grass had been tilled and replanted on Monday, the very next day after the booths were folded, stowed, and removed in vans and trucks, late Sunday.

As she turned west down Belgravia, Kathryn thought of the cyclical order that Élisabeth Vigée-Le Brun had brought to her old age: fall and winter in Paris amidst a cultural scene full of theater, opera, music, parties; in spring and summer she fled the city to live her days simply, close to nature in the countryside.

When Kathryn was a child, she had loved the academic excitement of the beginning of school and the robust fulfillment of autumn. By the time the leaves changed, the semester was in full sway. It was a blessing to have continuity in her life—first a student, then a teacher. Down through the decades, the rhythm of the academic year had given order to her life. Except for math, she had loved all her studies, literature best of all. Reading was pure pleasure, but in college, full of philosophical imperatives, she wanted to choose a profession that made life more possible for other people, in an essential—no, *existential*—way. *I want to do something that counts*, she had told Giles, the smartest of the smart. He had looked at her wonderingly, without comment. (And what was that pain she glimpsed behind his intelligence? She felt kin to him, essentially, yes, *essentially*.)

"In what way," their perceptive English professor, Dr. Abernethy, had asked the undergraduates, "are Pip of *Great Expectations* and Huck Finn alike?" No one knew. But she did know this much: that the answer, whatever it was, would be of tremendous importance to the young man across the aisle, to Giles, whose direction was all uncertainty. She held her breath. The skilled professor left a few moments of silence so that the students could adequately plumb the depths of their ignorance.

"Both are boys in search of a father," Dr. Abernethy had explained. And class ended.

As they stepped through the classroom door into the hall, Giles had said, without looking at her (she knew his eyes were glazed with tears), "So how can you doubt, Kathryn, that literature fails to do good in the world?"

I know, I know, she had answered.

If literature helped to still the confusion of just one extraordinary person, had it not earned its keep as an appropriate lifework? Yes! She had rejoiced. *Now she could take the path of reading and writing.* Yes! No need to be a social worker or a medical missionary. No need to worship the Bible, when literature also had its truths. Its essential truths. A truth that cleared the vision for one whom she loved, for she had loved Giles more than anyone. That was enough to justify the entire existence and study of literature. (And perhaps she could *write* fiction, too?)

Giles was dead before he turned twenty-one. A car accident.

Loss, loss, loss. Was that what she was cut out for? Death and divorce. Why? Why not?

Ryn told herself she was more experienced at divorce now; the loss itself was less devastating. But there was a silence in the house, and her soul felt saturated with disappointment. And of course her age made it harder to be alone. The quiet and narrow sidewalk of Belgravia Court felt comforting to her. Belgravia Court had its own hushed timelessness: no traffic, no cars even visible, a real retreat to an earlier era; here were narrow sidewalks with discrete little gutters running beside them and the lovely new emerald grass standing as upright as a boy's crew cut. Belgravia held change at bay. It was the domain of healthy pet cats lounging peacefully on porches or stalking birds. The birds and squirrels of Belgravia were wary, well versed in the nature of cats.

She paused to look at fish swimming in a small rock-lined pond. Even the fish in their orange and gold scales seemed dressed for autumn. Often cats perched there watching the fish, too. Kathryn had her favorite fish, a white, angelic one with a long, transparent tail. But there was something to be said for the brilliant red-orange fish, too, scales bright as jewels, reflective. The fish flinched when the point of a fallen maple leaf dimpled the surface of the water and settled there, flatly, to float.

There was Daisy's cat Lillian, a walking puffball, like the cat Humphrey had had to leave behind in Atlanta. Marie Antoinette would have liked Lillian; she might have used the cat to powder her face in a whimsical moment. Kathryn imagined Daisy's quick laugh at such an idea, and the light that would flash behind her brown eyes. She wished she would see Daisy now. Daisy had sent her an e-mail message, but in her effort to finish the first draft she had postponed answering.

She rounded the west end of Belgravia and started eastward, past the house with the split double door, bronze fox heads on each against the red paint of the doors.

Without once discussing it, Daisy and Kathryn agreed about certain assumptions of value: the fragility of every life, for example. Nonetheless, Daisy was unremitting in her moral judgments. Anyone who hurt another person was evil. But who knew the extent of extreme provocation? Ryn was more equivocal. Who knew the torment adolescents suffered from bullying? Ryn thought of her own Humphrey, his difficulties in high school where he was teased and bullied. Sometimes, as an adult, he bullied *her* a bit, verbally. But Humphrey had lived through the hard school days, though sadly another boy had not. What a tragedy that the two boys in the same high school had not known each other, could not have taken comfort in their sameness. At the university, Humphrey had found his own energy, freedom. *I just realized,* he had told his mother, *my name has the word "free" in it.*

She had felt proud of him. But how to keep him safe? From HIV or AIDS, from violence even within the community, from hatemongers among the straights, from predators, diseases, or accidents of any sort? She was thankful he had a stable partner, and they had been married by a Unitarian minister.

There in her tiny yard on Belgravia Court was a neighbor who always chatted with Ryn at the Fourth of July picnic on the green, whose name she could not remember. "Beautiful day," the woman said and smiled.

"Really lovely," Ryn echoed. Ryn thought the neighbor might be a nurse; she might have known Mark professionally. Ryn was glad the woman had not asked about him.

Before marrying #3, she had tried to express hesitation: married people take each other for granted, she had said. But he had insisted it would not be so. She had wanted their happiness, and he seemed more stable than #1 or #2. The fact that he was an admirable neurosurgeon, well respected in town, had appeal. With lovely eyes. What person, lying on the operating table, might not have looked up into his gentle brown eyes, at the last moment before the anesthesia set in, and felt some form of love?

She missed his large, warm body at night. *My heater,* she had called him affectionately when she cuddled up to him. Six and a half feet of him. And his soft, curly hair, such a pleasure to touch. She had always wished her own hair was curly; in Mark she had had the curls vicariously.

But often, like many eminent men, he was oblivious to anything but the needs of his own ego. Like Woolf's Mr. Ramsay in *To the Lighthouse,* he needed constant praise, doting admiration. The young interns gave him a lot, but it was never enough. She had banked on his loyalty, his integrity. Of course he was tempted by the young female interns in surgery; their lovely eye makeup visible over their surgical masks must have been alluring. She was still proud of the years of his loyalty, even if it had turned out badly.

Book had followed book: that was the problem. At parties, people soon wanted to talk to her instead of to him. After one party he had complained bitterly that a woman had said, "Surgery? How gruesome!" and turned away. She had promised him not to talk any longer than politeness dictated to anyone who brought up the subject of her own work. At that time, he had been loyal, and so would she be. They would grow old together.

Eventually she noted he had no patience with any illness she might have. He left the house as soon as possible whenever she was sick. Perhaps it was natural that he tried to avoid carrying germs to his patients, she had tried to persuade herself. Perhaps her little indispositions lacked the drama to make them of compelling interest. She felt shunned. At parties, or even at a restaurant, if anyone else was in the room or at the table, he never spoke to her or even looked at her. He wanted to erase her.

As a volunteer, he liked to go to jungles in Central America to operate. He did all kinds of surgery, not just brains, there: cleft palates, clubfeet, cysts. The unusual settings added spice to the routine, he said. He liked to serve without boundaries, and the nurse from Guatemala who lived on the Court encouraged him to visit her country. One day in the jungle he realized he was looking into dark eyes he could not deny. Someone who said she would tutor him in Spanish, show him a pristine waterfall, the elusive quetzal of the dangling tail feathers. Her body. A mole that worried her. *It was not really sex,* he had said, *but we touched each other. She cared about my feelings. We could talk in Spanish. She was the one who started it.* Not his fault. When they returned to Louisville, she had asked him to look at the mole again.

Ryn almost chuckled; she shook her head knowingly from side to side. Then the idea lost its humor. She sucked in her gut and lifted her head. While she walked, she ought to work on her posture.

Yes, Ryn admitted her failure. Her loss. Failures, losses.

After the divorce, they had tried to remain friends, but ultimately he withdrew. Too painful, she knew. She didn't blame him for that. At their last supper, he had talked for seventy-five minutes about what he had been doing. She had asked questions; she had wanted to know about his recent travels, the difficult operations he had performed. She had always liked hearing him speak the Latin names for the parts of the brain; it was a kind of poetry. Dessert was over; she had asked her last question. She looked at the smear of chocolate, dollops of meringue, and crumbs of piecrust left on her plate. Leftovers. He had scraped his clean.

"How have you been?" he asked nervously.

"I enjoyed seeing my brothers," she said.

"How are they?"

His questions dwindled. After five minutes, he announced that he needed to go.

It had been that way for a very long time. For him, seventy-five minutes of focused chatter; for her, less than four. He wasn't interested in her; sharing something of his life with her was an act of generosity on his part. In his own mind, he was not responsible in any significant way for any injury inflicted on anyone. Everyone made surgical errors at times, but for Mark there were always mitigating circumstances. It was a mental habit he carried from the operating theater into his life; he was never really accountable for causing serious damage.

Had she wanted that last post-divorce dinner with #3 to be a disappointment? Had she made it happen that way to reassure herself that it was not merely Mark's infatuation allowed to go too far but the whole quality of their own relationship that had made the marriage a kind of death to her spirit? Yes, she probably had. "You deserve the loneliness," she said to herself. She muttered the sentence out loud, with a stern German accent: "You deserf the loneliness."

You *deserf the rudeness*. An eminent professor, the guru of James's (#1) philosophy department, had spoken unpleasantly to a visiting lecturer. *Well,* the visitor had said, *I don't know if I want to answer a question couched in such rude terms.* The reigning professor had leaned forward and hissed into the face of the university's guest, *You deserf the rudeness.*

How James as a graduate student had liked to play that role, grinning impishly; how he relished the German accent, the professorial authority that was never to be his, despite his brilliance.

The universities never divorced her, never disappeared into the ground. They promoted her, raised her salary, expressed appreciation, sometimes gave her honors unsought. She supposed many of her colleagues took refuge from the stress of academia in their marriages, but she had found stability in teaching, in her students, open and eager, when life closed down on her. (She passed the façade of Daisy and Daniel's house, its lovely French windows behind wild rhododendron shrubs.) They were the exception among her friends, long and happily married, their children, likewise; they were now blessed with young grandchildren.

Here was the pink palace. A tall, turreted building painted long ago the color of Pepto-Bismol, where St. James crossed Belgravia before continuing to busy Hill Street. The three-story, towering house had once been a Victorian men's club—cigars, newspapers, business suits, probably prostitutes. During her tenure on the Court, she had liked two gay men who used to live there, both of them smart and sweet, full of friendship freely offered. They had been kind to Humphrey, like older brothers, when he was in high school and most in need of friendship.

Like her own house, the pink palace was one of only a handful of homes that had private swimming pools out back. She knew her pool should have been already covered for the coming winter. She was paying for a lot of gas calories because just maybe Yves had said, over a month ago (had he forgotten?), he would like to go for an autumnal swim in well-heated water. For many days, she had patiently delayed her writing to net out the yellow cottonwood and brown oak leaves floating on the surface of the water. Once waterlogged, the leaves sank to the bottom and turned black. Left uncared for, the pool could probably turn into a bog in just one season.

A happy couple were carrying groceries just ahead of her and having their own intimate conversation, glancing at each other as they spoke. Would she want to say to them: *I finished the first draft of my novel; I'm at loose ends. What's wrong with me, divorced three times? How do you two do it?* Would she just blurt out something inappropriate if she paused in her walking?

The woman, pretty and intense, Ryn now recognized as the daughter of a well-known sculptor, now deceased, and an artist herself; her partner, white haired, keen faced, and dashing, was a psychologist. Ryn wondered what it would be like to sit in his office. *Yes, I truly enjoy my work. My writing,* she would say, and he would ask if she felt compelled to write. *I wish I did,* she would answer honestly, and he would look at her a bit quizzically.

Failing to fall asleep at night, when quite young, sometimes she entertained herself by asking, *What was I just* thinking? *And before* that? *And before that?* She pictured a literal train of thought where each subject was represented as an open gondola carrying a load of details. She would ask herself what had linked the cars; how had one thought led to another; what was the spark in one thought that caused another to flare. She could trace the line of thought back to five or six subjects; never more, not even when she tried to keep a running tally as she waited for sleep. It interested her, the private movement of the mind.

Now she had rounded the east end of Belgravia Court; she looked across the grassy median again at the magnificent châteauesque house with a double staircase, each side scrolling down with a slight twist to the sidewalk; it was as much a sculpture as a functioning staircase. A breathtaking façade. Yes, she had taken Mark for granted, focused too much on her writing, her students, her friends, but she had not betrayed his trust.

When she had published her first slender book, she had looked at a basketball stadium filled almost to capacity with eighteen thousand fans and thought, *If only each one of them would read my book.* (Only a thousand copies had been printed.) She had thought it impossible to have as many readers as spectators at a single college game. But now it was many multiples of that. Not a university stadium full of readers, but a whole city's worth, and more.

When her breakthrough had come with her fifth book, she had asked the university president to introduce her at halftime at the basketball game. A person of true generosity, he had done just that, with only a slight glimmer of curiosity about her request in his nice eyes.

Taking her October walk, she laughed at herself and felt lighter. No need to be gloomy. She exchanged a friendly nod with a tall African American jazz pianist who lived on Belgravia. No need to think of the past, or of marital failures. Late last night, she had finished the draft of another novel. Next she would meet Peter in the park. She wondered if Peter had heard from Humphrey, in Sweden. If Humphrey were here, she and he would celebrate her completion of *Portrait* together.

PORTRAIT

FROM THE *BOULANGERIE* Maman has brought brioche with pleated sides and a glazed pouf. I almost want to paint the large brioche, it looks so delicious and its colors so rich. But is the crust a bit too brown, a bit too much black suggested? Black is not a good element in bread, though it may make the tip of a tart oozing cherry fruit seem more real in a painting, which is a funny idea, for what can be more real than real?

The odor of escargots baked in garlic fills our house, but I am more enchanted by the vegetables in the fish stew, the aroma of cooking onions, celery, and carrots. We are preparing for a large dinner party of Papa's interesting friends. The table has been enlarged by placing wide boards across it, and a lovely cloth over the boards. All of Papa's interests will be represented by the presence of our guests from the literary, philosophical, musical, and artistic worlds, even a scientist who studies the movement of fluids. The fowl will have a mushroom and truffle stuffing, with dried berries, and a great pile of haricots verts with slivers of almonds, and many

more fresh and delicious dishes. Papa says I'm to have a taste of the wine
and sit at the table, being twelve.

"Jesus went about his father's business when he was twelve," Papa
declares.

My mother glances at him with a slight hint of reproof in her countenance, for she is very pious, more so than he. She does not think any
human should be compared to Jesus.

"I only meant that twelve marks the coming-of-age," my father explains.

Étienne will not be at table but he will be present as people gather
and he will greet them like a little page boy. I have a new skirt with vertical stripes, thin black velvet dividing thin stripes of many colors, like a
dark rainbow, including deep mahogany, dark blue, maroon, and other
deep colors. Maman and I will sing a duet just before dinner, and we will
each play the guitar as well, as accompaniment. And the first guest is at
the door!

People gather and gather till the room is filled with so many different
fabrics that we are rather like a washtub, but I don't mean that, only that
the room is a confusion with a great swirl of patterns and shades. Étienne is
still so slight that he slips around the dresses with ease and people are often
surprised to see him appear and then very pleased, for he smiles and is not
the least shy but always has a compliment or comment that is sincere and
interesting; in both face and gesture, he is beautiful. I feel that I behave
very well, too, with similar glad manners, though my conversations are
somewhat more extended since I am older. Sometimes I catch Maman's
eye, and she shifts her gaze toward a particular person, and this is a signal
that I should not prolong the conversation but approach someone else. It
is very helpful because sometimes when conversing with adults, *I* am very
interested but it is more difficult to tell if the other person is being merely
polite or wishes to continue. I should very much like to have a salon and
give such parties myself when I am grown.

I am only a little nervous when it is time for our duet. "Let your heart
be light," Maman says. "No one here has so nice a voice or so true a sense of

pitch as you. Give yourself to the music." And then, bolstered by her praise, I understand how true her advice is: there is nothing to fear because I love the music and I love singing with her; I give my guitar a little strum, and I think of the shape of the music almost as though it is a shape and color I have not yet painted, and I enter completely into that world which is invisible and made purely of tones and rhythms. In this song the words almost don't count, but sometimes they do.

Papa looks down modestly while we sing, but as soon as we finish, his face uptilting is radiant, rosy, like the rising sun. His glance encompasses the room: he is very pleased and his eyes rest on us with complete satisfaction. Then we all move to the table, which is loaded with beautiful food, savory and colorful, and there is the brioche with its golden-brown glazed dome, and it seems a special friend, though a little overdarkened.

Even eating has its own rhythm and its own sweet sounds of silver utensils and china plates, and there are waves of aromas, characterized most often by the creamy fish stew. When Maman stirs the stew with the big ladle sometimes a curve of celery rises up from the broth, or the orange of a carrot round is visible in the milky liquid, or a chunk of fish. I have always admired the large size of the soupspoons, so important, at each plate, and I happen to watch as Maman sips from her spoon and then puts it down. Very daintily, she removes a slender fish bone from her mouth and places it on the side of her plate.

At that very moment Papa begins to cough and sputter. His face grows red, and everyone looks concerned. Maman breaks a fluffy piece from the brioche, and he takes it into his mouth, chews rapidly, and swallows. When eating fish, always have bread at hand, she has cautioned me. We watch, concerned.

Finally Papa says, "There, there, it's only a tiny bone, let us be anxious no more," and he tells a joke that makes us all merry again, but I notice he does not remove the bone from his mouth.

AFTER THE GUESTS HAVE LEFT, I ask, "Papa, did the fish bone go down?"

"No, dear child, it is still lodged, but probably it will go down while I sleep."

"But are you not uncomfortable?" Maman asks.

"Well, you could look in my throat. If you see it, perhaps you could contrive to bring it out."

The specially engaged waiters are still clearing the table of remaining food; all the fish stew has been consumed. Papa sits down and opens his mouth very wide. It is almost comical. But Maman sees nothing.

"Bring a candle," he says, "and let little Sharp-Eyes take a look."

It is a strange thing to look past his teeth and tongue. There are some bits of food, a sliver of carrot caught between two large back teeth (themselves like little hard, creased pillows), but even with the candle I cannot see far into his throat, which is a tunnel that disappears in a downward bend. Inside his mouth the color is faint pink, and then a redder pink, and the shape of the throat reminds me of a butterfly, but I see nothing of a fish bone.

"Well then," he says, "give me some more wine, and I'll lie down for the night."

IN THE MORNING, Étienne wakes me up (for the party has exhausted me) and his face is very serious. He tells me that because our father has swallowed a fish bone, he is in great pain, and then I hear his groans.

"He tried to reach in with a spoon," Étienne explains, "to scrape it loose, but the spoon only made him gag."

"Perhaps the bone came up with vomiting?" I ask hopefully, but my small, white-faced brother only shakes his head.

My mother appears at my room and tells me to come in my nightgown, that my father is calling for me. He wants me to look again in his throat. I am very frightened, but I go with good cheer and say, "I am here. I will try to help you, Papa."

My mother explains that he thinks with my slender, strong fingers I can reach right down his throat. Still in bed, he shifts his body into a beam of morning sunlight that is coming through a window. He nods encouragingly and opens his mouth again. He is wearing his white nightshirt.

With the sunlight, I can see very well into his mouth, but it has greatly changed. "It's very red," I report, "and the throat is nearly swollen shut." Even the root of his tongue is swollen, and the word *infected* comes into my mind, though when have I ever heard it?

"Try, very gently," my mother instructs, "to push the swollen tissue aside. Find the opening between the two sides and see if you can slip your two longest fingers between the flaps."

I nod. I understand that should I feel something sharp it is the point of the bone, and I must try hard to clamp my fingertips very much together and draw it out. My father's teeth are around my wrist, but I know he would never bite me.

Softly my mother expresses her astonishment that he does not gag. My fingertips feel nothing but hot, wet tissue. I hope for a pricking, like the prick of a needle, but I feel only a swollen softness. It is as though my fingers can see the red tissue. I am quick and thorough, and then I withdraw, for I know it must be difficult beyond nature not to gag.

"I felt nothing," I say, and I push down the feeling I know must be panic rising.

My father is panting, and my mother asks me to try again. Twice more I reach inside. As she hands me a cloth to dry my hand, she wonders if my brother's smaller hand might be better, but my father shakes his head no, and my mother says that the doctor will come soon.

ALMOST IMMEDIATELY HE IS THERE with his black leather bag, and he takes shiny instruments like scissors from it, and I am sent from the room. I grasp Étienne's little hand and lead him out with me. We go back into the kitchen, as far as possible from my father's room. But sounds of his suffering still reach us. We sit on short stools, looking into each other's eyes. I remember Jeanette and think that now I must be calm like Jeanette, for Étienne's sake. We place our wrists on our knees and reach our hands toward each other. Very tightly we hold each other's hands and wait. And wait. Our hands are moist. Étienne's hands are smaller, and I think of the three years between us.

"The bone has slipped beyond reaching now," Maman reports, and Étienne and I squeeze each other's slippery hands—"and the doctor must reach with his instrument as deeply as he can to cauterize the infection"— and now we leap up from our stools, Étienne and I, and fall into the circle of each other's arms.

Below Maman's eyes, the flesh is dark and puffed. Her face is stunned. "We were so happy," she begins, and then I put my arm around her waist and look up into her hurt face, and I say, "And we shall be again." But I feel my own face going numb even as I whisper the words, knowing they may not be true. I who have never lied, and yet—and yet I feel wrapped in God's forgiving love. That I have done right, uncertain as I am. God is inside me, saying *Console, console*.

"The doctor knows best, and your father is willing, but—" Here she stumbles, and I see that Nurse is behind her, and she is wearing a shawl and holds our wraps in her hand.

"Papa would like us to take a walk," I interpret, "Étienne and I, with Nurse."

Maman nods, and as she looks at me, two clear beads of tears form, cradled on the cusps of her eyelids, but the tears do not tilt over. She quickly nods affirmation and with her hands moves us into Nurse's care. Quite tenderly, Nurse wraps us, and I am grateful, for my entire body has gone cold. I hear the sound of chattering, a sound made by little Étienne's teeth, and I know he feels the same cold that I do, and we are alike. I clamp my teeth firmly together.

Nurse is full of ideas about what we must see: a certain arch in the park, a bridge over the river Seine, the twin towers of Notre Dame, and then we must climb up to have a view of the city. Close to the gargoyle waterspouts, I wish I could take one home to guard our house from danger. After we come down, the vastness of the city and the shape of the river stay in my mind. On and on we walk through the Jardin des Tuileries till Étienne begins to whimper like a younger child, and really he seems to have shrunk. Then Nurse takes us to a café and insists that we eat. "We must keep up our strength," she says, and even when we can eat no more, she orders a nut pie for herself and chews and chews.

It is midafternoon before we return home, and Maman greets us at the door saying that we must be very quiet, for now Papa is resting. We are too frightened to speak, but Nurse asks, "How is M. Vigée?"

Maman answers with barely moving lips, "He has suffered terribly."

Now I go to my own room, while Maman stays with Étienne. She knows I wish to be alone. I kneel beside my bed and pray that the Virgin will intercede for my father. I pray that his suffering will cease and then he will be comfortable, and then he will be well and happy again, and soon sit in his leather chair, and place the wreath of his words on my head, so lightly, his praise and his love. And his large, warm hand on my shoulder.

I pray again and again, the same prayer, till my knees ache and it is growing dark. Then I crawl into my bed and lie on my back, but I hear my father groan, and now I pray more quickly and briefly only that he will live and someday be happy again and kiss the ladies on New Year's and be happy and well with us by New Year's Day.

It is dark, and I hear Étienne saying that he wants to be with his papa, and then that he *must* be with our father, but I listen and hear no movement through the house, for if he is allowed, surely I will be, too. Still I understand, we are but children, and we can be of no use. When I hear the front door open, I imagine that the doctor has been admitted again, and later he leaves. And I wonder why my mother does not come and tell me anything, or even Nurse, but then I realize they must stay at his bedside and help him, that they know how best to care for him, and must not leave even for a moment. My whole body hurts, and my face has been made raw with tears.

I look at the small painting in my room of Jesus wearing the crown of thorns; his chest is open showing his sacred heart, and he points at it with one finger. He looks calm but I know he is suffering, for there is blood on his forehead where the twisted thorn branches have pricked.

Maman brings me soup to eat, but it smells of fish, and I cannot lift the spoon to taste it, but I warm my hands on the sides of the bowl. When I ask how he is, she answers only that he is resting. Then I bite my lips and make them ask, "But is he better?" She looks at Jesus and says, "Truthfully, Louise-Élisabeth, the outcome is uncertain."

The doctor returns, for now it is decided that the bone which was in the throat and causing pain has passed into the stomach and punctured it. Now there is infection within the stomach, and the only desperate recourse is to operate on the stomach itself. Again we are sent from the house.

I BARELY SEE MY FATHER during these weeks, he is so ill.

Another operation is thought to be the very last recourse. It is awful to try to live our lives while our father suffers, but my mother says he has great trust in the good doctor, and that he wishes the operation to be performed, as it gives him a chance to live.

THE NEXT MORNING IS HERALDED with a terrible cry. There is no doubt who it is who screams. I slide off my bed and kneel and pray, "Let him live, let him live, Mother Mary. Saint John, most beautiful, pure, and holy saint, remember my father and preserve his life!" But the screams continue, and the sound of great suffering fills the house.

Suddenly the door opens. My mother says quietly, "Élisabeth, go to your brother and hold him close."

As obediently and quickly as I can I run to his bed. He is curled into a little ball, sobbing. I lie down beside him, and he uncoils and I guide his head to my chest, and I cradle him close. He shudders with sobs. "Shhh, shhh," I croon, and gradually he becomes quiet, but I feel more sad than ever.

Silently, I only pray this: *Let him suffer no more. No more.* I would hold my father across my lap, if I could, as Mary held her crucified son. I would spread my knees to balance his man body. My tears would fall into his closed eyes, carved or painted, and give him peace.

My father's shrieks of pain grow quieter, then cease. I fear he has died. My mother is at the door. "He has asked for the drug to make him sleep. He wants to gather his strength by sleeping. Perhaps the fever will abate now." Then she adds that we, too, should nap, if we can.

Strangely, we do, Étienne and I together, as though our mere obedience will intercede in heaven and benefit my father.

WHEN I AWAKEN, the house is completely quiet. I hear only our breathing, Étienne's and mine, in the room. Without moving my body, I open my eyelids, and I see the wall is glowing with reflected sunset. The colors are very beautiful, rosy pink and tones of purple; there is a yellow the color of a healing bruise. Very carefully I turn my body so as not to awaken Étienne. I want to look out the window and see the real colors rather than their reflection on the white wall. The sunset is gorgeous, rich and blended. I do not know if paints or a painter could ever duplicate the subtlety of gradations as one color becomes another. And do we, too, when our life is over make a transition like that of one color to another? Do we change by degrees from our corporeal being purely to our spiritual being, just as pink can blend to gold? Purple is the royal color of resurrection, the triumph of Christ over death when even his body ascended into heaven. *And he shall come again to judge the quick and the dead.* I think of beautiful holy words and holy promises. *In my father's house are many mansions. If it were not so, I would have told you.* Perhaps it is not so terrible to die.

Something changes, and I slowly turn my head toward the door. Yes, a change in the light, for the door has opened. My mother is standing there; I see her gaze is also drawn to the window, and all the sky colors, and I turn my head to see it again because my father has said every sunset is unique, and really it is changing moment by moment. That is true. Now we have less of the rose and more of the purple and lavender, and I do not like these colors as well. Before it was perfect.

My mother calls our names, and I shake Étienne just a little so he will wake up. She looks peaceful and strong. She waits patiently, and we move slowly. I do not know what I dare not ask. All the words have fallen to the floor. I stand beside the bed and hold my hand out to Étienne; with his other fist he rubs his eyes the way he has since he was very young. First the knuckles into one eye, then the bent wrist moves across both sleepy eyes. I lead Étienne to the door. We are as quiet as our mother, and we both hug her, one from each side.

"Papa is awake," she says. "He wishes to see you again. And to say adieu."

The three of us walk together, touching each other as we move like candles carried flickering through the house to his door, which is open. Nurse sits in one corner, and there he is: very large in bed, looking much as he always has. He opens his eyes and smiles at us with puffy lips. His eyes are the same as always in the way he looks at us. When he speaks it is a croak and a whisper; his tongue seems too large and he is flushed red. He motions with his hand, and I know, or perhaps Maman tells us, that he wants us to kiss him. Silently but very fast—*we will not be too late!*—we rush to him, I to the closest side and Étienne quick as a wink and with a scramble up on the bed at the other side. I kiss him first on the cheek, again and again. I cannot stop kissing him. His skin is burning to my lips. He says *Adieu*, and we both say *Adieu* over and over, and he calls us each by name separately: *Je t'aime, Élisabeth. Je t'aime, Étienne.* And then he asks God to bless us and our mother, and then he closes his eyes. We wait. Once again he speaks: *Be happy, my children.* Together, we are very still.

Suddenly, our mother shrieks with grief and gathers us both to her heaving bosom and holds us close, and I sense something of the magnitude of what it is to be a wife. I know her bosom is rent! I think of the sacred heart, exposed, of Jesus and his halo of thorns! I sob for the loss of my father. When I try to embrace my mother, she seems very large. Her arms are very long and she folds us into her powerful passion, and we are shaken with her, to the base of our beings.

FOUNTAIN

AS KATHRYN HURRIED to meet Peter in the park, the waters of the fountain suddenly ceased to move.

THANK GOODNESS, SHIRLEY THOUGHT, *a little peace and quiet.*

TOO SOON, LESLIE THOUGHT. Why had the fountain been silenced? She had been reading Ryn's manuscript to the water music. The sound had helped her focus her mind. She stirred in her chair and regarded her Chinese cabinet. She looked at its multiple drawers and could not remember what had been stored where. And what was it, Leslie tried to remember, that she herself most wanted to write about, either in a suite of stories or in a novel? She had counted on the clatter of water to drown out other claims on her attention.

Again she returned to her balcony to survey the scene: ah, workmen had turned off the electric pump for some reason. On the sidewalk, a man nicely dressed in a suit was watching the workmen. He was a neighbor, Leslie believed, who lived on Belgravia. She would go back inside, to read.

AS DANIEL SHEPARD STOOD beside the pool of greeny water, gently rocking, he conjured up a larger shallow pool in the Luxembourg Garden of Paris. Toy sailboats navigated its surface. It was after Vietnam, coming home by way of Europe, that he had felt an impulse to visit the ancient cemetery Père-Lachaise. But it had given him no peace. The antidote to all the so-recent deaths in Vietnam had been little boys with their sailboats in the Luxembourg Garden.

After he returned to the States, he and Daisy had gotten married; they had gone sailing for their honeymoon in the Caribbean. Now it occurred to Daniel to buy a toy sailboat for his grandson—the perfect gift. Next week, when he and Daisy had the family over to Belgravia to celebrate Danny's birthday, he would hand him a blue sailboat with a white sail, cloth not plastic. Maybe they'd try to sail it here.

As he walked on toward home, Daniel watched a man wearing a blue cap pull on waders, then kick his foot up onto the wrought-iron railing.

ALMOST FORGOT THE NET, Jimmy Nettles thought. He dutifully collected his gear. A man in a suit stopped to watch. Then Jimmy threw his leg once more over the pipe bounding the top of the wrought iron. Holding his pole and net basket, he stepped onto the cement curbing that encircled the fountain, then down into the water. *A lot of fall leaves in the pond,* Jimmy thought. He swept the net through the water, collecting leaves before they could gum up the works.

NEAR THE NORTH END of the Court, Kathryn passed two towering hemlocks that flanked the sidewalk of another house the same way magnolias flanked her own walkway. The hemlock trunks were straight, with a somewhat hairy texture.

Time to cross Magnolia Avenue and enter the park. To wallow in the glory of autumn foliage. To spend a few moments with ex-husband #2, Humphrey's father, while he walked his dog. Like her, he was a lover of language and of story.

Peter was an actor. He had deserved to be a well-known actor, Kathryn believed; he was that good, that original. When he spoke, every word was shaped beyond mere meaning by intonation and emphasis. His modulation of pitch could nuance feelings for which there were no single words.

When an up-and-coming director, a woman who had her own sense of presence, came into his life, Peter had said good-bye to Kathryn and Humphrey to look for the fulfillment that should have been his fate already. He had broken both their hearts, but that was years ago. And he was sorry. His new wife had stayed with Peter a few years, then moved on to someone more cheerful, and Peter had been left to struggle with depression, nervousness, and addictions to cigarettes and booze that damaged his heart and lungs.

Over time, Kathryn had come to see him as a friend, a particular friend with whom she had had her only child, their beloved son so much a mixture of them both. And she felt Peter had suffered too much. It had been more than twenty years ago that despite their tears and pleas, Peter had left them. Never mind.

She sympathized with him; Peter had wanted so much to bring his own potential as an actor and artist to fruition. And who didn't want to do that? She knew she was boring sometimes—certainly not an exciting, dramatic person. In her conversation, unlike Peter, she had no sense of performance. She was excited about her writing, but that was between her and it. She adored her son and gave everything to him she could: unwanted shepherding, unflagging attention, and financial assistance. She sighed.

For decades she had treated her students with similar generosity, in terms of time and effort. Tired, that was how she felt. Exhausted.

Some of the students had become abiding friends.

Sometimes she longed for her mother: there, in that relationship with her mother, was the unselfish, congenial devotion that something in Kathryn had not just wanted but expected from a mate, though she herself had only so much to give to any of them before her own needs set in. Her mates had happily taken everything she had to give, and then, well mothered enough, they each had felt themselves ready for new adventures in the broader world. The mother-model, a dangerous role for a mate.

A few women had been attracted to her, but she'd felt only affection and admiration in return.

What did she want now from men? From Yves? As she walked into the street, the answer came as steadily as a two-pulsed heartbeat: companionship and passion. Why passion? She was nearly seventy. Yet it was there, that need, or at least the desire for desire. She thought of butterflies twinkling and hovering over determined Knock Out roses throughout the late fall blooming.

If Peter was merely her friend now, why had she never mentioned to him her sporadic but highly desirable dinners with Yves, when she went back to Montgomery, her fascination with his Frenchness as though it held some freeing and affirming possibility for her, heretofore not to be found in her American husbands?

She hoped Peter would be occupied by work tonight. At the Home for the Innocents not far from the Ohio, he ran a sort of volunteer acting class for the older kids that was somewhat therapeutic (perhaps for him as well). If he were at work, there would be no chance that he would see Yves come to her door. Did she want, greedily, in some sense, to garner attentiveness from them both?

Was she insatiable in terms of attention, or was it devotion, or admiration she craved? Some empty hole in her psyche or heart that needed patching if not filling? Insatiable, like Mark? Just as weak and needy as Mark the brain surgeon? As fickle? To be led astray by a young Latin American nurse in a jungle! And now to be so quickly married to yet another woman about whom Kathryn knew nothing. Absolutely nothing. She imagined her middle aged, definitely not old.

What Kathryn wanted was intimacy, to truly know and to be truly known. Mark had kept veiled (even from himself, it seemed) his inner-most longings and needs. Mark had neither wanted to know her nor cared about her inner life; he had shielded his own inner life from her, refused to discuss whatever introspection he harbored about matters of the spirit. Guardedness was almost a form of sexism with Mark. Like the aged Tol-stoy, had Mark thought that women were unworthy of understanding a man's spiritual quest? Without paying much attention, she finished cross-ing Magnolia Street into the south entrance of Central Park.

A girl in a plaid school dress was crossing the park ahead of Ryn. What was she doing walking here alone, the morning of a school day?

Pretty girl, pretty girl, a cardinal sang. Time for Ryn to pay attention to the fall colors; she had been so absorbed in writing she had almost missed the seasonal change—and that would have been unforgivable. Here was the park. The young girl over there, sturdy in red plaid, was maybe ten or so. She carried a fire-engine-red school satchel, and Ryn remembered her own plaid self at ten or twelve in the fall with her girlhood friend Laura, how each year before school started, they made a ritual of walking together down a wooded boulevard. Full of resolu-tions and excitement they had been: how hard they vowed to study, how devotedly they desired to be better students than they'd been, never mind the columns of Es (for Excellent) they always earned. They wanted to *really* learn, far beyond the requirements.

Ryn wished that she would be meeting Laura among the well-spaced trees of Central Park, instead of her ex-husband. While Peter and she were friends, and she certainly cared about him, not only because he was the father of her son but also because he was a genuine artist, original and con-fident of his unique vision, still she had to be careful at every turn not to say anything that bordered on advice or could be taken as a criticism. Lest she tread on his toes (and apparently she had done it continuously when they were married), carefulness and restraint were her watchwords.

With Laura, words had fallen down as naturally as falling leaves. Who knew from whose tree they fell, their colorful mingling of words? The effortlessness of their conversation! (Sometimes it was like that with Humphrey.) Words had bubbled out of Kathryn and Laura on all subjects, girlishly philosophical some of it.

How to imagine eternity? They had asked each other. Two willow wands, they were. Slender. She had liked the phrase, used it for Élisabeth. Élisabeth herself had used it in her memoir, *Souvenirs*.

PORTRAIT

W ILLOW WAND," Maman calls me. My father is dead.

    She rubs my shoulders and back as she has always done because painting sometimes fatigues. She whispers the phrase fondly in my ear. "Willow wand." We are seated in front of the dressing table. I glance up to look at Maman in the mirror. She smiles, and makes her eyes glow with sympathy and understanding. "Straighten up, my willow wand."

I smile wanly in return and then study my hands, lax in my lap. I love my mother. It is I who should be taking care of her, but she is brave. And I am crushed.

"Pretend you are painting us," she says, gesturing at the round mirror that frames us together. I look up again. The circle of the mirror echoes the curves of our heads. It is easy to understand why painters sometimes soften the rectangular canvas into a circle. I glance outside the mirror's circle and see the dull world of the bedroom. The well-made bed. I have no heart for drawing or painting. My fingers want only to curl tightly into angry balls of misery.

I love my mother, but she cannot see into my heart. My melancholy and grief lie inside me like a gray lake, one that can barely move. With a wink and a gesture of his hands my father could shine. Like the sun. On me.

Turn gray to blue, and make waters sparkle on tiptoe.

M. DOYEN, MY FATHER'S PAINTER FRIEND, is at the door. He is an awkward man and shy. I wonder that he comes alone. When Papa was alive, M. Doyen never came alone; he was never the first to advance an idea.

My mother makes him feel at ease. She invites him in, and he sits down rather tentatively in my father's leather chair. I am surprised that my mother has gestured at this chair. Usually she sits there herself, quickly, when callers come, and they sit around her. It has been months since Papa's death, and her habits of cordiality have returned. She wants the guests to be at ease, but the conversation lacks the interesting topics that Papa inevitably introduced. My father knew what was at the heart of each guest, and which ideas engaged the mind as though it were a heart.

When I leave the room, I hear Doyen say to my mother, urgently, "I am alarmed at her *douleur*."

I do not hear her soft reply, but my head droops even lower, for I have failed "to enter into the spirit of the moment," as my father would have prompted.

When I return to the room, Doyen says with surprising energy, "Élisabeth, would you bring me some of your drawings?"

"I've not done anything new," I reply.

"But it is exactly the old ones that I wish to see," he says.

In the room that I share now with my mother, I sort through the old drawings. I see my painting of John the Baptist: it is a little clumsy, to be sure, but the blue color behind his head still pleases me. I do not know if I could duplicate it. I glance around to locate the mortar and pestle I used to use for grinding pigments. The vessel is stained with a strange blur of the powders ground into its bowl.

Some of the drawings are architectural, copied from engravings of Rome. Here is the Pantheon. The drawing, from an interior perspective, is of the open dome with its oculus. The pagans wanted to let all their gods into this temple. The engraving had included clouds, visible through the oculus, that happened to be passing over the building at that time. Their presence makes clear the idea that the dome is open to the sky. It's only a drawing; if it were a painting the blue of the sky would make the idea more immediate.

Here is my sketch of another girl who likes to draw and paint: Mlle Boquet. She is very beautiful, and I have not fully captured that beauty, but still the overall expression—she was very friendly—is present, to some degree. I tried several times to sketch her, and here is a sketch of my mother, and one of the plaster head of Julius Caesar. And here is a sketch of the hand of Michelangelo's David. My father said that the real hand, much larger than this copy, which is only life-size, was once blown away from the figure with gunpowder.

Anyway, I gather up the better ones of my drawings.

As I enter the room, Doyen springs from the chair. "Let's go over to the table and spread them out," he says. "I am already full of eagerness because you are a talent, Élisabeth. Your father always recognized that, and he and I often spoke of it together."

I have enough sketches to cover the table. Those that are of the same subject, I place in a stack so as to allow more room.

M. Doyen immediately picks up the sketches of Mlle Boquet. There are seven or eight of them. Now he commandeers a wooden bench and arranges them in a row. He adjusts their order in the row, substituting one for another. "There," he exclaims. "Have I gotten it right? This is the order in which you sketched them. Am I right?"

I am curious, and I go to check. He is correct.

He points to three laid out along the center of the bench. "It was most difficult to get the order of these three correct because they were sketched, perhaps, on the same day?"

"How do you know?"

"That is easy. The shade of charcoal is from the same stick. But with each one you were mainly focused on a particular feature which is subtly rendered; the other features are more generalized, suggestive, though you have not neglected to try to be faithful to their essence." He waves his pointing finger above various features—her chin, the nose, her eyes—circling and reversing the circle as he speaks.

"Can you tell which followed which because of the sharpness of the line?"

"No, for between the second and third, you resharpened the stick."

I laugh. It is so surprising to laugh! "You are very perceptive, M. Doyen," I hear myself saying, and I am surprised again—such quick authority in my own voice! But fortunately I have not sounded rude in the least.

"I knew you would work on the nose first, then the mouth, and save the eyes, perhaps the most difficult and the most important, for the last."

"There are many attempts at each feature back in my drawer. I only brought out the better ones."

He clasps his hands over his little stomach and looks wise. "Of course, Mlle Vigée. Now tell me, in your own opinion, which, taken altogether, is the most successful sketch of your friend?" He waves the back of his hand down the row on the bench.

The word *friend* rings in my ears, for it does not seem quite true. Mlle Boquet is more an acquaintance than a friend. But I wish she were a friend. M. Doyen is waiting. As his hands rest on his stomach, he even makes his two thumbs chase each other round and round, and I remember the squirrels in the country at the convent, how they would spiral up a tree trunk, one in scrambling pursuit of the other.

I gasp, for I also remember the sad, kind eyes of Jeanette, and I wish that I could sketch them now, and I wish that I could see her again. While my thoughts have wandered, my eye has combed through the sketches and made its choice. Without hesitation, I know the answer. The best sketch is not the most recent one, the last one in the row, but the next to the last one in the row. The one just before it, third to the last, is almost as good. I remember the feel of the charcoal stick in my fingers, how one must let it be a separate thing, a trusted tool, and not clinch it too tightly.

"Would you mind, M. Doyen, saying first which one you consider most promising, and then I will say?" I am feeling more grown up and sounding more grown up than ever I expected. My request is couched in a friendly, almost warm tone. I sound confident, and it is surprising.

"Ah," he says, tilting his egglike head to one side. "There's a matter of trust and honesty here. Let me call in your mother." She enters the dining room, full of alert cheer. "Will you permit me, Madame, to whisper a number in your ear? And then your beloved daughter will do likewise. You must tell us if we have selected the same sketch."

My mother nods and smiles. She is pleased with her assignment.

Cupping his hand over his mouth, he approaches my mother's cheek and whispers his choice. Playfully, I clap my hands over both my ears to show that I have no desire to cheat. There is a bit of green paint on his knuckle that he has neglected to wash off. Then I go around to the other ear. I'm not sure why, for the fun of it. Each ear will convey its message and then they will meet in the middle, and the brain will *compare* them!

"You have made the same choice," my mother says, "as I am an honest arbiter! But I must say, I do not know why." She lifts her brow as though in inquiry. "Now each of you must explain your choice." She beams at us.

"I shall go first," M. Doyen replies happily. "The last one and the next-to-the-last one were both drawn on the same occasion, but it is in the next-to-the-last one that each element is most evocative, and the composition as a whole is most harmonious. Mlle Vigée is a good student and demands much of herself.

"At the time, the next to the last was the synthesis of all that she had learned, but she required of herself to try yet again, though what she had just accomplished is truly excellent.

"Now, however, with the last sketch, she is bored. She has already done her best. Perhaps a little tired, but certainly bored. She is continuing to work for work's sake. Perhaps the mouth is even a little better in the last one, but overall, she was ready to stop for the day after completing the next-to-the-last sketch. It is both professional and spontaneous. You must have thought, Mlle Vigée, with the next to the last, *I've got it!*

"Perhaps one *should* stop for the day when one has a special feeling of achievement. But she is a hard taskmistress, Mme Vigée, for herself."

I know that I am blushing. For in every word and in every tone, M. Doyen has expressed admiration and respect for me and for my work. I am speechless with pleasure till my mother reminds me that I too am to explain my choice and thus critique my work, using the method of comparison and contrast. I do so, starting with the overall impression. "The next-to-the-last painting simply has more *life* in it. It comes closer to suggesting the subject might move or speak . . ."

BEFORE M. DOYEN LEAVES, he suggests that I try a sketch of him, from the life. He has been so kind, and I see that my mother wishes it, that I agree to do so, but what I want more to do is to try to recapture Jeanette, who would have been, during our time at the convent school, really a young woman. I think I understand her much better now, but I will have to make that drawing from memory.

"M. Vigée always used to emphasize the importance of drawing from the life, as well as from the plaster models," Maman says briskly.

"And I wish to do the same," M. Doyen says. "Shall I stand for a full figure," he asks me somewhat impishly, "or only the head today?"

I smile. It would be fun, but not flattering, to draw the full figure with his round stomach and oval head. Those would be the structural elements pulling at each other. I wish I could draw his spinning thumbs! And instantly I think of how I might do that, with one cocked high (higher than would be natural) and the other thumb aimed at the web of the hand. That might work. I would need to move the clasped hands farther apart than they actually were.

"What is your disposition?" I ask him tactfully.

"Oh, just the head," he says. "I don't wish to task you. A quick sketch: the almost oval—but my chin is a little short, the forehead a little too long—I have noticed the imperfections myself drawing from a mirror. Do you do that sometimes? You always have a ready subject when you practice with your own portrait. So, an imperfect egg, with a bit of black fringe over the ears. Never mind the graying part. All black hair will be more defining for a quick sketch."

I fetch my sketch pad. When I return, M. Doyen is already seated in my father's chair.

"What about the wrinkles in your forehead?" I ask, for I feel very much at ease with my father's friend.

"It's so easy to overdo wrinkles. Have you noticed? Just a mere hint, I'd think."

When I've finished, he remarks, "Very refreshing." He says that he will come back in a week, and I can try again, taking more time. He and my mother stand at the door and chat a bit. He is a well-respected artist, and I feel encouraged by his visit.

AS M. DOYEN IS TAKING HIS LEAVE and chatting with my mother, I retreat to my drawings and then I sit down before my mother's looking glass. I am thinking of the advice to practice drawing and painting using myself as the subject. When I raise my eyes to the glass, I know immediately that I appear more well, more alive. But I am not the least bit prettier.

My forehead is far too large; my brow hangs over my eyes, and they appear to be peering out from a cave. I turn my body to the side and glance at my profile. I *am* bent like a willow wand.

At that moment, Étienne opens the door and runs to me with his arms outstretched, wiggling his fingers. He grabs me under the armpits and runs his hands along my ribs, up and down, tickling me hard, and saying, "I'm going to do it! I'm going to do it! I'm going to make you laugh!"

I shriek for him to stop, stop, but I am laughing, and it is a fun scene to watch in the mirror as it's happening, how we are tussling and laughing.

"I heard you laugh," he says triumphantly. "I made you. Now draw me, for of course I am exceptionally beautiful." And he strikes a pose.

I do take up a small pad, and I intend to draw, using a graphite pencil, a caricature of him with his nose stuck up in the air, as I might have drawn at the convent. I glance quickly at him again, to get the sweep. But he *is* too beautiful, and I cannot, for the sake of beauty, do anything but try to capture his lovely spirit.

As I work, the hand dictates that the sketch be delicate because of the tenderness I feel for him. I make him look more poetic than the robust boy he really is; he seems older and more thoughtful than a mere ten-year-old.

As I draw, my ribs remember his tickling. And that he was surprisingly strong. Though it was all in fun, I had to try hard to fend him off. It *was* fun, but I am quite thin, and my sides feel almost bruised from his enthu-siastic tickling.

"There!" I say, showing him my sketch. "What do you think?"

"Too angelic," he says, and sticks out his naughty tongue at my work. But he is smiling and I know he only teases.

Our mother comes in and I show her and ask her for an opinion.

"It's wonderful," she says. "So finely and sensitively drawn."

With her praise, I look at it again, and I see I have well used negative space, as my father might have said, to create the delicate feeling I had for Étienne. But I realize it is not really a true likeness of him. I pull it off the little notepad.

"May I have it?" our mother asks. I understand that she feels about him as I do, and that my sketch has caught something of that. We do not want the world to hurt him.

"You are so kind, Maman, to want this little work of mine," I say. I am grateful as I hand it to her. "I'll do a much better one someday, and you may have it, too."

I look in the mirror quickly, for the feeling I have inside me, here with my mother, is quite lovely. I hope something of that feeling will be in my face. But I am disappointed. In appearance I have not changed. I am really quite ugly. I sigh.

"Élisabeth," my mother says, a little nervously. "M. Doyen mentioned to me that he is acquainted with the art teacher of Mlle Boquet. He lives at the Louvre, and M. Doyen will inquire if you might be part of a little art class consisting of just Mlle Boquet and yourself, with Nurse attending. Shall I let him arrange for classes at the Louvre?"

"Yes," I reply, without hesitating. And again I am surprised at my own forthcomingness. Something in me is more ready than it has been before to part with my sadder part.

FOUNTAIN

THERE WAS PETER, at the crest of the rise, and Ryn hadn't yet fully
admired the two trees near the park entrance, their deeply grooved
bark streaked with orange, their gnarled bumps and bulges, or the corrugated green fruit lying like discarded brains under the trees. The Tolkien
trees, her friend Daisy called them. But there in the offing was Peter, handsome and pleasingly dressed—an untucked corduroy shirt, burgundy—
with Royal, his oversize white poodle, a particular friend of Kathryn. Still
at a distance among the maples cresting the slope, Peter's body and face
were turned in profile; from his back pocket billowed an at-the-ready plastic doggie-poop bag.

There; she was spotted, or smelled, by sharp-eyed Royal, who let out a
subdued whine, appreciative but not demanding, just loud enough to carry
a greeting and also to alert his master. Like a white hyacinth, the curly club
of the dog's tail vibrated quickly, and he shifted his front feet as though he
would like to run to her, though he knew to control his eagerness. When

Peter looked at Ryn, his face brightened, she could tell, but it was the stunning majesty of the poodle that compelled her attention.

Because of his size, Royal seemed uncanny. She always had to look twice to be sure she had not exaggerated his stature. Taller than a standard poodle, he was a dog whose shape and movement suggested the grace of a unicorn in a forest—it was the carriage of his head. Royal was white and covered uniformly with close-shorn curls. When he moved, he pranced as though he were the embodiment of magic, yes, a unicorn.

But wherein lay the enchantment of Royal? Amazing though he was, he suggested what he was not: he excited the world of wishes and imagination. Only a practiced enforcement of common sense prevented Kathryn from worshipping such an animal.

Kathryn waved, and Peter waited while she ascended the slope. She checked on the hemlock on the right, not yet losing its needles. It was a relatively new planting, scarcely half the size of the pair on the Court. Size, shape, color—how she loved to wallow in the visual world as an escape from the world of words. Wasn't the impulse to live aesthetically the same: to organize nature into the beautiful, to see texture, variety, structure; to impose or discover design where none was intended; to find *correspondance,* as the French Symbolists would say?

"Nice day," Peter called, glancing away from her up at the sky.

Peter rarely made eye contact right away. Theirs was always a kind of dance, finally meeting each other's eyes and minds and then a looking away, a backing off to safer distances.

"Yes." Timorous today, was how she sounded. She was never sure what timbre would come to her voice when she first spoke with Peter. Her attitude was unpredictable; she discovered her mood by listening to her own voice. He *was* her ex-husband; he *was* the father of her child. He could be tiresome; he could be compassionately insightful.

She glanced up at the sky, too, and saw gold and red, a maple pushing against the blue. *October blue, I call the hue.*

One of her best friends, Frieda, had once said that phrase, a friend long ago, at Huntingdon, her small, wonderful college in Montgomery. *October blue*—it was a phrase that could smite Ryn's heart, for the young woman who looked at the sky, smiled, and pronounced that pleasant phrase was long dead, a suicide. Loss, loss. Quickly, automatically, Ryn's heart shifted to college gear, became a bright, metallic artifact, something she had needed to have to survive the loss of Frieda and the accidental death of Giles. If she and Giles had married, would she believe now in the sanctity of the institution? Without doubt, she would. She liked to believe in the sanctity of things. Mark had promised her a mature heart, not a slippery sophisticated one.

Then she and Peter—how long had they known each other, nearly forty years—looked at each other's eyes there in the park, in Louisville, and he averted his eyes again and asked gently, "How's the writing going?"

"I *finished*. I took it to Leslie to read." Abreast, they began to walk down the slope as they chatted. Finished: vulnerable. The gracefully curved walkway was double width, perfect for two to walk together through the park. They looked around at the changing trees, the still-green flow of grass. "About midnight. Under a gibbous moon, I walked it cross the Court to Leslie." She knew Peter didn't want to read her work; she didn't want him to think she expected it of him.

He couldn't stand reading her work unless he was in a willing-to-serve mood. She never knew why or which mood, but she didn't want to trouble him in any case. Not about anything. Not even about her fiction, though his comments were pure gold. He always knew what was worthwhile about a piece, when a special sentence had flown sure as an arrow to the mark.

"That's pretty late to be out at night."

But she had finished her book. Because it was real, printed out, finished for this round, even at midnight she had been invulnerable. No. There had been moments of fear. And she struggled to believe the book was real.

"I don't usually go out that late," she reassured him. There was sometimes a streak of paranoia in Peter. She didn't want to say *unless I'm with somebody;* he might wonder with whom. A man? He was just getting his feet under him again after a bad bout. She didn't want to upset him, not in any way.

He spoke again, looking down at the paved walk, his voice full of gloom. "I thought I saw Humphrey's old boyfriend yesterday. Jerry." He meant *the bully, the fiend, the sadist.*

"Really?"

"I might have been mistaken," Peter said. "Red hair though. At a distance."

Jerry's hair was sometimes red, sometimes blond, sometimes its natural raven black. "I hope not," Ryn replied. Royal put his cold nose into the loose curl of her fingers, and she patted his topknot. His eyes looked steadily into hers with pure understanding. The dog felt what she felt. "I hope not," she said again.

"If he comes to the door, you ought not let him in."

"I know," she said. But she didn't know. Would it be better to talk to him? If he came to the door, it would not be to see her; it would be to ask about Humphrey. Maybe it would be best to tell him that Humphrey was married to his partner now and living in Sweden. If Jerry came to the door, it meant in some way he was haunted by his old attachment. Maybe it would be kind to tell him something that might release him.

"You can call me, if you need to," Peter said.

Royal licked her fingers. Just once, politely.

"I'll be all right. I have the alarm system." She didn't say the system had malfunctioned. A repair person would come sometime today. She didn't want to say *I have a gun now. Ellen gave me a gun.* She didn't want Peter or anybody to know she had a gun. It seemed a betrayal of all her nonviolent ideals to have a gun in the house.

Of course it wasn't loaded. But the bullets were right beside it. *These bullets are lethal,* Ellen had said in her matter-of-fact way, the steadiness of more than ninety years of firm living in her voice. She had shown Kathryn how to slide the cartridges into the chambers of the revolver. Ryn could almost see the finger bones moving beneath the skin of those dear, aged hands. *Lethal,* Ellen had said without the slightest quaver or emphasis. Ryn couldn't remember quite why those lozenges were lethal; perhaps they were hollow; the nose of some bullets was a dimple, but some were pointed; maybe that was why.

"Is your tenant's dog any good as a watchdog?" Peter stopped. Now he was staring at Ryn intently, right into her eyes. He looked almost like an old man, worried and grim. Weak. Peter's hair was mostly white now, but he still had plenty of gray in his forelock. Receding at the temples, not that it mattered, for anyone would register his western good looks, not those details.

"I once asked Janie that question. She said he's pretty territorial."

"Good."

With both hands she stroked Royal's curly ears while she waited for Peter to resume the walk. Royal's ears were vaguely woolly, with a soft nap. Janie's dog's ears were like leather flaps, and they rattled when he shook his head.

Actually Janie had said Tide was pretty territorial *about her,* Janie, not about property. Though Tide always expressed full-body wiggly enthusiasm for Kathryn, she didn't know if her part of the house was included in his jurisdiction, in any case.

"Is Janie mostly upstairs at night?" Peter pursued, but Ryn was only half listening.

Could it have been Jerry? She hoped not; she didn't want to deal with him. She had loved him once, when she believed in his love for Humphrey, but Jerry had hinted by e-mail, after Humphrey and he broke up, that he might want to blackmail Kathryn. She didn't know how or why, but she wrote him back the simple truth: *I've always helped you at every turn. I won't be spoken to in a rude or threatening manner.* He never communicated again. Still, she had gone to the local police and asked that it be a matter of record that Jerry should be investigated if anything . . . Probably he hated

Kathryn; she so clearly loved her son a billion times more than she loved
Jerry, though love had been there, at one time, for him. He was bright and
articulate, nimble tongued, though uneducated, comely in an interesting
way. *Was Janie mostly home at night?*

"You know," Kathryn said, "Janie's not afraid of the dark. Night and
day are the same to her. Tide is always with her. They come and go as
they please."

"'I'm Buster Brown,'" Peter quoted. "'I live in a shoe. *Arf, arf.* That's
my dog Tige; he lives in one, too.' Do you remember that commercial on
the radio?" Now they began to move along the paved walkways of the
park, past the scarlet maple.

"Janie's dog is Tide, not Tige."

Royal smartly led the way, but he never pulled at the leash. If they
stopped, he stopped. If they lingered, he sat down, chest up, head proudly
erect. His whole being was sweetly patient, alert. She thought of Butch, the
large mongrel Jerry and Humphrey had shared.

Not from witnessing the act, but from one of his comments, she sus-
pected Jerry had beaten the dog more than once. Butch had been curled up
in a far corner of his cage, and a heavy piece of lumber had leaned against
the wall nearby. "They don't feel like we do," Jerry had said authoritatively,
in the kitchen. When Ryn glanced at her son's teenage face, she saw it set
defiantly: he was on Jerry's side and tacitly endorsed Jerry's decisions, no
matter what his mother thought or said. Jerry was his lover, his new master. Ryn had hated her son's subservience to another man. It had made her
want to lead a cavalry charge, riding a silver-white horse, against the evil
smirk of Jerry.

"Yes, Buster Brown," she murmured to Peter. "Was he an orphan?
But I was devoted to the Lone Ranger." She remembered the days of
radio programs, back before television supplanted it in the living rooms
of America. She began to sing the *William Tell* Overture. Taah-ta-tah . . .
on and on she tongued the stirring tune. She knew she kept on ta-ing too
long, but she couldn't stop herself. It was an irresistible and irrepressible

sequence of sounds. She fell into step beside her son's father, while Peter, slightly embarrassed, endured her singing. It felt good to reach the end of the musical phrase, not to be cowed into breaking off prematurely.

As was usual, they saw other individuals and couples with dogs. Some had the ubiquitous plastic bags tied onto the leashes. Ample trash cans stood at reasonable intervals along the walkways to receive the contributions of the conscientious dog owners. Almost everyone in the area was perfectly honorable about picking up after pets.

Here came Kathryn's former student Remy, a nice middle-aged woman, with her blue-eyed husky. They smiled and nodded but did not stop to chat; the walk was a serious matter for the husky. Kathryn thought Remy might be curious about Kathryn's habit of taking a walk with her ex-husband, but Remy never asked and she was completely cordial. Remy had also seen Ryn occasionally with Mark (not lately, as Mark had stopped communicating) and with a few other men. Unfailingly careful not to stare, Remy was a dear, always considerate. She had already offered to hold a neighborhood reception for Ryn whenever *Portrait of the Artist as an Old Woman* came out.

(Do you want to invite Peter? she asked herself. No, he'd be uncomfortable. And why? That was a nosy question Remy would never ask.) Would there ever be a congenial man of Ryn's generation who did not feel threatened by her success? Perhaps someone much richer than she, or even better, a more successful artist of some type. And how would she like that?

Though spotty, the mostly untended park grass was still green, and it flowed on and on, dotted by trees wearing orange or red or saffron. A glimpse of the pastoral. That was the kind of music on the record player when she had mounted the dark steps that night, after the trip back from Huntsville, after Giles's funeral: Beethoven's Sixth Symphony, called the *Pastoral*. One of her brothers had placed that record on the phonograph, though he could not have known that his sister sometimes had thought of Beethoven's so-called *Pastoral* Symphony as the best music she knew for a wedding, should there ever have been a wedding for her and Giles. Had

Giles lived, could her life have moved with the untroubled, sure lightness of that music?

Back in the time of Giles (he died at twenty), life had seemed pregnant with hope. He had been dirt poor; he claimed he and his mother had put in the last cotton crop with a mule and a plow, though she doubted the literal veracity of that claim. Once she had written in a story that it was impossible to tell a lie; a lie merely told something else about you, a different truth. Giles had understood the kinds of truth wrought by art, literary or otherwise. With a nose worthy of Cyrano, whose words both Giles and, later, Peter sometimes quoted, Giles had embraced her mind and her sensibility, and she had loved his.

For one another, they had each wished the greatest possible success in the uncharted future. There had been no grudging tallying up and comparing of achievements; not enough living or accomplishment had been accumulated for that.

In Central Park, the walkway curved gracefully between double rows of pin oaks. Deeper into the green were a few lordly white oaks. How tall? Six stories at least. All the oaks were still green, oaks always being the last to change, as though they knew their somber brown could not compete with the glory of dogwoods, maples, sweet gums, and ginkgos. Kathryn's mother had read to her, as a child, a folktale in *Jack & Jill* that explained why the oak tree held its brown leaves so long; Kathryn hadn't much noticed nature till tutored by stories.

"I have my checkup tomorrow," Peter said, for now they were old, and Peter had had heart surgery. Kathryn took medicine for heart arrhythmia. And for thyroid, and blood pressure, and cholesterol, and thinning bones. At least her hair was thick and luxurious. *You have the best hair,* her forever-beautiful stylist always said, though Kathryn herself could never do a thing with it.

"Let me know what the doctor says," she said to Peter. Someone behind them was cutting across the grass; she relished the crunching of the leaves. The sound of the season eating its dry cereal. Half-asleep the fall still was, autumn lolling in the arms of latest summer. "Are you sleeping better?" she asked Peter.

"I never sleep well. Nobody does at our age."

I do, I do, she wanted to sing. *I read myself to sleep most nights, propped up in bed.* (Not last night.) *It's the best time of my day.* She wanted to explain: *I read only for pleasure; I want to stay awake, but I'm tired. My mind sways between consciousness and sleep; like a rocking boat, my mind dips this way, then that: I yearn for sleep; but I'm delighted to read. Back and forth, two sides of rocking pleasure.* It seemed amazing to her, too good to be true, this nighttime formula. *At night I read nothing but what engages me; too soon I tip all the way over and fall into downy sleep. Happy. Insomnia is opportunity.* She was brimful of pleasure, headed for sleep. But she'd already sung him that rhapsody, at least twice.

"Your e-mail said you had seen Christopher Plummer as Prospero," she commented. "In Stratford, Ontario."

"The consummate actor," Peter mumbled. It was the kind of mumble that was meant to connote reverence. Peter, an actor himself, for Christ's sake, could speak clearly. His mumbling meant she had to walk a little closer to his shoulder if she was going to hear, and she very much wanted to hear about Christopher Plummer.

"He's well over eighty," Peter went on. "But there was nothing of age in him. Sure-footed, supple, nimble . . . must have a personal trainer twice a day. No memory problems. None."

Kathryn knew it was better not to quiz Peter; just listen to the gravelly melody of his voice. She loved it when Peter found something or someone inspiring. His rare, hard-won praise glittered like a shower of diamonds.

"Plummer owned every line. Every line was nuanced—pitch, pace, emphasis—exactly the way he wanted. Perfectly calculated, perfectly spontaneous."

"Without flaw or blemish?" She was teasing him.

"Perfectly rendered. I felt in the presence of Shakespeare. Not physically. But Plummer embodied the essence of genius. The spiritual and artistic essence of Shakespeare, captured completely by Plummer."

Kathryn had never heard Peter speak so unequivocally. Not in forty years. Royal glanced back over his shoulder at her and smiled: she had opened the right topic. She waited another moment, then said softly, probably too soon, "I once heard a Rubinstein all-Chopin performance like that. It was in San Francisco in the early seventies. I was teaching in Idaho. I flew down just to hear him play. Rubinstein and Horowitz—they were the pianists my mother most admired. She was still alive then, when I had the teaching job in Idaho. I wanted to hear Rubinstein partly as a tribute to her. I couldn't afford the dollar and fifty cents to have new heels put on my shoes that year, but I flew down there and back. James was in San Francisco then; we were divorced, but he met me and we went together. Then I flew back to Idaho."

"Yes, well," Peter said dismissively of her journey to San Francisco— so long ago, to be sure, before he came into her life. "This trip to Stratford was certainly an extravaganza for me." Peter directed a stony glance at the distant treetops, as though they irritated the sky with their branches and their incessant need for more. More sunshine, more time, more rain, more money.

Now they were looking down the empty terraces of the amphitheater toward the permanent stage shell, two stories tall, woodland brown, with an ample number of door and window openings for any theatrical need. At the bottom of the slope where they stood, the stage backdrop rose flat, brown, and two-dimensional in front of the trunks of magnificent trees. An empty stage, *bare ruined choirs where late the sweet birds sang,* Kathryn thought. Why didn't the neighborhood children use the empty stage for playing? she wondered. Why didn't they devise their own stories and act them out on these empty boards? They didn't know how. No one had taught them.

Why didn't children playact here on the big stage in the park all year long, not just play on the swings and slides in the southwest corner of this available paradise? She ought to instigate the activity; give some of her time to Cochran Elementary, only four blocks south, to introduce the children to the fun of pretending and acting, the way she and Nancy had done spontaneously when they were children.

(The younger of her two older brothers, John, age six to her four, had taught her how to imagine: *They aren't benches anymore*—the long, ebony-colored piano bench, the shorter hard-maple vanity—*they're horses and the sofa cushions are our saddles.*)

Maybe the university would let her work with children one semester instead of teaching her usual class for advanced writing students. She should ask. How could they give her permission if she didn't ask? The dean would understand. The provost and president, too. She was a lucky academic to have such humane leadership at the top.

Looking at the open amphitheater, the stage with its stalwart backdrop of doorways and balconies, a natural, mature grove behind the set, and an immense golden ginkgo at stage right—surely a place to inspire any ambitious child or natural thespian such as Peter—Ryn said, "I wish you'd try out for Lear." She spoke as quietly as she could, wistfully, with no imperative in her tone. Every summer there was Shakespeare in the Park.

"'Blow winds and crack your cheeks,'" he mumbled.

Speak up! she wanted to say. She mumbled, "I know you'd be great."

"Think so?" He suddenly looked at her and grinned happily. The dog added his knowing glance. "I played Lear in college."

"I'm surprised some faculty member didn't grab the part."

"Why? They knew I was the best." Now he was impish. Totally cocky.

Harmony. Why did he insist that in some way their sensibilities were at odds? For all their spurts of congeniality, he must forever and a day be in some contention or competition with her (Giles had felt none of that). Why? She knew the outrageous answer he stubbornly maintained: it was because she grew up in the city, while Peter had grown up on a wheat farm in South Dakota. She was the city; he was the country. (But Giles had been an Alabama farm boy, with red clay caked on his heels.)

Just behind center stage rose Kathryn's favorite tree, towering over the open-air stage: a fantastical hemlock, a natural steeple. Its sheer size implied its importance, though it was never self-important. Its shaggy mate, stage left, a somewhat smaller hemlock, was also lovely.

"In her memoir, *Souvenirs,*" she told Peter, "Élisabeth Vigée-Le Brun quotes her little daughter, Julie, about the cypress trees of Italy. She was only seven. When she saw the cypress trees, Julie exclaimed, 'Those trees demand silence.' Élisabeth mentions in her memoir that she never forgot her daughter's words because she had been so surprised that such a young child could think in that way."

"Did you include that in *Portrait?*"

"No. I don't think so. You always have to leave out so much in a historical novel. But I always felt for Julie. One of the things that drew me to Vigée-Le Brun was how much she loved and appreciated her only child."

"Like you."

"Of course."

"Well, what do you think those hemlocks are saying?"

Kathryn looked at the feathery pair; she glanced at Peter, tall and straight. "I don't know."

PORTRAIT

WHILE I HAVE scarcely even begun to mature, for the sake of propriety, I am always escorted in my journey to the bric-a-brac shop kept by Mlle Boquet's father, and from there she and I have excursions for drawing lessons supervised by M. Briard, who has rooms in the Louvre.

So much better to regard the unique features of faces other than my own! I know now that I want to work with portraits in earnest, not just types, but individuals. As for myself, I am happy almost to forget that I even have a face; when I am absorbed in drawing or painting it is easy to forget myself.

With heads bent, Mlle Boquet (who is beautiful) and I, at her home or mine, spend hours drawing with charcoal, side by side. On cloudy days by lamplight, we draw natural objects we collect or plaster casts replicated from the sculptures of great artists. How to render the illusion of depth on a flat surface is the question.

Mlle Boquet and I visit not only the collections of paintings within the

Louvre but also in the Palais-Royal (especially the Italian masters of the Renaissance) and at the Luxembourg, which contains some of Rubens's great paintings. Nurse carries a picnic basket for us—the food, especially the hard sausage, is so very delicious—so that our pursuit of art, both regarding it and our own drawing and painting, is seldom interrupted. We eat when we are tired and hungry and then we talk and talk about what we have observed.

I consider my friend wonderfully talented; of myself I must say that my progress is so rapid that now I am being discussed among the artists of Paris, and the famous painter Joseph Vernet has made it his business to become acquainted with me and to encourage and advise me. Many of the artists, as well as intellectuals, knew my father.

I am especially grateful to know the Abbé Arnault, a member of the French Academy, for from him I am learning how to speak of all the sister arts, as well as of painting. He insists that I read great literature (not novels, of course). From this learned mentor I garner a vocabulary I would not otherwise possess, and more important, a way of seeing and understanding that is imaginative and aesthetic in relation to the other arts. I learn how to recognize moments of greatness in poetry and in drama almost as surely as I learned from my father the hallmarks of excellence in painting.

But it is in conversation with Mlle Boquet, over our picnic basket, that I feel most free, and I can integrate what I learn from my elders with my own nature. I am passionately devoted to Mlle Boquet because we share the same passion. We are connected at the core of our beings. She is fifteen and I am only fourteen, but we are perfect friends, and we share every idea. To talk with a congenial soul is surely one of the great pleasures in life: to have a dear friend! I do not long for any more. She is complete and perfect.

We also practice our art at home, individually. She has her father to encourage her, and my mother is unfailingly enthusiastic about my progress and the new acquaintances I am making in the salon world of Paris, sheerly because of my work.

ONE DAY WHEN I AM WORKING AT HOME, I try to render my mother's nose, but I cannot quite make it right. I am looking in our glass to inspect my own nose, hoping that comparing and contrasting will enlighten me. My nose has been my best feature, but I realize that my nose has become more attractive than it used to be. I look again. To my surprise, each of my features has improved! They seem actually to have moved about, as though my head had been modeled in soft clay and the sculptor had had a second, better idea. So surprised and pleased am I that I do not look at my reflection again, lest my improvement has been an illusion.

I realize that transformation must be gradual, if it is occurring at all, and I think change can best be tracked by examining my reflection at somewhat wide-spaced intervals, but regularly. I want to be scientific! I hit upon the idea of the Sabbath as being a time to check my physiognomy. Perhaps I may be able to join the tribe of the beautiful!

The Sabbath is the day my mother and I take special pleasure in being together. Mlle Boquet says she does not experience music as my mother and I do. Kneeling with my mother, we are invariably transported by the sacred music. And I pray ardently and privately for transformation, directly to God the Father, the Creator of All Beauty.

Perhaps it is the low notes of the organ that rearrange my face! I feel their powerful effect inside my body, a feeling of ecstasy, which I now think of as corporeal joy. I almost feel that I could leap up from the kneeler and continue to be propelled upward, to the top of the vaulted ceiling of Saint Eustache.

After my mother and I return from Mass, I allow myself to glance into the glass above her dressing table. Only then! (I abstain from practicing my art by looking at myself; at home, I use my mother or brother, whom I so much enjoy looking at anyway, as my models.) In my own features, each week I think I see something of my mother's beauty. Or is it only a miraculous residue within the glass itself of her image? I think I see something new and almost pretty in my own countenance trying to shine out.

Nearly every Sunday some aspect of my face has improved, or the whole configuration has become slightly but visibly more harmonious.

I notice that as my appearance improves, so do my confidence and my ability to charm in conversation. My ability to access wit and quickness increase till one day I think I am speaking with the aptness, alacrity, and ease of my father. "You remind me of your father," my mother remarks immediately. "You have almost the same modest curl at the end of your sentences that was so delightful in his speech. Something self-effacing and modest, for all its perfect aptness."

The flesh of my body as well as my face begins also to feel different: more rounded. Within my clothes, softness develops. When I put the palm of my hand and my fingers against my forehead, its bone seems gracefully curved. Against the inside of my eyelids, when I lower them, comes a slight pressure like luminosity (I fancy), and I am glad because my father often said a beautiful eye is made more beautiful when it projects a sheen of intelligence. Not every man of his day would have voiced that notion.

One day when I arrive a little late, and therefore flushed, at the door of my friend in the Rue Saint Denis, Mlle Boquet grabs my hand before I can take off my coat and leads me to the pier glass.

"Look at us," she says. "Now people will say you rival *me* in beauty."

And I see that it is true. In her objective mirror, because I am trying to be an impartial judge, I cannot say whose glowing face is to be preferred.

"I am completely changed," I say, but with as much wonder as vanity.

HUBERT ROBERT, WHO HAS BEEN in the presence of the king, has also taken an interest in my painting. My skill as a painter is bringing me many commissions despite my young age, which is most fortunate, for my dear father has left us nothing in the way of money. I have now painted the portrait of Count Orlov, a giant who was one of the assassins of Peter III, and also Count Shuvalov, who is about sixty, a charming, amiable man who enjoys the company of the best society, some of whom also engage me to paint their portraits. For Russians, they speak French remarkably well, but I have learned that French is spoken not only at court in Russia but in most of the capitals of Europe.

Because of my skill at painting, the foreign and some French notables include me at gatherings, a person otherwise of no consequence, and they do not condescend to me in the least, but always treat me with respect, despite my youth, as though I were their equal in every way. My mother is always with me, whatever the location of my work, so my purity is never impugned.

In addition to the well-connected Count Shuvalov, at the same time I also paint Mme Geoffrin, who is even more famous for her brilliant social life, which includes men of talent and discernment in the arts and in literature, as well as notable foreigners and the grandest members of the court.

I learn two truths from her. The first is that through dressing poorly it is entirely possible to look much older and less attractive than one really is. I guessed her to be a hundred, for she is bent and wears an iron-gray gown and a large unfashionable cap with great wings tied to her head with a black shawl knotted under her chin. But my mother tells me she is very far from one hundred.

The second lesson is that Mme Geoffrin has earned for herself a position of importance in society that no other woman occupies, though she has neither a good family, nor wealth, nor unusual talent. If such an achievement is possible without possessing particular intellectual or artistic gifts, it seems to me that if one did have talents one might surely win for oneself such a circle of friends.

Mme Geoffrin, because she had heard others speaking of my gifts, actually came to see me. It is very easy to like anyone who has a genuine enthusiasm for one's work, so long as he or she does not become too demanding of one's time, which belongs, after all, to the passion of work. But friendship is another worthy passion, and I can tell who is genuinely friendly and who is merely being pleasant. I like Mme Geoffrin, and I do my best in rendering her in pastels as interesting and somewhat more attractive than she actually is. She loves my portrait, and me. I can tell she would like to pinch my cheek.

My best portrait is that of my brother. One morning, as he is about to leave for his classes, his books bound by a leather strap that he swings up over his shoulder, he puts on his hat, opens the door, and looks back at me. "Stop!" I screech. "Stay exactly still!" and I pull out my book and sketch him rapidly. He loses nothing of his spontaneous brightness as I sketch him. It shifts only slightly to something a bit more mellow, perhaps less exuberant, but his *intelligence,* and *freshness,* and *affection* for his big sister who sketches him are all captured. Then I let him go, and I set about immediately to transform the sketch into a small oil portrait. I do not want to lose the joy, neither his nor my own. And I do not. It is there. Captured in oils: his bright glance from beneath his tricorne hat, the spontaneous turn of his body to say au revoir to me as he leaves for school.

These days, since my change, my mother is proud of my face and of the fresh, blooming appearance of my body, and she has begun to take me on walks on Sundays, after Mass, at the Tuileries. She is beautiful herself, and the two of us are often followed by admiring men. I learn how to discharge such admiration without giving insult, a skill, my mother says, that will keep me in favor throughout my career.

Though a young artist, I am paying our household expenses with my earnings as well as for my brother's schooling, his clothing, his books, and all the items necessary for a young man of ability.

Nonetheless, it seems that my mother believes it would be greatly to our advantage to acquire new and more expensive lodgings and for her to remarry.

FOUNTAIN

THE FRONT DOOR was standing open when Kathryn returned home from the park. Through the glass storm door, she saw Royce, her housekeeper's handsome son, who was vacuuming a rectangle of sunlight on the carpet. The rounded toes of Royce's shoes stood on the petals of large flowers woven into the rug. When Marie and Royce were in her home, she felt happy, at home with herself in a special, cozy way.

She had forgotten that it was the day for Marie and Royce to come, but Marie had her own key for use when Ryn was away or forgot what day it was. Marie was leaning over to dust the Marie Antoinette replica furniture in the entry hall, but she didn't look happy.

As Ryn and Marie hugged, Ryn asked, "What's wrong, Marie?"

"I was in this room by myself and that man used to hang out with Humphrey came by, asking me where y'all at?"

Ryn felt her body turn cold. "What did you say?"

"I said y'all moved away and we working for the new owners."

"What did he say?"

"He said how come the same furniture in this entry hall. And then I hollered *Royce,* and he come right down from mopping the bathroom upstairs, and I say, 'I don't think you met my son Royce. He all time working with me now.' Soon as he saw a strong young man coming down the stairs, Jerry say, 'Thanks, Marie,' and he turn himself right around and go down the steps to the car."

"An old Chevy, got a salvage door on the side," Royce said. "Out-of-state plates."

Ryn sat down. She felt drained. Dizzy with fear. She started to ask if they thought he'd be back, but nobody could know about that. Marie sat down, too. With her dustcloth, she automatically rubbed one of the bronze Egyptian busts that topped the front legs of the chairs and settee. "He might be planning to come back," Marie said without looking at Ryn. Ryn understood: Marie was warning her.

"How did he seem?"

"The same. Same as before." Marie paused. "Nice looking. Mean."

Ryn remembered Jerry's face. His intensity, his narrow keen features. When she first met him and his hair was black, she had thought Jerry looked like a muscular young Chopin. An incongruous appearance. But she had liked him; he was intelligent, a pleasant conversationalist interested in a range of subjects, eager to make a good impression. But he had turned out to be abusive; he indulged his rage, frustration, and disappointment on people who could not possibly defend themselves. On Humphrey. But Humphrey had had the courage to leave him. Finally. Without having been told any of that, Marie knew a menace when she saw one.

"Why you think that man coming back by here?" Marie asked.

Ryn gave no answer.

Stunned, Ryn got up to wander the house. It had been three years since she last saw Jerry, in Atlanta.

Jerry is looking for Humphrey, she could have replied.

Pieces of furniture brought up from Alabama calmed her bewilderment: her father's clock with its two stacked round faces. Solemn Roman numerals told the twelve hours; crowded Arabic ones circled the days of the month. At least Humphrey was in Sweden. She imagined hearing the clock clear its throat before striking, but she had not heard that sound since she was a girl. The room seemed to darken. The pendulum disk hung still as a full moon. Her eye moved to her mother's piano, a Baldwin with a beautiful bass sound.

So Jerry the would-be destroyer had come back to Louisville. Yes, light was draining from the house, all the colors going gray. Once he had said to Ryn, *Any contest between you and me over Humphrey, I win.*

As nonchalantly as possible, as though not even a feather were ruffled, she had gazed at his hawklike nose and replied, *Of course.* But her heart had drummed in her chest as fast as a sparrow's. Her reply had been politically savvy, she knew. What Jerry had said was true.

Wandering through the kitchen, she stopped to take an apple from the bowl centered on the table. She stepped down onto the floor tiles of the sunporch, where light was always brighter. Here the light held a melding of inner and outer worlds, but now it was not strong enough, not real enough to meet Ryn's need. She needed outdoors again. Quietly she unlocked the back door and slipped out onto the deck.

Golden brown. Very little was left of summer. Her gaze surveyed the remains of the perennial bed beside the blue-green swimming pool. Near the deck she registered a late spurt of richest ruby from the Ingrid Bergman, the tall hybrid tea of her first rose garden. *I always promised myself a rose garden,* she thought. She drew in the heavy fragrance of the lavender rose, Heritage. She bit into the waxy red of her apple.

Where have you gone before for help? Not here. Not to Nature in its backyard manifestation.

She remembered only last month when she had knelt in her bedroom to pray for the life of her dying friend, someone she had known since childhood. She, a writer who had not prayed for years (except when she thought Humphrey in danger), had prayed on her knees, not to God, for she could not pronounce that name, but to the universe. *Dear Universe,* she had actually uttered, sotto voce. And she had asked for the life of Lallie, dying.

The apple was soft, but not mealy, thank goodness; remembering Lallie, she chewed. Full of flavorful juice; white inside and deep red outside, those colors speaking essence of apple. Like a cow with a cud, she chewed. Lallie would have smiled at the comparison. Lallie, whom Ryn remembered as a wiry girl of ten or eleven, her hair in two thick black braids, her dark eyes full of girlish, wry intelligence, Nancy's close friend. Young woman Lallie in her wedding dress, leaning forward to cut her cake, her brow as pure and as graciously curved as any Madonna by Michelangelo. Lallie in her sixties, costumed as Virginia Woolf, as Woolf had appeared in the photograph on the cover of Hermione Lee's great biography, even with a cigarette held jauntily at the end of a long black stem, ready for a joke.

Lallie. Dead now. Lying in her coffin. Her animated zest for every moment, stilled. Gone.

What had Tillich written? Ryn looked out toward the fence at the back of her garden, past the warm swimming pool to the bronze crepe myrtles planted in a row in front of the high fence. She lifted her gaze to regard—higher than rooftops—her across-the-alley neighbor's half-bare tree of heaven billowing sparse yellow, big as a cumulus cloud. Not October blue, but a paler, thinner blue, this western sky beyond the rooftops. Yes, this was the color of the thin day-veil that masked the dark universe.

Paul Tillich, the theologian, had written of the God beyond God; the God that appears when God disappears. Perhaps he meant the universe beyond the Hebrew sky god. A problem had been the persistence of the old word *God* used for Tillich's new idea of God, she decided. But what was the right metaphor? Clearly Tillich had chosen the word *God* hopefully, wanted it to serve as bridge, not barrier.

Again she bit into the satisfying apple.

Ah, she had it; at last she had it! Already she had had the new term, though she hadn't recognized it. Now she had come to that place again and recognized what she had half understood and uttered for the first time in praying for Lallie: *dear Universe.* The God beyond God was the merging of metaphor and actuality: that vastness and magnificence ratified by science, its distant wonders brought to us by the long eye of the Hubble telescope, called the universe. *Dear Universe; dear* for the necessary anthropomorphic touch. (Had Jerry really been inside her home?)

Anybody could get to Sweden, if determined.

Fear, now and immediate, for the safety of beloved Humphrey, her only begotten son, was what had caused her metaphysical mind to leap. As it had when she feared for Lallie's life.

So God's best name was Universe, not as an abstraction but as a vivid and visible, yet illimitable and incomprehensible, reality. Behold! Yes, that was what the eye was for. No wonder she had prayed to the all-encompassing, ever-fecund vastness of space. Perhaps she could do it again—whatever. Imagine ultimate realities? And more successfully? she hoped, ruefully.

For now, there was the tasty juice of apple, the commingling of red and white, and the sight of her garden, which would be even better next year (God willing she should live so long and be well), and behind her, her home that she loved, in the neighborhood that suited her the best of any of the world, that contained Daisy close at hand on Belgravia and Leslie just across the Court on the other side of the fountain. Friends! Friends who were neighbors; many neighbors who were genuinely friendly. Here was a home that sheltered her father's clock and her mother's piano, her aunt's china cabinet and her grandmother's rocking chair, the artwork of her son, the books written by her friends and brothers. And most of the books she had read and loved since she was a child were treasured here, waiting on the shelves in her library, just one arched doorway away from her bed. Freedom! Freedom and home were here, now.

And what of that bed? Gigantic, expansive, a ship, a plump-pillowed cloud, that bed.

Here outdoors on the deck was the bright air of harvest all around her, and the blossoms of red roses bigger than ever, swollen with the perfection of their form.

She bowed her head in gratitude. She smiled. This gratitude was for her last husband, the most recent and the most unforgiven, who let her buy the house from him, over five years. Never mind what else had disappointed and hurt her of his doing. At least never mind for this moment.

A sharp and happy yip followed by an *arf*, then quick footsteps, sounded from the brick walkway on the north side of the house that connected the front with the back. Janie and Tide had returned home from their outing.

Though not yet visible to Ryn, Janie's voice called out, "Fair game! You're outside!"

"How did you know?" Ryn called.

"Tide told me, of course." The rush of young woman and guide dog, her hand on his stiff harness, came around the side of the house into view. Tide was the russet color of an autumn leaf, short-haired, some sort of hunting breed.

"*Arf* is dog for Ryn?"

Janie laughed her exuberant, bubbling laugh. "Nope. Body language. He gave the Ryn-wiggle all down his back. I felt it." As they flurried up the wooden steps to the deck, Tide leaned eagerly into his harness. His friendly tongue (broader and warmer than that of elegant Royal) licked Ryn's hand; the swift, accurate arms of Janie gave her a hug as though they were two schoolgirls. Yes, there was always something younger than her age about Janie. Was it because the blindness had come upon her when she was only twelve that her viewpoint and enthusiasms remained young? And Janie always treated Ryn as though she were younger than her sixty-nine years, as though Ryn were full of unspent life.

But the question Janie asked, "Are you feeling all right, Ryn?" held concerned anxiety and compassionate maturity in its tone.

"How did you know I was upset?"

"The way Tide licked your hand. He gave you the healing lick, instead of the happy lick. The caring lick. Also by your voice."

Janie held a flimsy plastic bag with two heavy cartons of milk and a can of something; the strap of her purse crossed her slim, strong body.

"Tide ought to be canonized as a saint."

Janie replied that Ryn shouldn't flatter the dog, and Ryn said that an old friend of Humphrey's had come to the door and asked Marie about their whereabouts. "Actually, an enemy now," she added.

"You're not afraid of him, are you?" Janie asked.

"A little. More for Humphrey than for me."

"But Humphrey's not here."

"I don't want to see Jerry. He'll want to know where Humphrey is, and I won't want to tell, which will make him angry. I don't want to have a confrontation."

"You're right, you can't tell," Janie said. "Not if you're afraid he might hurt Humphrey."

How quick and to the point she was. In agreement, Ryn lifted her eyebrows, as though Janie could see the gesture. Still, Ryn thought she probably had nothing to fear, though Jerry had hurt Humphrey physically. She knew she had a tendency toward paranoia, especially toward men about whom she herself harbored some violent feelings, men from whom she turned firmly away because they had betrayed her trust.

"You have to trust yourself," Janie said passionately. "Trust your intuitions."

That was the world in which Janie, not Ryn, lived. Janie's world hung from the thread of heightened sensitivity to touch, sound, odor, taste—the slight rattle or the whiff of a particular aroma, the shift in the terrain under her feet, subtle signals concerning if not Janie's safety then the nature of her surroundings that a sighted person could ignore.

"Is this a day to make potato soup?" Janie asked cordially. Her voice had a juiciness to it, like an autumn-crisp apple, not a potato.

"Not cold enough," Ryn replied. "We'll do it after Thanksgiving."

"But before Christmas," Janie urged. "It can be our Christmas present to each other."

"Perfect." Ryn recalled that Janie had no spare money for presents, and yes, the soup would be delicious; they'd freeze individual or double-size portions, have its mealy savoriness through January and February.

"The leaves are good and crunchy underfoot," Janie said.

"Do the squirrels tempt Tide?"

"No, he's a good boy, aren't you, Tidy?"

"Do you think he'd bark if somebody tried to get in the house? In my part?"

"I don't know." Her voice expressed perfect doubt. It tilted toward neither a subtle *yes* nor a cautionary *no*. The timbre of her speaking held a precise balance. "I guess you need to work now?"

"I finished the book last night," Ryn said. "Yves, the Frenchman from Montgomery, is coming up to visit."

"I wish I could read your book right now," Janie said rapidly, and then, without pause, added, "Has Yves been here before?" Janie had rented the upstairs apartment for only the last year.

Absentmindedly, Ryn shook her head. And then said, "No." Once before he had canceled on the very day scheduled for his arrival.

"I didn't think so. Then I know you need to get ready," Janie added cheerfully.

With one fluid gesture, she and Tide turned. Smooth as synchronized clocks, they stepped down the wooden stairs from the deck to the brick patio. Before rounding the corner of the house Janie called back, "It's great you finished the novel."

Staring into the thinness of air, at the empty corner where her friend and tenant had disappeared, Ryn suddenly called out, "Have you ever fired a gun?"

All in an instant Janie and Tide suddenly materialized again, standing there on the brick patio beside the corner of the house.

"Ryn, if you ever feel afraid," Janie said, "just yell as loud as you can. We'll be down the inside stairs in a flash."

"Have you ever fired a gun?"

"Do you have a gun?" Janie asked.

"Yes, Ellen gave me one the last time I visited her in Alabama. She said she used to go anywhere she pleased at night, with the gun in her raincoat pocket. She gave me some bullets, and she had me practice loading it, but I didn't fire it. She said I ought to take a class; the police give lessons at a firing range."

"You should take the lessons," Janie encouraged. With the tip of her tongue she seemed to taste the air, then lick her lips. "Daddy taught me how to shoot, before I lost my sight. At ten, I was an expert marksman."

The words dissolved into the air; the air became fluid and bore them away. They left the two women standing in their space, the older woman on the wooden deck, the younger woman, with her wavy black hair, slender, graceful, strong, standing on the bricks. Her hand rested lightly on the hoop of the stiff leather harness worn by her dog.

Slowly Kathryn added, "I'm actually a very good shot. I found out accidentally. James and I were on a ship crossing the Atlantic. He wanted to trapshoot off the fantail. I was amazed because I hadn't touched a gun since I was a child. I never missed. Or, rather I quit before I ever missed. He called me Annie Oakley."

PORTRAIT

M Y NEW STEPFATHER is a man who wears my father's clothes, without even taking them to the tailor for alteration. My father's clothes
are much too large for my mother's new husband. And yet he is a jeweler
and doesn't want for money. In addition, as is his right by law, he takes for
himself all the commissions I earn.

I tell myself it doesn't matter. It is the painting itself I love. I would
probably do it for free. In a sense, I *am* painting the portraits of foreign visitors and important members of society for free, since I receive no remuneration. My mentor, the painter Joseph Vernet, is in a fury about the greed
of my mother's husband, and he has advised me to grant my stepfather,
whom I hate, an annuity under the condition that I am to keep some of my
earnings for myself.

It is my mother whom I love, and I have painted a new portrait of her
in oils that is the talk of Paris. I wanted to capture all her ripe vividness,
but in a way that makes her almost veiled, mysterious. I am afraid that my

stepfather might make my mother miserable in some way if I withheld anything monetary from him. My loyalty to her is unswerving because I see that she needs it. Perceiving that she has not chosen well, I vow never to do anything through my own behavior to give her discomfort.

Immediately after the new marriage, we move from Rue de Cléry to Rue Saint Honoré, where we look out on the terrace of the Palais-Royal. It is an advantageous new location. In that popular and fashionable garden, where my mother and I often walk, we frequently see the Duchesse de Chartres strolling with her ladies-in-waiting. She always looks at me in a very kindly way, and it turns out that she has seen the painting I made in oils of my mother, which was being much discussed. She sends for me and commissions me to paint her, and she speaks highly of me to her circle of friends. Soon I am visited by the Comtesse de Brionne, the Princesse de Lorraine, and a great many of the great ladies of the court. My career as an artist sprouts new wings.

These great ladies treat me as though I am not quite an ordinary human. I put on no airs, I am sure of that, but they seem to think . . . I do not know what it is they think, but they are kind and curious and somewhat in awe of me. And I do not quite know what to think of them, either. It surprises me that my tongue always knows what to say.

While many men, also, from these royal circles flatter me and seek my company, I am too absorbed in my painting to pay any attention to them. I know it would be wicked to respond, for my mother's piety has entered the marrow of my bones. Thus my art and my religious principles, instilled at an early age, protect me from dangerous romantic temptations. My mother always has my best interests at heart, such as taking me out in public but making sure that I am chaperoned so that no hint of gossip could ever be uttered about me. She speaks to me about such things when we are together in the room we share; from down the hall, we hear the stentorian snoring of her husband, but he is far away. I dread it when he raps three times on our door, and my mother goes to him.

I am painting all the time. I never hurry but I work long and steadily.

At end of day, I am happy that I have been able to create worthy work. And I learn, always. A new face, a new dress, a different fabric—everything teaches me, and it is as easy to learn as it is to walk across a room.

MY DEAR MOTHER GUARDS MY HEALTH as well as my reputation. I am terrified to learn that my friend Mlle Boquet has contracted smallpox. I press my hands together and implore my mother to allow me to go to the bedside of my friend, but she absolutely refuses. Her firmness is fascinating to me: it is so unbending. Her love strengthens her like a steel ramrod. I feel giddy going up against her with pleas full of my love for my friend, and about my duty as a friend. She is unyielding and has not the slightest temptation to give in to me, she who so often treats me as an equal.

Maman suggests we send Mlle Boquet a tribute, a lovely basket of fruit, and that I include in it, perhaps, a watercolor on a nice card stock.

This I leap to do: it is a spontaneous depiction of me (from the back) painting the very basket of fruit that we are sending. Cherubs flutter above the curve of the basket handle and hold a ribbon banner between them that reads *Health and Happiness*.

I begin my prayers for my friend at sunset and remain on my knees until midnight. It is a clean half-moon in the sky, and I think that should she die, I would feel like half a moon. I feel much drained and my knees can hardly unbend from my long vigil. It is true that I have been so busy in my studio that I have not seen Mlle Boquet for perhaps a year, but she has always been nestled in my heart, with the dear memories of our sausage luncheon baskets at the museums of Paris. Perhaps the fruit basket will remind her of those times, though only now do I myself see the connection.

I hear that Mlle Boquet receives many kind attentions from people of all walks of life because of her sweetness.

WHEN MLLE BOQUET RECOVERS from the smallpox, we rejoice that her beauty is not much marred; very soon she is quite well again. And soon after her recovery, she is married to M. Filleul. The queen appoints her the gatekeeper at the Château de la Muette, which of course is a post that involves a pleasant stipend. And so my friend has made her way in the world because of the kind attention that her illness stirred, since she was young and beautiful, and through her marriage.

As soon as I can, I visit her in her new capacity as gatekeeper and greeter, taking with me my sketchbook and pastels. What an honor to live in such a palace! At first I am full of joy at merely seeing her again. However, with increasing disquiet, I cannot help but notice that her interest in talking about paintings is not very great, and my sketchbook of recent work receives only polite attention. My friend's thoughts seem scattered and lack the intense focus that so enlivened our conversations when we were young.

Thinking she might have misgivings about her appearance, I take her hand and say, "My dear friend, you do know that you are unscathed on your face by the pox?"

"Yes," she answers. "I wore thick gloves from first to last, to prevent scratching and scarring, even when I slept." She does not look into my eyes as she speaks; instead her focus is on a rather conventional bouquet of yellow roses.

"And are you quite strong again and confident in your health?"

"My marriage is a great comfort and blessing to me, though I miss the daily devotion of my parents, who had such hopes for me."

As she enunciates this rather stuffy speech, she begins idly to turn the pages of my sketchbook again, which includes a few landscapes. "Sometimes it is a great relief to sketch the face of nature," I say gently. "She is always fresh and surprising." But then the question bursts out of me, "And what of your painting, my most cherished friend?"

She looks me full in the eyes and says, "Since my marriage, I have given up art altogether."

For a moment I am struck silent by the impact of her revelation.

She goes on, "And do you have a prospect of marriage, my dearest friend?"

"Truly, I don't think much of it, or even want it," I answer. "But my mother is married again."

I FLEE HER RESIDENCE at the grand Château de la Muette as though from a cage. At my home I seek out the quiet gloom of the bedchamber I share with my mother. As soon as I lay myself on my couch at the foot of my mother's bed, my eyes fill with tears. Almost immediately I bounce up again, like a carriage spring, thinking, *Where are my paints?*

I am filled with a great urgency to return to my work. Quickly, I reposition my easel so it is near a window which frames a mere square of light falling on the trunk of a tree—a most delicious, absorbing, and *spare* piece of geometry—and commence a sketch with chalk on the canvas.

My interest is in the pure light against the rough bark texture of the tree, and how the square of light embraces the curve of the trunk, and how that square is at an angle from the rectangle of the canvas. I rarely have time to render nature in oils; that time-consuming medium is reserved for the portraits. But I love nature. Today I want to say that nature is important; painting is important. They go hand in hand. I do not live simply to marry. It is *my* nature to paint—anything in the world I wish, even a square of light on a curved surface.

THIS EVENING I WALK OUT with my mother and stepfather to Vauxhall for a concert, followed by a spectacular display of fireworks. My heart expands with each explosion of color flashing against the black of night, and I consider how one might render such brilliant hues on canvas.

After midnight—I hear nearby church bells—finally weary, when I lie down for sleep on the couch at the foot of my mother's bed, I see again the pale face of my friend who has given up art for marriage; quickly I replace her visage with glorious expanding colors, fireworks, red and gold making their mark on the countenance of night, and I summon up the memory of the stirring drumbeats of the tympani in the orchestra concert. Though my couch is narrow and uncomfortable (I have never minded my mother's gentle snores), I feel grateful to be in my mother's household. Not married. Free.

IV
MIDDAY
Old Louisville

FOUNTAIN

LESLIE'S MIND LOVED digression and parenthesis, and she had fallen into a reverie about beauty and the role it had played in her life. Old Louisville and St. James Court in particular invited reverie.

In her own young life in Montgomery, wearing beautiful dresses, fashioned by her mother, had marked Leslie as worthy. She had come to believe in the potential of beauty not only at school but also at church, the moment her minister in the pulpit had quoted words from the book of Solomon: *My love is black, but comely.*

How that minister had savored the pronouncing of those English words: *black,* like a stick of licorice to be licked; *comely,* like something delicious to be swallowed.

After church Leslie had whispered to her grandmother: "I want to sing in the choir." But what Leslie wanted was to relish the cadence of language, all language; she wanted it to be made juicy with song, some syllables stretched and sucked; some trilled off the tongue or summoned up from deep in the throat. *Comely:* she knew what it meant, though she had never heard the word before; what it had to mean; a word kin to *becoming,* as in that ribbon *becomes* you, what a *becoming* dress. If she could not be a minister with potent words in her mouth, at least she could be a singer in his choir.

"It would be good for you, baby," her grandmother had said. "Hold that chest up high and belt it out. You stiff, Leslie. Music ain't no stiff poker. Bow and sway. Bend your knees. Feel the music in the soles of your feet. Snap your fingers and clap your hands." Her grandmother took another large stitch in the wall hanging she was creating, of sunflowers. Her eyes no longer permitted fine work, but she could stitch big and bold.

Leslie's mother added, "Keep your mind on the Lord, praise his glory."

The minister had looked at Leslie when he spoke of *black* and *comely.* It was only eye-flirting, but she caught the spark: the way you're dressed, your body (twelve years old), your skin, your voice, your hair; all of you is a thing of beauty and greatly to be desired. The idea had changed her life. All the way to the marrow of her bones she believed that beauty was power and with power you could do anything. You could sing and dance and study and get elected, and smooch and say no.

She knew she could go off to college after high school, and she would, for Tuskegee was just down the road from Montgomery. Her mother and her grandmother had saved for it, and she had no siblings. Even her own pennies and dimes had gone to the account since she was a small child. Every penny and every dime she was gifted or earned.

The first time she and a carload of high school students from Montgomery drove onto the campus, she looked at the sky and felt the gigantic cloudy head of Booker T. Washington was smiling down at her, saying, "Lower your bucket, where you stand." And she vowed to work harder and to learn more than any girl ever had before on that campus.

To feel the power of beauty was to prepare for love.

Leslie fell into something like love for the first time when the youth director from a progressive church back in Montgomery came out to campus with a car full of undergraduate white students. Study buddies. How happy they had all looked: a car full of sunshine, and the driver the purest ray of all. They were to be paired up: black and white who shared the same interests. Despite her love of music and her excellent progress as a singer (she was learning an aria from *La Bohème,* "My Little Hand Is Frozen"), she was an English major, and she was paired up to study with a white girl from Huntingdon College, Kathryn, who believed, like the rest of the group, that integration of the races was just and necessary for the welfare of everyone. And it was taking too long. Kathryn, not an entirely new acquaintance, for they semirecognized each other, but someone she already knew a little at the instant of meeting or remeeting: a misfit girl, like herself, someone whose mind was stamped in different tissue. Leslie looked at Kathryn and thought, *We're smart and nothing will stop us. And we will be friends forever, Ryn.*

That had been true, but theirs was a friendship that waxed and waned over the decades. Sometimes they were very much in touch with each other; sometimes the lines of communication went down—for years at a time in their late thirties and forties. But the lines remained viable, and either could pick them up at any time, and they could continue where they'd left off. As they approached their sixties, they had shared more and more of their lives and interests. "Now we're as close together as the letters *K* and *L*," Leslie said to Kathryn the evening after moving into the condo.

Leslie believed in the sincerity of the white college students from the moment that the young youth director, a seminarian, enunciated the study-buddy idea. It was not the words, but the glow in Benjamin's eyes and the radiance of his face that made her believe. He was white, tall, and thin—not prepossessing in his appearance, except for the radiant goodness in his expression whenever he looked at you. From the trunk of his car, he took a large framed painting of Jesus, standing tall in a white robe, his white hands raised, and the sleeves falling back from his forearms; the chestnut brown eyes of Jesus were the color of Benjamin's, but Jesus had long hair and a kind beard.

"This is my favorite painting of Jesus," the young minister said. "I'm going to bring it with me every week. I want to prop it up on the table against the wall. When we work together here in this room, in the spirit of love, we are doing his will." Later he told them there were many ways to try to please God, not just one certain way.

Over a period of time, Leslie saw that their leader was always warm, always steadfast in his goodness. He showed no favoritism to any person as an individual. Who was black and who was white was never an issue, in his eyes, from the beginning. Five or six years older than any of the students, Benjamin was clearly their guide. Friendly, but not their comrade, more adult than any of them. And he was engaged to be married.

Once Leslie boldly asked him, though the question seemed more natural than bold: "How did you get so good?"

"I don't think I'm so good," he said.

"You don't just act good," Leslie persisted. "You are good."

Once Zeke, who was the darkest of the students in the study group, asked Benjamin, "How come you don't ever invite us to come to church here?"

Benjamin smiled and said, "You're certainly welcome to come, if you'd like to."

"Would we be seated with the rest of the congregation?" another young man looked up from his book to ask.

"I don't know," Ben said.

When Leslie remembered his voice, she heard the warmth in it. The warmth and love were always there. Whether he spoke with certainty or uncertainty about what others might do, he knew how he felt.

Soon after the young men had questioned Benjamin about the depth of the welcome the white church might extend, Ben asked if any of them played a musical instrument. He had a lot of friends who played various instruments, he said, and they were willing to be teachers. One of the young men said that he blew a horn. Leslie said, "I already play the cello." And Benjamin had asked if she'd like to play in a quartet, or a trio.

Zeke asked, "How come you want us to take up music?" And Benjamin had said it was because, sometimes, in music you could express both feelings and ideas that could not be translated into words. "How about boxing?" Zeke persisted. "You think we oughta take up boxing?" Benjamin had said he didn't like violent sports, or any violence.

WHEN THE TUSKEGEE STUDENTS went back home to Montgomery after their freshman year, Benjamin used his car to help them move. Before dropping each person at his home, Benjamin explained that he meant to keep the study group together over the summer, using a room at the church he served as a youth director.

Benjamin the good. Leslie could see him now, after so many years. She could see him so well because once she had taken his photo. At the end of summer, Benjamin was sitting on the corner of a pipe railing on a terrace behind his church, chatting. He had looked perfect, his large, lovely hands loosely clasped; it was a moment of being perfectly himself, and Leslie had grabbed her little camera.

"Hold still," she had said, and he had tried, but just before she clicked the shutter, his eyes had squinted slightly. But still it was a perfect picture. The photo had caught a moment as it moved, but nobody in the world but Leslie would ever know that a half second before Benjamin's beauty was even better because his eyes had been at ease.

A half second earlier, that was when she should have pushed the button. His appearance in that moment was as clear a picture in her memory as the photograph. When she remembered, those two split seconds were both real again, and the moment seemed to recur, taking its own original time. A sliver of eternity: that was what she had felt when she looked through the camera lens at Benjamin sitting on the pipe-rail corner of the terrace, above the dusty garden. She liked to think that he existed now in that eternity. Always had, always would, because of his generous spirit.

After she took the picture, she told him and the others the secret she had kept all summer: she would not return to Tuskegee. She had been accepted as a music student, in performance, in cello at Curtis.

He looked her straight in the eyes and said, "I'm so proud of you, Leslie." His eyes lingered on hers. "That's a really great music school. Way up north." And then he asked playfully, "How did you get so good?"

She answered, "I'm not that good. Not really."

NOW LESLIE WAS ALMOST SEVENTY, but Benjamin had died before he was fifty. He had never married, after all, despite two engagements. It was almost as though he were Leslie's son now. If only one could reach out and save him. Ben had become a pediatrician, not a minister. When he knew he was dying, he had requested that any memorials be for children with AIDS. Not only good, Ben had been fearless. True to his nature.

Leslie recalled that Kathryn had worried a great deal about AIDS during her son's teens. Leslie did not regret never having had children.

Leslie had married twice, each time to a person who was abusive. The first had been physically abusive (Leslie hadn't stood for that long), but the second spouse had mainly wanted the inequality of dominance. It was something he felt the world owed him. He needed to believe that he was the important person in their relationship. But when William insisted they move to New York City, she had been glad.

She decided to leave Curtis, and she got a teaching certificate and then a teaching job, and she loved the ethnic variety in the school where she taught. When creeping age scared William, he had come to believe that there must be more to his life than loving Leslie. He had begun to nag and criticize; he puffed himself up with his own importance and tried to make Leslie feel small: Leslie shouldn't do anything except what bolstered him and the fulfillment of his desires. Once he fired a tennis ball so hard and fast across the net that it hit her shoulder before she could move out of the way. He liked for her to iron his underwear.

Having retired from teaching high school English, Leslie had wanted to write. She felt that all her life she had wanted words to be like clay in her hands. And she had published a book, a short novel that Kathryn said was finer than anything she herself had ever written. The day her book was published, Leslie moved out, away from William. She went back to teaching as a substitute, filed for divorce, and saved her money. After a year, she decided to move to Louisville.

One book. Now for another. Living across the street from Kathryn would help Leslie keep her focus. She would live a quiet life and do the things she most wanted to do.

While Leslie had loved Benjamin, now she wouldn't call it *being in love*. (After all, he had been engaged.) But it wasn't quite being in love because she didn't want anything from him. She just wanted him to be, and for her to be in his presence.

To be in love, she now realized, required at least the hope of reciprocity, of mutual need. Benjamin was complete as he was. She had nothing that he needed. With surprisingly little pain, she had given up the idea of being in love and simply loved and admired him. It surprised her now that she'd had that much sense.

Leslie put down Kathryn's manuscript and walked out on her balcony. Across the court, Janie and her dog emerged from between the houses; Janie had two limp cloth bags for groceries hanging from their handles on her forearm; she would be on her way to the Root Cellar quasi-organic grocery at Hill and Third. The dog glanced across at Leslie but never hesitated or gave any acknowledgment. He stretched his nose forward a bit. A squirrel leapt from the canopy of one maple tree to another, and a gold leaf dropped down. Leslie admired the purposefulness of Janie and her dog. She felt something of herself mirrored in the scene across the Court. She had moved here purposefully, but now she really wanted to rest. Just to be. Where had Ryn gotten all that "go" in her nature? No matter who was betraying her, or who died, she wrote.

Mirror, Window; Mirror, Door—that had been the title of Leslie's book, a set of linked short stories that together formed a novel. She liked to think of a window as a device—actually she preferred the word *machine*—for subverting the opacity of a wall. A window was the magic membrane through which outside and inside could share their worlds. But a door! Ah, by means of a door one could transport oneself from one world to another.

Mirror, Window; Mirror, Door: it sounded like an incantation to Leslie. Transportation, not communication, was the real magic. She had taken herself out the door of her bad marriage and into a better world, here on St. James Court, a special community. She reentered her flat and the waiting manuscript, *Portrait of the Artist as an Old Woman.*

Yet, she dawdled. Here was her furniture, so satisfactory, and she saw herself among it. Satisfaction! That was the watchword for how she felt about being here, in her flat on St. James Court, high up on the second floor. She smiled to think that a New Yorker would not consider this very high at all.

Leslie believed that across the street Ryn had found her own brand of satisfaction about being precisely here, though she had entered her last marriage with the expectation of its lasting forever. Ryn was hurt by her divorce, but Leslie felt liberated by hers. Perhaps as Ryn's eighteenth-century artist had felt. She, too, had been divorced. Élisabeth's divorce had been politically mandated by her émigré status; she and her husband had remained cooperative friends.

Having already looked at Vigée-Le Brun's paintings on the Internet, Leslie had immediately begun to discriminate among them. She especially appreciated Vigée-Le Brun's depictions of artists: of Hubert Robert, the painter of ruins, and of Joseph Vernet (both male painters had been Élisabeth's guides and friends), and a self-portrait holding her own artist's palette, prepared for the act of painting. Those were her best paintings, Leslie had decided.

Vigée-Le Brun's paintings had entered history, and her work was exhibited, Leslie had learned, at the Louvre, the British Museum, the Hermitage in St. Petersburg, the National Gallery in Washington; with scattered paintings in many other museums, in Minneapolis, St. Louis, Fort

Worth, and Sarasota. When Ryn had first spoken of her interest in the painter, Leslie had made a special trip to the Met to see her work there. Ryn had said that Élisabeth's passion for painting did not abate as she aged. It sustained her to the end.

So what if she herself, Leslie, was aging! Everybody aged. She was free. She saw herself clearly. She knew she had little inclination to try marriage again; she wanted to relish her independence. To be alone, divested of that particular marital misery, was a triumph.

After the end of Ryn's second marriage years ago, she had come up from Louisville to New York to visit Leslie. Devastated by Peter's defection, Ryn had nonetheless made good progress toward recovery and a sense of well-being, partly for the sake of Humphrey, who was still a little boy.

On television, Leslie and Ryn had watched the Kentucky Derby together. After the race, Ryn said to Leslie, "If only I could learn how to change my lead, like a horse. I can lead with my need or I can lead with my sense of independence, in relationships with men. If only I could lead with the independent leg."

Leslie had told Ryn she was a Thoroughbred. She could change her lead.

Leslie felt free free free, perched on her balcony higher than Venus standing on a clamshell dais, skimming the surface of the sea. The sounds of the fountain, the rushing of water, were frisky and potent. There were many things Leslie wanted to do (her own writing) this scrumptious autumn day! She would savor every minute of it. She did love every minute of it.

And she had a fireplace here! She could tickle the ribs of winter with her own orange flames. Didn't she see a grayness moving in from the northwest? Rain? Winter would be a good time to write a novel, something with sustaining length. Even Kathryn had said the transition from writing short stories to a novel had been difficult; it had taken time. Of course Leslie didn't have time stretching ahead of her. But she had a new home, a new start, new energy, and the presence of a friend who had been a member of Leslie's life.

WHAT HAD RYN TOLD HER now in the way of advice? Be patient. An idea will come to you, and when it does, seize it, even in the middle of the night. Don't take notes or make an outline; leap into the writing itself, and write until you drop.

The right idea had not yet seized Leslie. She was suspicious of her characters. She didn't want to give herself to them. She didn't want to love them. Perhaps if her life had left her something other than disappointment about intimacy—the husbands? But there was Ryn, thrice divorced, writing away, new projects always knocking at her door.

If she couldn't leap on the novel train, Leslie thought, she'd tarry in the station with a series of thematically linked stories. Ah, that idea was like a revolving door: she went in it and out again, then back in. Not linked through the characters, as *Mirror, Window; Mirror, Door* had been.

Over the cascade of the fountain, Leslie heard loud, unbridled laughter, something raw, erupt. Across the Court, workmen were carrying something on their shoulders as they walked between Kathryn's house and the lovely, baronial, turreted place to the south. The new owner, an exceptionally handsome and pleasant man with a shiny bald head and attractive black eyebrows, walked quickly behind the work crew.

He and his wife had found the house on the Internet and moved to Louisville from California, saying Old Louisville was the best-kept secret and the greatest real estate value in the nation.

Before the Californians' arrival, no one had seen any furniture on the front porch or any human enjoyment of that lovely verandah, not for decades. Ryn had said she used to see the old woman owner, who rented out rooms, standing on the porch; always wrapped in a thin gray sweater, she looked cold, and she sometimes called out to neighbors or visitors passing on the sidewalk in the hope that they would come up her steps and chat a bit. Fifty years earlier, May had been one of the movers and shakers, a founder of the St. James Art Fair.

RUNNING HIS HAND OVER HIS BALD HEAD, Brandon felt embarrassed by the boisterous laughter of his workmen. St. James Court was such a sedate place. He liked that about it; people were friendly but far less casual than neighbors in L.A. The woman with the husky and her husband—they lived down the street in the house with the terra-cotta roof—were truly convivial. One summer evening, sitting on her porch with a glass of wine, the woman had promptly invited Brandon to join them. "It's cocktail hour," she had said gaily. They were both easy to talk to, full of zest for what was happening in the neighborhood, and they encouraged him to get involved, too. He knew Sallie would like them, once she could join him in Louisville.

Suppose they weren't a fit here in Louisville? It was a big deal just plunging into a strange city.

When he had asked the woman next door, the writer, so is Louisville in the South or the Midwest, she had said that she had had the same question when she moved here. "It's the South," she had said. "Those trees in my front yard are southern magnolias, but they don't grow much across the river. In southern Indiana, they get spring a week later than we do, and it's colder there in winter. The Ohio River divides the South from the North." She had been talkative that day, as though she were trying to be welcoming.

But she seemed a moody person. Usually she just nodded and said hello, took no time to chat. Sometimes she wandered aimlessly around her pool and backyard, not doing any work, though there was clearly a lot of work that could be done back there to good advantage.

Today she uttered a mere *Hi*. She looked abstracted. Not that he wanted to talk anyway; he had supervision to perform. Probably writers were generally moody people. Off in some dream world. He wondered how hard it might be to spend so much time alone. But she always looked right at him, with friendly eyes, as though she understood what it was to be another human being.

I'LL DIE, KATHRYN THOUGHT, glancing up at the very large tree over the deck, *if the cottonwood ever dies.*

Suddenly she heard the new neighbor calling to her over the curved arm of brick wall. "What does the fountain have to say?" He was smiling as he stretched his face up over the brick wall. He was pleasant, and his head looked polished.

"Keep on truckin'," she answered.

He laughed. Then he added, with a knowing look, "I saw you out front last night. Looking at the fountain."

Kathryn didn't know what to say. Why shouldn't she go out at midnight if she wanted to?

"What's her name?" he added. "The fountain lady?"

"Venus."

"Like the planet? Did you see the planet?"

"Venus comes up in the early evening."

Workmen, having left their burden inside, passed noisily behind their employer and moved toward the street again. They put their boots heavily to the walkway, with a certain emphasis, too heavily, Ryn thought.

"Stargazing, then?" her neighbor continued.

"I was looking at the moon. I like to keep track of the phases of the moon."

"My wife does, too. She says, 'Full moon. Watch out.'"

Ryn thought, *Yeah, well, I don't have to worry about that anymore.* Maybe he believed she was younger than she was. Most people did. At the point when most people found out her age, they just stared at her quizzically. Then she would usually say, *I've drunk from the fountain of youth. My mother did, too. She once passed for fifty when she was eighty.*

"Putting in some new drywall," he explained, turning away.

"Good luck with it," she called to his back. Descending the stairs from the deck to the patio, she felt careful and fragile.

AT THE BOTTOM OF THE STAIRS, Ryn placed her hand on the round wooden newel ball and let herself fall back into thought. Was it an unwise idea just to stop, to let herself pause, midstep, to think? Stooping, she fingered the seedpod of a spent hollyhock blossom beside the brick column. But had he—the neighbor—actually asked her what the fountain had said to her?

Not everybody would have asked that. So now there was this filament of connection between them. *What had the fountain said to her?* He had offered a human connection and she had been too self-absorbed, worried about Jerry's visit, to respond to it. Alone so much with her writing, she needed human connection: that glance into the eyes that said I live, you live, we understand, this is all. She needed that. It made ordinary living meaningful. *I'm a human. Unique. I see you are, too. We share something. Something impermanent. This moment. That is all. We perish.* Then she added of her neighborly encounter, *Let it be forgotten. As a flower is forgotten.*

Or an autumn leaf. Only sometimes she saved them, tucked them between the pages of a book. She would find them later, very flat, like a thin piece of tin, but the color miraculously preserved. Although she would try to remember, she would be unable to reclaim the moment when she had seen the leaf on the pavement or ground, took it home, and placed it in the book.

She hoped Yves would come to visit in the evening. They had agreed on it, but why didn't he call to say he was on his way? This uncertainty reminded her of travel when she was a child. You didn't waste a long-distance phone call then to say you were doing what you'd already said you planned to do: start out. Maybe it had been that way in France, too, when Yves was growing up, and he'd held on to that habit of mind. Surely, he would call if he weren't coming.

But did she really care? No, not really. She was too old now to care much about connections that lacked the heft of mutual history. But about people she'd known in college days, though they'd broken or forgotten their connection, still, if they were suddenly remembered, or sent her an unexpected e-mail, or even were mentioned in passing by someone else, somehow, then she would care immensely about them. It was as though that long-ago affection had been put in the bank and gathered compound interest, and now it all came rushing out—like winning the jackpot at a slot machine in a Las Vegas airport, the coins of affection pouring out over her cupped hands, spilling into a messy pile on the carpet.

Let Yves live the life he wanted to live. But she wouldn't be trodden on. Too little evidence of affection or simple consideration, and he would be forgotten. Without regret. Without much regret, anyway.

And suppose Jerry showed up again, after Marie and Royce had finished their work? She didn't want to see him. Back when she thought his presence made her son happy, she had felt a lot of warmth for Jerry. Now, uninvited, he was coming to her house, asking questions, posing himself as a threat.

How she wished Humphrey would just suddenly appear at the door to surprise her! "Hi, Mom," he would say, and she would exclaim, "I thought you were in Sweden." She would be dazzled with happiness. Her son! Home to see her.

Without conscious volition, Ryn's fingernails tore off the husk of a hollyhock's seedpod to inspect the seeds stacked on their edges in a neat circle. Here was the embodiment of a plan for survival. Who would think a thin husk, buried in snow, would be a sufficient coat to keep the seeds viable through the winter?

THE DETAIL OF THE SNOW made a bitterness form at the corners of Ryn's mouth. In Montgomery, they had all been in love with snow. Even in their first-grade readers they had loved the pages that pictured northern children playing in the snow: their snowmen, their red cheeks as they sat (in the beloved reader near the top of the left-hand page), on their sleds, ready to go. Now those were *real* children. Sometimes she and her friends heard it had snowed in north Alabama, or even as far south as Birmingham, where the last of the Appalachian mountain chain unraveled into nothing. But a hundred miles farther south? Montgomery? Not likely.

And then the miracle: it snowed all the way to the Gulf. It was snowing in Mobile and in New Orleans, the radio said. Even college students—she was at Huntingdon by then—borrowed trays from the college cafeteria and looked desperately for some slope to use for sledding.

How Frieda's dark eyes had sparkled that white day! Her closest friend, after Leslie. (But Leslie had left Montgomery to study music in the North.) *We can fit, we can fit,* Frieda had insisted. *Both on one tray. Sit between my legs. Scooch closer.* And Ryn had scooched close, in a rapture about the whiteness of the snow. *Now I've got you,* Frieda whispered in her ear and leaned forward and kissed her on the cheek.

Broad daylight, in the glittering snow! One woman pecking the cheek of another. But it was all right: other college students rubbed snow in each other's faces, clung to each other to stay upright, wore socks on their hands (nobody owned mittens) and made snowballs which left half the snow sticking and caking onto the thin, cotton socks. The sheer, extraordinary fun of it! Everybody had loved everybody that day.

Ryn glanced around the spent garden. The pool steamed senselessly into the autumnal air. The garden was dead, or dying, or resting. She would go inside. She would telephone Peter and tell him that Marie and Royce had talked to Jerry. Quickly she passed through the iron gate and up the stairs to the deck. While she was out, walking in the park with Peter, Jerry had come to the door. Jerry had been inside her home. She tried to digest that fact. Loitering on the deck, she swept her fingertips along the rough wood railing.

She remembered Frieda's guitar and her song of Molly Malone: *She wheeled her wheelbarrow / through streets broad and narrow / crying "Cockles and mussels, alive, alive-o!"*

A mockingbird lit on one of the brick walls around the patio; the bird turned its back to her and lifted its tail. High, and higher. What insouciance! It was as though the bird was mooning her. She smiled slightly: as though it were about to shit on her precious memories. *In Dublin's fair city, where girls are so pretty* . . .

Back then when Frieda had sung the Irish folk song of fishmonger Molly Malone peddling her wares, none of them did more than faintly dream that they would ever see Dublin, or any other of the capitals of the world. Yet, as it had turned out, Ryn had traveled the world. But now she would traverse time instead of place, back to Giles's face, alive and happy months before the auto accident, his shining eyes when Frieda sang, *'Twas there I met fishmonger Molly Malone.* Ryn smiled. Grammar school, high school, college friends in Alabama, were all still real to her; she saw the glow of their youthful skin, their cheeks, and their bright, direct eyes. When Frieda's song turned to lament the fate of Molly Malone—*she died of a fever, and none could relieve her*—they had felt how sad the inevitability of death, but it was a long way away from any of them; death was in Dublin. Death was nothing imminent. Not around the corner for Frieda, for Giles; only for Molly Malone, who had lived in another time and place.

Her ghost wheels a wheelbarrow

Through streets broad and narrow

Crying "Cockles and mussels, alive, alive-o."

On the carpet, they all drew closer together. Sometimes Frieda changed the words to sing "alive, a-love, O!"

A FEW YEARS AFTER COLLEGE GRADUATION, when Ryn visited Frieda and her husband and young child in New York, it would snow again. In the apartment, they would gather around their window with the best view of Washington Square six stories below. Frieda, half out of her mind . . .

Yes, Frieda half out of her mind, Ryn saw the scene again, knowing what would happen next and next. Because she would feel Frieda's breath on the rim of her ear, and words would be whispered like puffs of breath into Ryn's ear: *Remember when it snowed in Montgomery?* Both Ryn and Frank would chorus that they did remember, but Frieda would go on speaking as though Frank were not even there, as though she had erased him, *And you let me hold you?* Straightening his body, Frank would remark stiffly that it was time to put Francine to bed, and he would carry the little girl into another bedroom.

Frieda would seize the moment to say to Ryn that she loved Frank, *but I love you more. I want you more.* And Ryn would say that it was impossible, that she didn't feel that way about Frieda, not physically. And Frieda would say mysteriously, *The body is the only reality. The body knows best.*

But my body says no.

My body knows better than that. You'll never know a man who can love you as completely as I love you.

I don't believe that, Ryn would not say. But I do love you, Frieda, Ryn would say. Really I do. That she would say. Accept what I do feel.

Not enough.

It's not a little thing, friendship.

The situation was impossible. Frieda lived in a cocoon of pain and Ryn in a net of helplessness. When Ryn asked herself what could she do, she could imagine no remedy. She would lose herself, she knew she would; her selfhood would become irreparably broken if she loved Frieda not physically, but sexually. Why was Ryn not merely afraid but intuitively certain that she would not be able to reorganize some essential core of her being if she weren't true to her own nature? Her limits.

So Ryn would leave New York to go south as far as she could go, to the panhandle of Florida, to walk the soft beaches of sugary sand. It wasn't really warm there in February; you'd have to keep going—to Sarasota, or Miami or Key West—to get to real warmth, but at least it wasn't Washington Square with the wind clacking the ice-laden limbs against each other. It had sounded like a macabre dance of bones, of knitting. And so she had fled, had found a safe hotel near turquoise water at Destin.

In the middle of the night, the hotel phone rang. She must have mentioned the name of the hotel.

Just say one word to me, Frieda's voice entered her ear. *Say "yes."*

Ryn had exploded in tears. No. She sobbed. I'm so sorry. No.

Ryn had slept late the morning after that call, but she went downstairs in time to have a good breakfast. She felt drained and empty, but relieved that she had taken a stand. She deserved to eat, to buy an expensive breakfast. Waffles with pecans, and scrambled eggs with patches of cream cheese blended in. Fresh orange juice. Even hot, milky coffee. She thought, *This is good.* The conventions of a substantial white tablecloth, silverplate utensils, and the bourgeois brightness affirmed her sense of normal—normal for her. *This is all good for me,* she thought. *It tastes good and I like it. That was the end. Things are settled now. I'm all right. I said no. Frieda will find somebody, a woman, who is right for her. We'll keep our friendship.*

The image of Frieda and the joy of being her friend came back in full measure.

As she unlocked the door of her room, Ryn heard the phone ringing. She fumbled with the key, but the phone rang on and on. Surely it would stop before she reached it. When she put the receiver to her ear, she heard Francine screaming in another room. Frank's voice made words enter her ear; it was as though he had thrust his tongue in her ear. "Frieda jumped."

YEARS AND YEARS AGO. But still real. Squeezing her eyes shut, Ryn pressed the palms of her hands against each other, hard, till they trembled. Then she opened her eyes and slowly parted her hands as though opening a book, its pages joined in back at a spine. She half expected to see a pressed leaf. She half expected to see a splotch of red. Perhaps a stiff maple leaf, intact, preserved, fine-cut edges. No. Only her own blank palms to read.

The mockingbird twitched her tail this way and that, small jerks left and right. Ryn cherished the fact that Frieda had been part of her life. Frieda had been rich in the capacity to love: men, women, children, the elderly, foreigners, those who suffered. The richness of her thought and feeling had made her death all the more painful. Once Ryn had seen a pomegranate broken open, in Calcutta, atop a pyramid of fruit, and remembered Frieda's heart. Inaccessible, rich, inspiring. Ryn sighed. The mockingbird decided her direction and flew away.

Look at what you have! Ryn's world seemed to say, but did the world console, or accuse?

I have no blood on my hands, Ryn thought. Again, she pressed her palms together and opened them. I did the best I could. I had the right to preserve my own sanity.

She could hear her stalwart friend Daisy saying decisively, "Of course her death wasn't your responsibility! You weren't even there."

And what was it about the completing and letting go of a novel that brought remembrances and a longing for Frieda and Giles? Ghosts, not demons. After she finished a first draft, that space between books was a crack through which came the unresolved, and the impossible to resolve, and losses, pain, regret, longing.

Yes, sometimes after finishing a draft, there came a disconcerting vista: a great blank basin, sun dried and fissured, and all the waters of memory and imagination gushing upward to fill the barren bowl. The sinking of the sun was a hard time for all fish, Hemingway had written in *The Old Man and the Sea*.

The time after finishing a book had often been a difficult time for Virginia Woolf: voices, some form of insanity, rose up from slumber then, to haunt and torment. The mental illnesses were linked with Woolf's traumas: her half brothers' sexual explorations of her body, the deaths of her mother, her half sister, her beloved older brother Thoby (fictionalized as Jacob, as Percival), and her father, a member of the established literati. But that last death, of Sir Leslie Stephen, had also been a liberation. How much did anxiety about the public's reception of her books figure into Woolf's recurring illness? Was hoping for their appreciation too excruciating?

Ryn felt joyful over finishing her books, usually. Hopeful, but not anxious. When she let go of them, she felt a rather sturdy faith and fulfillment in what she had created. Some reviewers felt a new book should be much like the earlier ones—a reviewer's error, not Ryn's. But after the novels were finished, she wanted life to fill her. Not a good time to be alone.

The antidote was to live in the day: to embrace friends close at hand who could support her, Leslie, Daisy and Daniel, Peter, for Peter was her friend as well as her ex-husband. It wasn't often that she thought so far back in her own history as to mourn again the loss of Frieda, or Giles.

Someday Humphrey would come home, or he would invite her to visit in Sweden.

I love you so much, she let herself say softly into the backyard air, even though she knew it was sentimental. Sometimes she let herself be sentimental, superstitious. What did it hurt? The air was a good mailbox for a message: didn't it circumnavigate the globe? Pursing her lips, she smacked a kiss into the air.

"For Humphrey," she said boldly, and turned to go inside.

As she turned, her eye caught the face of her nice neighbor staring at her, concerned, from his back steps. Had her words traveled to his ear?

Her hand reached toward the doorknob; time to hide; she would pass from the outside to inside.

When Marie had told her of Jerry's visit, she had felt the thudding of her heart. From inside her chest, its beating had shaken her. Did Jerry think he could harm Humphrey? She would never allow that. She would shoot him first.

Ryn hurried up the stairs, for now she was alone, brave enough to face inside what she must face, through the library, through the arch, to stare at the bed, where—had it been for the last time?—she and Mark had lain.

YES, IT HAD BEEN GOOD that last morning, their lovemaking. Whole-hearted, it had seemed. (Yes, with force of will she had pushed away what she knew, walled it off.) As though nothing had happened. (But it had.) But love was done for the day.

Done and then unexpectedly undone.

While she had lain quietly, without demand, beside her husband, a wedge-shaped blade that would not be denied had dropped between them. At first, she had felt a gush of warm, surprising tears (she was still nestled close) and then her own sobs, and she had moved to the edge of the bed because lying beside him, as though nothing had happened, was impossible.

Grief had grabbed her lower lip and tried to pull it over her chin, tried to turn her face wrong side out because then if she faced him maybe he would see. Maybe he would see and say whatever it was that could mend her. So she showed him her face, herself shocked by what she felt happening to her face, the painful distorting. She turned to him, begging in a whisper, *Look at me, look at me! See what you've done to me.*

I thought we'd had a nice time together.

We did. We have. (But *see: see me now. My face is wrong side out, grotesque.*)

I'm sorry for whatever pain I may have caused you.

(Whatever!)

(Whatever pain!)

She wheeled back to the side of the bed, grasped the hem of her nightgown, and began to tear it upward. One long strip and wailing and then another.

He slid out the other side and walked around her, not looking at her, intent on moving toward the bathroom. "You'll need to cry like this two or three more times before you get over it."

Look at me, she had sobbed, saying nothing more.

ALMOST TWO YEARS LATER, and still here again was the need to face it, even this triumphant day: she'd finished a novel, one over which he had no influence, except, except. Except the way, with a wave of his will, simply by remarrying (it was his right), he had made the waters close over her head, seamlessly, as though she had never risen from the depths, stood on mere foam, open-armed and openhearted, believing in his love.

So here she was again. Upstairs. Ryn stared at the broad bed.

There was where sweet love had been: this capacious bed now dressed in snowy white. But what meaty truth and bitter pith must she extract and swallow? What was the message she had rushed to this place to read?

There must be something new to see; was it time to look again, not at her deep past, not at her real fears for Humphrey, but simply at her own recent past? There must be something she had not understood before.

Well, he was gone. Nearly two years. Really gone. But only recently had he made it clear: she had been quickly and easily replaced.

Long distance, a consoling friend had said into her ear: *Men replace; women mourn.* She had not thought him an ordinary man. (And of course, some men mourned; some women simply replaced.)

What it meant was that for a time, too long a time, she had just been the woman, the wife; there had been no value put on her uniqueness.

Buy new sheets. Plant the rose garden herself; carry out the garbage.

Loss, but now the gain? Her gain?

It was a gain: this fact that she needed to face. She had not been treasured.

ON BELGRAVIA COURT, Daniel Shepard sat in his study and worried about his wife. He had taken half the day off from work to revise his memoir, or was it to become a novel?

He wanted to write about growing up in Africa, in Nairobi, the child of missionaries, about when he had decided to participate in tribal rituals: how he prepared himself to take a spear to confront a leopard in the bush. How he had lived in Africa in two worlds—a God-drenched one; a sun-drenched one.

But memory conjured up the enticing aromas of the mission kitchen, not the hot dust, where the gifted chef had concocted a cornucopia of pastry to be filled with almond-flavored crème. Daniel thought, *All right then, to the kitchen, with butter and eggs and flour and cinnamon.* Let that be the subject.

Still, he made no headway with his writing by switching from one subject to another, for he remembered too vividly the sad face of his wife, who was planning to visit her mother in the nursing home. How could he focus on writing anything when Daisy was suffering?

On the bulletin board above his computer, he had posted some words from T. S. Eliot's *Four Quartets:*

> *We shall not cease from exploration*
> *And the end of all our exploring*
> *Will be to arrive where we started*
> *And know the place for the first time.*

Daniel thought that might happen when he went back to Africa, to the land he'd first known; he might know himself then, understand both his restlessness and his content.

He had asked Daisy not to go so often to visit her mother, and she had agreed and thanked him for his care of her, but even so, of course the trip was always there, waiting for her. Daniel offered to go in her stead, and had done so, but when questioned by Daisy, he had answered truthfully that no, her mother had had no idea who he was.

Daisy had inquired, "Did she ask about me?"

"She did."

"What did she say?"

Daniel had put his arms around his wife and replied, "She asked if I knew her daughter."

Immediately he felt Daisy's hot tears coming through the cloth of his shirt to his shoulder. Perhaps, when Daisy came home, he would offer to go there with her. To be some support, at least. Yes, he would do that, but first he would go out and get some flowers for Daisy, as a surprise. Perhaps he would hide them on the third floor, and then when they got back from the nursing home, he would fetch them and surprise Daisy.

Yes, he could imagine how her face would brighten, how she would smile at him.

WHAT PETER WANTED was a second chance. He sat down, alone with the dog, on a park bench to enjoy the autumn splendor. He would watch and count the fluttering descent of five red leaves. Five scarlet maple leaves with their fine-cut serrated edges. Yes, a second chance with Kathryn, with Ryn. That fluttering, wing-wounded wren. It was amazing that while her marriage to the neurosurgeon crumbled, she'd been able to finish her book.

But she was hard like that. Way back when they had been married, on the way to the hospital before Humphrey was delivered, she had insisted on stopping at the post office personally to mail a manuscript to meet some contest deadline. He had hated that steel in her. How she had trusted only herself to do it. And how often she had not guarded hours that could have been used to write (or to do something for him) just to read a manuscript for somebody else. Even when he advised her to think of her own need to make pages, she was wasting time that way. But up against an actual deadline: *She would make it. She would not be late in a way that canceled out the worth of her own effort.* Half bragging, she had told him she had printed out the last page of her dissertation and made it to the defense one minute before it was due. She was her own personal melodrama queen.

Certainly no one else, not those so-called dear friends eating up her time with their needs, cared that much whether she made her deadline or not. Certainly, he didn't, for he would have cared about her anyway, even if she had not been a quite successful writer. Maybe more. Struggle was noble. He'd struggled always with the self-serving Philistines.

Peter sank his broad fingers into Royal's curly topknot. Kathryn had a strange affection for the dog. And the dog went crazy with joy whenever he saw her. Sometimes Peter was so mad at her, the way she overenthused about nature, the particular color of the sky, the way a cloud billowed, a potpourri of colors on the pavement (there was a lovely scramble of gold and brown at the tip of his shoe). He crossed his legs. Sometimes he just wanted to get away from her as soon as he saw her. It was folly to want to mend things between them. He couldn't anyway. She was completely skittish. Like an unbroken colt, but pushing seventy.

Probably she would remember, if she ever did feel so again, that he was a jewel like no other (she had said that once), but then would she also remember that he had not been as kind to her mother as he could have been. Should have been. But stopping by the mailbox on the way to the delivery room! Making him detour to the drive-by post office! He could still hear the clunk of the cast iron drop-shelf as it swallowed her precious contest submission.

She hadn't won the contest, either. It would be nine more years before she would publish her first little book.

His shrink said he ought to forget her. Go forward with his life. No doubt she would, again. She had before. She had that terrible Forward gear. But he always knew exactly how she felt. She was ambivalent toward him. Something, her genuine admiration of his talent, did make him special and irreplaceable to her. They'd had a child together. That meant a lot. But it was more than that.

Over there by the huge oak was a pale little girl by herself walking around and around the park. Her expression was serene, though, a bit dazed. She was both remarkably pretty and remarkably well dressed in a pastel way. Artistically dressed she was, in a coat heavy enough for winter, fashioned from large fuzzy patches of wool, lavender and apricot, a sort of ruffle at the hem and large loose loops edging the collar. Sometimes Peter sketched possible fashions of women's clothes, really ideas for costumes in various plays, something that would catch the spirit for contemporary audiences for a character, like Miranda, out of Shakespeare, but this park visitor was purely a little girl. He had no interest in such a figure. And she was already dressed to perfection in ways he couldn't have imagined himself. Quite young, maybe seven, wandering. Another child, in red plaid, was kicking purposefully through the leaves. Lone children—strange, but not his business.

One of the problems with Ryn was that she had no sense of style. She dressed for comfort, as though she were wearing the leftover corduroy shirts her brothers had outgrown. She didn't get the importance of style. When she tried, it turned out usually to be all wrong, or with one feature glaringly wrong. Occasionally she did hit the jackpot, and then she was breathtakingly and surprisingly attractive. Peter or even their son Humphrey had more sense about women's fashions than she did. "I'm out of sight writing most of the time, anyway," she would say gaily.

He had never said, but you could dress for me. *I* look at you.

Peter studied the toe of his shoe and the scattered leaves. Nature's confetti, he thought. The toes of his shoes, Italian, were scuffed. He'd want new ones soon. He sighed.

"Hello, Peter," and there was Daisy, with two dogs, both mongrels, on leashes. Her pretty round face was smiling at him, glad to see him. "I'm driving the team today," she said lightly. "Daniel's going to the farm, cutting wood for the winter." The mongrels pulled in two different directions. Royal looked away, bored, displayed not even a twitch of interest in his fellow dogs.

"You're looking well, Daisy." She really was. Though partly gray, her hair was groomed becomingly, and she wore small drop earrings, gold with a subdued green stone.

"I was just thinking about you," she said. "Didn't you say you'd like to move out of the condo?"

"Out of Old Louisville, actually," he said. "Maybe across the river, southern Indiana." Once you got beyond the knobs, Indiana was flat like parts of New Mexico. He felt closed in among the mansions and old trees. It would be nice to see farmland in the distance, under a great lid of sky.

"That's what I thought you said. Shall I be on the lookout for you?"

"Something small and cheap," he said, remembering Daisy was a Realtor. "With a fenced-in backyard for Royal so I can just let him out the back door."

Her dogs had decided to tangle their leashes while she chatted.

"He's so stately," she said of Royal.

"That was quite a nice gathering," Peter went on, "over at Ryn's, last winter. Even a little fire for the literati of Old Louisville."

"You read so well," she said. "It was wonderful to hear a real actor read a new play."

"So when'll your book hit the screen, Daisy?" Peter meant the *little* screen, the computer, the iPad, the Kindle, the Nook—not the Hollywood one—and Daisy knew it.

"I'm not sure," she said. "There's always something to adjust. One of the nice things about electronic publication. You can just keep on revising. We've settled on the title, *Where the Heart Is*. Daniel says he'll take it away from me—"

"Yes, best just to let it go," Peter advised.

"Of course he's teasing me—" Daisy interrupted herself. "What do you think that girl is doing in the park? She should be in school. She has her books . . . Excuse me. I think I'll just speak with her."

Off Daisy went with the two dogs more or less in tow toward the child in the pastel coat. The other girl had disappeared. Royal glanced at Peter. He put his long nose down on his outstretched paws and sighed. "Bored, old fellow?" Peter asked, but he watched Daisy cut across the yellow-and-gold-leaf-covered grass to intercept the girl. *Hello, there . . .* Daisy's voice drifted back to him.

The child stopped in her tracks. She hugged her schoolbooks to her chest and stared at the grass, stock-still, while Daisy approached her. The two dogs ran ahead, split apart, at the girl. A whole shower of scarlet leaves fell in front of the scene like a curtain, but Peter could see Daisy had made the dogs cooperate. They stopped, came back, and flanked the little girl. The dogs wagged their tails but maintained a respectful distance. Clearly Daisy was talking to the little girl, whose face was tilted up, her whole attention focused on Daisy, telling while Daisy listened. Then the child handed her something from her pocket, probably a cell phone. Daisy switched the leashes to one hand and held out her arm. The girl walked into the open arm, leaned against Daisy, while Daisy squeezed her shoulder and drew her closer. Then they began to walk. Across the grass, straight toward Peter.

He stood up to wait for them, as did Royal. Daisy's face showed calm control, but a certain remoteness, too. The girl, perhaps she was eight years old, was studying the ground again.

"This is Juliette," Daisy said to Peter, "and this is Mr. Peter. Peter, she's gotten some very bad news. She and her mother accidentally switched phones, and she's received a call from the hospital that her father's died." Daisy's voice was perfectly matter-of-fact, but suffused with understanding.

"An accident?" Peter asked.

"No," the word suddenly broke out of the girl. "He's been sick a long time. We knew he was going to die." Then she threw herself against Peter, and he held her tight as she sobbed.

"There, there," he said. "I know, I know. It's so tough." He patted her shoulder. "We're so sorry." Then he held her and rocked her while she sobbed. He cradled the back of her head with his large hand. Royal looked up at the sobbing child and whimpered, then licked her dangling fingers.

Over the child's head, Peter's eyes met Daisy's, and he knew they were thinking and feeling the same pity and regret and acceptance. And Daisy was thanking him, too, though no thanks were needed.

"Stop it," the girl finally said irritably to Royal. "You've got me all wet."

"Here's my clean handkerchief," Peter said. "Wipe your hand."

They waited while she cleaned her hand to her satisfaction and then patted Royal's head.

"Now hold my hand," Peter instructed. "We're all going to walk down to Belgravia Court to Mrs. Shepard's house, and she'll call someone for you."

"I didn't want to go to school." Instantly, the child was sobbing again. "But I didn't want to go home. I thought if I just stayed in the park—if I was in the park, maybe my daddy, my daddy wouldn't be dead now." Her sobs racked her body.

Peter held her close, but he started them walking south again, toward Belgravia.

"I know," Peter said. "We understand."

She walked beside Peter even while she gasped and blubbered. Holding Peter's hand quite firmly, she looked up at him and said, "And I thought I might be in trouble—"

"Juliette, you're not in a bit of trouble," Daisy said. "I'll take care of everything. I promise. You can trust me."

"Thank you," she sniffed.

They didn't talk anymore. From time to time the girl sniffed. Checking for cars, Peter escorted them across Magnolia into St. James Court. From time to time, Peter hugged the girl closer. Just as they were passing the fountain, the girl hesitated, hitching up their progress. They all paused to look over at the fountain, but then the girl's eyes shifted to study Peter's face, as though to memorize him. He returned her gaze and smiled a little, as a grandfather might.

"It's a statue of Venus," he said, projecting his voice confidentially but loud enough so that she could hear him over the sound of the water falling like hard rain. "The goddess of beauty. In ancient Greece, they believed she was created from the foam of the sea." His voice conveyed a soupçon of both wonder and incredulity as he pronounced the last sentence.

FROM HER BALCONY, Leslie watched the three people and the three dogs disappear behind the fountain and its veil of waters, jetting, falling, till the group reappeared on the other side. She was sure that was Peter, Kathryn's ex, with his royal poodle, but having been in the flat less than two weeks, she wasn't sure about the mother and little girl. The woman looked familiar, but Leslie didn't think Kathryn had friends with a young child. They made a nice group, though, those three people, moving smoothly along to the counterpoint of two exuberant middle-size mutts darting around erratically and the measured march of Peter's aristocratic poodle. Yet the trio moved in perfect unison. They glided along, despite the distraction of the dogs.

What was it that made the group seem somber? Ah, the man, Peter, had his arm around the little girl. Like two unequal dancers, his stride slightly shortened, hers conscientiously lengthened, they moved forward in step, a little behind the woman with short gray hair, whose head was held high. *A noble head, like a Roman matron,* Leslie thought.

She glanced across at Kathryn's second-floor library window, and she saw that Kathryn was standing there, her hands pressed against her hips, her head tilted down, also watching the little parade on the sidewalk pass her house. Leslie turned away.

Kathryn needs me to read her novel, Leslie recalled. But she was right to delay. You had to be in a balanced mood when you read for other writers, or you'd project your own mood or needs onto their work.

THERE'S PETER, KATHRYN THOUGHT, and he's helping Daisy with some mission of mercy. A lost child, perhaps. Not the same little plaid schoolgirl Ryn had seen earlier, the sturdy, know-it-all ten-year-old. Another child, prettier, more tender looking, wearing a woolly coat in soft pastels. Seven or eight years old. Stylish. Peter of the sympathetic heart. Peter knew how people felt. It was part of his talent as an actor, but also his empathy bespoke the kind of quick, imaginative person he really was, despite being grumpy and evasive a good deal of the time.

YOU CAN CLIMB ANY TREE, the little scholar in red plaid hiding in the park told herself. She had found a way to clamber up the stage shell and then transfer to the lower limbs of the giant hemlock nearby. She had named the hemlock behind the stage the Steeple of the Park, and she knew the word *sanctuary* and applied it to this place of squirrels and birds. Hemlock branches were not very sturdy, but she was light. She loved being among their green feathers. They were thick enough to conceal her and soft to touch. From her vantage point in the tree, she had watched a little tableau of adults, dogs, and a pretty little girl. Now the dogs and the three people had crossed Magnolia and were almost out of sight, stopped at the fountain.

She thought she had seen the little girl once before, visiting her church: First Unitarian Universalist. She had noticed the three dogs many times: the poodle was stuck-up; the brown dog was a crybaby; but the black dog was rich and mysterious. His head was shaped like a wolf's head, and he was deeply black but with a white flag on the end of his plumy tail to signal he was really gentle as a lamb. He smiled when he was happy. He had seen her up in the tree, but he hadn't told anybody.

She had to be up in the tree to read her book. She had to play hooky. *Hooky,* it was a very old-fashioned word; her grandmother had told her she had always wanted to play hooky, but she never had. So Alice decided she would inhabit that word. She preferred to read her own library book, *The Three Musketeers,* rather than go to school. Milady had been imprisoned, but she was so clever and so beautiful that Alice believed Milady could probably convince her jailer to release her. Alice felt sure it would happen, but the suspense was thrilling and hypnotic, and Alice's sureness was mixed up with a dreadful hope against hope. If she were ever in jail, she would need to know how to escape, how to sway men.

For just a moment her gaze flicked up the tall straight trunk of the hemlock. Like an arrow, it led all the way to the sky. And then there were clouds. After she finished *The Three Musketeers,* she would read the sequel *Twenty Years After.* After that came *The Vicomte de Bragelonne,* in twenty volumes, but the library didn't have it. Her parents would not let her have an iPad or an iAnything. The little girl below, who cried, had a cell phone.

But Alice was happy with her thick book up in a tree. She loved how thick it was.

When she looked up at certain kind of clouds, she imagined that she could walk among the clouds, soft and thigh-high, like huge cotton balls or sea foam, like bushes made of white light, and behind the bulges like bushes were hidden short stacks of volumes of the *Vicomte de Bragelonne* series.

She loved short stacks of books. They were beautiful. When she was little, she had played at arranging stacks of books in different ways, in different orders of thick and thin and turned at various random-seeming angles.

RYN HAD MET THE LITTLE GIRL in the pastel coat before, the child walking with Daisy and Peter and the dogs.

With her mother as chaperone, the girl had knocked on Ryn's door selling Girl Scout cookies. Quite some time ago it was, but she was wearing the same coat then. The little girl had had porcelain skin, a really beautiful child. Her bright red hair overpowered the soft colors of the coat in a striking way. During their talk of thin mint cookies, the girl had suddenly taken a quick breath and delivered the information that her father was in Rochester. The fact seemed just to tumble out of her.

"Is that Rochester?" she had asked, pointing at a watercolor in Ryn's foyer of a woman in a long dress standing on a roof walk in Nantucket.

As she replied, Ryn had noticed that the colors of the girl's coat complemented the hues in the watercolor. "It's a painting of Maria Mitchell. She was the first person in the world to discover a comet using a telescope," Ryn had explained to both the girl and her mother.

"That was a long time ago," the child had noted, having registered the woman's long skirt and the sailing boats in the harbor.

"That's Nantucket," Ryn added.

"You're the writer, aren't you?" the mother had asked.

"Yes, I am," Ryn had answered. She noticed the resemblance between the mother and daughter then, though the mother's skin had lost the delicate tints and tenderness of her daughter's.

This had to be the same little girl walking with Peter and Daisy and the dogs, but now Ryn saw only their backs, the child's tumble of long hair against her coat. Far down the sidewalk now. Going to Daisy's house perhaps. Ryn hoped nothing was wrong.

What would it have been like to grow up being so enchantingly beautiful? Bright and sensitive, too, the girl of the beautiful coat, the little Scout, had seemed, commenting on the painting. When she had been pregnant with Humphrey, Ryn had rather hoped for a little girl with red hair, like Peter's hair.

Even when she was a child Ryn had known she was different from her peers—not that she was beautiful. Some other immutable reason. When she was with a group of kids, her main ambition had been to fit in, to pass for normal. Only when she was with a single, special friend, with Nancy or with Laura (sometimes including Laura's sister Margarita) or with Wanda, or Barbara, the violinist, did she feel at ease and fully herself. When she learned about the strange ability of the chameleon to conform in color to its environment, she had realized "I am a chameleon," and felt ashamed.

She knew she had changed to fit in with each dear friend, yet with each one of them, she had the immense pleasure of inhabiting some facet of her true self. She had not aspired, or even wanted, to be normal—that she understood to be beyond possibility—but only to *pass* for normal.

Turning from the library window—Daisy, Peter, the little girl had all disappeared—Ryn thought of Mark yet again. Did she need to salvage what had been good in the marriage? No, she thought not, though that had been important to do when the long marriage to Peter ended. She stood in the open arch between the library and her bedroom. Uncertain, she gazed into the bedroom again.

Now should be a free day, a day of liberation. She knew the lesson she had learned, staring at the blank bed: Mark had not valued her, not as a unique person.

PLACING THE PALMS OF HER HANDS against each side of the arch, she swayed forward and backward, sometimes leaning forward into the bedroom, sometimes rocking back. She looked at the smooth bed, its whiteness. It hurt her that he had replaced her quickly, but she had already faced that. And wasn't she thinking of replacing him now? Hadn't she invited Yves to visit? Now that the book was done, on schedule. Now that she had time to pour herself into another life?

She would fix lunch, tuna salad on a toasted whole wheat English muffin, with low-sodium tomato soup. Stalks of celery. She would hard-boil two brown eggs. It was a usual writing-day lunch, but she would serve it on her good china, the Haviland. Rather happily, she headed downstairs toward the kitchen. She hadn't used the Haviland since Mark moved out. "Of course you can have it," he had said angrily. "The house, too. It's all yours. Now are you appeased?" Of course he had meant she could have the house if she paid him for it, with value added for the improvements she alone had funded.

While the eggs were bouncing in the pot, the thud of the door knocker echoed throughout the house. Glancing through the half-length leaded glass sidelights was woolly Royal, nose pointed up, eye directed inside. Peter was stopping by. Something he never did, especially not after they'd had a walk, unless he'd forgotten something.

As she opened the front door, she explained that she was just fixing lunch and would he like to join her for soup and salad.

"'Fixing'?" Peter said. "Is it broken? Fixing lunch? You Southerners never learn. Make. You *make* lunch. It's a creation, not a broken wagon wheel." He looked impish and young, starting over, as though he'd forgotten about the walk among the autumn leaves of the park.

Ryn forbore asking him about the child and Daisy; he wouldn't like to think that she was supervising his life. She mentioned the eggs boiling on the stove and led Peter and Royal back toward the kitchen, Royal's toenails clicking on the polished oak floor. "Guess I should have his nails clipped," Peter said. "I don't walk him enough." Peter's condo was mostly carpeted; he wouldn't have noticed the telltale sound there.

His leash unsnapped, Royal moved purposively with a princely bounce in his step through the foyer, past the living room piano and the large painting hanging over it, back to the spacious kitchen. Ryn rather wished Royal would look at the painting: it deserved his notice.

"Do you like the painting?" she asked Peter.

"Very large," he said. "Colors of Chagall, composition of Matisse. Nice combo. Trapeze artists."

"Notice the area for the audience is almost as large as the arena at the top of the tent."

"Okay."

"And the trapeze bars have no lines attached. The troupe flies without wings, so to speak."

"Okay. Now I know how to look at it. So it's a metaphor for all artists." His voice was tinged with resentment, and there they were again, off on the wrong foot with each other.

"I'm inordinately proud of it," Ryn said, by way of apology.

"So naturally you want people to appreciate what you appreciate about it." His statement was no more than partial reconciliation; he sounded resistant. "To see it your way," he murmured.

"Humphrey encouraged me to buy it."

"So who's the artist?"

"She's from Louisville. Joyce Garner." Ryn led the way past the painting, past her father's clock. *She's the real thing,* Ryn thought of the Louisville painter. *A successful artist who trusts her own energy. A happy person.*

In the kitchen, Peter pulled out a chair from the table and sat down.

Royal trotted out to the sunporch and lay on the tiles in a block of October sunlight. He was bored with their conversation. Sunshine, sunshine sinking its fingers into springy curls, that was what Royal wanted for himself. He wanted the sun to scratch him with its fingers.

Ryn hated the way she let herself be absorbed in the pretend psyches of animals. It was as though she didn't quite believe in herself as a human. "Did you read that mystery Rick wrote? *The Ecstasy of the Ani-*

mals? I always loved that title. I would have bought it from him if I could.

"It's about being set free," she added, but Peter seemed absorbed in his own thoughts. She cracked and peeled the hard-boiled eggs, ran the can opener around the six-ounce tuna can, took the mayonnaise from the fridge, and mixed up the salad.

"I don't know that animals are all that eager to be free," Peter said. "It's a hard life to fend for yourself." She noticed his lips looked dry and parched, but there was a glow about his face. Some of the fresh audacity of just dropping in to visit at lunchtime still brightened his expression.

As she poured the soup, she was careful to give both portions equal amounts of the diced tomatoes. Because Peter enjoyed arty, handmade things, she had gotten out the bowls she had bought at the St. James Art Fair, instead of the Haviland.

"Nice bowls," he said with unqualified appreciation while she put the food on the place mats, woven of rich fall colors, russet and harvest gold. She didn't like things to match overly much.

"Actually I was thinking you'd like them," she said. The hand-thrown bowls each swirled together a clayish russet with midnight blue. "Did you go to the fair?"

"Yeah. I wanted to let Royal strut his stuff. It's good for him to be admired."

At his name, Royal had turned his head to watch them talk about him.

"Aren't you afraid of making him vain?" she teased. But Royal was not vain; he was just himself. She enjoyed his proud carriage, but it was his expressive face, both intelligent and understanding, that she loved. As she sat down across from Peter, the kitchen telephone rang.

"Go ahead and answer it," Peter said, so she did. Almost no one called her on the house line anymore, but she kept it for the security system. Right into her ear, as though he were down the street, instead of on a rocky shore in Sweden, she heard the voice of their son.

"Humphrey!" she exclaimed. "I was just thinking of you." (Of course she was always just thinking about her only child; Peter had another boy

from an earlier marriage, but Humphrey was her one and only.) Peter held
out his hand as though to take the phone, and she nodded and smiled at
him: yes, she'd hand over the phone in a moment. She asked about Edmund
and about the weather, genuinely interested in both. (*Fit as a fiddle* and *surprisingly still warm.*) To know Humphrey's context was to make him seem
all the more real. It was so very pleasant to hear his voice, for him to say
anything at all. All at once she both listened to him and thought of what
she wanted to tell him. She would tell him that the fall colors were gorgeous, that they had walked in the park, maybe that she had seen a little
girl in red plaid with a heavy load of books that reminded her of herself and
how she would go walking with Laura, scuffing their feet in the leaves, and
oh, that she'd finished the first draft of her new book—

"Does Dad happen to be there?" (*How full and rich,* her son's voice.)

"Yes. Yes, he does happen to be here. Royal, too. Just a minute—" And
she carried the phone around to Peter, who was positively beaming.

"What are you working on?" Peter asked their son, for her ex took a
lively interest in Humphrey's work as a sculptor.

Humphrey's answer was long, and Ryn watched Peter's expressive
face responding. Feeling shortchanged, she began to eat her soup before
it got cold. In his kitchen chair, Peter changed his posture, somewhat restlessly and impulsively, as he listened. Probably Peter wasn't getting to talk
as much as he would have liked.

She would have liked to hear what Humphrey was saying, but she
knew how she always cringed when anyone announced, "I'll put you on
speakerphone." It was the old chameleon in her. What she said was carefully adjusted in subject matter, sentence style, tonal structure to her particular listener. She imagined Humphrey felt the same way she did about
having a conversation over distance with more than one person. On book
tours, sometimes people would ask her the audience question: "Who do
you write for?" She'd known the answer since Alabama college days when
she was just beginning to write stories. *I write for a person just like myself who
has not yet read my book,* she would respond, slowly, so the listeners could

follow her ready answer. Nearly always there was a slight twitter or some other expression of surprise. She supposed it sounded narcissistic, but it was true. That Peter was finally speaking into the telephone snagged her attention, and what had he said?

"Humphrey, it looks like I'm going to play Lear next summer at Shakespeare in the Park. Maybe you and Edmund can come back over."

"What?" Ryn exclaimed, surprised and smiling.

Phone glued to his ear, Peter shook his head slightly and smiled back at her; Peter's listener was clearly intended to be Humphrey.

"Demented, I'll play him as demented. Alzheimer's. That's what a contemporary audience can relate to . . . No, he won't lose grandeur. Pity and terror, Greek ideas of tragedy. It will lead to that. Divesting himself of his position and power as king, that opening scene? It's a sign of dementia. His paranoia about being loved by his daughters, that, too."

Yes, Ryn could see King Lear played as having Alzheimer's or some sort of senile dementia.

Ryn was patient; she loved it that Humphrey and Peter had special parts of themselves in common, talents that she lacked, but she was beginning to feel left out. Humphrey had called *her,* for God's sake, and she'd barely gotten to say hello. She thought of the way Mark always excluded her. If he was talking to a relative on the phone, he had always gotten up and walked out of the room. He disappeared her from the scene. Yes, of course some things were private. She wondered if she should mention that Jerry was in town, had actually come out to the house looking for Humphrey.

Peter suddenly spoke to her. "Humphrey's running out of time. You want to talk again?"

She held out her hand for the phone and said directly into the mouthpiece, "It would be great if you and Edmund could come back in late June, early July." His answer was a short *Maybe so,* and she asked about autumn in Sweden, which turned out to be already over. Maybe Humphrey would come back for *Lear,* next summer. She wouldn't urge him again, though she said, *That would be great.* Then she mentioned that she had finished the first draft of her new novel and taken it over to Leslie, who had moved to Louisville recently.

"That really is great, Mom!" Humphrey's voice swung fully open with pride and enthusiasm.

When she asked about Humphrey's work, he said he was making a series of foot-high clay sculptures of old-timers at work. Mixed media. The work object was represented with snippets of the actual task: a miniature piece of fishnet, a piece of shoe leather—and then he broke off to ask what was the title again of the new novel. When she said *Portrait of the Artist as an Old Woman,* they both chuckled.

She felt sure that they simultaneously recognized the congruence of their subject matter. "Do a little sculpture for me of an aging woman at her writing," she said, and he said he would, one with a laptop at a desk. Suddenly she thought it could look kitschy, but she didn't say so.

He signed off saying, "I love you, Mom. I'm really, really proud of you for finishing the draft," and she replied, "I love you, too." She wouldn't tell him about Jerry.

Probably Jerry would come and go, and that would be that. "Well, that was a pleasant surprise," she said to Peter. "Do you want me to heat up your soup."

"No, this is fine," he answered. He began to eat rapidly. Royal came in from the sunporch and sat sedately beside his master.

"I'm glad he called while you were here. And Lear! Did you know that earlier?" She wondered why Peter hadn't mentioned it when he first came in the door. They had only chatted about the trapeze artists painting.

"On Belgravia, Royal and I were walking a little girl and Daisy back to Daisy's house, and afterward I ran into Josh Bomhart, the director. He stopped me right outside Daisy and Dan's house, and he offered me the role on the spot. He'll call my agent."

"Terrific! You'll be terrific. Huge congratulations."

"Then Humphrey called on his cell, so I told him about Lear, outside

Daisy's, but I couldn't hear what he said. Static on the line. I told him give me time to get back to your place and then call on your landline."

Quickly Ryn stuffed down any disappointment, just as she always had throughout their marriage. Then Humphrey hadn't really been spontaneously phoning her up. So Peter had saved the big news about the Lear role for Humphrey, even though she had been wishing it for Peter just that morning. Just this morning, with all the autumn leaves floating around them, in the park, while they walked the paved pathways, the idea of Peter playing Lear had come to her like an inspiration, out of the blue. And she had shared it, immediately. But what did the sequence of events matter; Peter was going to get to play Lear in the park. Yes, it would be a triumphant moment in Peter's career. And he would be splendid (if only he didn't fall into that low-key conversational mumble). Who knew who might come to the performance, what it might lead to?

"I'm really happy you get to do the part," she said again to Peter. And she was.

When Peter was almost out the massive front door, he paused, looked back over his shoulder, and gave Ryn a wink. Did Royal give out a throaty little arf at the same moment, or did she imagine it? At any rate, it was clear Peter was feeling good about himself.

STANDING IN THE ENTRY HALL of her Belgravia home, Daisy hung up the phone and said to the tearstained little face, "Your mother will be here to get you just as soon as she can. It won't take long. Come sit on the sofa with me while we wait."

Such a pretty child, she thought, so much suffering so young. Daisy's gray-and-white long-haired cat came rubbing against the girl's ankles.

"You can pick her up," Daisy said. "She's a special kind of cat, a rag-doll cat. When you pick her up, she's as limp and flexible as a rag doll."

"Really?" the girl asked, but she hesitated to stoop down.

"When we sit on the sofa, Lillian will come over to us." Knowledgeable about the ways of both cats and traumatized little girls, Daisy took the girl's hand and led her from the entry hall to the living room. They paused to watch through the French doors a golden shower of ginkgo leaves raining down onto the grassy median. The girl's gaze shifted to the silver tea service on the coffee table and back to the gold fluttering just outside.

"Are those windows or doors?" she asked.

"They're windows, and we don't walk through them," Daisy explained, "but they do open all the way down to the floor, like doors. And we call them French doors. It's confusing. Would you like me to open the French doors?"

The girl looked up at Daisy and whispered, "Maybe the leaves will blow in, if we open them." She smiled slightly. Quickly, she added politely, "If you don't mind."

"Wouldn't that be nice?" Daisy said, and she opened both French doors to their widest extent. "When Daniel and I first moved here—Daniel's my husband—the first thing we did was open the French doors. Then we sat on the sofa and had a glass of wine, and people said hello to us as they walked by on Belgravia Court."

Daisy spoke in a warm, confiding tone to the child, but she watched her closely, highly aware that she stood between the little girl and her sense of desolation. Daisy was grateful that she had her home to offer as a temporary refuge. In the absence of cars, Belgravia being a walking court, this place felt more timeless, intimate, and comforting than St. James.

"We live on Fourth Street, but sometimes we walk over here. I like the goldfish pond in front of the house down there." She pointed. "Once we looked at a house for sale on Belgravia that my daddy really loved, but my mother said we'd better stay put."

"Here's Lillian," Daisy said quickly. She swooped down and put her hand under the cat's belly. When she lifted her, the cat drooped down on both sides. "She's ve-e-ery limber," Daisy said slowly, arranging the cat against the girl's chest.

"She's so soft and deep," the girl said, holding her close with one arm and petting her head. "She already loves me, yes she does." She arranged the cat onto the other side. "Is this more comfortable, kitty Lillian?" Then she arranged the cat again so she was right in the center.

"Now she's comfortable," Daisy said.

"I like her best right here. Right against my heart, aren't you, Lillian kitty?"

Daisy smiled and said nothing. When Lillian began to purr, Daisy felt softly pleased with the cat.

"My daddy would love Lillian," the girl said, and repeated herself in a kind of crooning while she stroked the cat. "Yes, he would. My daddy loves Lillian. He loves her so much." She stopped petting the cat and looked directly into Daisy's eyes, while the tears streamed down her cheeks. Her rosy lips parted a little, and Daisy could see the slightly scalloped edges of her teeth. A small wail like the tearing of silk came from the girl's mouth.

"Oh darling," Daisy said, "come here and let me hold you." Lillian leapt away as the girl put her arms around Daisy's neck and snuggled herself against Daisy's breasts. She sobbed and sobbed. "There now, there now," Daisy said. "You're going to be all right, Juliette. I know how you miss him." Nothing in Daisy's calm strong voice echoed the fact that her own mother was dying perceptibly, day by week by month, of Alzheimer's.

While she soothed the child, murmuring to her and rubbing her back, Daisy watched Lillian move to a chunk of sunshine and wash the long white fur on her bib. For a moment, Daisy closed her eyes and remembered her own girlish glee over the wet sandpaper tongue of a cat licking her neck. She wondered if her mother would enjoy holding Lillian-kitty. Probably not.

The girl lifted her head suddenly from Daisy's chest at the sound of high heels on the sidewalk and said, "That's Mommy." She sat up and began wiping her cheeks with her fingers.

"You can go in the bathroom and wash your face, if you like," Daisy said. "It's just beyond the dining room, off the little hall to the kitchen." The girl hurried off in a purposeful way.

When Daisy greeted the mother, a pretty, professional woman in a fall suit with a lace collar and brown patent-leather pumps, Daisy said that the child had been pretty confused and upset, but when the little girl came back in the room, her face refreshed and her hair neatly in place, she seemed the picture of composure. She had pulled herself together for her mother.

"Mommy, I'm so sad about Daddy," she said. Almost ritualistically she went to her mother and hugged her. "Let's go home now," she said.

The mother was full of thanks to Daisy and flustered concern for her daughter. Daisy saw gusts of the woman's own grief sweep over her, but she was the mother and a capable adult, and she clung to her role. Before Juliette turned away at the door, she spoke to Daisy with the same kind of poise Daisy herself often used in facing an uncertain world. "Thank you so much for helping me. And Mr. Peter, too."

"I'll tell him for you, Juliette," Daisy reassured. To the mother, Daisy added in her richly timbred, rather formal voice, "Let us know if we can be of further help." Then she closed the door firmly.

Daisy felt drained. She looked around her lovely home, was grateful for it, and took a deep breath. There was a lot to do. Daniel was packing to go to Nairobi with his brother; the brothers were the sons of medical missionaries, and Daniel had not been back to Africa since he was nineteen. When Daisy picked up Lillian from the floor, she marveled again at the animal's pliancy and the fineness of her gray-and-white fur. After she kissed the cat's pink nose, she said, "Well, Lillian, you were a good girl," and put her back down on the rug. Daisy remembered that the bananas, waiting in the blue fruit bowl on the kitchen table, were now perfectly ripe, and she went to fetch one to take to her mother.

The clock struck one, or was it twelve thirty? Or even one thirty? Daisy sighed. She'd better stop by the bathroom before she drove to the nursing home. She hated using their facilities; it almost seemed that she belonged there when she used their toilet and washed her hands at their sink. She supposed she would belong there someday. A lot of people would unless there was more money for more research for Alzheimer's. Ryn's mother had it, too, but Ryn seemed to be going strong; she was nearly seventy, six or eight years older than Daisy. When the disease was undeniable, Ryn's mother had been about eighty-four, like Daisy's mother. Her own eighties were a long way off, Daisy thought.

In the tiny powder room, Daisy discovered the little girl had picked up a lipstick from the shelf over the diminutive sink to draw a picture on the mirror. Outlined in red, with waxy pellets adhering in places, Juliette had drawn the face of a girl crying. The tear shapes were colored in completely and resembled drops of blood streaming from the child's round eyes.

It was a startling picture, vaguely African. Daisy stooped a little so that her own face was congruent with the red drawing. Now her own eyes appeared to be weeping blood.

She decided not to clean the lipstick off the glass for a while. She would show it to her husband. As soon as he saw it, Daniel would say, "Well, obviously, she's hurting for her daddy." While Daisy was agreeing with Daniel's interpretation, some of the terror in the drawing would dissipate. Probably Daniel would go on to say, "Here, let me just wipe this off for you," and very efficiently—would he use soap, shampoo, tissue?—the lines would blear under Daniel's moving hand, then fade to a mere smear, then disappear.

Daniel's hand itself would blur, always efficient and ready to do anything he could to make things easier. Hadn't Daisy heard a church bell strike one o'clock? But there was Daniel now—not gone to the country after all.

"PETER," KATHRYN CALLED AFTER HIM, from her porch, though he and the white poodle were already descending the three stairs to the public sidewalk. Royal turned his head to look at her, but Peter just stopped and said, "What?"

All right, she had irritated him, interfered, placed herself at the controls.

"What about the little girl?"

Now Peter turned to face Kathryn. There was a soft wonder in his eyes. "Daisy was taking care of her."

"Why?"

"She just learned her father died."

Had someone died in the park? Kathryn remembered an unshaven old man curled on a bench. Homeless. Asleep, she had thought.

As though he followed her train of thought, Peter explained, "The girl's father died in the hospital, but she'd gotten the message in the park. Cell phone."

"Oh." Without saying good-bye again, Kathryn reentered her home and closed the heavy wooden door against the world. She leaned her shoulders and the back of her head against the wood. Her heart was beating fast as she remembered what it was to lose a father.

In her psyche Kathryn knew she still cradled that bereft inner child, but she had also had another self as companion—a little trouper, stalwart and strong willed. An explorer. She stood up straight, breathed deeply, and opened the door to the Court again. Yes, she could hear Leslie practicing the cello, a mellow sound. Like the smell of autumn apples, juicy, plump, blushing.

V

IN THE
FRENCH MANNER

PORTRAIT

B ECAUSE OF THE PLEASURE (and attention) my mother and I receive strolling the grand boulevards and enjoying the summer concerts of Paris, my stepfather has taken a small house in Chaillot, away from Paris. It pleases him to call this place "the country" and to imprison us there on weekends so that we cannot enjoy the advantages of Paris. There are no trees in "the country," and the sun beats down on the so-called garden relentlessly. This sterile place is in no way worthy of the name "the country." My stepfather has planted some haricots and nasturtiums, but both refuse to grow in this hostile environment.

The garden itself is divided into quarters, and each weekend young men come to the country to practice shooting birds. They are such poor marksmen that I fear they will accidentally shoot me. Even inside the house the racket from the continual gunfire plays havoc with my nerves. Certainly I cannot even sketch with my hand jumping like a rabbit at the surprise of yet another blast from their guns. I cannot think or even have a conversation with my mother. It is torture, of a sort.

"Gunfire," my stepfather says, "a kind of country music, heh-heh."

When my mother's friend Mme Suzanne and her husband come to dine with us at Chaillot, they witness the state of terror and boredom in which we exist. My stepfather interrupts every interesting conversation to change the subject to a trivial one, and he does not give us two minutes alone with our old friends. It is another sort of torture. But while my mother diverts her husband, Mme Suzanne seizes the opportunity to whisper to me that next Sunday, they will return and rescue us.

BETWEEN BLASTS OF SUNDAY GUNFIRE, I listen for the approach of horses and go to the window to look out. When I see our friends approach in a tiny conveyance, I cannot stop myself from announcing, "Here they come," in an excited tone of voice. "Heh-heh," my stepfather agrees, but soon he will have to swallow his glee. Even as we greet our friends, they absolutely insist that we go on an excursion, and they whisk us away immediately (their conveyance has room for only four) to the castle and grounds of Marly-le-Roi.

They convey us from limbo to fairyland!

Behind the castle at Marly-le-Roi, fountains fall in cascades from a mountain to form sparkling streams upon which swans swim. Summer houses flank the castle and are joined to one another by luxurious arcades of honeysuckle and jasmine. The four of us, in our little party, inhale deeply, all together, and then smile with delight. Here is a place that smells like "the country."

One of the jetting fountains rises to such a height that its plume disappears into the clouds. The castle itself is a vision of ethereal loveliness, but at the same time it possesses the grandeur of the Sun King, Louis XIV. For the first time I realize that here on earth a place of magical enchantment might actually exist. Many times I whisper the question into my mother's ear: *Is it real?* And she always replies, looking deeply into my eyes, "Quite real."

I see a shadow in her expression, not all joy, when she remarks on what is real, and I realize that equally real to her is her commitment to my unpleasant stepfather. He is not a brute, but he is oppressive.

Marly-le-Roi is a place I will keep in my heart. When I need to be swaddled by peace and beauty, I will think of what humankind and nature have created here. Along with the Church of Saint Eustache, for me, the gardens of Marly-le-Roi will always be the hallmark of a sanctuary.

MUCH AS I LOVE the excursion that took my mother and me to the true country, I know that I must also have the city. Upon my stepfather's retirement, we have moved to an enormous mansion, which has been divided into many apartments for families and some businesses as well. What sustains me is my bright-burning desire to paint and paint and paint. At nineteen, there is a convergence in me of stamina, knowledge, curiosity, and determination. Whenever I return to Paris from an excursion, I find myself renewing my vows to learn the complexities, subtleties, and finally the power of my art. Each year I want to surpass in quality what I have achieved the year before. I wish that I could travel to Italy and to other centers of art to study the masters there. What lessons I would bring home!

I have confided my wish to my mother, and she has given me a surprising reply.

"While I cannot wave a magic wand and transport you to Florence or Rome," she says, "I can make it possible for you to see some works of the masters without leaving this mansion."

Of course I ask my glowing-with-pleasure mother how this might be possible.

"In this building is the atelier of an art dealer who trades in the paintings of the old masters. I shall inquire if we might visit."

MY MOTHER IS TRUE to her word, and the very next day we knock at the door of M. Le Brun. My mother has learned that he is not only a dealer in fine art, but also a great-grandnephew of the famous Charles Le Brun who painted gigantic murals at Versailles for the Sun King. We have never been to Versailles, of course, but Le Brun is a name that has survived in history in connection with monumental art.

I watch my mother's knuckles rap on the door, and I memorize the image because I feel intuitively that what lies beyond this door may augment my art in a real way. While I have seen collections of paintings exhibited in grand museums and also admired great paintings in a few private châteaus, beyond this door is the hoard of an art dealer, and it is housed under the great roof of the very place where we already live.

M. Le Brun greets us pleasantly, but my ears close as my eyes open. On his walls, or displayed on easels, or even propped on the floor and leaning against an artfully carved sofa or chair, are splendid paintings, many of them by old Italian masters of the Northern School. They are arranged and displayed not simply to present their glory as individual works of art but also to complement each other, and above all to make the viewer love and want them all. The paintings are for sale to the highest bidder, and each of them excites the viewer in a most calculated way so that one wants not just to appreciate but also to possess their grand beauty.

I am like a twig swept away by a stream of color. All my patient habits of viewing at museums are overwhelmed. I cannot fasten on one of these works without being drawn to another. Here is a shade of cerise that awakens everything feminine in me, and here is a use of the color brown—like burnt sugar touched by sunset—that causes my mouth literally to water. The scroll on the arm of this chair alerts my eye to a painting that I think might be an early Titian, luminous, with loose brushwork, but isn't that the Flemish work of Rubens on the wall! How Rubens makes the eye travel the canvas! But I am so greedy! My eyes dart everywhere as I glide on the wings of Mercury through the collection.

"Oh, may I come again and again to study these glorious works?" I blurt when I return from my survey to my mother and the proprietor.

There is a silence in which I feel my future may be denied me.

Quickly my mother says, "My daughter would benefit so greatly, Monsieur, if it would be no inconvenience for you, if she could come back, along with myself, for you can see by her ardor, that she is quite overcome and cannot take in the lessons that she would learn here all at once."

M. Le Brun answers in a measured and courtly fashion. "While your daughter is already a fine artist, as all the connoisseurs of Paris know, if I might advance her career in some small way by providing access to my paintings to you, dear Madame, and your daughter, I would be only too pleased to do so."

At the end of his speech he bows his head modestly with a slight smile at the corners of his mouth. He folds his hands in front of his body and fastens his attention on my mother, radiant with gratitude. I understand that I am free to extend the moment of my enjoyment of the bounty of Italy.

I have never been asked, nor have I ever wanted, to conceal my wonder at something beautiful. As I tread softly among the paintings, I make no effort to curb my admiration or pleasure. I am a bit giddy.

Then the three of us walk more slowly, yet again, through the rooms, with M. Le Brun sometimes murmuring an informative comment. I am not unaware of the thickness of the carpet under my feet.

When we return home, I go straight to my cot, lie on my back, and close my eyes. I want to remember, as precisely as I can, what I have seen. I brush aside my memory of the furniture and rugs in the sumptuous atelier and strive to furnish my mind only with the paintings. I know that if I but let myself enjoy their memory-images to the highest degree, important lessons will be attendant on that pleasure. There were so many! And all of their venerable mastery was new and overwhelming to my eyes. The experience differed greatly from revisiting work in a museum over and over, such as the *Mona Lisa* at the Louvre. At the atelier, sometimes I recognized a master's technique, sometimes not. And M. Le Brun said we may come again. He also added that the collection is constantly in flux, which both terrifies and thrills me.

M. LE BRUN OFTEN SENDS WORD to my mother and me that he has a free half hour or so, and that if we should want to step over, why, then, we should come. Sometimes he reports that he has a new acquisition that really almost no one in the city has yet seen, for it just arrived from Florence or Siena. Equipped with such titillating knowledge, I enjoy conversation at salons more than ever before.

I begin to chat rather freely with M. Le Brun about what I see in this or that painting, especially if it holds a new discovery for me, and in some ways these casual conversations are as unguarded and pleasant as those I had with Mlle Boquet when we were going to art school together at the Louvre. Amazed and delighted by the achievements of the great, I learn and learn. My renaissance occurs in this atelier.

In my own studio, I feel myself fully fledged as an artist: I paint and large fees flow into the household. I am happy and sure of myself.

I feel myself to be the equal of M. Le Brun. Though I have not traveled, my eye, as a practitioner of art, is the equal of his as a connoisseur. Thus there is a spontaneity and naturalness in our conversations that fills the gap in my life left by my dear friend Mme Filleul's (née Boquet) defection from art to marriage.

When I inquire if M. Le Brun himself has not been tempted to take up the brush, he begins to blush and to exclaim that while he has, it would require him months to accrue enough courage to show me his work. He says he is a rank amateur. Of course I am curious, and before the occasion actually arises when I am allowed to view his work, I think about what might be tactful to say. At this point, I am quite aware how rare genuine talent is. In no way do I want to offend this man who buys and sells great art.

When my mother and I do view his work, I see what somehow I had already intuited (otherwise why would he not paint instead of buy and sell?), that there is a woodenness about his figures, and, honestly, there is little to praise, except in moderation. Into my silence he says in a genial manner, "I see, dear lady, that your tongue dies in the presence of my paintings."

My mother quickly notes, "I especially like this one."

I am gratified by Maman's selection. Possibly a self-portrait, "this one" is indeed the most pleasing one of the group.

"And I agree," I add honestly.

"Perhaps you could be persuaded to be my instructor," he says.

Again my mother saves me: "Oh, dear M. Le Brun, Mlle Vigée has such a long list of people waiting for their own portraits or those of their daughters to be painted and by certain dates, that I'm sure my husband would not allow her to take time for giving lessons."

He immediately bows his head politely. The truth is I have no desire to teach. I simply want to paint and learn. I want to improve my own knowledge and skill. Maman knows and respects that I wish to be a practicing artist, pure and simple.

Then I allow myself a small lie. "It has always been the act of painting that gives me satisfaction, whether others warm to my work or not. You must not be discouraged. It merely takes practice to improve."

"But truly," he says, "I myself, like you, Mlle Vigée, have no surplus of time, either in terms of life or business."

It strikes me as a somewhat curious speech, but I hasten to compliment him. "Your atelier is by far the most attractive in all of Paris. Your collection is truly superior, and you display the paintings as well as the fondant maker displays his sweets. Whenever Maman and I come through your door, it is as though we have entered paradise."

Now he bows deeply and murmurs that I am too kind. He offers to show me a little Raphael that has come into his possession. The use of red and green in this painting thrills me with its freshness, and I exclaim with true candor, "Thanks to you, M. Le Brun, I will never see or use those colors again in quite the same way."

AFTER WE LEAVE THE ATELIER, Maman remarks, "You are certainly appreciative of his inventory, my daughter."

"What a shame that he has little talent as a painter," I reply.

"But does that matter much?"

I am surprised at her remark. "To me, if I were he, it would matter a great deal."

"As he said, he is a dealer in art, not an artist. One painter in a family is probably enough."

I am shocked. "What can you mean, Maman?"

"Did you not catch his hint? He said that he had no surplus of years. He is seven years older than you at twenty. You said it makes you sublimely happy to frequent his abode."

"As a visitor!" I exclaim, but even as I object, I know it would be not only pleasant but inspiring to live among such paintings. One would not need to own them. And to travel to foreign countries, as well.

"Would you not be happier in your own place?" She holds my astonished gaze only a moment and then quickly looks away as she continues. "You and I would not be much separated by such a small distance. Still under the same roof. We could visit each other even when it stormed or snowed."

This last idea of hers cannot be refuted. I say nothing. But to be married! Why? It is nothing I desire.

AS TIME PASSES, my mother does not press me to develop an interest in M. Le Brun, yet I am made to know a marriage to him would please her. Can I be sure my own work would in no way be hindered? My mother implies that it would help me to sell my work even more widely and better to be married to an art dealer, but I feel I am already doing remarkably well, quite independently. But another idea, evolved entirely by myself, is a sobering one. I realize my mother's own marriage might be more happy if I were not under her roof. This consideration causes me to take special care to be polite and cheerful whenever I am in the presence of my stepfather, but I have always been scrupulously courteous to her husband, no matter the rage and rebellion within, for her sake.

I must say it takes little effort to be cheerful when my mother and I are under the ceiling of M. Le Brun's atelier. He is conversationally interesting, lively, and full of good spirits. At times, he reminds me of my father in his savoir faire. Other times he reminds me of my brother in his naturalness. Étienne, as a promising young student, is much about the city with his friends these days, and I realize that I have turned to M. Le Brun for conviviality.

M. Le Brun has a pleasing appearance. He is of average height, with black eyes, eyebrows, and hair. His eyes are intelligent and keen, and his high forehead also adds to his look of intelligence. He is lively, yes, charming in almost every utterance, and quickly witty. He is at ease with himself as a successful man who is still ambitious.

And he makes it clear that he admires me, and even that he desires me. To my own wonder, I find desire awakening in myself, or at least a curiosity about desire. He communicates his interest in a perfectly decorous way. I know of his attraction because his eyes shine when he looks at me, and his lips part in a slight smile.

Strangely, it is when I am in church with my mother that I experience an overwhelming desire to please her and to make her life happy and without care. Wonderful music, whether sacred or profane, makes me want to marry! Our Church of Saint Eustache is famous for its organ, and from time to time, renowned musicians come there to perform secular music. For any such grand concert, the mood is as devout as when people come to Mass, because the audience anticipates being in the presence of rare and transcendent music.

Most readily, my mother and I embrace the opportunity to attend a performance by a descendant of the Bach family of musicians, from Leipzig. With the first piece, music composed by Buxtehude, we feel gloriously enlightened by harmonies and rhythms of an almost antique era. Because the organ concert occurs in the afternoon, Saint Eustache blooms with colored light. Together the music and the church become a bower for dear memories, and I am recalling how once my father took me to see the back of this church with its exuberant flying buttresses in the Gothic manner and how next we walked around the building so that he might show me its more classical façade. He spoke of these two different styles of beauty. Then he asked me, "To which tribe do we belong, my gifted daughter, the exuberant or the restrained?"

I answered, "To both. We restrain the expression of our impulses in public, but inwardly we leap for joy, just as these buttresses leap from earth to support the structure." He told me I spoke truly, for myself, but he was one who preferred to spring forward joyfully, in public or closeted.

My mind jumps forward to New Year's and how he loved to kiss the ladies, but with that thought comes a revelation I would not have had as an innocent child. I think that probably my papa was not faithful to my mother. Not that she ever complained or criticized—not by the slightest glance.

Unrestrained by the fact that we are seated in church, I reach across and hug Maman's shoulders against my own body. My tears well up. I think it unfair that my beloved mother should not have been treated with utter loyalty, and my own appreciation of her swells. I think of the devotional light in M. Le Brun's eyes, and their soft fondness for me.

At that moment, the organist announces that he will perform the J. S. Bach Toccata and Fugue. From the instant of commencing, the opening figures pierce me with their power and urgency. I almost want to cry out! And then they are repeated in a lower, more earthy register, and then still lower, as the chord begins to build itself into a tower of sound, more magnificent than any I have ever heard. Then all this power dissolves into airy puffs of short phrases.

Like filigree, the toccata makes my skin feel titillated, as though touched by the lightness of a wispy web. If I feel teased by the toccata, then I am fulfilled by the ramifications of the fugue. Never have I experienced more glory: more complexity, more subtlety, more relentless grandeur. Not in music nor in the visual arts.

As the music engulfs and tumbles us, one by one members of the audience began to rise in reverence, and as they stand their eyes fill with tears. My mother and I turn to each other, seeing one another through glazed eyes and sharing our souls. Almost by their own volition, our bodies rise, and we join the others to stand and lift our faces. It is as though we are stretching upward like plants, and when we cannot grow taller, our gaze continues upward into the vaulted ceiling of Saint Eustache. Our gratitude makes it difficult to breathe, for we know the extremity of our privilege in hearing this music.

When it is over, we sink back into our chairs, exhausted. I slide to my knees and pray, giving thanks to God for his gifts.

EVEN THE NEXT DAY, I feel made of different stuff. I am almost too exhausted and too exhilarated even to paint. My hand trembles when I pick up the brush, for I feel unworthy. The music of Corelli once entered my spirit in a way that made me spin; his variations on a theme titled "La Folia" has this wild and insistent power, but the Bach seems to contain the breath of God, not some human frenzy. I think of the word *ecstasy,* and I think I must have experienced a moment akin to that of Saint Teresa of Avila.

Because I am restless and frayed, I ask my mother to walk with me in the gardens of the Palais-Royal. I think the large, generous trees will refresh me. She sees my state, and despite the unusualness of walking so soon after lunch, she violates my stepfather's expected routine to walk with me. In private, we talk of the music; we try to find a language adequate to its genius.

She understands, for something of the rapture continues in her as well. To fail to find adequate language frustrates me. I think of the word *ravishing,* but I keep it to myself, as a secret. While I am not bold enough to utter it, I believe it is the most accurate term for that music. Obliquely, my mother mentions the Bernini sculpture of Saint Teresa, in Rome. My eyes shift from the grand trunks and their shaggy canopies to the smaller trees of the garden, pruned and stately in the manner of Le Nôtre. Geometric. In them, nature has submitted to order. I wonder if the huge old trees are

Gothic, and these carefully controlled ones classical. I begin to feel more steady, and more like myself. Maman advises me to take a small nap when we return to our apartment, and I am glad to accept her advice.

AFTER I HAVE NAPPED for nearly three hours, I sit up and rub my eyes as though I have awakened to a new world. I look about me at my mother's room, at her dressing gown on the bed, and feel the proximity of my stepfather and how we are confined always by his sensibility. But I feel better. The nap has refreshed and quieted me.

It is time for a light supper, and we have eels, which I especially enjoy. My stepfather is quieter, and he even makes an effort to be friendly. My mother seems happy, too, and is attentive to me in ways that only she knows, with special warm glances. We are enjoying a crème brûlée when my stepfather clears his throat and says, "What is your disposition, daughter Élisabeth, toward the art dealer, M. Le Brun?"

"What do you mean?" I ask.

My mother replies, "Late this afternoon, while you were resting, he has asked permission to marry you."

"I've scarcely thought of it." I am amazed, and I see the calm happiness begin to drain from their faces.

"But you and I have spoken of the possibility," my mother says, very gently.

"He seems well off," my stepfather interjects. "According to your mother, he has a worthy stock of fine paintings."

"It seems to me," I venture, "that they do not sell very rapidly."

"Perhaps if he had a wife, heh, who herself is an artist, he would be connected to the arty part of society, heh?" my stepfather asks, rather gruffly. "Have you had other offers?"

"I am so involved with painting," I answer truthfully, "I have had no time to think of marriage."

"There's no need to decide at table," my mother says. "I mentioned to him that no answer would come till morning. But I would agree he seems well off, with his fine rugs and furniture."

When my stepfather says, "I leave it to you two, entirely," I am surprised and pleased. "It will be a loss to the family for you to marry. Remember that. But I don't stand in your way, since your mother seems to wish it."

"Really," she extends her hand to me, "I wish only for your happiness. I have never seen any ill temper in the man. He is convivial, like—like your brother."

"I am glad to have some time," I answer.

AFTER SUPPER, I ANNOUNCE that I will sit up and read by the fire. Rather tactfully, my mother retires to our bedroom and my stepfather goes to his, to leave me alone with my thoughts. "Wood is nearly as dear as silver," he says. "Please be sparing, heh-heh?" I settle myself by the fire as though to read Racine's *Andromaque*. My mother brings me a woolen wrap from the bedroom so that I might not grow cold as the fire burns down.

As I look at the orange-red embers, they seem almost like fruit to me. I wish to bite them, though reality is a sure restraint on that impulse. But I see in their glow a metaphor for my heart, for my inward life. I am very happy.

I feel that I could fan that ember within myself forever. That it would never cease to glow as long as I live, if I can paint. If I can hear music, either heavy with meaning or frothily delightful, like court music. If I have my mother and brother to love me, and interesting acquaintances who encourage and support me. Who appreciate my talent.

And does not M. Le Brun appreciate my talent? Does he not value it and me, in several ways? I could have a studio for my work, adjacent to my own bedroom. I almost smell the turpentine. I envision a stack of linen canvases, on stretchers, blank, and waiting to be sized. I could have a bedroom with its own grate.

And what of marriage? I stir in my chair, for I can feel that my body stirs toward that idea. It is natural. I feel no shame. Since the Garden of Eden, desire has been part of the human lot. And childbirth. I do not fear childbirth. It too is the lot of womankind. My mother is happy in her motherhood, and I feel I would be as well. It would take its place beside my work.

And M. Le Brun, in particular? Perhaps if I had paid more attention to those young aristocrats who tried to divert my eye, I would have found someone more enticing. I like their gracefulness. But I am a commoner. My mother has never encouraged an ambition to marry out of my class. My talent alone admits me to their chambers. And would continue to do so, I believe, if I married M. Le Brun. Or at least to admit the notables to my own salon.

He wishes to marry me. He has chosen me. He is a charming man, vivacious, and in possession of a certain family pride, through Charles Le Brun. And I do not enjoy living under my stepfather's roof.

The small log breaks apart. Fire drops like liquid into the ashes. Despite the frugality of my stepfather, I rise and add another piece of wood. I think of the valuable carved and gilded wooden frames that enhance the paintings. I particularly like the Spanish dentate molding. Again, it makes me want to bite, and I smile at this strange response, associated, I suppose, with appetite. I know that I do have an appetite for love.

It is that exuberant, leaping part of me. But would not marriage provide its own restraints and limitations? I cannot doubt that. But I know that I flare within. I flare for my work, and nothing can prevent that. M. Le Brun has no wish—I am sure of it—to divert me from painting.

Yet I am uncertain.

WHEN MORNING COMES, I see that I have fallen asleep in the chair, as though I could make the night of my indecision last forever, and my mother is gently shaking my shoulder. She whispers my name and asks me if I have decided.

I come to my senses slowly. My eye falls on the ashes in the grate, a lovely silvery gray, before my thinking comes into focus. She is speaking to me.

"My daughter, few people are ever entirely certain about marriage. It is natural to hesitate. But beauty does not last forever. You tax your beauty like no young woman I have known. Not even servants work so hard as you. Hour after hour, you toil without relaxation—"

"Art is not work, Maman," I interrupt. "Not in that sense. Not to me. It is my privilege. It is the natural desire of the talent with which I was born. Since I was a little girl, at the Convent . . ." Suddenly I see the sad but encouraging eyes of Jeanette, my friend, age twelve to my six, age seventeen to my eleven. I think that she would not have chosen the celibate life, had she a choice. She would not have chosen the restraint of being a nun. Did she not make of me something of her own child?

"To marry is itself just as natural as talent," my mother is saying. "I would not see you deprive yourself of the womanness that has given me great joy."

"And sorrow, too?" I hold her gaze.

She looks away from me. I know she will find a way to tell the truth.

She says, "In my children, I have found nothing but joy."

"And you think it best, and it would give you peace, should I accept the offer of M. Le Brun?"

"I think his devotion, his worship at the altar of art, and his genuine admiration for you, both your talent and your person, your spirit, bode well. I think that should you ask time for more consideration it would quell some of his ardor."

"And what of ardor, Maman?"

"I think we, male and female, find our own ardor. I cannot answer for you. I would advise any bride to go to her bed with happy anticipation."

"But ardor? The word has a Latin root. It means to burn." I stop speaking to feel what is within myself. Desire flames through me. I cannot deny it. "I burn," I confide.

"Then we will give M. Le Brun good news?"

I try to say yes, but my tongue is reluctant. I nod my head in acquiescence.

AFTER WE COMPLETE OUR *PETIT DÉJEUNER,* after we have spoken enthusiastically about my future, about how close I will yet be to my family, after we have speculated about the creation of my salon, after we have summoned M. Le Brun and my stepfather has given our answer, with a certain air of style and pride, to my suitor, I smile at M. Le Brun, and a wave of happiness illumes my face. I feel quite warm.

The man falls to his knees and a thousand thanks tumble from his lips. Though it is morning, he enthusiastically calls for wine, and we all have a small glass and toast the event to come. He sits with us and eats fruit tarts with great relish, even a bit messily, and he leaps up to embrace my parents several times.

I am most pleased when he launches into a description of how the three rooms of his atelier can be rearranged into two, and I shall have the room with the north-facing window for my studio. I clap my hands with glee. He goes on to describe the little chamber adjoining, how it can be my boudoir, while he will retain the large bedroom, and he asks if that will be a pleasant place, and I ask if it has a little fireplace, and he confesses it does not, but he has an ornate brazier that can be brought in and set on tiles, and I promise I will certainly not sulk over such an arrangement, and such rapid arrangements make us all quite convivial.

"Will you give her a little painting for her boudoir as an engagement gift?" my stepfather suddenly asks, which seems rather too pointed a question to me. M. Le Brun's eyes shift to my mother's face. Quickly she asks me, "And which would you choose, Élisabeth, if the choice were yours?" and I answer immediately, "Oh, the small Raphael!" and M. Le Brun rolls his eyes in comic fashion and says, "Would that I could, but it is already promised to the Duc de Vaudreuil." And so between us my mother and I have saved him the embarrassment of having to promise me what would surely be an extravagantly expensive gift. M. Le Brun jumps to his feet and kisses first my mother and then me on the cheek and asks my stepfather, "Have you ever seen two such charming and gracious women?"

Then our conversation turns toward the date of the wedding, and I mention rather soberly that I should like to finish several portraits beforehand. My mother looks worried and my stepfather absolutely grimaces, but M. Le Brun says, "Neither at this time nor at any time in the future will my own urgent desires come between you and your work. I know that you are who you are because of your brush, and I applaud and admire you for your industry."

I see and hear that he is utterly sincere.

My mother exclaims, "Oh, you are a very good man, so unselfish!" but I note a new shadow of anxiety on her brow, for I have studied and painted her many times, and I am quite sensitive to the nuances of her expressions. Perhaps she thinks I may be urged to work too hard, but I believe M. Le Brun knows it is my nature to work.

We continue our celebration, and then I turn happily to my painting, before the afternoon is gone. I think of my friend Mlle Boquet and how her marriage displaced art, and I am sad for her. Her error, perhaps, lay in her choice of spouse.

WHILE I DRESS FOR MY WEDDING, I have great trouble arranging my hair in a way that pleases me. I have always dressed my own hair, not only to save money but also because as an artist, no one can twist, pin, fluff, or in any way arrange it so well as I can. I have finished the promised portraits, and the New Year has arrived, yet I can scarcely believe the date of my wedding is here. It seems too soon, this year of 1776. I have not thought properly about the step I am about to take because I have been absorbed and committed as never before to the last portraits I shall paint as a virgin.

My hair is rebellious. I have watched my mother put up her own hair, and so learned all the tricks of combs or fixatives (I have always detested the idea of powder in human hair when it can have its own glorious luster). As I grew older, Maman sometimes listened to my suggestions or allowed me to fix her hair for her in ways that flattered the shape of her face or brought out her eyes or lips and surprised her. "I didn't know I looked like that!" she would sometimes exclaim before the glass after I had finished my arrangement of her coiffure.

Nonetheless, for all my practiced skill, on the day of my wedding, I try first this style and then that and cannot satisfy myself, and even begin to fear that my husband will look at me and think, *Oh, she is not as pretty after all as I have always imagined her to be.* My fingers actually begin to tremble, and I become much fatigued and thoroughly frustrated with myself in my indecisiveness.

My mother flutters about telling me again and again that one attempt after another is in fact perfect and should be let alone, until finally, giving up hope that I should ever please myself in the matter, I ask her if she would be so kind as to perform the task.

She murmurs, "Nothing could be such an honor as to dress your hair, my precious daughter, on your wedding day." I close my eyes, so that I will not be tempted to criticize or direct the operation.

When, with her permission—she is just atomizing a cloud of scent around my head—I open my lids, my eyes first meet hers and see the tender triumph and pride in her countenance, both maternal and artistic. Even before I inspect my image in the mirror, I spontaneously exclaim, "How beautiful!" and then I hear myself offering more words to my mother as my eyes look into my own reflected eyes. "You are truly an artist yourself," I say appreciatively.

The style is an excellent one, perhaps a little more severe than I would have made it, for I like a certain calculated disorder of tendrils and curls. I let myself become soft as a kitten; nothing in my expression suggests the focused, almost hawklike eyes of an artist at work, those eyes which I have

witnessed in myself accidentally, recently, over the shoulder of a sitter in
some extraneous mirror.

We put on our warm wraps, for it is January. As we walk toward the
carriage waiting to transport us through the Paris streets to Saint Eustache,
I ask myself, shall I get into the carriage? Shall I mount the step? Shall I
really allow the carriage door to be closed so firmly, with that resounding
whack, behind me? I shiver, and my mother places an arm around me as
though she would warm me and quell my qualms.

I half wish that a wheel would roll away from the carriage and that it
would kneel down on one side, and then I could jump out and run away.
But where would I run? The only place is back to my stepfather's domain.
We pass the mighty Notre Dame, with its unfinished square towers, and I
pray, "Let this day and this deed also remain unfinished, for I am content
as I am and need no marriage spires to point heavenward." I think of how
in medieval times one could run into such a church and shout "Sanctuary!" and no one would be allowed to drag you away into the street. But a
church is not a painter's studio, and perhaps no one would bring me canvas
or paints or brushes there—I imagine a pitying dove winging her way to
me, sequestered in one of those high towers of Notre Dame, with a paintbrush in her bill.

All the while my mother coos and soothes me as best she can and tells
me she is proud of me and what a doting husband M. Le Brun will prove
himself to be, for *Is he not also a worshipper of art?* and *Do not you and he have
the same household gods?* My pious mother blushes at invoking a pagan image,
and she quickly rearranges the idea to ask is my groom-to-be not devoted to
the beauty of art? None of the paintings he owns, she says, is as radiant or
pretty as I will be, at the altar of Saint Eustache in my bridal gown.

When I see my soon-to-be-husband standing at the rail, I do think how
stalwart and well he looks, a charming alternative to my stepfather. Most
reassuringly, at the moment our eyes meet, M. Le Brun's face shows affection and admiration and also, somewhat disquietingly, the look of raptur-
ous pleasures anticipated. Nonetheless as the nuptial questions are being

asked to me, still I debate with myself, "Shall I say *yes,* shall I say *no?* Shall I, must I, *now* say *yes?*" And I do.

I do say *yes.*

AT HOME, OUR HOME, in flickering light, I see myself as I must appear to him, my new and ardent husband.

He sees me propped against a wall of pillows, each with a wide band of lace to embellish the open end, and the high, dark headboard of his bed (for he has taken me to his own large bedroom). The headboard is carved, with a row of Gothic points across the top. My gown is gleaming satin with a graceful curved scoop neckline setting off the top of my bosom and my neck and face. I know my lips are parted and a little cloud of breath hovers and passes back and forth across my lips, sometimes outside, sometimes warm against my tongue and the arch of my mouth. I know this because he makes me wait while he stands there, his hands reaching toward me.

And then I see him as he is.

There is scarcely any residue of wine on his lips, for he wants no incapacity of body or consciousness to mute the experience; with wide and bright eyes he approaches, fully relishing his own alert eagerness to pluck the flower of my maidenhood. His clean and blazing white nightshirt with gathered sleeves fits him loosely and is open at the throat, and his bare forearms and hands stretch happily toward me.

We study each other's faces for a moment, like the painters we both are. In the light from three tapers, I am satisfied with his manly face: his cheeks with their ruddy glow. A little fire burns in the grate, for it is January. His pleasant nose; his lips that smile a little at me with tender encouragement and friendship; but above all the expression in his eyes makes me feel seen and appreciated. So *this* is marriage, I think, this warm, unguarded intimacy!

And at that point we do but look at each other! But looking is not a casual activity for either of us.

He calls me his love, his charming bird, the mistress of his heart and life. I gulp in his words and realize I have raised my arms in answer to his and stretched my fingers, flattening them back to make my receiving palms the outposts of my welcome. My hands are almost pink in the light, and immediately he names me to be his pink rose, his delight, and he speaks of the rich chestnut of my hair. It is a courtship of colors, but every color is a code for the yearning and hope for happiness that we feel.

As he takes a slow step forward, I notice his knees beneath the hem of the short gown (he wears no lace, his linen is smooth and plain). I have never seen a man's bare knees before and have not imagined their rounded strength, for his posture is crouched a bit as he advances. I am so stirred by his body that all in one gesture, I throw aside the comforter and quilts and bedsheet that have been covering me as high as my waist and at the same time feel myself kneeling on the bed and opening my arms yet wider and lifting my bosom toward him. I care nothing for demure waiting propped up like an inert doll but become alive and animated by love and call him my splendid spouse, my divine M. Le Brun. My voice drops to a whisper and I tell him that I want him, that I am nearly dead for wanting him to claim me.

He is upon me in an instant, kissing my face and smelling of pear water, his clean-shaven cheek a novel texture brushing now and then against my cheek. Then he halts in this mad rush of passion and simply holds me dearly and tenderly against him. I can feel his heart beating, the very life of him, and he holds me close and strokes the top of my head and lets his fingers play in my hair till I am impatient for his passion to come to me again. How artfully he leads me to renounce virtuous restraint, to leave that girl behind and to be filled with the desire to be made fully a woman and his wife. I feel myself becoming the slave of this carnal desire that never before has possessed me to any degree whatsoever. I almost want to beg him to take me, to take me now.

But he is kind and patient and artful: that I realize and fully appreciate as we embrace, and tumble, and cast off even my slippery satin negligee and final shift (he makes a moment of untying the white ribbon at the neckline of my gown), trusting him to choose when I should be complete. I know nothing but mad joy and admiration for this large male body (how strange and enlightening to touch a man flesh to flesh and experience his full strength and weight, his bone and muscle). Almost I feel that I am some classical maiden, and he a god in glorious human form.

I have never been an accomplished dancer, preferring to sit and listen to music in its purest state, but on this wondrous night I have no thought about how to move my body or when. All is natural, and in everything I follow him with grace and pleasure. Beneath him, I seem to glide from one side of the bed to another, and to find myself on a pillow or on my side, or the two of us rolling weightlessly, as though we are finding our bliss on the clouds. Only our own bodies are real to us; everything else, even material objects, seems to have disappeared. Ah bliss, ah bliss!

My husband gives me pleasure unbound, and it is as beautiful as any symphony. It roars through me like the deep tones of a pipe organ, like the breath of God.

And the moment itself! That moment when he enters me and makes me fully wife is the crown of my joy. If there is pain, I do not feel it. I want with all my being to get for my own pleasuring exactly the pleasuring I have gotten.

AFTER HE HAS CROWNED ME with our success and joy, he whispers, *Only a moment now of sleep for me, and I will quickly return to you.* And so he sleeps. His breathing changes into something of strange depth in his unconsciousness, and for not more than five minutes, admiring him and loving watching over him, my eyes are fixed on his face and closed eyes. I feel both trusting and trusted so that it seems an honor to wait, and those few minutes are delicious ones. True to his word, he awakens, opens his eyes as though his mind is still lost in slumberland, then slowly smiles at me. He reaches up his hand to caress the curve of my face and says, *My beauty.*

Soon he is kissing and caressing all of me again, to my delight, and I exchange my own touches for his, but to my surprise he draws us to a pause. He says we should eat and drink a bit, and he gestures toward a tray covered with a white cloth that sits in front of the fire. I agree. (I would agree to any suggestion he might make.) Quite efficiently he dresses me so that I will not be cold and flips his own nightshirt over his head so expertly that I laugh as his head emerges and the gown settles on his shoulders. So we are concealed from each other again, and already I understand that this is a good stratagem for us both, for it sets up a desire again to rid ourselves of any clothing and for flesh to have no barrier between flesh and flesh.

But for now, sitting across from each other in front of the fire, other appetites arise. He unveils a dish of beautiful fruit, some cut and some intact, including a spray of grapes; and two cut-glass goblets of red wine— how those two glasses please the eye as their facets flash and glitter—and a board of cheese, including the blue-veined variety from Ambert, made of cow's milk, that is my favorite. Even the shining knife for cutting the cheese seems enchanted as he prepares an oval of bread for me. I reach my fingers to take it but he stops and shakes his head and carries the dainty to my lips. When a crumb of cheese sticks to my lower lip, he pushes it inside my mouth with the end of his large finger, and even goes deeper inside to rub the tip of my compliant tongue. So I understand that as husband and wife we are to feed each other.

While we delight each other with the small combinations of fruits, nuts, and cheese, and even hold the goblet when the other is to drink, we talk. We talk of paintings, and once he gets up to fetch a scarf to tie around my hair as it was done in a certain painting. And then he puts my arms into other pieces of clothing that happen to be around, and shawls on my shoulders, and ties about my waist till I am almost a mountain of clothing. How my body laughs against that swaddling of fabrics of various textures and types, either artfully draped or tied in a clumsy, masculine way. Finally he stands up and takes off his own nightshirt and puts it over my head.

With no more shame than Adam stood before Eve, he stands naked before me, the firelight flickering on his flesh from nose to toes and toe-nails. Then he pulls me to him and encircles me and all those wraps and waist scarves and his own shirt, and kisses me first tenderly and then rapa-ciously till his chest is heaving under its thatch of virile hair. Still he is in complete control. Standing back a bit, suddenly at arm's length, he remarks that now he is naked and wanting, and I must be made so, too.

When I reply, "Please," the timbre of my own voice, suffused with desire as it is, shocks me, for I have meant to make a decorous utterance. But he smiles at me with the kindness of a brother, and I am swept with a greater longing that has a feeling of warm safety in it. Though I start to lift his nightshirt over my head, he stops me, and explains that it is for him to disrobe me, as he has placed the garments on me.

Ah agony of waiting, for he is very methodical, as we stand beside the little fire and the table with the remains of our picnic, and he kisses and teases each part as though it alone were enough. Sometimes I moan with pleasure. Once I giggle and push him away a little but quickly bring his hand back to that place. Every gesture pleases, as though it all were a dance.

He saves my breasts for last, and then I think I will faint for the joy of his lips upon me. While I am half swooning, he tells me to stand on his bare feet, and together we make our progress to the bed. I feel the arch of his foot under mine, and then our whole lengths press together, though my height is not equal to his, flesh against flesh, as he slowly walks us across the carpet to the bed, I rather clinging to my god.

And so we celebrate our wedding night, on and on, with one theme and many variations, and with fun and good talk, too, and plenty of rest to allow our already satisfied bodies to rekindle themselves. I hardly know whether I sleep first or he does, but he lets us sleep long and fully. He brings yet another glass of wine to my lips while I lie drowsy in bed. He may have put some potion in it, so thorough, long, and replenishing is my sleep.

Thus we are eager and refreshed when we have slept and awaken yet again to bright glimmers of noonday sun coming through the cracks in the drapery. It is a new step in our pleasure to see each other in steady sunlight after the flickering, shadowed night. Yes, there is blood, the badge of my virtue, staining the sheet. We care nothing about unsightliness. For my part, there is no blush of embarrassment. Ah, he covers the place with a lacy pillowcase so that he may lay me down now against clean linen. That pleases me, too. And it pleases me to receive him again.

BECAUSE OF THAT HONORABLE RUSTY STAIN, I feel I have graduated to a more real understanding of what it means to dwell alive within the house of human flesh. And all the colors and textures to be seen about me please me. This nuptial morning, I am happy to be an artist who is a passionate wife. I feel all my powers increase tenfold, including my prowess as a painter.

VI

A CELLO IN THE
AFTERNOON

FOUNTAIN

HAVING HEARD A CHURCH BELL bong once, Ryn assumed that it was one o'clock, or one thirty, and the first day-after-completion was half over. She remembered a time when she lived in the Highlands, opening her car door back then and finding the air was full of the clangor of church bells. Something awful had just happened (she couldn't remember just what), but she had taken the church bells as though they were a force of nature sympathetic to her mood. The pathetic fallacy: she knew the literary name of such a delusion, but still the church bells battered her heart in a way that seemed appropriate and made her feel less alone. Was it grief over her mother's Alzheimer's, or over something Peter had confessed? Or even a death? Perhaps a young friend of Humphrey (she thought of her own youthful horror and disbelief at the loss of Giles). She couldn't remember. Just the clangor of bells through the magnolia leaves.

The church gong was striking again? *Open the door and there's disaster.* Time was the escort of death. Perhaps now it was only one o'clock;

surely not one thirty already. These days it was not unusual for Kathryn to be unhinged in time. She didn't wear a watch anymore, even though her mother had given her an easy-to-read nurse's watch and Kathryn had treasured it for decades. Her iPhone had replaced the wristwatch, though she didn't glance at the phone frequently the way she had with her watch. Her brother John, who was retired, had stopped wearing a watch. She admired his gesture greatly: unshackled, it meant.

Growing up in Montgomery, Kathryn thought of her father as the keeper of time, for only he wound the mantel clock that now sat silently at the heart of her own house. Suddenly she vowed she would have the clock repaired. She wanted to hear it tick; she wanted to hear it clear its throat, just as she had as a child lying awake but very still in her bed. And then the resonant gong. Her young little body was restless. Was it twelve thirty, one, or one thirty A.M.? It was deep night in Montgomery and why couldn't she sleep? No one must know. And so she would tell herself a story, a saga that had gone on and on throughout the years of childhood. Her body lay perfectly still, not restless, while she imagined. No one would guess she was a wicked girl whose conscience barred the door to sleep.

She felt very stupid now: uncertain if Yves intended to visit or not. But yes, it had been quite definite. Yves had said he was coming today, and so he would. They were both mature enough not to have to check and recheck such a commitment.

Once back in the kitchen, she saw that Peter had thoughtfully carried their lunch dishes to the sink. She looked at the place mats, russet and gold, and thought of Humphrey's voice over the phone. He had sounded confident, happy, a bit in a rush. Things to do. A new series of clay sculptures. What she liked best about his idea was the size of the pieces: significant, about a foot tall, but not so large as to be difficult to box up or relocate within a home. Humphrey's projected sculptures would be about the size (heavier, of course) of a short stack of good, hefty books. She had written a few like that.

She bent to load the dishwasher. Didn't everyone hate stooping to the

dishwasher? She understood some dishwashers were now built like drawers, at a reasonable height. Probably someday a kitchen would be banks
of drawers, all of which were dishwashers, and each set of dishes would
have its own drawer and stay in it always, removed just to be used at the
table, then returned dirty to the washer-drawer. Or maybe dishes would
be invented with a surface that never got dirty; one to which no trace of
food clung. Or dishes would be edible, and one would just eat them along
with the rest of the food. She would be dead by then, she hoped.

Actually she was in great physical shape. There was nothing that caused
her trouble: she could bend or stretch or climb, even run, at will. But she
didn't ski anymore or skate. If she fell, she broke bones. Both feet, a shoulder, even a finger, and that had been fifteen years ago. She had lost weight,
but Peter was too heavy. Had the play director thought of that? But Lear
could be a big man: a big wreck of a man—powerful, childlike, helpless.

Peter! That wink! Cocky and happy! Shakespeare's King Lear to be,
no less. She hoped he wouldn't mumble, mistakenly thinking that a low
voice showed gravitas. But there was no way on earth she could warn
him about this tendency. Acting was his bailiwick. If she tried to give him
advice, he would be furious about it, even after the show. His resentment
would smolder forever. She supposed a director would tell him, but then in
the performance, Peter might be moved to play it his way. Surely not! She
sighed and felt tired.

And why not, she'd been up till midnight finishing the book. It would
be a pity to be tired when Yves arrived. When one scheduled the day, tired-
ness was worth considering if one was approaching seventy, no matter
how much younger than that she looked. (So people said. But less often
now than they used to.) She wouldn't go back upstairs; she'd already made
that pilgrimage, faced the empty nothingness that her marriage to Mark
had become.

Oh for the wide, pale-green, down-filled sofa on the sunporch! How
convenient and lovely it would be to nap there. Since the sunporch door
was covered with a security grille, she wouldn't feel the least vulnerable,

even if someone could look in and see her asleep on the sofa. And she'd cover herself with the nice woolen throw that her dear friend, the second Nancy, had given her for Christmas, a piece of folk art made from sewn-together large patches of old sweaters, recycled. Casual and cozy. And what was it she had decided to wear for greeting Yves?

When she lay down in the light-filled room, it wasn't Yves she thought of. How young Peter had looked, though his hair now was thoroughly white. She remembered when his hair was red, an amazing burnished copper color. Humphrey's hair was paler; it seemed to have sand mixed in. It was good to lie down.

As she began quickly to fall asleep, she thought how wise she was to decide to nap though it was something she very rarely did. And she would dream—of the real Peter or the way she had transmogrified him in fiction? Some of both would be most soothing, most satisfying. *Transmogrified:* she liked the gritty feel, the *grif* part of the word.

She was glad she was like the resolute girl in red plaid, carrying the load of schoolbooks like a stout cudgel . . . not *resolute, resilient*. That was the word her mother had used when she admired Kathryn's framed high school graduation photograph. *I admire your resilience,* her mother had said, holding the framed photo at arm's length. Nothing about looking beautiful, which was what Kathryn longed for. Oh well, maybe her mother had exclaimed, at first, *How pretty you look!* But her considered opinion: well, that involved the idea of *resilience*. Kathryn at seventeen had been utterly surprised. If she wasn't resilient, perhaps she had better try to learn to be so. That was what she'd thought. And she had known, even then, that looking pretty, even if she had received the compliment, wasn't the same as being beautiful.

After they had made love, when they were young—yes, it was their first time together—while Peter lay on his side, sleeping, his red hair glowing like copper, in candlelight, she had thought him *beautiful*. This is what it means to embody beauty. She had never seen a man so completely and unfalteringly beautiful, but part of that beauty had a barb in it, it must have had, for she had felt a stab of pain as she admired him. She had thought, *Why, he's as beautiful as a Confederate soldier.* But he wasn't a southerner, and she had nothing but contempt for the idea that the death of a young soldier was in any way beautiful. All such deaths were in vain and represented the failure of elder statesmen to protect their young. The old lie, the poet Wilfred Owen had labeled the Roman memorial motto *Dulce et decorum est pro patria mori.* Wilfred Owen, homosexual, noble, truthful; it was never sweet and seemly to die for one's country. Perhaps Owen only needed another decade to be the equal of John Keats. Owen had died in the last week of combat during the First World War, a week before the armistice.

Lying on the pale green sofa, Ryn stirred against the slab of down cushion. She wanted dreams, not thoughts. But thoughts were dreams, too; at least they were infused with imaginings. Thoughts leapt from image to image like stepping-stones across the stream of feelings. Felt-thought, she knew of no more apt phrase for the processes of cognition.

And there lay Peter in her memory, the sheet pulled up, but his round naked shoulder there, golden, more beautiful than marble, and his burnished hair. The light caught his high, defined cheekbone, his beautiful jaw and perfect chin.

She dreamed there was a storm, pounding rain and strong wind, and where was she? Not here, not now, but they (she and someone) were sheltered inside a glowing lamplit house from the dark of the storm, cuddled together. Now at her typewriter, yes, that's what they used back then, but for a moment, her hand turned masculine and she held a feather quill such as Charles Dickens surely used, and she glanced out the window, glad that the storm had cleared and she was no Lear in it, but there was a warning glimmer of lightning in the bluing air, and she knew better, much better, than to go out too soon, for she had been told the story. She saw her friend's son, a ten-year-old, after the storm had cleared, sent out to ride his bicycle, with his friend. Straddling their bikes, the boys were cautiously waiting at a street corner, when a late talon from the sky struck one of them and his bike to earth. Only his friend left standing and alive. The horrible pity of it. If only, if only . . . the child had been told to wait. *Wait a minute or two,* someone might have said. Ryn had been told the story, but (she stirred) not really soon enough, not when she was a young mother and might well have dressed and ventured out too soon after a storm, with Humphrey. When she was a girl she should have been told, she had needed to know how lightning could strike after a storm.

Again, in her dreaming, she saw her hands above the typewriter, no, she was writing by hand with a slender red fountain pen—a Christmas gift from her mother—and it was high school, when penmanship mattered. She had always loved her hands; they *were* beautiful and she had never seen any woman's hands she preferred to her own. Waking suddenly, she glanced up at the sky, and it flashed its silver palm at her, and she knew the lightning was never over, nor could it be, no matter how distant the growls of thunder.

She turned on her side to face the back of the sofa and pulled up the woolen squares cut from the backs of various sweaters—how had its creator accessed the courage, looking at old and dirty sweaters in a second-hand shop, to believe that they could be artfully redeemed, purified of any defilement, made softer and cleaner than new—snuggled under the Christmas gift of her friend. Warm, protected, sleepy and sleeping. With palm to palm, she wedged her hands between her knees. Yes, earlier she had locked the iron-scrolled security door between the sunporch and outside. Having an awareness of being asleep, of resting, doubled her pleasure as she lay half dreaming, an awareness of soft warmth, of being cradled.

WHILE KATHRYN SLUMBERED on the celery green sofa at the back of her house, the sun moved himself around to warm the glass room, which had been created, after all, with the idea of boxing some of his power. The sun's beams fell first on Ryn's face and almost woke her. In her sleep, she mumbled something about "The Moon with the Sun in Her Eye," which was the title of a book of poems she had published with her small press.

She smiled as she napped, felt happy as a cat, and her half-conscious brain enjoyed the satisfaction of the title again, for it was astronomically true that the moon was like a bright eye *because* she reflected sunlight, *and* having something in your eye somewhat blinds you, *and* certainly there were intimations of feminism in the idea. The feminine moon's ability to see clearly where she was and what she was about had long been obstructed by the dominance of the masculine in her universe. *What a fine title!* But how fine the sunshine felt on her face. Ryn smiled in her sleep, though quite suddenly her hand flapped up to her eyes as though she were swatting a fly. Resting where it landed, her fingers splayed across her face.

Ineffectual. Sunbeams still shone through the spaces between her fingers. Quite unconsciously, she rolled onto her side so that she faced the back of the sofa. What was the difference between dreaming and writing? Between memory and imagination. The brain was one; she felt both at one with the sun while she dreamed and also that she was as smoothly delicious as a slice of chess pie moon. She swallowed. Warm, warm and lazy was she, a gray cat on green linen.

In the front of the house, the house telephone rang. Someone was calling who didn't know that these days Kathryn mainly used her cell. The phone buzzed and purred, but she slid deeper into sleep and paid the phone no attention. A message was left. Crickets were eating the wheat.

The sun stepped around the room, down Kathryn's turned back; the solar light splashed onto the thick blue rug, dark as midnight, onto the potted gardenia raising its topiary head on a single long stalk, its dark green, waxy-leaved branches pruned into a stylish ball. And the ficus with its three-strand braided trunk: it was pleased that the sun had arrived. How many winters now had it survived?

Nine or ten, the ficus had lost count, but the point of pride was that her bushy top had held its own, in spite of the fact that the sunporch was chilly in winter. During the summer, the potted ficus dominated the wooden deck, but autumn was her favorite season. She liked being special, being brought inside and sheltered by the glass room.

Really the ficus was quite the envy of the giant cottonwood outside—though he was forever stalwart, close to the sunporch, whether bare in winter or bedecked with large spade-shaped leaves—because the ficus sat green and cozy inside until spring was shouting her name, actually banging on the iron of the security door.

What was that banging? It was at the front door. Someone was pulling back the door knocker and letting it drop against its plate over and over. Rudely persistent. What a clangor of brass on brass. Kathryn sat up on the sofa and rubbed her eyes. What now, and where was she anyway? In a forest surrounded by greenery. No, the carpet was as dark as the night sky, and now she must walk on it.

From the back of the house to the front, she would not hurry. That was the way those who were approaching elderhood got hurt. Slipped and fell and broke, they did, when they felt compelled to hurry. For the sake of a nimble future, Kathryn had been practicing being very careful. Through the kitchen—oh, the lunch dishes were still in the sink—into the living room past the curved purple sofa, almost a soft sculpture in its own right. Through the door leading to the foyer, past the dainty, reproduction eighteenth-century furniture (green and rose stripes with pale blue classical motifs) reflecting Marie Antoinette's furnishings at Saint-Cloud. Could Yves have arrived so soon?

That thought focused her mind. It could not be more than midafternoon, and she was still dressed like a slouch. No makeup. Knowing she must be ruffled from her nap, she quickly smoothed down the back of her hair.

When she glanced out the sidelight beside the massive front door, Ryn saw the person was a stranger. A man. He looked reasonable enough. Clean and dressed appropriately. Surely not drunk. Boldly she unlocked the door and opened it. (Taking a survey? Desiring directions? Bringing a check for a million dollars as on the old *Millionaire* TV program? Who couldn't use that?)

"Hello," she said, in a firm neutral voice through the screen. He returned the greeting and gave his name, but with her usual perversity at such moments, Kathryn failed to pay close attention. He was standing on her porch, now what did he want? That was all she cared to know.

"I used to live in this neighborhood," he said. (Yes, people often came back to St. James Court for some nostalgic reason or other, but always to utter to a current resident the fact of their own former connection to this enduring, beautiful place.) "And I actually learned a good bit about the history of this house."

She said nothing. Surely he didn't expect to be invited in, though she sometimes did, for the sheer fun of it, invite people in, perhaps a harmless-looking group of three excited aging women snapping photos of the façade, people about her own age, or older; yes, she would invite them in, show them the first floor, just to indulge her whimsical impulse, to partake of their happy surprise. But this man wasn't old enough to be invited in and, besides, he was alone.

Into her silence, he went on. "For example, did you know that a woman who lived here jumped off the roof? Jumped from the third floor and killed herself."

Kathryn looked steadily past him (seeing nothing, not even the fountain) and said in exactly the same voice she had used for *Hello*, "*No*, I didn't know that. But I'm rather busy now, and I don't have time to chat. Goodbye." And she closed the massive oak door.

What in the world could he have wanted? That ordinary, reasonable-looking, not-tall man?

Maybe he thought she wanted to get her house onto the Old Louisville Ghost Tour. But she did not. As Halloween approached, such groups could be seen at dusk, a spooky clot of people moving along as a unit, pausing before this mansion or that, netted together by the cheerful, vital voice of their leader. A woman had jumped from the roof! She wasn't surprised.

Actually she had thought of it herself, if things got too tough physically and life seemed pointless. But that couldn't, wouldn't, happen. Not so long as Humphrey lived. It frightened her to think that Humphrey might have considered jumping from the flat mansard roof sometime when he was a roly-poly twelve-year-old, miserable to the nth degree, and uncertain about his sexual orientation. Why would some stranger want to tell her such a thing?

Today should have been a day of relaxation for Ryn. That was the kind of day this was. A time that afforded time: to walk in the park to admire the lavish autumnal colors, to watch the fluttering descent of leaves (saffron ones; crimson ones). Claiming for herself a nap—that was the very kind of thing to embrace on a day after the work of several years had come to completion, or, at least, had defined its end point. (The End, Start Over.)

But who would the woman who had jumped have been? Someone like herself, thrice divorced? No, that kind of marital record hardly ever happened years ago. And that jumping from her roof had to have occurred years and years ago. And had she jumped from the front or the back of the house? Her own friend, her college friend so long ago, had jumped in January, in the dismals of gray, bedraggled January, in New York.

Certainly old writers—the pace of thinking slowed, grew more sober—could forget even characters created in the blaze of their imaginations. In Joyce's smithy of the soul. Tolstoy had forgotten not characters but the laws of his art and descended into didacticism of an unhinged sort. When William Faulkner had visited the University of Virginia, he hadn't been able to remember in which novel some of his characters had appeared. In herself she noticed she was taking a greater pleasure in abstractions as she aged, a kind of nimble glee about being able to use them well; she was like a frog, leaping from abstraction to abstraction as though they were lily pads. She thought of the giant lily pads of the Shaw Botanical Gardens in St. Louis and old photographs that showed a single pad bearing the weight of a long-skirted Victorian woman.

Having closed the front door with a firm push, and another sealing push with the palm of her hand, and a turn of the bolt, Ryn walked determinedly into the guest bathroom. She leaned over one of the twin sinks and the bland tile counter to look herself in the eyes. The commanding horizontal blank of a single mirror stretched itself in a reflecting swath eight feet along the wall and four feet high.

"You forget things," she said to herself evenly in the long mirror. "It is hard for you to form new short-term memories. You know that is one of the early signs of Alzheimer's." It actually seemed a bit odd to be talking to herself this way. So she winked at herself, and then went on, not without wit. "You read it in Wikipedia, and you know it actually is true. You've seen it in your own life. I repeat, Kathryn Callaghan—that's you, old girl—*has trouble forming new short-term memories.* A new person has to register in some way that actually matters to you, or you forget him or her. She thought of the thousands and thousands of dear people into whose eyes she had looked during the multiple book tours. She wanted to remember each of them. Those readers who had bothered with her. But she couldn't. And the mere effort of gratitude had cost her, slicked her memory. She spoke on: "The memory reservoir expected in normal, merely polite society is leaking out of your brain through your right ear." She grinned at herself, and then her voice surprised her with the sound of whispering. She listened.

Timid, secretive, and frightened, her voice registered in her ears. "It has gotten worse: since the trauma of Mark's betrayal, and the divorce." She wanted to end her soliloquy on a more positive note, so she said, "Your freedom has cost you."

Freedom. Strange; it had been the watchword of her college days, under the influence of existentialism. And here it was again, waving its hopeful, threadbare flag.

Now was a time of freedom, of opportunity, for her.

In the long, bright, clear mirror, Ryn watched herself kiss the end of her finger. Then she placed the finger on the reflection of her lips in the mirror and made her exit.

Reclaiming the living room as her domain, she sat in the twirly gray chair. It was from the same family as the sculptural purple sofa (so contemporary!); this gray chair and its fat gray crescent hassock suited her body always more comfortably than she was expecting each time she sat down in it. Resting in the twirly chair was like going out and having a better time than one expected. Or meeting up with a friend unexpectedly. How pleasant that seat was!

Freedom: a heady concept left over from the sixties. In college, idealistically in search of philosophical truth, they had embraced Sartre's idea of freedom as a troubling part of existentialism; and in the cause of racial equality, they had sung for freedom in the streets. But now, to Ryn, *freedom* suddenly seemed fresh again: a banner for some sort of needed rebellion. Maybe she was just being terribly old-fashioned. She needed to bring herself up to date. Read more magazines; maybe watch the news on TV. Read best sellers and book reviews again.

She believed she would subscribe to the *Atlantic Monthly* today. Yes, as a way of celebrating the completion of her new first draft she would give herself a magazine subscription, several of them. Now she would have time to read again (but something true-hearted, not fashionable), something other than her intense study of Vigée-Le Brun and the culture of the painter's long lifetime, 1755–1842. Would Ryn herself live so long?

On her left hand, a tiny wart, like a seed, had formed under the skin of her middle finger, in the center of the whorl that made up the fingerprint; she checked it with the pad of her thumb on the same hand. What a minute reality it possessed. Something to test, something to consult from time to time. The grain of wart was still with her, slightly larger.

Suddenly impatient, she threw down her hand. Testing a wart was worse than contemplating her navel.

She wanted to be out of her big, empty house and inside Leslie's condo where everything was new and contemporary, pale and smart, blank, not this color-saturated red-blue jungle at the heart of her house. She rose from the gray chair and headed for the door. Leslie would never jump off her balcony or the top of her building. If she wanted out, out of misery, she would find another way out, land on her feet, be seen fashionably walking the sidewalk, head high, moving forward at a meaningful clip.

As Ryn turned the key to lock her front door, she heard the wispy strains of a cello, a Bach sarabande. And here were the colors of autumn splashed all down the Court; more red and compatible oranges, gold and brown, bits of pink, and some tenacious green. No sign of the man who had knocked. Across the Court, Leslie was practicing the cello. Though she was inside the condo, the open door to her balcony allowed the music into the Court. She's not reading *Portrait*, Ryn realized.

The single, yearning line of the cello wove itself into the strands of falling water. Listening, Ryn paused on the cusp of the semicircular porch steps.

Bach had written six of these suites for unaccompanied cello. Leslie was starting the short, slow sarabande of the third suite over again; there was the rolled chord, that moment when Bach dives for richness to support the purity of the single line, and suddenly Ryn was extraordinarily happy, as though a ladle had dipped into her heart and found a liquid reservoir of shimmering gold. The mingle, the beauty, the power, the truth of the music! And she was there to hear it at just this moment, like no other.

Like dye, the sound of the cello saturated the fabric of everything. Midafternoon and the fountain, standing on a porch above the quiet street, the brilliance of the trees. Everything partook of Bach's sarabande, a slow dance derived from the Spanish and Italian *zarabanda*. Of course it was an autumnal sound; it had its own consoling glory, its own poignancy, its own heritage, the unexpected cocking of a wanton's hip.

Stain me, Ryn prayed to the stately sound, *saturate my soul.*

VII

THE ART
OF LIVING

PORTRAIT

A S SOON AS WE ARE MARRIED, M. Le Brun asks that we keep the
marriage a secret, for he is engaged to the daughter of a Dutch dealer
in fine paintings with whom he is conducting a business arrangement
involving a good deal of money. He asks that I agree to silence about our
marriage until the business can be completed. I choose to comply.

While the marriage is a secret and yet the possibility of it is in the air,
several friends come to visit me while I am with my mother in her apartment. They speak urgently in front of her, and indeed Auber, who is the
crown jeweler, is my mother's friend as well. To me, he says, "It would be
better if you tied a millstone around your neck and jumped into the river
than to marry M. Le Brun." My mother blurts, "Why?" and the jeweler
tells us my already-husband is a gambler and loses large sums of money.
My mother gasps, and I fear that she will lose her composure.

Before I am two weeks wed (and the fact is still a secret), we are called
upon by three women of high society, each of them young and beauti-

ful and full of knowledge about eligible young men. One is the Duchesse d'Aremburg and another the Portuguese ambassadress, for I have met them at supper parties involving the Princesse de Rohan-Rochefort, the Princesse de Lorraine, the Duc de Choiseul, the Duc de Lauzun—all those salons and members of society who have welcomed me simply because of my talent and achievement. The Duchesse d'Aremburg, without giving her reasons, states simply, "You must not marry Le Brun, for he will make you unhappy." Again, my mother covers her mouth with her hand and struggles not to burst into tears.

As soon as they leave, I take her in my arms and say, "There is no need to worry. I have my painting. As long as I can paint, I will always be happy." I am sure it is true. All the more reason to throw myself into my painting. My happiest hours have always been those when I stood or sat in my chair before my easel.

But when I am alone, I realize that the need for secrecy and the unfortunate information and attitudes revealed have cast a shadow over my marriage. I remember that my mother was able to create a happy home, as many women bravely do, even when the situation is less than perfect. To compromise is itself an art: first one must cheerfully lower one's expectations in any area where change is unlikely.

I work every day till nightfall, when the lack of light stops me. I accept invitations to the theater, which I adore, and to supper parties and to the countryside. I enjoy these activities to the fullest, knowing I have spent the day with my passion.

Like my stepfather, my husband receives all my commissions, which is his legal right. He has great need of the money, for he not only gambles but he also has an uncontrollable passion for extravagant women. His gifts to them are the fruits of my labor as well as his sales through the atelier. I refuse to be bitter. I prefer to accommodate myself to the truth and not to have illusions about my marriage, which is finally announced. And the deal is done.

Unlike proximity to my stepfather, it is no burden to be in the presence of M. Le Brun. He has an obliging nature. Not only is he pleasant, he is in fact kind (if one makes exception for his gambling and philandering, and the subsequent disillusionment). His manner and indeed his nature are a mixture of sweetness and gaiety. I refuse to hurt myself by harboring either bitter disappointment or low jealousy. I vow to appreciate what is best in him, and to give myself to the good pleasures with him and with witty and charming friends, to the theater, to conversation, to music, to nature, and above all to art.

We have discovered that M. Le Brun does not own this mansion; he is a mere lodger like my family, though he led my mother and myself to think Lubert was his. To augment my earnings (which are now very considerable) from my portraits and other paintings, my husband asks me to take on students.

MY MOTHER AND I are closer friends than ever, for without dishonoring the memory of my father, she has implied not only are we mother and daughter (with many shared memories) but sisters in managing the art of marriage. What else can one do but embrace and refine manners that enhance and favorably affect the inner being? It is for a woman's own sake that she lives a life beyond reproach of any sort, and that she recognizes, treasures, and enjoys true friendship for its congeniality.

When our lives need refreshing we often go together to Marly-le-Roi. We like to visit that sanctuary on Sunday afternoons, as we did that long-ago day with Mme Suzanne to escape the "country garden as shooting gallery." Not only the Marly grounds but also the nearby château and park of Sceaux with its ancient trees have been made open to the public by the generous Duc de Penthièvre.

Soon after our arrival at Marly-le-Roi, as my mother and I walk arm in arm along the broad paths between the great trees of the park, we feel more at peace with the world. As though we were a pair of sheep, we dip in and out of pools of shade and splashes of light and gaze appreciatively at the still-dewy sward. There *are* sheep, clean and bright, to be seen, and occasionally we also see shy deer. In this natural paradise, between the dark trunks of the oaks, one occasionally glimpses a flurry of dainty dresses in the distance and graceful ladies floating along.

Around one bend, to our surprise and instant trepidation, we happen to come upon Queen Marie Antoinette strolling with several of her ladies. All dressed in purest white they are, and for a moment I think a small group of clouds has come down into the park. They do not seem like real people but like a confection, or like zephyrs, each of them with a prettiness of figure and face that appears visionary.

Immediately my mother and I change our direction so as not to intrude on their private pleasure, but just as immediately the queen calls to me, acknowledging me even by name!

"Please," she says, with exquisite politeness, "let us not inconvenience you. Please continue your stroll as you wish, along this walk or any other that may please you here at Marly."

My mother and I thank her graciously, but of course we do not tarry as though we are expecting more conversation.

"To the lake, then," I say to my mother, for that is the part of the park I prefer to any other. While geometric parterres of small flowers flourish like carpets in the open sunny area close to the château, I like the more dreamy glades that have nothing of symmetry about them. Perhaps I want the queen to have a vague idea of my aesthetic sensibility by mentioning the lake as our destination. Beside the lake, which I have already come to love from another vantage point, we now find the most beautiful trees—noble, graceful, immense—that I have ever seen in my life. They seem to me to be the essence of the earth, mediating between us and the blue of heaven.

This day, with my mother, having just enjoyed proximity to the queen and her ladies and lingering among the huge old trees beside the lake, I am in a special rapture that I vow to hold in memory, for it is more precious than a casket covered with jewels. It proves that despite vexation—

and who does not experience annoyances in life?—there are redeeming moments. One must embrace them. By doing so, one is true to one's own nature; one is creating a self that is sufficient unto itself. I believe that is the way for me to live happily.

I ADMIT I DO NOT LIKE TO TEACH. I do not have confidence that what is true for me will be of value to others. Most of my students are young women but older than I am. It is difficult for me to assume an unnatural air of authority and stuffiness, and so I fail to gain the respect that one must be accorded if one is to teach well. I try to do my own work while they do theirs, but I am constantly interrupted by the need to offer advice about how to paint eyes, noses, and faces. Form divides itself into mere technique. I feel like an accomplished writer who is required to teach youngsters the alphabet, or an actor capable of transporting everyone in the theater, who is asked to teach children to speak a word.

One day recently, before I mounted the stairs to the old hayloft M. Le Brun has rented for my teaching studio, I heard joyful giggling. My young ladies had attached a rope to an exposed beam, and they were having a high time swinging about. I scolded them as best I could about wasting time and about their failure to take the opportunity of lessons in a serious manner. However, the swing was a temptation, and I tried it out myself after ousting them. Soon I was laughing unrestrainedly and they were enjoying the spectacle of their teacher flying through the air.

Afterward, I gave a lecture on Watteau's painting (asking them to recall it by memory) of a young lady, outdoors, swinging. My dear papa, who excelled with pastels, was much influenced by Watteau, and I think that he might have been proud of me if he could have heard me lecturing and seen me standing before my students; however, he would have taken far greater delight in my own painting of portraits and my acquaintance with the notables I have been engaged to paint.

I must say that I have had one student of real talent, the youngest of the lot, named Mlle Émilie Roux de la Ville. Mlle Roux de la Ville is fascinated with human skin, as I am, and she practices diligently to catch its innumerable variations.

IT IS THROUGH the recommendation of the queen's friends Comtesse de Polignac and her lover the Comte de Vaudreuil, both of whom I have rendered in oil portraits about which they expressed the greatest pleasure and satisfaction, that I am invited to the queen's private apartment hidden in the labyrinth of the Château de Versailles. Through the recommendation of these powerful people, to whom I will always owe my gratitude and loyalty, I am invited to paint the portrait of my most gracious sovereign.

M. Le Brun has given me a thousand pieces of advice about how to comport myself so as to win favor, and while I have listened to him with the courtesy and respect due a husband (as I have always made it my rule to observe despite my disappointment in his profligate spending of large sums on gambling and on women), I intend to forget all of his counsel. Of course this portrait will bring the largest remuneration we have ever known, but it is not for gold that I tremble. I tremble because I am so thoroughly and deeply honored by having been deemed worthy not only to receive the commission but also merely to be invited into her presence.

I have dressed myself with the utmost care, choosing the colors that complement my eyes and my hair, which has a natural hint of red in it, like the chestnut berry, and I have arranged my hair myself, as I always do, with special care for special moments. It's as though I am creating myself for the occasion to come, as I assemble my appearance. Today my hand has been a happy one and a confident one. Oh, I can hear the puffery in my own inner voice, but I *need* a draft of bravado, for soon I shall see and be seen, not by accident but by design, by my sovereign.

My hair falls loosely in natural curls, and I wear a rose gown shot with thin brown stripes, but the brown dye has a hint of red about it.

While the carriage is conveying me to Versailles, I look down at the colors of my dress, rose red and chestnut brown, as though they both contain and bespeak all my hopes for success with my interview and with the work to come.

When I see the queen in the sumptuous surroundings of the Château de Versailles, I instantly make my curtsey, long and deep. She is dressed in magnificent white satin, a court dress with wide panniers, and I am dazzled by the reality of her presence. My eyes seek the relief of looking away from her into the weave of the rug. She is like an orb of light! She has sent for me!

Her voice finds my ear, and it is as quick and light as the song of a bird. She invites me to rise.

"I think that we are friends already, Madame Le Brun. You and I are the same age, and we have some of the same friends. You *are* the friend of my very dear friends, who have spoken of you with warm fondness and admiration for both your person and your talent as a painter."

For only a moment, overcome by the naturalness of her kindness and by her lavish and generous words, I look down again, but this I must not do, for my eyes are the emissaries of my own inner gifts. When I look at her again, I show her my spirit.

But I am no casual observer. Immediately I am struck by the quality of her complexion, for it truly is dazzlingly transparent, and my first impression of her extraordinary radiance is not caused entirely by either the shock of being in her presence or the shimmer of her gown. While she has something of the long chin of her Austrian forebears, her mouth is mobile and expressive. Even beyond the tones of her complexion, it is the carriage of her head and indeed of her whole body that suggests her royal lineage.

"It is almost hard to believe we are the same age," she says, "because you seem so fresh and youthful. I like your natural curls, and I rather wish the court custom of dreary powder were not a necessity." With cheerful audacity, she adds, "How do I look to you?"

Ah, she breaks my silence with a direct question. But it is a kindly, lighthearted question to which there can be no incorrect answer, that is if I can keep even half my wits about me. Strangely, I remember my father at our old home, how he would pause a moment sometimes before answering a question directed to him by D'Alembert or Diderot.

"As any queen would give her life to look," I say, and I am surprised at the confident, even confiding, warmth of my own voice. It is a brown voice ruddy with life, like the rich back of a viol. "Not only as a queen but as any happy and virtuous woman would like to appear, so you appear to me—full of life and goodness."

"But can you paint such abstract qualities?" she inquires, and I realize that she is a woman of quick wit, that she likes to tease and playfully, harmlessly to challenge those she counts as friends. Dare I think as much? This friendship she spoke of in her first utterance—I do feel its glow and its ease brightening around us.

"If you will forgive me for saying so, I believe that I can, with my paints and with your most gracious permission, embody something of the grace and goodness of Your Majesty."

"In truth, the reputation of your extraordinary skill is well established. You understand far better than most painters"—the palms of her hands lightly smooth down the shimmering white silk of her robe—"that our surfaces are nothing without the animating spirit that lies within."

Although my impulse is to amend her statement, for my art depends on my belief in the integrity of surfaces and the unity of the self, I say, "Your understanding of these matters makes me wonder if you have not yourself occasionally taken up the brush." And I realize that I am no longer afraid; it is possible to think in her presence. I have asked a question of her as naturally as though she were indeed a friend.

As she sits, she tosses a pink shawl across her lap, and the sheen of the silvery pink silk acts like a mirror and throws a delicate pinkish tint over her incomparable skin. Since I am standing while she sits, I see her face from a new angle, one that emphasizes her blue eyes, both their quiet kindness and the lively sparkle that perhaps one notices first.

I think that she is a woman fully comfortable with herself and who both is enjoying and intends to enjoy every moment of her aliveness.

"In Vienna, my sisters and I were given lessons in drawing and in painting and in all the arts. Do you have sisters?"

"My friends have been my sisters, Your Majesty." I am thinking of Mlle Boquet.

"But it is the art of dancing that most delights me," the queen continues. She smiles at me with the very thought of dancing. "My feet are more talented than my hands."

"I do not exaggerate to say that no member of your circle whom I have painted has failed to remark most enthusiastically about the beauty of your dancing, and of—"

Here she interrupts me to say, "And of my carriage." With those words she rises from her seat, lays the pink scarf across a nearby table, and pretends to be giving unseen friends a little lecture. "My dear friends, no doubt you who let nothing at court go unnoticed have remarked that I have two ways of moving myself across a room, that is, of walking, of perambulation." She is witty and charming, pretending to be pompous. "When I am with you or with my family, I walk in such a way as to express my happiness, my sheer happiness that I am in your company. On the other hand, when I wish, I use another carriage to impress viewers with my dignity. I employ that method of propelling myself forward or backward or on the diagonal as though I stand on a little wheeled platform. There is no disturbance or expression in the upper body that suggests my feet are even moving. I move like a minor goddess." She frowns slightly. "But is there then, dear friends, a stiffness about me?" By extending her open hand, she pretends to address her circle of ladies. "Perhaps we should let my newest friend, the most beautiful and admired artist in Paris or the whole of France, be the judge."

"I am overwhelmed by your kindness. Please do not ask me to judge you, Your Majesty." I smile at her and cock my head a little to one side as though to avert my eyes. I am playing, too!

"Would you like a lesson in how to walk like a queen?"

"I think that I must walk like an artist, but one who is most happy, most honored to be in the presence of her queen."

"But come and walk around the apartment with me. Let me put my hand in your arm."

"Your Majesty is quite well, I hope."

Here she blushes a bit, drops her chin a little, and looks up at me from her lovely blue eyes. Why, what could cause a queen to blush? My lips part with a tiny pop, for *I think I know.*

There is a particular reason why the skin of the queen has a heavenly glow. I believe the queen is pregnant! I am flooded with joy at the thought of it. All France will dance with delight. Seven years of marriage have passed with no heir, and the populace has begun to grumble with impatience. I am most sure that there was no lack of willingness on her part to consummate the marriage.

"May I merely say, my dearest new friend, that I have never been more well or more happy in all my life."

There! She has told me without telling me. I see in her a person of both truthfulness and discretion.

"This little apartment is quickly seen," she said. "Let us stroll in the great rooms and get more acquainted with each other. I shall play the role of your guide, just as Louis XV—Papa-Roi, I called him—escorted me when I first came here from Austria—became my guide to the wonders, paintings, murals, and statuary of the château. But here we'll pause before the glass and make comparison. What do you see? Can you look at us, side by side, and let words serve as though they were your paintbrush, rendering the two of us?"

"Because color is the most vibrant part of painting for me—"

"Yes, I have heard you described as a colorist."

"I note that we are created from different palettes, for you are blond, and I am brunette."

"That is safely enough said!" she candidly replies, but with that mixture of teasing and fun that I'm sure will be characteristic of much of our conversation. But it will not be all of it. I shall see to that. For she is pliant and genuine enough to want to reveal something of her depths to one who honors and truly loves her.

"And you are taller," I add.

"And you are more slender," she says. "In our colors and stature, we are opposites."

"If I might speak freely, I would describe us as complements."

"Both of us move in the circles of the greatest refinement and privilege that France has to offer." Now she is speaking more thoughtfully. She is capable of focused introspection. "It is right, natural, and fitting that we should both be present at the court of Louis XVI. But there is a difference. I am here by the right of birth, as the daughter of the empress of Austria. And you are here because of your talent and your own efforts to employ that talent. You make your way by the gift of God, and it was also God's gift that I was born to a life at court. I think us equally fortunate."

I answer her with true and honest humility. "Your Majesty makes too much of me."

With this sentence she squeezes my arm, almost pinches me. "Your sentence echoes one I myself once uttered."

While I do not dare to question her, I pray that she will continue in her confidences with me.

"When I journeyed from Austria to France, to be wed to my most dear husband, the caravan stopped on an island in the middle of the Rhine River. It was a location thought neutral, politically, neither Austrian nor French, and it was there, through a special ritual, that I was to abandon my Austrian identity and assume a French one. I was still only fourteen years old.

"My Austrian ladies relieved me of my Austrian clothing so that I was for a moment as naked as any baby who comes newborn into the world, a simple human. All my Austrian jewelry was removed and even my little dog was taken away, for he was deemed to be a sort of Austrian citizen.

Then I was tenderly dressed again with French robes. It was a moment of transition, not without pain for all the joy and honor I felt as the bride chosen for the future king of France."

Here she pauses, and I know that I am trusted indeed. Has she ever mentioned to a single French soul that she had felt pain in giving up her allegiance to all things Austrian? I hope not. Though I would never betray her nor betray her confidences in the slightest manner (I will tell my husband that I had been made to understand that I must never describe or repeat any scene or conversation to which I was privy at the court of Versailles), in this moment I wonder if it is wise on her part to be so frank with me. I am quite sure (and I hope) that usually she is more discreet. But I think she wants me to know her story so that I may have a better chance of painting the soul that lives within her body.

"Even my name, of course, was changed, for at home—"

Yes, she even uses the word *home* to apply to Austria! I fear for her: too quickly she lets herself be natural and trusting, without subterfuge.

"At home, I was Maria Antonia, and it was by that name that my ladies called me as they undressed me on the little island in the Rhine. They were like bright butterflies in their beautiful Austrian dresses, and it seemed that their wings beat around me and fanned my cheeks with whispered love and gracious compliments. 'You make too much of me,' I said to them, for I did feel humble at my selection and at my opportunity to contribute to the peace of Europe. 'You make too much of me.'

"And those are your very words, my dear Madame Vigée-Le Brun, to me, just now. It is the proof of what my heart already told me, the moment we looked into one another's eyes, that there would be a special understanding and compatibility between us."

"Oh, Majesty," I say quietly but with all the ardor of my artistic nature, "you do me such honor that I fear I will faint with happiness."

With that utterance, she quickly kisses me on the cheek, but she begins speaking again immediately as if this gesture that seems the seal of favor bestowed upon me is not even a moment to be remembered by her.

But no doubt I do her injustice with this thought, for she is sublimely sensitive to the feelings of others.

"Look up," the queen instructs me, for she wants me to see the painting on the ceiling of Mars, the god of war. "I was shocked that his chariot is drawn by wolves, the first time, the first day, I walked beneath this scene. May the dogs of war never draw this Roman god across the skies of France. My marriage was meant to ensure the peace between Austria and France, ancient enemies."

"Among my plans for paintings," I confide, "is an allegorical one that will depict Peace bringing back Abundance. Two figures of women, one blond and one brunette."

"Then think of me," she says, "when you represent Peace, for my person and my presence here serve that cause."

But I already know the blond figure will represent Abundance in my allegory, and the simple brunette would stand for Peace.

As we pass through the stately public rooms, I see other rich paintings from the time of Louis XIV that Louis XV explained to my noble queen when she was but the dauphine, newly arrived at Versailles, among them *Victory Supported by Hercules Followed by Plenty and Felicity*, which extends the same sentiment of my painting *Peace Bringing Back Abundance*.

The only awful mural among those on the ceiling is that of *Terror, Fury, and Horror Seizing the Earthly Powers*. At those images my queen trembles, and I experience her tremor through our linked arms. I remember my father's speaking of how the world we knew was soon to be turned upside down.

My own favorite of these mythological scenes is *Venus Subjugating the Gods and Powers*. Her chariot is drawn by doves and rests upon a cloud. She is half unclothed with bare breasts. Of course Venus is the goddess of the beautiful, superior to all other gods, and she is my icon. Naturally, the chariot of Beauty is drawn by those emissaries of peace, the doves.

"When I first stood under this painting," the queen reminisces, "on our way to Mass in the chapel, but newly married, you can imagine my feelings of inadequacy as we regarded the lovely breasts of Venus. Though I was fourteen, when some women have already acquired their womanly shape, my chest was as flat as a shield. Papa-Roi sensed my discomfort, for he said to me as we looked up, 'I cannot imagine anyone more like yourself in loveliness than Venus, the queen of Love and Beauty.' "

"Beauty is indeed a great power in this world," I say.

"I would rather embody Peace than Beauty," she replies seriously, "but they are connected. A queen has more power for peace, if she is admired and loved for her beauty."

"But did not the beauty of Helen spark the Trojan wars?" a male voice asks behind us.

Instantly I deduce it must be the king, and I bow as low as possible and do not dare to look at him. By his footsteps I know that he is passing by us, and he is accompanied by several other pairs of stockinged and well-shod male feet. "Enjoy your time among us, Madame Le Brun," he murmurs as he passes. Now is not the time for presentation, but I allow myself to glance at the retreating figures of the king and his retinue. One turns—it is the Comte de Vaudreuil, whose portrait I have painted—and winks at me.

I am horrified and aghast, but I hear a slight chuckle from the queen, for she is the intimate friend of the Comte de Vaudreuil and the Comtesse de Polignac (they who recommended me to her), and people say they are all quite merry together. Another minister also turns to glance back at us, and I think he may be the Vicomte de Calonne, said to be astute in matters of finance.

I wait for the queen to speak to me. I feel almost turned to stone, immobilized by the powers around me. In all of Europe there is no palace more grand or more important than the Château de Versailles, and I who command only a few rooms in a mansion on Rue de Cléry am now defined by these walls.

"Another day," the queen breaks my silence, "we will walk together to the chapel, perhaps while the organ is being played, and you will enjoy those sacred Christian paintings, which these Greek pagans only prefigure.

"Your own paintings are always secular portraits," she adds. "I think you do not paint sacred images of the Virgin or of Christ our Lord, or of the Creator? Or even the saints?"

"That is true," I say, though I remember when my brush transformed John the Baptist into one of my father's friends. "My brush would falter before such subjects. I must look with a literal eye upon my subjects. My inner vision is not strong enough."

I am amazed to hear myself saying these things to the queen of France, for I have never thought them before, not even to myself. For a moment I think this must be a great failing on my part and that God is surely displeased with me. "For my own edification," I reply almost in my own defense, "I paint the landscape in watercolors. It is my relaxation and my refreshment to do so. An act of reverence. If I cannot paint our Holy Father or his Son, at least I can paint his creation. I am ever full of wonder at natural beauty."

"We each have our talents and our inclinations," she said. Her voice modulates from a somewhat pontifical key to a soft confidentiality. "No one is expected to excel in every way, but to be ourselves fully. My hope is that by the end of my life, I will fully know myself and live honestly and bravely with that knowledge, unswayed by others."

I am struck silent by the sincerity of her wish. It amazes me that one so young and lovely would be speaking of the end of her life. I hope with all my heart that she bears future life within her now, and that for years to come she and the king will be surrounded by the many children of France.

"Dear Mme Vigée-Le Brun. I wish for you long life and health and happiness."

I feel as embraced through her simple, soft, and warm words as I would if she had thrown both arms around me. I am stunned, however, into formality. "I cannot find the words to thank Your Majesty enough," I say.

"When I paint Your Majesty," I say, though the phrase first forms in my mind otherwise—*when I paint you*, I would have said—"I will strive to capture something of your naturalness."

At this she laughs, a trilling bell-like cascade of happiness.

"Then I must tell you, beforehand, what fixes my gaze when I am in the chapel. Can you guess what aspect of deity, when I first enter the chapel on almost any occasion, my eyes seek out? And not only seek out but return to again and again while the organ is heaving its mighty notes and piping its delicate flutes, and the incense is doing its aromatic work, and the voices of the choristers chant and intone their Latin, and I sit, stand, and kneel in all my polished finery?

"On the grand chapel ceiling is a painting of God the Father, Creator of Heaven and Earth, most majestic, with a white beard and in his celestial robes. He hovers over us as we look up.

"The artist has painted God barefooted, and what I most love to see is the bare bottom of God's foot, the very sole of his foot. It is shaped exactly like a person's bare sole, with little lines, like wrinkles, something one rarely looks at on the feet of others. In the chapel, we are far below God, but because of his high position and ours beneath, with clouds not much in the way, we are able to see the bottom of his foot, so like our own, and to love him and worship him."

AS WE PROMENADE back through the stately rooms toward the queen's apartment, though we chat as we walk, I look at everything with the intention of stocking my memory with these privileged objects of Versailles: wall coverings, carpets, chairs, desks, mirrors, tables, vases, clocks, even tassels and sweeps of fringe; the parterres and fountains outside, the pleasant, sunny vistas tantalizingly glimpsed through the windows, especially the great fountain of Latona with her children Apollo and Diana. However, it is the work of painters hanging on the inner walls of the Château de Versailles that shouts for my attention.

I study especially the various portraits hanging in their magnificent frames of the royalty of France, for it is in portraiture that my own task and my opportunity lie. My spirit whooshes up like a fountain with the knowledge that my work is almost surely destined to hang on these very walls—I know it, for these works do not surpass mine—and that what I paint will in my own lifetime gain a measure of immortality here. It is an intoxicating idea.

Ever sensitive to the enthusiasms of her guests, the queen causes us to stop before the full-length oil portrait of Louis XIV, in which he has thrown his royal robes to one side in order to display his shapely leg, made a focal point not only by its central position but also by the brilliant white color of the stocking he wears. Strikingly erect, this king of France wears no crown but presents a commanding, arresting, and haughty pose. The attention drawn to his magnificent leg is only somewhat balanced by his face and its frame of a curly dark wig.

"I paused here with Papa-Roi," the queen muses, "when I was fourteen, to admire his grandfather, Louis XIV. It seems very long ago, yet it is but ten years. And my Papa-Roi is gone now, and we are here instead."

I wonder if she notes the cruelty in the painted face of the aging Sun King. Certainly, I do. But it was during his reign that the greatness of France rose over Europe and gave us our preeminence. I notice the way the foot of Louis XIV is turned, and how well the red color of his high-heeled shoes has retained its brilliance.

"Do you sculpt as well as paint, Madame Le Brun?"

"As a child. Sometimes using the mud of the garden at the convent where I was educated. I would gather up the clay soil to mold a duck or rabbit for the pleasure of my friends. But human faces were ever my obsession, and I drew them everywhere. On the ground with a stick and in the margins of my copybooks, for which I was punished by the nuns."

"All the same, let me point out to you this marble bust of the Sun King by Bernini, when the king was young."

As soon as she has led me to this work, I exclaim my admiration. She has chosen well in making sure I experience this miracle in marble, and my heart warms toward her as a perceptive and caring person. I marvel at how at ease she has made me feel.

"He lives," I say. "Though his flesh is but cold marble and of an unnatural hue, the sculpture compels him into life." I am thrilled to think that Bernini's own hand held the tools that chiseled, carved, and smoothed this very bust from a block of marble. I wish my mother were with me to see it.

"Sometimes I think sculpture has quite the advantage over the flat canvas," she says.

"We live in a round world," I agree. I do not say my thought: I am so used to looking at paintings, which have their own verisimilitude through the art of perspective, that it seems unnecessary to me to have literally the third dimension.

"This visit we have become acquainted," the queen says. "Next time you will set up your easel, and we will begin. But I have heard that you sing well, so now let us enjoy a duet together. Something of Grétry's?"

AS I AM ABOUT TO ENTER the carriage that will convey me away from the Château de Versailles, my progress is arrested by a gentle touch at my elbow. It is a girl, thin, a bit dirty and rather ragged, but with a face of unusual delicacy and sensitivity, partly because of her thinness. Through her transparent skin I can see the blue vein that curves close to the jawbone. She asks to speak to me for a moment, and I readily nod my permission as I ask her name.

"Jeanne Marie," she answers. "I am a seamstress."

"Is there some way I may be of use to you?" I ask. The footman in his immaculate wig and splendid livery is gripping together the three thin legs of my easel and placing it in the carriage, along with my stretched canvas, loosely but carefully wrapped in tissue.

"I think you must be a friend of the queen," she says.

"As is each of her loyal subjects," I readily reply, "but perhaps not in the intimate sense that you imply."

"Is it you who are painting Her Majesty, and do you paint mesdames, as Mme Adélaïde Labille-Guiard does?"

"I am just beginning a portrait of Her Majesty," I reply, but I feel uneasy. Who is this personage who knows the names of artists and those they paint? Might she be some sort of spy sent here by a member of the court who wishes to know too much about the queen's choices and plans? Despite my feeling of slight alarm, the girlish unguarded part of me proudly and confidingly adds to the information I have already given. "This is the first time I have been invited to come here."

Instantly I feel the blood drain from my face: how has this girl led me into such unguarded disclosures? For I am the most discreet *salonnière* in Paris. No one can trip me into divulging information better left unsaid.

As though to implore aid, the girl presses her hands together, and I see that between her palms she is holding a tiny garment fabricated from thin white batiste. It is tucked in front and a band of finest lace encircles the neck. "I have made this gown myself," she whispers, "a gift for the queen and for her infant to come. Perhaps you would take it with you now and present it on my behalf to the queen, when next you come to paint."

How is it possible this girl suspects, as do I, that the queen is newly pregnant? No one, not any member of court who frequents my salon, has even begun to hint at such a thing. And how did I know? Something in the queen's complexion, which so transfixed my appreciation, and something of the joy in her eyes. I shake my head and say in as kindly a fashion as I can, "My dear, I could not dare to presume."

The girl presses her hands together almost ecstatically. "Then perhaps you would like to buy it from me for your own use?"

"But—" There I stop myself. It is no business of this seamstress to know that I am not pregnant or that I am, or to presume I wish to purchase a gift for someone else. But is it possible that I, too, am pregnant, and that this waif can see in me what I saw in the mien of the queen? While the little garment is wonderfully made, quite artful really, it does not seem entirely clean. There is a grayish cast to the fabric.

"Have you quite finished with the little dress?" I ask. "Do you consider it ready to sell?"

"Madame, it is finished as to stitchery, but—" Here she looks down, and she rubs the back of her hand under her nose. "I know it should be laundered." Now she looks up into my eyes again. "Something told me to bring it to this place at once. I think it was the Holy Spirit. The idea formed in my mind that I was not to tarry. Madame, I promise that when the dress is laundered and spread on a bush in the sun to dry, and ironed of wrinkles, then this will be a dress fit for a royal child. You will not find smaller or more perfect stitches anyplace in France, and the ideas for its shape and the lace, too, are like no other."

I am quite amazed by her ardor and no less so by her faith. When she spoke of the Holy Spirit, I thought of Bernini, not of the bust, which I have just seen, of Louis XIV before his dissipation but of the evocative engraving of Bernini's sculpture of Saint Teresa of Avila. I know that I will buy the little garment, for I wondrously believe that perhaps I myself am with child or will be soon.

"Will there be a full moon tonight? Have you noticed?" I ask her.

"Madame, it was three nights ago. Tonight the moon is waning. Its back will be hunched."

Ah, I have been so excited and absorbed by the prospect of coming to Versailles that I forgot to notice the absence of my menses, which arrive each month as regularly as the full moon, unless . . .

I reach into the placket of my dress for my pocket of coins. I know there are not many coins in it, for M. Le Brun gives me only a tiny allowance each month. Inside my skirt, my fingers bump against my own thigh, and the prodding and groping surprises my leg. I had almost forgotten that I had a body, other than my hands and eyes; this mystic child seems somehow disembodied—her thinness. Could it be that she and her family are starving?

As I empty the purse into my hand, I look down at the little seamstress and ask hopefully, "Is it enough?" for I know she has spoken the truth about the value of her work.

"It is more than enough, Mme Vigée-Le Brun."

"Take it all, Jeanne Marie."

Her lips part but she makes no sound. Nonetheless, the gratitude in her hungry eyes speaks for her.

Woe be unto the girl in France who hears divine voices, my own inner voice warns, and I spontaneously remember an earlier Jeanne, Jeanne d'Arc of bygone times.

After I climb into the carriage, I sit heavily upon the bench.

I hear my father's voice, with tears in his eyes and his voice cracking with joy, who tells me, "You are an artist, my child!" Today his prophecy is fulfilled, for I am indeed commissioned to paint the queen of France.

Somewhat ruefully another voice within my head tells me, *Yes, and you are a woman, too, with a husband who has pleasured you, and you with a body well prepared for childbearing.* Involuntarily I place my hand beneath my bosom. My fingertips rub the fabric of my dress, deep rose and brown, maternal colors. Suddenly I long for fresher hues, something of light blue and celery green and sunny yellow.

Would it not be nice to mother a little boy with hair as full of sunshine as the head of a summer dandelion? I ask myself. I am in a state of wonder.

My encounter with the prescient little needlewoman has almost shoved aside my elation that I have been commissioned to paint the queen of France. The thin child's prescience is something I can hardly doubt, for it echoes my own happy intuition about the queen's pregnancy. I am more happy for her than I am for myself, for I know that the demands of pregnancy will take more from my work than I would like, no matter how sunny the child. The queen, the darling, will benefit enormously if she gives birth to a child, especially if the babe should be a boy. For the sake of the family into which she has married, for the sake of her own status, for the sake of France, and one may say for the sake of all of Europe as well, the queen's pregnancy will be the most joyous possible news.

I am pressing the dirty little garment against my mouth as though it were a lawn handkerchief, as though I am about to use it to wipe clear my own tears of joy for the happiness of the queen of France. Taking the little dress by its shoulders, I give it a hard shake within the carriage, but that does nothing toward removing its grayness. Dust is so thoroughly worked into the weave of the fabric that I know it will require soap and scrubbing.

I imagine the young girl sewing beside a window for hours and even weeks. Yes, so much care has been taken with the work that the cloth must have been touched and maneuvered many times by her talented fingers. Still, the garment has no worth if it cannot be made pristine. Should I have let her learn that lesson? I sigh.

It is very easy to ruin a work of art. Or to mar it through some impulse to hurry or because fatigue makes one careless. For now there is nothing to be done but to fold up the tiny gray batiste garment and put it away. I spread the little dress on my knee and fold it in half lengthwise, a soft bend that I do not smooth into a crease. As I softly fold up its length into thirds, something in me rebels against handling cloth less than clean, no matter how delicate its workmanship. Now it is a square shape about the size of my palm. Well, I shall place the garment inside my pocket. I note how truly light, almost weightless the thing is, as light as if it were a stack of folded cobwebs.

And the little seamstress, she was but a wisp herself. My impulse was correct to empty my purse in her hand.

Now the carriage is passing, and I within it, across the wide entrance pavings before the Château de Versailles—marble, then cobblestones. I have spoken with the splendor and grace of Europe; I have seen wan poverty, tantamount to starvation. Through the streets of the town of Versailles, I ponder these visions, and beyond, onto the road that will take us through the countryside back to Paris.

VIII

A CELLO IN THE AFTERNOON

(continued)

FOUNTAIN

THERE WAS ENDLESS SORROW, the cello said, and yearning, but also full-throated fulfillment. A lone woman had jumped from Kathryn's roof; her own parents were dead and buried; but friendship was at hand, and Kathryn could claim it. Down the curved steps, somewhat carelessly she went, with a clatter, an urgency. No need to be isolated in uncertainties.

Long ago a student of Kathryn's (the brilliant Aleda, now dead of cancer) had written a poem euphoniously titled "A Cello in the Afternoon." Those two different but equally elongated *o*-sounds, that was part of what she had loved about Aleda's title: cello, afternoon. And Aleda would have loved this moment: a real cello in the afternoon. Now. The enveloping elegance of St. James Court. The elasticity of time.

And there was Kathryn's beloved fountain, Venus by day, goddess of love and beauty. Her verdigris face seemed triumphant against a sunny ceiling of sky blue. Oh, the fountain of St. James Court: how it refreshed—

green against blue—how it both satisfied and inspired, as she crossed the
daylit Court, pulled by emanations of a cello playing Bach.

As she crossed the Court, Kathryn was tempted to drop some gold
trinket into the grassy ring around the fountain, something that might be
found years and eons hence, by archaeologists (perhaps with faces evolved
to green or blue) so they would know the ancient goddess was still worshipped and offered tributes by a populace far beyond her time, but Kathryn wore no jewelry at all, unless she was dressing up. Amethyst, ruby, and
gold, the jewelry of the trees.

She felt she was holding Time, lightly, appreciatively, by the throat. If
Humphrey were here on St. James Court, she would present him a bouquet of long-stemmed autumn leaves, encircled by her hand.

BY OPENING THE DOOR of her building, Shirley, the resident from the
third floor of the St. James flats, made it easier for Kathryn to enter the
condo building. When the door closed, the resonant tones of the cello fell
as through a funnel down the staircase. "I just love to hear her sawing
away on that bass fiddle." Shirley's words followed Kathryn as she hurried
up the interior stairs. "Don't you?" When Kathryn reached the landing,
she found Leslie's door ajar, and the last note, rich and full with vibrato,
was being released into the air. With her hand on the doorknob, Kathryn
paused and thrust only her head into the room.

THE CELLO SECURED between her knees, Leslie slowly opened her arm,
theatrically, lifting the tip of the bow away from the strings in a wide arc.
"Welcome, stranger," she said, all warmth in the timbre of her voice, in the
tone of her skin.

"Been writing," Kathryn said. Already she felt brighter.

"I know. Been reading." Leslie spoke happily, as though it were one of the
major joys of life to read what Kathryn had written. "But I'm barely started."

"I promised myself I wouldn't ask you about it if I let myself drop in. A social call. How are things going *for you?*"

Loosening the bow at the nut, Leslie said, "The book is pure you." She smiled.

"It's supposed to be Élisabeth. The reader should forget me. How is it pure me?"

"Lined with silken sentences."

"You look happy to see me," Kathryn replied.

"Well, of course I am." And for a moment the two old friends simply beamed at each other, Leslie with the cello between her knees.

"Do you remember," Kathryn continued, "what Woolf's Mrs. Dalloway wanted from life? That people should look happy when she entered the room."

"And that Evelyn Whitbread, the estimable Hugh Whitbread's always ailing wife, never did look happy when Clarissa arrived."

"So you're really and truly moved in?" Kathryn asked. "Here to stay?"

"I think so. I intend so. And yourself?"

"I've been on St. James twelve years, but who knows what life might bring?" Kathryn felt excited and eager. "But I want to be sure of you."

"How fair is that?" Leslie asked, smiling again.

"Critics and readers, too, always say that all my books are different."

"And they are, but they're all you," Leslie replied.

"I hope I'm not turning sows' ears into silk purses." How was it possible, Kathryn wondered, for anyone, for Leslie, to look fresh and graceful every moment of her life? Woodsy, by which she meant *natural,* though sophisticated. Like a doe in the woods, Leslie was, with wide dark eyes and chiseled cheekbones, a quiet, alert, self-contained expression, unless she was speaking. "Then *Portrait* is okay?" Kathryn asked. "So far?" Now she was pushing when she shouldn't, so she rattled on. "I took a little nap on the sunporch—it was midnight last night before I came over—but my nap got interrupted."

"I saw you out earlier with Peter, walking Prince." Leslie gestured at one of the marshmallow beanbag chairs dressed in soft, white leather.

As Kathryn sat down, she fingered the surface of the leather squash chair: pebbly. She would have preferred something more sentimental, a cuddly, brushed nap. "Royal. The poodle's name is Royal. You sounded great on the sarabande."

"Prélude allemande, courante, sarabande, bourée gigue. I messed up the sarabande the first time, too distracted."

Ryn eyed the cello and the cellist as though they were one beast, a study in browns, wood and skin, though Leslie's curly-frizzy hair had puffs of gray in it. "I came out my front door just in time to hear you starting over."

"A title idea came to me for a story while I was reading your book," Leslie said. "'The Death of J. S. Bach.'"

Ryn's attention wandered over the furnishings. Everything seemed freshly placed; everything was aesthetically pleasing and could be savored a great many times without losing its charm. No clutter.

"A new short story." Leslie's glance was bright, eager for her friend's interest. Levering the cello forward from between her knees, Leslie stood up and carried the instrument by its neck to the rigid case standing in a corner, upright and open. "A triumphant story, actually. At least as deaths go." Retracting the endpin, Leslie slid the instrument inside the case, secured it with a strap, and closed the lid, as though it were a door. She sat down again opposite Ryn on the edge of the straight chair, pressed the palms and fingers of her hands together, placed the wedge between her knees, and leaned forward.

"Part of a story collection based on lives of the composers, *Moments Musicaux*."

"Americans might have trouble with the French title," Ryn warned, but already she was thinking of great performances she herself had witnessed. Moments that should be immortalized.

This was the way of their conversations: they branched and branched, but usually they kept track of their branchings and could return to the point of juncture to redirect their topics.

"In 1968," Ryn began, "when I was in London with my mother and James, we went to hear the Russian orchestra at the Victoria and Albert Hall." James had sometimes called her *Piggle*. "The Soviet Union had just invaded Czechoslovakia, and they were scheduled to play the Dvořák Cello Concerto with Rostropovich as soloist. He was still with the Soviets then." As Ryn told the story, Leslie rose, and Ryn followed her into the kitchen, talking.

Ryn knew that Leslie knew Ryn wanted her to fix a snack, that Leslie could do it with ease, that Leslie would be happy to fix something good for her—simple or elaborate.

"When the orchestra began, the audience started shouting in English, 'Freedom for Czechoslovakia!' and in Russian, 'Freedom for Czechoslovakia!' The rafters rang with it, but the conductor conducted like mad, and the orchestra played like mad, and some people shouted, 'They're just musicians!' and 'Let them play!' And the audience quieted down.

"Then after the Dvořák, Rostropovich came out by himself to play an encore. He played the Bach sarabande you were just playing."

Leslie stopped, leaned back against the stove, listening.

"It was the saddest thing in the world, the way Rostropovich played it. It was so clear that he was offering an apology for what his country had done."

"Terrifically moving," Leslie murmured. "You should write that story."

"It was a wonderful moment for the three of us," Ryn said. "All of us loving the timeless music so much and being so much a part of that moment." She remembered how James had held his face lifted, his large nose tilted as though he were breathing in the music. And her mother, with a slight set smile, determined not to be moved to tears. Her mother, glad she was alive, in London for the first time, fulfilled in that moment. For the sake of the trip, Ryn had paused in her graduate studies, taught in Muscatine for a whole year to earn the money—a trip to Europe for her mother, and for James and herself as companions. "Of course Rostropovich defected to the U.S. later. Became an advocate for human rights globally."

Leslie took the teakettle to the sink to fill it. "Like Casals," she murmured.

Moments Musicaux. Ryn recalled Leslie's French title, an allusion to Franz Schubert's *Moments Musicaux,* and felt bad to have sounded a cautionary note about it. "How big a collection of stories?" she asked Leslie.

"Maybe just six. A slender volume." Her eyes twinkled with the phrase *a slender volume.* When they were freshmen in college together, they had both said how lovely it would be to meet a young man on campus with long legs, his back against a tree, reading a slender volume of poems. For Ryn, Giles had been that young man, well discovered.

There had been the college Daniel, too (not Daisy's husband), not slender and long-legged but with the desired sensibility, despite his compact body. An organist and choir director, alive in every fiber of his being, a lover of Wordsworth. Quick, full of discerning empathy, but politically conservative. Kathryn's soul had divided, loving them both, ecstatically, chastely, first Daniel, then Giles.

Leslie had married mature men of practical sense, capable of success, socially viable, but men with secret vices under their respectable surfaces. The first marriage had postponed the completion of Leslie's education for decades.

"Apple cinnamon tea?" Reaching high, Leslie took ivory, gold-rimmed cups from their shelf. She popped two poppy seed muffins (strange flat seeds, pale, paving their crowns) into the toaster oven.

"Actually, I'd rather have hot chocolate," Ryn said. "I'm upset. I'll make it," she offered, "if you've got any cocoa." She felt guilty that Leslie was always "doing" for her. It seemed vaguely racist. Or was anxiety about being racist even more racist? But Kathryn was inept in the kitchen.

Leslie promptly took a canister of designer cocoa off the shelf and handed it to Ryn. Till Ryn spoke of what troubled her, Leslie would quietly wait, but Ryn fussed with the chocolate and the sugar, measuring them, getting milk from the fridge, till finally Leslie asked, "What's upset you, Ryn?"

Ryn explained that a stranger had come to her door to ask her if she knew that a woman had jumped to her death off the roof of Ryn's house.

"Maybe he was making it up." Leslie looked into Ryn's eyes to test the hypothesis. "This is an old neighborhood. Probably every possible human and inhuman act has been committed here. Let me make the chocolate. Just like in the suburbs. Every house, not just yours, probably has been connected with a death, and a birth, and a wedding. And a huge business coup, and an utter failure. Didn't the poet Madison Cawein go bankrupt in your house and move over here?"

"Yes, the apartment over yours. In 1914."

"Shall I put a dash of pepper in the chocolate, Mexican-style?" When Kathryn nodded, Leslie shook cayenne into the palm of her hand, then pinched up a tiny quantity and sprinkled it into the pot. A few grains fell on the glass stovetop. Ryn passed the long-handled wooden spoon to Leslie, who took up the stirring. "Don't let it boil, even a little," Leslie said.

"So what is it—" Ryn asked in a solemn key (she could say anything to Leslie); "—so what is it that holds a person together?"

"In difficult times?"

"Especially then, but not just then: what is the necessary and always present, to varying degrees, glue? I heard Mark is getting married again."

"Love and beauty," Leslie answered. She glanced up from swirling the chocolate; her face was lovely, completely open and sincere, her eyes surprisingly dark; then her gaze turned back to the spoon stirring the hot cocoa.

"Well, now, you *do* have them," Kathryn responded quickly, glad that Leslie passed over the news as though it didn't matter. Never mind Mark, on to ideals.

"*Aphro*dite at your doorstep," Leslie laughed, turning toward Ryn, primping her hair, and cocking her hip. "Pun intended." In that moment of vanity, the unwatched chocolate frothed up in a matrix of cloudy, brown-tinged bubbles.

"Watch out!" Ryn exclaimed.

Leslie lifted the pot from the burner and the bubbles collapsed.

"It'll still taste good," Ryn consoled.

"Not *as* good," Leslie said, and shook her head. "Should I start over?"

"Of course not, silly. Ever onward."

Leslie poured the chocolate into the ivory cups, and their embossed golden edges shone like twin halos presenting disks of cocoa.

"Tuxedo—isn't that your china pattern?" Ryn asked.

"I bought a whole set of Tuxedo in New York. But they don't make this style of cup anymore. These were my grandmother's." Leslie placed the warm muffins onto a cream-colored plastic tray with a bend that formed handle-like edges.

Following Leslie down the hall, Ryn remarked that she didn't really regret any of her three marriages. How could she? They had led to this. "It's a beautiful neighborhood," Ryn babbled on. "Totally devoid of pretension, as unself-conscious as a grand old tree." Ryn wanted to be like her neighborhood. What was to regret?

They settled themselves on the balcony behind the wrought-iron railing. "This is my favorite perch," Leslie said. "One time my therapist asked me what did it feel like, enjoying a conversation with a woman friend, with you, for example."

"What did you say?"

"I said"—her tone was suddenly confidential, ecstatic—" 'It makes me feel as though *I get to fly.*' "

Exactly so. Kathryn's eyes brimmed with happiness. Conspirators, they glanced at each other. Leslie took a neat, decisive bite of the warm poppy muffin. "I regret both of my marriages," she said matter-of-factly. "They were mistakes." She sighed, but she did not look unhappy. "Bad choices. Mistakes on my part."

"Truly?" Ryn questioned, for Leslie's words frightened Ryn. Life had failed, if her friend was unhappy.

"Yum, that's good." Leslie licked her fingers. "I love warm muffin, that minute crunch of poppy seeds, almost indiscernible. Yes. They were mistakes. Bad judgment."

"But you seem fine," Ryn said. And so Leslie could do that: fully regret, but not bitterly, not in a way that blighted the present.

"I am."

Ryn usually felt compelled to soften the past, to salvage something from it that kept it from dwelling entirely in the land of woeful error. Leslie was more honest.

"When I finished the book, I had to think about his marrying again. Then the Mark-ache rushed in. I believed we'd be together till one of us died." Oh, it was no problem, ever, to mention death in conversation with Leslie. They believed in death. "Once I was in love with a man," Kathryn digressed, "a Vietnam vet. What I realized was that I wouldn't be afraid to die, if he held my hand. I've never loved anybody else like that." She paused, wondering what it was about Will that had engendered such an idea. No, she hadn't loved Mark like that; Mark cared nothing for her inner life. Will had known her for who she was. She hadn't suited him, finally, but she had felt known, affirmed, anyway. "But I thought Mark and I would be there in some almost-acceptable way for each other." She hesitated, then added, looking at the floor, "I've been thinking about Giles and about Frieda." She had been much younger then, at college, back in the sixties; she'd met Will in the nineties.

"Do you miss them?" Leslie knew about both Giles and Frieda, what had happened to them.

"They died so long ago, when I was very young, I don't think of them often," Ryn continued, "but sometimes there it is. As fresh as it was nearly fifty years ago. I remember them perfectly, variously. I treasure every memory." She took a moment to imagine Frieda's face again, her dark eyes, the slight, mysterious smile when rising thoughts or feelings were coming into focus, and Giles's sharp nose, his quick glance, something breathless, caught off guard, uncertain and appealing, for all his clear intelligence.

How much resilience did she have left? She contemplated the fountain, the cascade of water, the thin, sky-climbing jets from the conch boys. "Now I realize Mark valued me the least of any of my husbands. My thoughts and feelings, who I was, had little interest to him. I had to look that fact in the face today. It hurts. Not to be seen."

"Well, we have to value ourselves. You know that." Leslie spoke matter-of-factly again. Yes, she was straightforward and truthful about hard facts. She was courageous in a way Ryn was not. Leslie was like the painter, Élisabeth, in that way; it was something Ryn loved and needed about Leslie.

"Once when I was crying," said Ryn—she didn't mention the pivotal importance of the terrible moment—"I asked Mark to look at me because I couldn't believe how my mouth felt, as though my lower lip had been pulled down over my chin." Ryn kept her eyes on the fountain, the still beauty of Venus in the midst of the living water. She didn't want to cry. "Something was contorting my face. I got up to see for myself. To look in the bathroom mirror. Horrifying, the way my lower lip curled almost over my chin, as though I were trying to devour myself."

"The mask of tragedy."

Ryn sniffed. She refused to cry. This day was to be a happy day, a triumphant day. "He scarcely glanced at me. Over his shoulder he said I'd probably have to cry like that several more times before I got over it."

"Till you got over it?"

"He didn't care how many times I turned wrong-side-out. He didn't care how it hurt. I'd never seen him so callous about anything. He likes to come on as supersensitive. When he said what he said, his tone, then I knew I couldn't get over it. It wasn't about morality, adultery; it was about total betrayal and uncaring ignorance of who I am or what's important to me."

"But now he's not with you. And you are going to get over it." Leslie was perfectly firm.

"It made me feel like shit today."

"I know. I'm sorry."

And Ryn knew Leslie knew, and so it was over.

"This is partly a postpartum attack. You've just produced another book."

"I'm always happy when I finish my first drafts," Ryn wailed. "I buy things!"

"Yes, but it's mixed, isn't it, the feeling of finishing. A little ambivalent?"

No, Ryn didn't think so, but maybe that was the way it had been for Leslie when she had finished her book.

Leslie extended the index finger of her left hand for Ryn's inspection. "I'm working on developing a callus, from my practicing."

"Are you enjoying it?"

"I am. I'm just playing pieces that I once played very well. I'm sure I'll get it back faster that way than tackling something brand-new. I want to build the calluses gradually. I'll probably not get as good as I was, but who knows? It helps me with my writing."

"What about the Bach story?"

"Yes. 'The Death of Bach.' I don't know if it's true or not. If it's not, I'll frame it with a character who needs to imagine Bach's death the way she, or maybe he, needs it to be. We write about what we need to explore, don't we?

"When Bach was dying—you know he was terrifically prolific and end-lessly inventive—he was composing a piece he called 'Before the Throne of God I Come.' He was too weak to scribble, the story goes, so he had one of his sons there at his bedside with a feather pen and tablet, and he dictated from his deathbed to one of his musical sons.

"In the scale, they're tones, notes named for letters of the alphabet, 'b' and 'a' and 'c' and in German there's a tone represented by the letter 'h,' a label we don't use.

"So, Bach is on his deathbed—a son taking dictation—creating music to the end, 'Before the Throne of God I Come,' and then he spells out his name, *B, A, C, H,* with the letter names of musical notes. Then he stops. And then Bach actually dies. Of course that's not the end of the story as I'd write it. It would be an awful ending for a short story. Just the seed story."

"Yes, you couldn't end the story there. But say why not." Now Ryn was excited. Always it was all right to push Leslie, always Leslie had already questioned, tested her own conclusions.

"Because I don't believe it. As an ending."

Ryn took a sip of her hot chocolate. Now almost tepid. The thickened skim floating on the top, which she relished, stuck to her upper lip.

"What do you think?" Leslie asked.

"You made me imagine the scene, the deathbed, the pillows stacked up. In the eighteenth century, everybody slept propped up. Only the dead or the poor lay flat. Of course the point of view you tell it from will make a difference."

"I know. I could tell it from the son's point of view, or from Bach's. Or some fictive character. Stylistically, the texture will be crucial. The story will be short. Maybe have moral weight to it the way the late Tolstoy stories do, like 'How Much Land Does a Man Need?' "

"I think your idea is wonderful. Write it. Write it today," Ryn urged. "Never mind reading *Portrait*. But I don't much like the late Tolstoy stories. Too didactic. Totally engineered in a mechanical way to make some moral point. That's why you can't end with Bach's dying. Your story is about transcendent aesthetic experience. Spirituality, not morality. But I do love 'The Death of Ivan Ilyich.' Have you read that?"

When Leslie said she hadn't read "Ivan Ilyich," Ryn told her that she would love it. "It's told retrospectively. Ilyich is already dead in the beginning. You should read it before you write 'The Death of Bach.' 'Ivan Ilyich' is about the power and the spiritual importance of empathy."

"Too bad you couldn't teach it to Mark."

"Ivan's peasant servant truly empathizes with Ivan, so finally Ivan is able to empathize with his little son, who is frightened that his father's dying. After Ivan experiences empathy, accepting and giving it, he becomes human. He can die."

"I suppose Mark didn't get enough empathy extended to him when he was a kid."

"I gave Mark lots and lots of empathy. Really I did."

"I know you did. Maybe it was too late. In his case."

For a moment they both rested in the peace of friendship.

"I wish I could be like my friend in Minnesota. She notices every-thing, *enjoys* everything. Reading, travel, music, flowers, weather. Lynn's an original. We e-mail each other often; we used to travel together a lot. She's been chronically ill for a dozen years. When she's well enough, she enjoys all kinds of folk dances, even Scottish dances, leaping up into the air. Everybody wants to be in her group. She ignites everybody."

"Lynn? You've told me about her. Invite her down." Leslie smiled warmly at Ryn.

"I have. She likes to take walks around the lakes, in St. Paul. Last win-ter she wrote me that she had seen two birds, close together standing on the ice. One was a crow and one was a seagull. They walked along, chirp-ing, as though they were talking to each other. Lynn knows I want her to visit. But she has her own rhythm."

"Like your Élisabeth Vigée-Le Brun."

"Don't you love that about Élisabeth as an old woman? She has her own sense of order. Winter in the city; spring and summer in the country, at Louveciennes."

Leslie nodded toward the sentinel oaks at the entrance of the south segment of the Court. "I haven't read that far. Where did Élisabeth spend the autumn?" The sentinels still held brown clusters of leaves, shaggy and determined.

"She was a colorist. Probably she waited to go to Paris till she felt win-ter chill. Then she'd want velvet, the heavy silk of the drawing rooms, the thick rugs. She was like Lynn; Élisabeth relished everything. When she lived in Russia, Élisabeth marveled at how warm the aristocrats were able to keep their homes. Citrus trees thriving in tiled sunrooms. The rooms perfumed with pleasant incense."

"I haven't gotten to that part yet, either," Leslie said.

"I might have forgotten to include the description of how Élisabeth marveled at the indoor warmth. I suppose I should go home so you can get back to reading?"

"You don't have to. I'll finish today for sure. I'll want to think it over,

sleep on it, make some notes before we talk. Come over about midafternoon, tomorrow, and we'll sit here and talk. *Portrait*'s not as long as your
books usually are."

"I know. I'm getting older, I could say." How delicious the chocolate
was but a little too cool now, like chocolate milk for a child. Really, she'd
like to pour it back in the pot and heat it up again, but she knew that would
be an imposition on Leslie. "But actually, I wanted it to be short. Joyce's
Portrait of the Artist as a Young Man isn't very long. I wanted this to have
a similar size. I wasn't trying to overwhelm the great male master with
sheer number of pages."

"Male chauvinist? Or just a creature of his times?"

"He only feels Catholic guilt for going to prostitutes. He cares very
little in that book for women as human beings."

Leslie said nothing. They had argued about Joyce before; they could
agree that the opening of his *Portrait* was brilliant. His sensitivity to childish language—the moocow.

"Who is anyone great, as an artist," Ryn went on, "if she or he doesn't
transcend the prejudices of her own times? Think of somebody like John
Stuart Mill—his autobiography—he lived well before Joyce; John Stuart
Mill respected his wife and women in general as equals."

"You mainly tell Élisabeth's story methodically, chronologically," Leslie observed.

"I wanted to give her her whole life. The length and devotion of her
life to her career is part of the point of a portrait of her as an old woman.
Joyce is all about the excitement and miracle of finally managing just to
resolve to get started. An equal wonder for any artist is in sustaining joyful
work."

"Of course Joyce did, in actuality, in his own life." Leslie liked Joyce
more than Ryn did.

"But that's not the focus of his *Portrait*."

"Well, he was a relatively young man when he wrote it, and you—"

"Yes, I'm about to be an old woman. Many people would say we are old women." Ryn grinned. "Look, there's Daisy, sans dogs," she added, nodding at the sidewalk beneath the balcony.

"Maybe I'll get to know Daisy better," Leslie remarked.

"Shall I call to her?"

Ryn suddenly realized she wasn't ready to go home, to haunt the house by herself. The image of Ellen's snub-nosed revolver, sequestered inside gray cloth, came to mind. Because the cylinder was swung open, one side of the soft storage bag bulged out like a deformity. In a corner of the drawstring sack, six hollow-nosed bullets and three pointed ones loosely nestled together. And suppose Jerry were to come back, and her alone in the house. He hated her, she knew. He hated that she'd been able to work hard, to become a success. "Shall I call to Daisy?" She could tell them both she felt afraid of Jerry? Or just tell Daisy later? No. Neither. Why worry Leslie or Daisy?

What a pleasure to talk with Leslie, to reconnect. They *had* flown; their spirits had sailed.

Ryn didn't want to stop; she didn't want to leave her perch on Leslie's balcony. Add a new element instead. Daisy.

"If you like, invite her up. Do it," Leslie answered.

"Daisy," Ryn called, her voice swallowed by the volumes of air.

At first Daisy looked around uncertainly, so Ryn called again. Remembering that Daisy was a little deaf in one ear, sometimes, Ryn shouted more loudly the third time.

When Daisy looked up toward the balconies, both women waved.

"Won't you, please, join us?" Leslie called.

"Certainly," Daisy answered, making sure her voice carried.

To Leslie, Ryn said, "I'll just run down and let her in. Want to put the teakettle on?"

After clattering down the steps (you're being careless again, she admonished herself; want another broken ankle?), she held the entrance door open.

She gave Daisy a warm squeeze and told her Leslie had been wanting to get better acquainted. "I finished my book," she told Daisy. "We're celebrating on the balcony in the fresh air and admiring the fountain."

"Congratulations! That's wonderful," Daisy answered, her voice eager.

At the landing, Kathryn was surprised to run into Shirley again, from the third floor.

"Reckon y'all are having a regular party today," Shirley commented, almost hopefully.

"Not really," Kathryn answered. "Leslie has been wanting to meet Daisy." With that Kathryn opened the door and gestured to Daisy to step in.

Quickly Shirley asked Daisy, "Who was that little girl you were walking with?"

"She was just a little lost child," Daisy answered firmly. "That's all taken care of now. I took her home with me for a little while until we contacted her mother."

After Leslie's door was closed, Daisy said softly, "I'm afraid someone feels left out." She rolled her eyes toward the closed door. "But I do appreciate your not inviting her. My hearing seems to be acting up."

PRACTICALLY SLAMMED THE DOOR IN MY FACE, Shirley thought. Not so friendly today. Oh, the hoity-toity Dr. Writer was pleasant enough if you met her on the street, but she never asked anybody inside. Howdy-do, and that was it. And Daisy had been a neighbor when Shirley lived on Belgravia, but now that Shirley had had to move, well, she might as well be dust under their feet. The flats were good enough for some people, but what about an ordinary couple, like Trevor and her, near retirement age? Shirley closed her eyes at the idea of retirement. She saw a black wall. They'd lost a third of their retirement money when the economy went bad.

Quite on purpose, Shirley stamped up to the third floor, but her eyes were full of tears. She hoped they heard her, that cozy little trio!

Better to be angry than sad, she thought, wrenching open her condo door and slamming it shut behind her. Now that reverberated, for sure! She would sit on her balcony. She would time them. There was only one front door, and Ms. Callaghan (people said her third husband had left her) and Mrs. Shepard would have to go out it.

Goodness, it was high up here. Enough to make a person feel dizzy. High and very bright, for the third-floor balconies, having no other stories above them, were open to the sky. Clouds were moving in from the southwest. That was the direction tornadoes came from, but these clouds were like white heaps of meringue; nothing menacing there. Shirley herself felt like a small, upright thundercloud. But the northwest sky *was* turning gray. Nobody else had such a view as this. Perhaps royalty commanded this kind of vista. Who was that guy in Texas who got up in a high tower with a high-powered rifle and picked people off, one by one, below? He was a groundbreaker, the first lunatic to decide to just kill strangers at random because the world was a rotten place. Which university? The idea had trickled down to schoolchildren now. What was wrong with education? People were lucky she wasn't like that. Still she could understand how they felt, those snipers and suicide bombers. She wondered if the whole world would ever go to war again.

Shirley sat down in one of the iron spring chairs. Getting it up to the third floor had been quite a challenge. She had carried it by one arm, and Trevor had carried it by the other. Although they had laughed about it, the method had worked. Whenever one of them was tired, they stopped and rested, balancing the clumsy chair on the edge of the steps. She checked her watch. She wouldn't waste too much time on lookout. Even though it was mid-October, up here the afternoon sun was almost too hot. Three o'clock. The trees were fiery; the red leaves like fury consuming itself.

At a quarter past three, an ice-cream truck came down the Court, broadcasting "Clementine" in a tinkling bell version. "Oh my darling, oh my darling, oh my darling Clementine. You are lost and gone forever . . ." But that's not true, Shirley thought, not of anyone she had ever really loved. Both her parents were still alive, and all her siblings. Her husband enjoyed his new job; he was cheerful nearly every day when he came home from work. He said he was getting used to the stairs; the climb was good for him. It was just the house that was lost, the place she had loved so much on Belgravia Court.

Placing her hands beside her mouth to make a megaphone, she called out, "Ice-cream man, ice-cream man, I want some!" But the truck and its music were making too much noise. You had to be down there waving at him to make the ice-cream man stop. The truck didn't even circle around the south end of the Court to come down her side of the grassy median. Crossing Belgravia, it just went on out the south end of St. James onto Hill Street.

But someone below was shouting her name. When she looked down, she saw Daisy, both her hands placed like parentheses beside her mouth.

"Come see me sometime soon," Daisy called.

Shirley shouted down, explaining she needed to get started on supper before Trevor came home, but Daisy didn't seem to understand. She put one hand behind her ear. Finally she shouted, "I can't understand. Just come see me, soon."

To indicate she understood, Shirley nodded her head up and down vigorously. She had forgotten Daisy was a little deaf—not bad, but sometimes she liked to be close to you and looking in your face while she listened. The noise of the fountain was louder than rain. In return to Shirley's gesture, now Daisy nodded her own head up and down to signal that she, too, understood; then she fluttered her hand in good-bye and turned to walk toward home, back to Belgravia.

So the trio had had their little party. It hadn't lasted long. Nice of Daisy to holler up an invitation. Not too high class, but that was one thing about Daisy: she knew when to ignore all that and just be human.

AFTER DAISY LEFT LESLIE'S CONDO, Ryn lingered yet another moment. She sensed there was something else Leslie had intended to say to her, but they'd gotten distracted. Yes, she loved the digressive nature of their conversations, how one thing led to another, but wasn't there something else she needed to learn from Leslie? Ryn remembered an old metaphor about her congeniality with Frieda. *Our minds are like two meadows,* she had told Frieda, *with no fence in between.* Yes. How free, how verdant, it had been. And just this afternoon, Ryn remembered, Leslie had said about their conversation: *It's as though I get to fly.*

"End of day is a natural metaphor for end of life," Leslie suddenly said. "In the morning, we wake up to consciousness from some other place. At night, we leave consciousness. In between, a day holds something of the variety of life, something of our generosity, something of our failures. It's a natural shape for narrative."

RYN NEEDED METAPHOR, something that could contain it all.

Outside, by herself, she looked at the fountain, the scrolled underside of the chalice and the surface of the receiving pool with its myriad bowls of dancing water. She would walk some more. Maybe over to Third Street to admire the mansions there. Perhaps she would walk till it was nearly time for Yves to arrive. Well, she'd save a little time to shower and change clothes. And what was it—the glue that held it all together—when you had to face the terror?

IX
VIGNETTES

PORTRAIT

WHEN I FIRST HEAR THE EXCLAMATION "Why, she paints like a man!" I am pleased; I take it only to mean that my work is truly excellent. But insult is also intended, and the innuendo, indeed the idea is expressed overtly, that my brush is my manly part!

I cannot help but note that it is soon after I have been commissioned to paint the queen that a rumor is bandied about at court and among intellectual and artistic circles that I do not do my own work, but that a man has done it. A woman could not have done so well, they claim. I think some women in these groups might accept my talent were I more ugly than they. I think some male painters would be less aggrieved if I did not command more lucrative fees than they.

My gender makes up part of my individuality as an artist, just as it does for any man, but we are distinctive for the *complexity* of our individuality, of which gender is only a part. For some that consideration of gender may be minor (I think it is for me), but for others major. My teachers have been men, as were most of the old masters; no wonder there are traces of "masculine" technique in my work.

The dear queen, because she is powerful in her own way, is the victim of much more vicious gossip about her person. Men are frightened of our power; hers as a monarch, daughter of the powerful Empress Maria Theresa of Austria. Antoinette is labeled *l'Autrichienne* by those who criticize her. But what is shockingly disgusting is that Antoinette is depicted in cartoons as a harpy, or as a hermaphrodite, with both male and female parts. They want not just to slander her but to suggest she is unnatural, a monster with monstrous powers, someone to be hated.

I am also slandered morally as the mistress of the minister of finance, the Vicomte de Calonne, whose portrait I painted. While I consider it one of my most successful works, the work was painted in bits and pieces, due to his busy schedule, and he scarcely had time for even a conversation of any depth. Rumors include the idea that he paid me with some sweets known as butterflies, each wrapped in a banknote of large denomination, and another slander is that my fee was high enough to bankrupt the entire treasury and the money was delivered in a pie! The truth is that M. de Calonne paid me only four thousand francs, which one may compare to a fee of eight thousand from M. de Beaujon for a painting of similar size and detail, which no one considered an extravagant payment.

"YOUR BABY WILL COME TODAY," my experienced friend tells me.

"But that is impossible," I reply, "for I have someone sitting for a portrait today, and my subject arrives soon for her appointment."

My friend would not be dissuaded, but my whole body (ponderous but so what?) leaps upward from reclining to sit ready before my easel and to dwell in the delight of my work. Despite my readiness for work, my friend insists on sending for the doctor. She assures me that I will not have to look at him till the crucial moment, for she will hide him in our home so that his presence will not offend me. Indeed, I am so absorbed, as usual, that I forget he is in the house.

Thus Julie is born, after a good day's work, with the odor of turpentine for cleaning my brushes still on my fingers when I first hold and love her as herself. I cannot describe the joy I feel when I first hear the voice of my child, her small cries.

WHEN I LOOK IN THE MIRROR, I see no hint of masculinity in my visage, and I determine to paint a self-portrait that will depict my nature aright. While I have a dual identity, that of new mother and also of artist, I look merely like a young girl, and that is my truest nature perhaps.

I am standing by myself, a bust portrait, looking straight out at the viewer. It is 1781 and my baby is very young. I am alone in the picture: I wear a white blouse and it fits close to my neck and falls in three simple ruffles; my blouse and my pale face comprise the center of light which is surrounded by darkness, for I wear a black hat that blends with the brown background, and a black lace shawl curves around my shoulder.

A cerise ribbon bow is planted among the ruffles of my blouse. It is a very pert and girlish bow, pleased with its own crispness. When I painted Marie Antoinette for the first time, in a dress with very wide panniers, there was a similar bow placed lower, one that blended with her ivory dress, and my bow chimes with hers.

In my self-portrait below my breast, there is a wide cerise band that matches the ribbon bow, but the sash is in shadow and not of much importance in the composition, except to help mark the bottom of the painting. The third use of the inviting cerise color is used upon my lips.

The most beautiful part, and the most beautifully painted part, of the picture is the opal earring that hangs from my right ear. The other side of my face is in shadow. On the illumined side of my body, below the pretty earring, the form of my right breast, small but pleasantly rounded, is clearly suggested by the way the blouse fits me. My face shows a hint of a smile just beginning.

Perhaps I wish to say, through this painting of 1781, *Though I am now a young mother I still look like a girl, for the neckline is high and modest; I am still myself; I paint with serious ardor.* I label this painting *Self-Portrait with Cerise Ribbon.*

I PARTICULARLY RESENT THE IDEA that I am extravagant when my husband is the extravagant one, and against my advice he is having a house built for us in Rue du Gros-Chenet. M. Le Brun is in a holy fury about the rumors of extravagance, which only serve to ignite him to wild flights of fancy. "Let the rumors fly," he declares. "After you die, I shall build a pyramid in my garden that reaches to the sky, and I shall have engraved on its sides a list of all your paintings. Then they will know how you earned your fortune." I try to chuckle at this fantasy, but it is disconcerting for my husband to imagine me dead, while he spends on. I wear muslin and dress my own hair, and I don an elaborate dress only when I visit the Château de Versailles to paint the queen. Here at Rue de Cléry, he consigns me to a small antechamber and a bedroom, which also serves as my salon. It seems not to matter; friends from all stations of life are eager to be invited to my salon in my bedroom or to attend a small supper in the anteroom.

On these occasions, when he wishes to attend, M. Le Brun is also a convivial part of the company. He takes great care with his appearance. In the summer months at home, he dons a white damask coat, often with a shawl collar. His stockings are also white, but the buckles on his shoes are gold. His breeches are made of expensive Oriental nankeen. Perhaps it is to fit in with the nobility that he powders his hair when he knows I detest powdered hair.

WE HAVE BECOME TRAVELERS! For the sake of purchasing new acquisitions for M. Le Brun's business (paintings owned by Prince Charles are being auctioned), we are traveling in Flanders and Belgium.

In Antwerp, as soon as I see the Rubens portrait of the famous *Chapeau de Paille*, I feel inspired to treat light as he has treated it, in a painting of my own. Rubens uses two light sources, the ambient daylight and also the bright direct rays of the sun. The simple daylight, then, becomes "shadow" in the interplay, and the highlighted parts are the direct sunlight. In order to embody what I have just learned by viewing Rubens's portrait, I commence a new self-portrait. I *feel* that I do dwell in daylight, while I am working on this self-portrait. In Brussels!

It is glorious to be out in the world, beyond France, and there is a freedom in the very sky which I've rendered behind my figure in this self-portrait. I feel that I am myself. I have stepped forward, in this self-portrait, as an artist, for I hold my palette and brushes in my hand as I paint them.

How better to learn a technique for matching the inner life, the emotions, with their outer representations than by painting oneself? Then alone does one know the truth of the inner matter and of the putative match appearing on the canvas. Certainly any painter tries to enter the soul of her subject through the imagination, but that inner reality of another is actually inaccessible, in the visual arts, except as it is expressed in bodily gestures or in facial expressions we fancy we have learned to read. Only when one is painting a self-portrait can one check for accuracy between what one is feeling and what is rendered on canvas. As an artist, I feel free and full of joy, of self-fulfillment.

Even while my hand does its sure work, my mind compares and contrasts this work to my *Self-Portrait with Cerise Ribbon*.

Now I do not look self-contained or thoughtful; I look confident. Joy is alive in every stroke of my brush. I am wearing the same opal earrings in both paintings, but this time the viewer can see both of them, for I am looking straight ahead into the daylight.

I'm wearing now a straw hat (not a black hat) with blue, white, and red flowers encircling its flat crown. The brim of the hat swoops in a lazy *S* sideways over my brow and is quite fetching. The hat brim prevents the direct light from illumining part of my face. There is, loosely defined, what one might perceive as a curved shadow across my face, but it is actually the ambient light. The brightest part of the painting, in the direct rays of the sun, shows my right cheek, my neck, and my bosom. The neckline of my dress is no longer modest and girlish but dips low, and a white lace collar ripples around my bosom revealing a young woman's décolletage. The bow is loose and wilted, used, not crisp.

In the earlier painting, my hands, lest that excite envy, were not even included. What is important now is that, in my left hand, I am holding my color-laden palette and a bouquet of paintbrushes; and my right hand, which is near the bottom of the painting, is open and relaxed, ready to pluck a brush from the bundle and commence work. The colors on the palette are the same colors as those of the flowers on my hat. The painting says, "Yes, I am an artist, and as for those flowers on my hat, why, it is I who have just painted them."

This painting is glorious with color, authoritatively used. Someone might say I was influenced by Rubens, and that would be true. But his lady in a straw hat is looking up in a coy fashion, while I look fearlessly forward. My painting says my hands are more interesting than my bosom. His does not convey this idea: quite the opposite. His says: Here is a coy woman with a lovely bosom; mine says: Here is a woman who is an artist; her hands are the instruments of creation, and she chooses to re-create herself, here, on this canvas.

And that shade of blue that I have achieved for the sky? It is the sky I loved as a little girl, bold and confident, supported as I was by both my parents; it is the sky behind the painting of John the Baptist on the wall of the Church of Saint Eustache.

But my lips! Yes, they are the Cupid's bow of the fresh girl-mother, but the smile is definite and inviting. Why? I have been treated to great courtesies, M. Le Brun and I, by the Prince de Ligne, who is the most seductive man I have ever seen. In return, I smile at him and his world, and even at Rubens!

Not for a moment would I betray the standards inculcated in me by my mother (never mind the loose behavior of our husbands), but I am free to feel what I feel. I am free to enjoy and, with sympathetic vibration, to validate the joy of congeniality.

Yes, I am forever yoked to my husband, but this is the art of living: to feel what I feel; to be in no way repressed, mentally or emotionally; and to find the means both artistically and personally to let out the light that is within me.

How glad I am, at last, to travel with my husband, and to see the world beyond the borders of my country. To have painted *Self-Portrait with a Straw Hat*.

WHEN I SHOW THIS PORTRAIT of 1783 to Joseph Vernet, the mentor of my maiden days and now my friend, he wishes, on the strength of it and others, to nominate me as a member of the Académie Royale de Peinture.

A M. Pierre opposes my admission because he does not believe in including women. It is pointed out to him that Mme Vallayer-Coster, a flower painter of genuine talent, has been made a member. Genuine lovers of art created a petition in my favor, and they circulated a verse: "To rob you of your honor / One must have a heart / Of stone, of stone, of stone"; the verse puns on the name Pierre, meaning stone.

As my entry, I submit *Peace Bringing Back Abundance,* which as an allegorical painting ranks higher in the categories of the Académie than does portraiture. And I am admitted.

I like so much my self-portrait in a straw hat that I also paint one of the queen in a straw hat and wearing a simple muslin dress. It is such a simple dress that some viewers are indignant and claim that I have painted her disrespectfully in her nightgown. That I should show disrespect for the queen is absurd. Muslin is her own favorite garb, which she always wears at the Petit Trianon where she is most at ease with her friends, away from the atmosphere of the court at the Château de Versailles. She also wears muslin (as I do) to save money. A court dress requires thirty-six yards of silk. But the silk merchants have risen up in arms, saying that the queen is ruining their business, by her example. The queen meant only to do good for the country by guarding its treasury.

Using the same three-quarter-length pose, I paint her again (much more formally) in blue silk trimmed with white lace; in both portraits she is holding a pink rose, the emblem of beauty, but to me she is far more beautiful in the simple white frock. I also paint her closest friend, the Duchesse de Polignac, the lover of the Comte de Vaudreuil, in muslin with a simple pink sash at her waist. She is, indeed, very pretty.

YES, THERE BEGINS TO BE some repetition in my works, some might say, but if one were to listen more closely, one would actually hear a conversation among them. One painting comments on and often extends the ideas of another.

But to try something entirely new, I decide to paint two ambassadors from India, whom I glimpse at the opera. I love to paint flesh, and theirs offers complexity in a new key. I remember my talented student, Mlle Émilie Roux de la Ville, and wish she too could see and paint the coppery flesh of the father and son from India. I send them a note of request, but they reply that only by direction from His Majesty will they consent to pose for me, for they have been sent to Paris by their emperor, Tippoo Saib.

However, with the help of His Majesty and by agreeing to come to their house, I do gain access, painting first one and then the other, while the paint is drying, back and forth. I am in a kind of paradise of exoticism, and I feel that they bring the sun and earth of their country with them. I enjoy their drapery, of course—they are dressed in white muslin gowns, embroidered with flowers worked in gold thread, and wear tunics with loose sleeves folded back and elaborately decorated belts and hems—but it is my greatest pleasure to paint their faces and necks and hands.

While the son assumes a standing pose for his portrait, with his hand on his dagger, I paint the father, who has a splendid head, seated. Of course their flesh, bones, and expressions vary, just as ours do. They are a study, though in separate frames, of comparison and contrast, and I feast on them and learn with voracious appetite.

My friend Mme de Bonneuil is curious about meeting these ambassadors, and I am able to arrange through the interpreter that she and I be invited to dine with them. To our amazement, we eat on the floor, lying down beside the table. They serve us with their own bronze hands, lifting the food from the dishes with bare fingers and using their palms as cups. The feast includes a dish of sheep's feet with a highly spiced white sauce. Eating the food that is a delicacy to them is very difficult for us, but we make merry nonetheless, and we teach them to sing a popular French song.

Unfortunately, at our last meeting, another difficulty develops. One of my two subjects, Davich Khan, the son, refuses to let me have his portrait after it has dried. He believes it is hidden under his bed, and he says such concealment is necessary because the image lacks a soul. A valet tells Davich Khan through an interpreter that His Majesty wished to have the portrait, and he has delivered it to him. Davich carefully and deliberately picks up his dagger to kill the valet, but the interpreter is able to explain that in Paris one may not kill his valet.

It concerns me that he felt his image lacked a soul, but perhaps something is askew in the translation. Perhaps in his country, a soul is imparted to an image by the two staying in the same room together for a certain period of time. Or perhaps some ceremony is performed, or permission granted from the sovereign or even a deity. In any case, I am very glad to have the portraits, one of which I give to His Majesty and one of which I keep for myself. I keep the father, for I have less upsetting associations with him than with the son and his dagger.

LEAVING MY OWN BRUSHES to languish while I teach is a great strain, and
in a cheerful way I point out the hardship to my husband. It is more profit-
able, I remind him, to make trips to the homes of aristocrats and ambassadors. Eventually M. Le Brun sees the simple truth of my statements, and
since commissions are ever pouring in, he agrees with me that I no longer
need to waste my time trying to be what I am not. With all my heart I
embrace my roles both as painter and mother, equally, but I am not a painting teacher for those who lack commitment or passion or both.

Because my paintings are hung in the annual salon (since I am now a
member of the Académie) next to the work of M. de Ménageot, the igno-
rant associate me with him and assert he is the true author of my work.
Anyone should be able to see that, while I respect his style of paintings, it is
not at all like my own. His are composed in a classic historical style, with
an emphasis on drapery.

My work becomes so much in demand that I schedule three sittings a
day, although by evening I am really too fatigued to continue to paint. I
develop a stomach disorder, and I become very thin. My friends suggest to
the doctor that I be required to rest after lunch. To retire to my bedroom,
draw the curtains against the light, and lie on my bed, waiting patiently for
a nap, does indeed help me to sustain my strength.

Only in the case of painting a self-portrait does one learn the fine
points of truly capturing the inner life, but sometimes there is also a social
or political motive in portraiture. Because as a woman painter who paints
as well as a man, I continue to be a puzzle or a threat to many, I decide on
a self-portrait that displays evidence of maternity. In my next self-portrait,
I include my little daughter, for is she not proof that I am a mother and
that I pose no threat to anyone?

I CALL THE PAINTING *MATERNAL TENDERNESS* in opposition to those
slanderers claiming I paint so masterfully that surely my paintbrush is a
penis! No, I am a mother, this painting says. My head is tilted awkwardly

to one side, the better to nuzzle up to Julie. My expression is simpering and stupid. With both arms and both hands I am holding my little girl tightly to my bosom, too tightly. The most truthful thing in this painting is Julie's expression. Her eyes ask, "Why is my *maman* clutching me so tightly when usually I am free?" The turban around my head looks something like a floppy halo, as though I were the Holy Mother clasping her babe.

I LIKE MUCH BETTER the portrait I paint in 1784 of the Comte de Vaudreuil. Sometimes thinking of the Prince de Ligne, who was so kind to M. Le Brun and me in Brussels by sharing his great collection of Rubens and Van Dyke, I paint the Comte without restraint, rendering his countenance just as sensitive and handsome as he really is. I owe him a great deal for recommending me to the queen, and I am determined to represent him more appealingly than ever before. The queen grows ever more friendly with the Comte de Vaudreuil and the Duchesse de Polignac.

I have also met now the Swedish nobleman Axel von Fersen, whom the queen adores. He is known as the most handsome man in Europe, and I am glad I am not asked to paint him, though I like him very much. The English call the Swedish nobleman "The Picture" because he is considered the almost-too-good-to-be-true image of masculine perfection. But it is the wit and social liveliness of the Comte de Vaudreuil that have captured my heart.

If one has self-confidence, then either the repression of a tender feeling or its expression through observing all proprieties can make the moments at a supper or a salon sizzle with life. The mind is like an acrobat.

As an act of self-indulgence, I engage a model to pose at my studio as a bacchante. She is entirely nude, except for the skin of a leopard draped across her thighs. And so I paint two "skins," one of a wild animal and one of a very desirable woman. One of her elbows rests on the round arm of a civilized sofa. The other arm is lifted over and across her head, exposing that entire side of her body and her breast to the brightest light. The breast is treated as one sometimes treats a face (as I treated my own face in the girlish and modest self-portrait after the birth of my daughter); that is, with a sharp contrast between light and dark. In a face, the nose divides the two realms. Here they are divided by the nipple.

The face of the bacchante would be in light, except the shadow of the raised arm falls across it in the most interesting and unexpected way. Her face is made interesting with shadows thrown not by a hat brim but by her own naked arm. The dynamic of the painting is contained between the bent elbow of her raised right arm and the nude bent left knee; that dynamic from high to low is crossed by an opposing dynamic arising from the lower right corner, the skin of the leopard crossing the thigh and on up. Her smooth white body is crossed by the spotted skin.

What a vulnerable place that is beneath the raised arm that reveals and raises the breast.

THE PORTRAIT I PAINT of the queen for the coming salon, in 1787, like *Maternal Tenderness,* depicts her with her children. She is dressed in red velvet, seated, with her firstborn daughter, Marie-Therese, leaning lovingly against her shoulder; the dauphin stands close by, and her second son is in her lap. I had also included the infant Sofie in her crib, but when she died I was asked to paint over her, leaving only an empty crib, which the dauphin points to in a heartrending way. I have saved the pastel sketch of the bundled infant. I consider offering it to the queen, but I think it would wring her heart to look at the image of her daughter whom she has lost.

No mother has loved her children more than the queen; she has spent as much time with them as possible, and for this she is criticized by the court, as she prefers the company of her children to cards and gambling. The court considers such time to be squandered and refers to those tender moments as the queen's "dissipations." At this time, the hearts of the populace are hardening against the queen, so much so that I begin to fear again the prophetic words of my father, coming home late from New Year's conversation with the philosophes, when he told my mother that our world should soon be turned upside down. I feel a nervousness beginning in myself, not just my stomach, but my whole being. I find, during this period, that I am more consoled by dinner parties, by opera, and by theater than I am by nature.

Merely the frame for the painting of the queen and her children is ridiculed for its extravagance by the hostile crowd when it is carried, empty, into the salon. They are the same mob, I daresay, who had protested the queen's portrait when she wore inexpensive muslin and a straw hat. I am afraid to be present when the frame and the canvas are united and displayed to the public, but my dear brother, Étienne, rushes to let me know that the painting of the queen in red velvet with her children is much admired.

Nonetheless, in a few days, hostility has mounted and the portrait is removed. In its place appears a crude sign which reads *"Madame Déficite."*

Perhaps it is because our own times have become frighteningly unruly, with passions unleashed, that we begin to turn back to the classical periods of Greece and Rome, when beauty and truth counted for more. And yet I have always been greatly influenced by Rousseau, who puts much emphasis on feeling and the inner life; I regret some segments of society have adopted him for their own use to justify behavior that is not only unruly but vicious.

WHILE I AM RESTING one afternoon after lunch, my beloved brother comes to my apartment to read to me some excerpts from the *Voyages du jeune Anacharsis en Grèce,* for Le Brun-Pindare (not related to my family) is coming to my supper party and is scheduled to read verses to us from his own translation from the Greek of Anacreon. This evening we will be treated to language depicting what life was like in ancient Greece. As soon as Étienne finishes reading a description of a Greek dinner, recipes, and sauces, with his inimitable enthusiasm he suggests that we try some of the recipes this evening for our party. We shall taste Greece! Étienne is irresistible in his zest for life, and I send for my cook.

Together we settle on one sauce for the fowl and another for eels, Greek sauces, one of which features pork fat, salt, and vinegar. As we talk I receive a note that the Comte de Vaudreuil and his friend M. Boutin will be late in attending this evening. I am sure a shadow passes over my face at this information, for my observant brother asks me if I have received bad news. His gaze is rather too penetrating.

"Not bad news," I reply, "but an opportunity. We will be eating Greek food, we will hear poetry in the Greek manner, and it occurs to me to dress some of our pretty ladies, who will arrive first, in Greek costumes. We will become a living painting, and those who come late—they do not arrive till ten—M. Vaudreuil and M. Boutin—will receive the surprise of their lives. They will believe themselves literally transported to another time and place, one that we would all like very much to inhabit!"

"Explain in more detail," Étienne urges, and he looks at me as he did when we were children and I was the big sister, almost magical in her ability to conjure up new and exciting activities and adventures. "Are you not, dearest and only sister, trespassing on the territory of literature? Is it not the power of drama, even of the novel, to transport one to another time and place?" He himself writes plays.

"All the senses shall have their role in the miracle," I reply. "The food will smell and taste divine. We shall have music *à la grecque* for the ear, our costumes for the eye, poetry for the mind. The reading of poetry will transport us yet again. It will be like having a painting represented in a painting. One enters one frame of reference only to enter another. It will be delightfully confusing, such that the latecomers will be forever in our debt for having created such a surprising spectacle. I do not think reality will ever seem stable to them again!" Of course I am exaggerating, but only a bit. I do almost believe that I am a conjuror of sorts.

At that moment, as though to confirm my occult powers, who should step into the immediate vignette but one of my neighbors from within the mansion, the Comte de Parois. And *he* is the possessor of a fine collection of authentic Etruscan vases. In a wink, he enters the enthusiasm of the moment, and his servants, like a troupe of genies, transport his treasures, quite a number of bowls and vases, from his apartment to mine.

From this array, I choose a selection, notable for its delightful variety, and then assemble them into a new vignette of an interesting and harmonious nature. I clean and wash the vases myself, very carefully, and then arrange them again on a bare mahogany table. What an earthy but noble display of textures, of wood and ancient clay.

To bring the whole picture together, I have a large screen placed behind the chairs, and I drape the screen, securing it here and there so that the background is uniform and pleasing. Of course, I have a large supply of all sorts of drapery in my studio. Next I have a large lamp suspended from the ceiling above the table so that the entire tableau will be appropriately lit.

How delightful to construct life! Yes, the theater has the illusion of such, but here my medium is reality: it will include us as ourselves, doubled by our roles. One will doubt the focus of his eyes, and ask himself does he see his friends or ancient Greeks?

Charming Mme Chalgrin, Vernet's daughter, is the first to arrive. I take her hand and lead her laughing into my studio, for she misunderstands and thinks I am going to use the flesh of her face as a canvas and superimpose new features upon her. "Not quite," I say merrily, "but something like. All of you compose my canvas, and with this drapery you will become almost unbelievably Greek. You know my mother has been a hairdresser, and I too shall practice that art upon your head, *à la grecque.*" Mme Chalgrin is amazed and a bit incredulous. But when I take her to the long mirror, after my work is finished, she gasps and reaches out to touch her image to see if it is real. Of course her fingers encounter glass, but she believes her eyes.

Next to arrive is the great beauty Mme de Bonneuil, who accompanied me in eating sheep's feet, along with her little daughter, who will be a companion for Julie. As was my father's custom, I take care that my daughter has the opportunity to meet and to hear the conversation of my own friends. Mme de Bonneuil is transformed in a trice! Even more enticing as a Greek woman! And then comes my beloved and talented sister-in-law Suzanne, both singer and actress, who has the most beautiful eyes in the world. As soon as each lady arrives, I costume her and arrange her hair. Athenian ladies all, from top to toe!

As soon as our guest of honor, the poet Le Brun-Pindare, sets foot in my apartment, it is off with his powdered wig, and we ladies fluff out the natural curls he has, close to his ears, and I even promise to produce a laurel wreath fit for a poet laureate to put on his head, for in my studio I have just painted the young prince Henry Lubomirski kneeling before a laurel bush with its crown of leaves on his head. That painting is called *The Love of Glory.*

Straightaway, this laurel crown is fetched for our poet, and I also send again to the apartment of the Comte de Parois, for he owns a large purple cloak, which completely transforms Pindare into the Greek Anacreon. When the Marquis de Cubières arrives, I dress him and he sends for his guitar, which I have Étienne gild so that the guitar becomes a golden lyre in less than ten minutes.

Of course I do not neglect to take care with the costumes of M. de Rivière, the brother of my brother's wife, Suzanne, and also my famous guest Chaudet, the much-admired sculptor. We are finally about twelve or fifteen in number.

I do not have much time to spend on my own costume, but that does not matter because my dresses are always simple white tunics (some call them smocks), to which I add quickly a diaphanous veil and a circlet of flowers for my head.

But in preparing the costumes of my darling little Julie and her little friend Mlle de Bonneuil, I take the utmost care and delight. They both become exquisite, irresistible, delicate Greek sprites. Julie has a transparency about her that shows the clear sparkle of her intelligent and original spirit. It makes my heart ache to look at their perfect, childish beauty and softness. These children have a vulnerability that displays no awareness of its own innocence. Amidst all our artifice, I want to weep that such natural charm can exist, for a while, on this earth. I feel something of the confused delight that I wish will wash over the unsuspecting latecomers.

At half past nine, we are all so pleased with ourselves and so full of anticipation in regard to the effect we feel sure we will make on the latecomers that we take turns playing the role of someone who has just entered who suddenly beholds the Greek scene, a table surrounded by beautifully attired Greeks. One by one we each leave our seats, exit the room, and return, so that we may enjoy the original and picturesque effect made by the others who remain seated. When each spectator turns and beholds the tableau, his or her face is swept with wonder, even though we around the table have witnessed the same expression on previous spectators, several times in a row.

I observe, "This tableau vivant from classical times melds two of the art forms we all adore, that of painting and that of the theater, and, in addition, it partakes of real life as we are enjoying it in the moment." They agree with my words, but it is difficult for mere words to convey how thrilling and fulfilling this charade already is for each participant.

At ten o'clock, as I have expected, knowing how meticulous the Comte de Vaudreuil is in all his appointments with me (even sending a note if he is to be late), we hear the carriage arrive. Quickly both doors to the dining room are thrown open, the visitors from ancient Greece assume their seats around the richly gleaming table loaded with Etruscan pottery, and we commence to sing Gluck's chorus "Le dieu de Paphos et de Guide," with M. de Cubières playing his lyre.

When the Comte de Vaudreuil and his companion enter, I see sheer astonishment such as not in all my life have I ever experienced before. For a moment I fear Vaudreuil will lose his wits. He even wipes the back of his wrist across his eyes, such as my brother used to do, very young, when he awoke. I am fulfilled to have evoked such amazement, disbelief, and pleasure on the face of any human. Vaudreuil is lighted with delight, from within.

WHEN I PAINT JULIE and me together again, Julie is two years older, and I am seated, and she has just run to hug me. My arms protect her, in the portrait, but my hand clasps my own wrist, with her inside my arms. It is 1789, a year for historians, if not history painters: people say it is the year of the French Revolution. Julie and I are going to leave not only Paris, but all of France, with her governess. In this painting *Self-Portrait, Holding My Daughter in My Arms* I am completing the circle with myself, which includes her.

She is embracing me as much as I am embracing her, but we are each thinking our own thoughts, and they are quite different. Now Julie's mind is beginning to be her own. I am wearing a loose, flowing gown in the Greek style, a reminder of that wonderful, spontaneous, very inexpensive party *à la grecque* I gave for my friends. My shoulder and part of my back are bare, vulnerable, and real.

My face and my body say hopefully, almost shyly, to the world, "This is my beloved child; be tender with her."

Though our departure from revolutionary France is imminent, I try to make it appear that all is normal. I set up my easels with some unfinished work, the better to create the illusion that I am resigned to remaining in Paris. These unfinished portraits for which I have received commissions I regard with regret. M. Le Brun has already spent the amounts I received as retainers.

M. Le Brun has given me a small purse, and we have agreed I am to leave Paris with only eighty Louis, though I have earned for him millions by this time. In order to protect his business as an art dealer (especially the extensive holdings of valuable paintings by eminent artists), my husband has affirmed again his decision to remain in Paris. Being aware now of the

increasing lawlessness of the populace, I doubt that he will be able to protect his holdings, but I admire the courage and tenacity represented by his
decision. We each decide our own fate.

WHEN THE TIME FOR DEPARTURE grows near, Paris is seething with a
special unrest. In gestures quite unusual for them, citizens arrange their
rags carefully over their shoulders as though they were dressing up with
rich scarves; they congregate and gossip to an extraordinary extent, exciting themselves, drinking to excess, cursing, spitting, raising their skirts
and shamelessly relieving themselves publicly rather than absenting themselves for even a moment from their particular companions and their dis-
course. With impunity, men steal not only food but also hats and shoes
and even chests from shops, and then fill the chests with other booty. They
shake their fists under one another's noses. It is as though the winds of
change are winding themselves up for an explosion of destructive energy.

As night falls, a tattered mass begin to move as a unit toward the southwest. I am baffled by this movement, as though all the bees are senselessly
leaving the hive together, till one of my servants explains their purpose
to me. The mob is marching to the Château de Versailles to confront the
queen and king. Faster and faster, they pour through the streets of Paris,
like a hemorrhage, toward Versailles.

Stunned by acute anxiety for my royal friends, I stand at the window and watch the dregs of society leaving Paris all through the afternoon and evening. During the dark of night, I pull a chair to the window
facing southwest, half expecting to see the glow of flames, but there is
none. I try to focus on the brave flicker of a nearby streetlight. Earlier
the lamplighter ignited the little flame with his long wand, then threw
his tool down on the pavement and, with a swagger and a glance at me,
joined the marchers. Eventually I doze in my hard chair, with my cheek
propped up by my hand.

After dawn, the cry of a rooster wakes me; dazed and full of sorrow,

I stir in my chair. As soon as I open my eyes I begin to witness a flow in the opposite direction of individuals and groups walking from the south-west. The number of pedestrians grows, and they walk closer and closer together till finally I am looking through my window at a mass of moving shoulders and heads, their legs and feet being completely concealed. The faces of the mob present a tapestry of emotion. Some appear jubilant and wild-eyed; others look sullen and satisfied, and some seem frightened and breathless. Coming toward me in the distance is a coach drawn by multiple horses, and I realize the mob is its vanguard.

The market women and shopkeepers of Paris have surrounded the coach bearing our monarchs, but they are not the only escort. The car-riage drawn by six matched horses is preceded by severed heads mounted on long wooden pikes, heads severed from the necks of two members of the royal Swiss Guard, for a hat has been placed atop one's head. The two severed heads, gory and ghastly to behold, present two quite different responses to the calamity that has claimed these once living humans. The eyes of the one wearing the hat of the Swiss Guard are closed serenely, and his calm head moves through the air with a certain still dignity. The other head stares with wide eyes, the gaze fixed in horror and disbelief. His hair is loose. Waved back and forth in arcs atop its pike, from this head I watch a single brownish drop of blood sling free and fall downward toward the paving.

A bystander holding his member in his hand pisses into the moving spokes of the carriage wheels. Some of the mob have smeared blood across their foreheads in a mockery of the rites of Ash Wednesday. The coach draws ever closer, and I can see inside, for the curtains have not been drawn.

Inside, my lovely queen has turned to stone. Her face is still and calm, framed by the carriage window. It is as though she has been painted for the eons in tints delicate and subtle in great contrast to the coarse garb and faces surrounding her. Her skin like porcelain, her bearing calm, somber, and proud, she seems to have come from the moon or some other celestial body.

Instinctively, I reach out my hand toward her, but of course it cannot enter the world of a painting, of illusion. Inside my home, my fingertips encounter the window glass, cold to the touch, and my hand falls help-lessly to my side. By slow degrees, the imprisoning carriage passes, and I also glimpse the king and the children of France within.

At the back of the magnificent carriage ride two footmen, their finery splattered with mud. Someone grabs the leg of one of them and pulls him crashing down into the street. I turn my head. To think, how easily with a push or the jerking of a leg, one can be brought low. Discarded.

For a moment my mind registers only blankness, for I have closed my eyes and almost lost consciousness, but the sensation of the fingering of the fabric of my own skirt restores me to reality. *Too fine, too fine,* my fingers tell me, and then my mind recalls that I have already taken the precaution of preparing the dress of a commoner for myself and for little Julie as well. Like commoners, we will sit safely inside a common stagecoach, not a pri-vate coach, I reassure myself. Yes, I know the means of escape, and I have a talent for acting.

Far ahead now, beyond my vision, the queen, my friend, in the noble carriage (I recognized the cage immediately as a borrowed one, belong-ing actually to a certain marquise) is being conveyed, I feel sure, toward imprisonment, perhaps death. Before me limp the wretched of the earth: exhausted, starving, dirty, chilled to the bone but with a terrible victory in their bloodshot eyes. Persistent but intermittent gunfire echoes in the dis-tance; however, I have become so used to the sound that I scarcely remark it. Much more frightening is the low growl that rises from the streets with-out ceasing.

TODAY WE LEAVE. I am glad that I have already bidden farewell to Mlle Boquet, with whom I learned to paint when we were quite young, now Mme Filleul. I have tried to tell her of the images of the horror to come that have appeared so vividly in my imagination, how terrible visions blot out the visage of anyone who sits or stands before me, posing for a portrait. I have seen these visitors sitting patiently beyond my easel as being washed in blood. I believe in these involuntary visions. The visions are so vivid, they must be prophetic—though I would not blaspheme. During my visit I tried to warn her, my oldest friend.

Mme Filleul said to me, "You shouldn't leave, my dear friend. You are making a mistake. I am going to stay because I believe in the happiness the Revolution is going to bring to us."

X

LOUVECIENNES

or, An Old Woman Among Spring Trees

PORTRAIT

I MUST LET THESE OLD EYES look about and be grateful for the air and light. That I survived. And yet survive.

My woods are full of violets, and honeysuckle will soon bloom. This is the true countryside—sweet scented, for I have trod on chamomile—beloved by all who believe that God's love is present in the awakening of the earth. For many years now, the simple sight of a child is like looking at spring for me, and I am overcome with joy at the replenishing of life. Without turning to allegory, no painting can really capture the joy of nature I see about me in this green-blue moment. Occasionally there is a breeze that causes the light to flicker. Ah, I can render a dappled shade with my brush, but to make light flicker—that is beyond me.

My last image of the queen in life is the one framed by the carriage window, her beautiful face like a mask of tragedy; the surrounding mob; their awful emblem of liberty being two severed human heads hoisted high on pikes.

Not that last image—tightly, tightly I squeeze shut my actual eyes though it is the mind's eye that unveils that horror. Not that, Memory! Instead, let us conjure up Marly-le-Roi, as it was then, a tranquil and serene place, nature's own rustic fairyland. But after my return, after the Revolution, I visited there. I know that Marly-le-Roi has been reduced to rubble.

Here at Louveciennes, nature has a wildness about her, and my trees have not achieved the grandeur of those at Marly, nor are we so parklike here; in my old age, I find that disorder and unbounded nature also have their attractions. I have hung a shard of broken mirror on the trunk of a chestnut tree. Or, rather, I have had a servant do so. When I want to see my visage framed in fronds of pale spring green, I look into this mirror fragment. It once hung whole, at Versailles, I've been told.

I wish that simply for my own pleasure, I might have painted that meeting at Marly-le-Roi of my mother and myself with the queen and her ladies all in white, but I would have moved the location slightly to include those serene and gracious trees beside the lake in the background, for the trees, like people, leaned toward each other, in congregation. Perhaps I would catch something of the dappled shade falling on our faces and dresses in the painting. It need not be too large; indeed, I want its size to suggest intimacy. The painting would be a window, a peephole, on a time and place, seen from a distance.

It would be like catching a cloud. Or, I could paint myself as I am in this moment: an old woman, with something of her former beauty still recognizable in her face, standing beside a chestnut tree in the wood at Louveciennes. I step forward, reach out, and now my hand cups a low-growing branch full of blossoms. The arrangement of the flowers suggests a chandelier descended from its ceiling and a woman cradling the panicle of blossoms in her left hand, as I do now. (After all, my right hand must hold the brush, but my right hand has often painted my left one.)

An Old Woman Among Spring Trees: she is gazing to the side, at the natural chandelier, not at all at the artist. She is quite unaware that she is the subject of a painting. The skin of her hand is somewhat curdled because she is old, but I would paint it so that the hand itself looks rather like a cluster of small blossoms.

Why not? A metamorphosis, such as Bernini sculpted for Diana when she was so hotly pursued by Apollo. I suppose my pursuer is Father Time, with his sickle and hourglass.

I walk on in the woods of Louveciennes, carefully but without anxiety, for I have a very good history of circumventing personal accident or even overt danger. As I take a step or two on the mossy path, I watch the sway of my skirt and how my toes nudge out from beneath the hem as I walk. I am wearing lavender shoes today. I would prefer to be wearing no shoes at all at the hour of my death. To travel its mortal path, the spirit need not be shod.

What does enchantment mean but to be relieved of the ordinary and the less-than-pleasing by something delightfully surprising? To be free to be oneself.

Chairs, like stations (stations of opportunity and pleasure), are placed about in my woods, should I want to sit. To rest or to paint or sketch. Some of the wooden chairs have grown moss on their arms. I will be happy to see them again, my friends the chairs.

Habit is like a smooth stone, a keepsake, in the pocket, delightful to the touch. It comforts.

My fingers find their way into my hair now, as though they were searching for something hidden there. No, it is to touch my scalp and the hard, curved bone beneath and the brain and mind beyond. I am trying to touch my own essence. To understand. To accept. To find the unity of self that needs to be apprehended before my own passing from the sunshine occurs. How I do love and have loved the light! The simple light. I think it is the darkness of the grave that is the most oppressive thought about death.

I remove my hand from the tree and smile at the reality around me.

The sky has darkened to a more mature blue, as the day ages. What a fine thing is a day! Its journey mimics the dawn and the dusk of our lives before the night. I have always loved the night and appreciated the respite it gives my eye from the constant stimulation of color, but oh how glad I am in the morning. Every morning I awake to exclaim, *Alive! I am yet alive, and here is the world, my home, waiting for me.* But where have I been at night? My eyes closed, my brain shut up in the cave of the skull? Is the night a round, dark portal to death? How can I fear it?

I have seen so many die too soon, their lives not yet lived. That will not be my fate.

WHEN MY NIECES COME TO SEE ME this evening, I will feel almost as happy—not quite, it is quite a different satisfaction—as when I was their ages. Still I relish the froth of social life. I cannot regret too much my connection to M. Le Brun, for it is through him that I know Eugénie Le Brun (now Mme J. Tripier Le Franc), whom I have guided in the art of portrait painting. From that ancestor Charles Le Brun, who decorated Versailles for Louis XIV, *she* has inherited more of the artist's hand and eye than ever did my husband, her uncle, though that blood did make my M. Le Brun (let me credit him again) an insightful connoisseur and art dealer.

My dear niece and student Eugénie is a success, admired for her likenesses and the delicacy and precision of her line. Some of that delicacy she learned from me, for it is a characteristic that can be taught and acquired. They speak of the richness of her colors; I did not try to influence her palette, for those choices must come from within the soul. In my best work, I use a palette close to that of Van Dyke. I like clarity and brightness. It is not so much richness through color that I would aspire to capture but joy, life itself, the brightness that light discovers. The very brightness of brightness.

This light here at Louveciennes could spawn a school of painters whose delight it is that we live on an earth kissed by sunlight. Even the shadows have their color. They are pockets in which light hides her secrets.

And to the woods and the wild softness of nature I have come again, soon to be visited not only by Eugénie Le Brun but also by the daughter of my brother Étienne, Caroline. My gratitude to each of these nieces, who do so much to enliven my days, is unbounded. Through them I experience maternal emotions again: those feelings of sheer pleasure that they exist and are within my sight so that I can enjoy all the nuances of their natures and also their immediate interests and hopes.

In the countenance of Caroline, I see something of my beloved brother, whose death was such a blow, but Caroline is also the embodiment of her mother, Suzanne, whose vivacity and expressiveness resided in her wide, intelligent eyes. Caroline follows her mother in her interest in music and both her parents in their interest in the literary arts, especially the theater. In the good days before the Revolution, my dear sister-in-law Suzanne often played leading roles in performances at my salon, and of course dear Étienne made a name for himself as a playwright.

It is for her overall charm that Caroline so delights the heart—her conversation, her music, her vivacity—while Eugénie has not forsaken her painting despite her marriage and understands my artistic nature as only another artist can do. In the two of them, I see two different aspects of myself, the woman who so loved the society of writers and musicians and the woman who best defined her passion when wedded to her brush.

And where would my Julie have fit between them? Oh, they would have made a place for her as friend, and more than that, as cousin who shared the blood of each, and between them they would have set her on a happier course. Like Caroline, my Julie was of a literary bent, even when she was a child, and she wrote not mere stories but an entire novella by the time she was nine.

I but blink and the present replaces the past, or vice versa.

Now I follow my walking path downward through a lower, damper part of the woods of Louveciennes where the yellow flags bloom in the late spring, but it is too early for them in May. Here are the aromatic narcissi to greet my nostrils. Something sharp and pungent, almost cutting. They seem fragile scattered hither and yon among the great trees. They will never grow even as tall as my knee. And I see the last of the purple crocuses, too, starting to wither, their petals thin and dry as tissue paper.

Knowing I would walk this day to this particular natural temple, I asked that an extra folding chair be brought here and placed in the shade. And here are the cushions, of a dull green velvet so as not to disturb nature's harmonious colors. Here I will have my reverie. I will recall the truth of the difficult days with Julie, my fragile child. This morning I conjure up my Julie—pain and all—for this evening I shall be visited by Caroline, my brother's daughter, who is always so loving to me, who has, in some sense, become my daughter after the loss of my own, and even more so after her loss of her own parents.

During the days of my exile from France, throughout my sojourns in Italy and Vienna, the journey through Prague and Berlin, and our long residence in St. Petersburg, I kept Julie ever at my side as she grew from child to willful young woman. On the other hand, I was not present during the maturation of Caroline, my dear brother's child, now woman, whose life has been so much more natural and happy than that of my Julie. Perhaps Julie would have better found her true sense of self if I had not been ever present in her life; perhaps if I had left her in a convent school in Italy (after all, I was sent to the sisters in France when I was very young), and she had not been in Russia as she became a young woman, she might have had a longer, better life.

After we fled France together in the common stagecoach and reached Italy, I gave Julie the advantage of an education that many would have envied, for it went far beyond the course of study even Rousseau had recommended in *Émile* for Sophie, who was to become the suitable companion of Émile. For Julie, I hired tutors not only in music, which was common for young girls, but also in writing and geography, and in the study of foreign languages—Italian, of course, as we were residing in Italy (and traveled much of its geography together, including Milan, Rome, Spoleto, Florence, Siena, Parma, Venice, Verona, and Turin); she had masters also in English and in German, which was the favorite of her languages.

Above all, Julie enjoyed writing stories; sometimes when I would send her to bed in the evening, she would get back up in the middle of the night, secretly, to work on her stories, some of which showed a stylistic command of phrases or an investment in some human's situation that would cause the reader to want to know more. As she wrote Julie tended both the fire of stylistic originality and the fire of human curiosity, for she knew instinctively that excellent writing must embody both aesthetic and humanistic aspects, as even the greatest art in any form must do. Of course Julie also had an aptitude for art, but I think in this area she was overawed by my own work, or perhaps simply by the attention that was given me because of my work.

I regret that I did not have the skill as a parent-artist that Bernini's father had, for the son gladly took his father's instruction and surpassed him, which the father was delighted to recognize. But Julie had the will, perhaps inherited from her father, to live her own life as it pleased her and her alone to do. As she matured, my interpretation of reality became less and less welcome to her till finally, in Russia, I had to abandon any attempt to guide her, not to lose her altogether. Since I could not control or even help to shape her choices, I made the decision to try to support her, for above all I wanted her to feel that my love was ever with her. No human being has ever been more dear to me than my daughter.

How gladly I would have given my life for her happiness, if that had been a bargain offered by fate. How gladly now, amidst the violets and fading wild crocuses of Louveciennes, I would lay me down on the moss and die, if she might rise up and be reborn in this verdant spring. It is not that I am unhappy; it is not that I do not value life—every drop of it is precious to me; so long as I have eyes with which to see the light, that act alone makes life precious and rich—but given a choice, life is a present I would hand from myself to my Julie, with a smile and eyes aglow.

From my chair my gaze lifts from the pale greens of the renewing earth to the pale blue skies and the thin clouds forming there. They are like veils stretched across the blue. When I look at the sky, I recall the words of little Julie when she first saw the sea; Julie then felt free to express all her delightful thoughts to me without hesitation, and I'm sure I never did anything but applaud such spontaneity.

Must I forever defend myself about my own guilt over Julie's unhappiness? I wanted nothing but joy and fulfillment for her.

When we left Rome for Naples, where Julie first saw the sea, she exclaimed, *Sais-tu bien, maman, que c'est plus grand que nature!* That is, she was so surprised by the immensity of the ocean which she had not seen before, except represented within the framed perimeters of paintings, that she said the sea was *even bigger than nature,* getting her categories confused.

When I look at the sky, either the day sky full of sunlight or the night sky sprinkled with stars and the moon, I do think that *it* is even bigger than nature, but that is because I am thinking of the God who created the firmament and its vast beauty.

I believe that during our time in Italy, Julie was a happy child, one who met the wonders of nature and of art and architecture with an open soul. She continued so during our sojourn in Vienna, which is where we were in 1793 when the terrible news came of the execution of Marie Antoinette.

Walking! I have come to the woods to walk and to paint, to muse and remember! But this spot does not please me. I'm restless. I need to find some mushrooms for our table tonight. And so I'll look for a woods not quite so shaded, one penetrated with splotches of light, but not too bright, over closer to the estate where Mme du Barry had her charming abode. Perhaps I'll sketch the mushrooms huddled together, having a conversation among themselves, before I gather them. I'll place a leaf in the composition for contrast. An oak leaf, certainly curled and brown now after its winter, with spines at the tips. They would provide a fine contrast to the roundedness of mushrooms. Something spiky up against the benign humps and fleshy stalks. All rather monochromatic, which suits charcoal anyway. Charcoal is such an old friend.

At the horizon line of a green meadow, I see the curve of what is surely the grandfather of all mushrooms! But wait, no mushroom at all! It is the crown of a bald man's head, and there's his face. A country man, very old, he walks with a twirled stick, one that grapevine has squeezed and forced to grow as though it were a baroque artifact, Bernini's columns inside Saint Peter's!

And I am hurled down on the ground in a wink.

I must have stepped in a gopher or mole hole of some sort, and here *he* is in three winks, squatting down beside, his age-spotted face quite close to mine, inquiring if I am injured.

I am not, but I have no inclination to try to stand. I do arrange my akimbo self into a sedate posture.

He retreats a bit and speaks in rural accents. "How may I best help you, Madame?"

"I don't believe I require any assistance," I reply, "but thank you for your kind offer." When he makes no reply, I add, "I've fallen in a shady spot, I see. And I'll just rest a bit."

"Mushroom hunting, I suppose?" he inquires.

The hoop handle of the tight little basket is still about my wrist, but one side is rather smashed in. He nods at that minor calamity.

"In the old days, I would mend that for you, for I was a basket maker."

I smile and say cheerfully, "The old days for me would have been far longer ago than for you."

"Do you think so?" he asks, and then he tells me his age. He is two years older than I. This piece of information causes me to brighten with pleasure, for I rarely meet anyone as old as myself.

"Yes, I made baskets of all sorts," he goes on. "Even the baskets that went under the skirts of the court ladies and held them out to the side to make the ladies look wider in the hips."

I laugh out loud, for I never thought that that was the reason for the fashion of my youth. That first portrait I made of the queen, in white silk, she was wearing wide panniers.

"To make them look capable," he adds.

"Capable?"

"Capable of much childbearing, you know."

Suddenly I feel very sober. "Yes," I say, "that was very important among the aristocrats, and especially for royalty." Two hundred people had crowded into the bedchamber of Marie Antoinette to witness her giving birth that first time, and the good king himself had smashed out a window so that she might have enough air to breathe, for the crowd was close to suffocating her as she labored.

The old man reaches out, picks up my sketchbook, and regards it solemnly.

"So, you remember those times when women wore baskets on their hips?" I ask him.

"Yes, I remember you."

"Remember me?" I say this as gently as I can. I do not wish to challenge him, or any old person whose memory might play tricks on him.

"You are Mme Élisabeth Vigée-Le Brun, the artist," he says, handing me my sketchbook.

How quickly and hungrily my eyes search his face. I almost see a glimpse of my brother, Étienne, in his alive eyes, and then he resembles M. Le Brun, my husband. Vaudreuil? Would he have come to this? Would he arrive yet again in my life? I saw him in England, after I left Russia. He was quite destroyed. His son was dead. But this is not Vaudreuil. "And who are you, Monsieur?" I ask, full of timid wonder.

He pronounces a name I do not in the least recognize, but then he explains, "I was, briefly, near the end, the French valet to the Swedish gentleman, the one who tried to save the queen and king."

"Axel von Fersen," I say, and then my lips close.

There was no name more sacred to the queen. I would not ask, nor would this rural gentleman tell, I feel sure, anything that might define the exact relationship of the Swedish count to the queen. Though the top of his speckled head is bald as a mushroom, the side locks are long and straight, and he resembles a gnome. He is more shrunken by age than I.

When I stir to rise from the grass, he says, "May I offer you my hand?"

But I settle myself again and say, "Do you recall where you saw me? Was there an occasion when we were in the same room together?" The man seems like a genie to me, for he has the ability to make real in my memory a time and place I have absolutely forgotten. He can give me back a piece of the past. I am extremely curious and delighted. "Would you be so kind as to tell me where and when you saw me?"

"I saw you here, at Louveciennes. You came to paint the portrait of Mme du Barry."

"I did indeed, three times. I wish that I could remember having seen you."

"I was only a workman on the property. I had not yet risen to be a valet. It was only on the eve of the Revolution that I rose."

I think how disappointing it must have been for him to have fallen back into his old position as laborer, but his face is not that of a man who has been disappointed by life. Saddened, perhaps. "I was only lately thinking about the queen," I say. "I painted her many times."

"I was never in the same room with Her Majesty," he replies. "But I saw your picture they took down from the salon. The one in her nightgown."

"She was not in her nightgown," I explain. "That was the style of dress, a simple muslin dress, with a sash. No panniers. She was wearing a straw hat. Remember?"

He shakes his head. *No.* "I remember the painting with her children. And the little empty crib. It was at the salon, too."

I say nothing. I notice the brown spots across the dome of his head, like a plover's egg. The conversation has become too painful. That was the last official portrait I painted of the queen, as a kind mother, in soft red velvet, with a sumptuous footstool and tall ostrich plumes in her hair. A state portrait, three children and an empty crib.

"How is your daughter?" he asks.

I can feel the blood drain from my face.

"Your little girl who came with you when you painted the du Barry?"

"We traveled Europe together. She married a Russian count." I hesitate. "She died in Paris, still a young woman," I say, glancing at the sky. Then I look directly into his eyes. "I arrived in time to say good-bye."

"And did she have children?"

"No."

Because I see concern in his nice brown eyes, not just curiosity, I add, "She died of a chest congestion and fever." I begin to rise. "And your family?"

"My wife was executed in the Revolution. She was seamstress to Mme du Barry and thought to be a sympathizer. Mme du Barry was very kind to her, as she was to the little slave boy Zamore, who betrayed her when he was a young man, before the tribunal. My wife was young enough to have been my child. I am a lucky man, for I live with my great-granddaughter, who loves me. I made baskets."

We both stand—I lightly take his hand—and prepare to part company. When he wishes me success in finding mushrooms, I tell him that I think I shall go straight to my watercolors, that I want to paint the bend in the road, around the willow trees before the approach to the house.

"I noticed the chestnuts are blooming freely," he says. He's very small. The top of his head comes perhaps to my ear, but he looks well, only a little stooped in the shoulders as a man would whose work positions his hands in front of his body. I have never painted a commoner at his work, but I think it would be a lovely picture, and the thought makes me feel happy. As though in response to that happy thought, he speaks again.

"I remember your little girl very well because she came out into the garden, where I was pulling spring onions."

I am amazed, and I stare at him in disbelief. What gift is this that he so casually gives me?

"She was so friendly a little girl, a regular darling. She asked if she might have one of the onions I was pulling. I plucked up a nice shoot from the ground, and I sliced off the roots with my knife, and peeled back the husk so it was slick and slippery for her. She put the bulb between her teeth, and bit it right off."

My heart brims with happiness. To see her again! In the sunshine of a garden! What an image, what a treasure, my little accident has given me!

"Just before she went in the door, she turned and said, *"Merci beaucoup, M. Jean-Jacques."*

Now I must turn away, lest I weep for joy. I say as I turn, *"Merci beaucoup, M. Jean-Jacques."* Dazed, I retrace my steps till I find one of the woodland chairs to rest in.

WHEN JULIE WAS SEVENTEEN and we arrived in St. Petersburg, she was charming in her person, possessed many talents, and had acquired a very good education because of her prodigious memory. She had large blue eyes, sparkling with freshness, a slightly upturned nose which added to her liveliness, with a very pretty mouth and pretty teeth. While she was not tall, she was slender without being too thin. Her manner was one of easy grace; at the same time she had a lively mind and could remember everything she had learned either from her tutors or from her own reading. Her natural aptitude for painting and also for music added to her accomplishments: she had a lovely voice and sang beautifully in Italian, while accompanying herself well on either the piano or the guitar.

My mind skims over the thoughts without the words, the narrative of Julie.

I thoroughly admired her bright spirit, intelligence, and responsiveness to art, literature, and music, and it was a joy to be in her company. Although in St. Petersburg I was hard at work at the easel every day, except two hours on Sunday morning when I allowed visitors to come to my studio, I wanted Julie to enjoy every pastime that pleased her.

One of her pleasures was to participate in the Russian sleighing parties, and sometimes I let her stay overnight with the Countess Czernicheff and her family without me.

At their home she met the secretary of Count Czernicheff, a M. Nigris. He was about thirty, of pleasing build and face. (A sigh escapes me as I sit here. Perhaps I should take up my brush and watercolors, should give myself to the scene before me.) Nigris had sweet manners and a certain melancholy manner which young and innocent girls often find intriguing. To my daughter, he seemed pale and interesting, and he wrote very well, as one might expect of a secretary. He also drew a little, but he had no truly remarkable talents. Nor had he family of note, nor fortune. Nonetheless, my daughter heedlessly fell in love with him.

Most regrettably the Czernicheffs encouraged her infatuation. As soon as I realized her state of mind, I asked about M. Nigris. Some spoke well of him, but others spoke ill of him, and I felt much confusion because I did not want to spoil my daughter's happiness without good reason.

Even before this crisis occurred—for they wished to become engaged— my own friends had said to me of my treatment of my daughter, "You love her so much that you are blind; far from her obeying you, you obey her and indulge her wishes." My greatest wish was to see her happy. When my friends tried to warn me, I replied, "Can't you see that everybody loves her?" as though their admiration for her excused my indulgence toward her and my wish for her to enjoy life and its opportunities to the fullest.

With this attachment to M. Nigris, however, I was not so blind. I saw it closing the doors to happiness and opportunity rather than opening them, for there is no going back after such a choice. Because this was such a serious situation, I tried to persuade my daughter of my point of view. I told her with much ardor that in every respect this marriage, if allowed to take place, would make her far from happy. She was so excited by the prospect of this romance that she never stopped to think that I was vastly more experienced in the ways of the world. She did not understand that I spoke against the engagement only because I loved her so much.

Her governess, Mme Charrot, who had ridden with us out of Paris and had been with us all this time, took Julie's view of the situation and did all she could to poison my daughter against me. This same Mme Charrot had let Julie read romantic novels behind my back, and that of course caused her to trust only her feelings and sensibilities and totally to ignore good sense. The Czernicheff family and their friends constantly tried to persuade me to allow Julie to have her way. The more I tried to reason with her and persuade her not to leap headlong into an ill-considered marriage, the more secretive she became. The more I thwarted Julie's dream of romance, the more estranged we became.

Her friends "confided" to me that her passion was so strong that she would even elope with this M. Nigris and marry in secret if I did not consent. I did not entirely believe this, for he had no money and I discovered the Czernicheffs themselves could barely pay their bills. They even had the effrontery to question me on behalf of M. Nigris about what size dowry I was prepared to endow upon my daughter. On this front, the ambassador of Naples became their spokesperson and asked for an amount that far exceeded everything I had. I had left France without any fortune, leaving all my earnings in the hands of Julie's father, and I had lost a great deal that I had earned in Italy when the Bank of Venice failed. But by working hard, I had earned again, just in Russia, a considerable sum.

Julie was so unhappy that her appetite decreased. Before my eyes I saw her grow thin and frail. Then she fell ill. I had nursed her through other illnesses due to the cold Russian winters, but this was entirely different. When I sat beside her and chatted with her then, or fed her hot soup with a bowl and spoon, her eyes always looked lovingly at me. A bit of sparkle would come to her face and appreciation for my attentions. Now when I entered her room, her face darkened and she looked more ill than ever. She refused any cheer or encouragement that I offered, and she cut short any expressions of love that I proffered as insincere and worthy only of scathing irony and disdain. I felt her very life was slipping away.

For her to marry, it was necessary to receive the consent of her father (despite my being her support and guardian). I had heard from her father and from others that in France, there was hope that our daughter might be married to the painter Guérin, whose reputation and promise had even reached me in Russia. I had welcomed that idea, but when I clumsily (I'll admit) suggested this alternative, she thrashed her head back and forth on the pillow, and the tears gushed from her eyes. She refused all food the rest of the day.

The next morning, seeing the anguish in her eyes, which were ringed with dark circles, I told her that I would write to her father, M. Le Brun, and ask on her behalf for his consent to the marriage. I did write him, saying that because we had but one most dear child, we should sacrifice all else to her happiness.

After this letter was sent, I was most relieved to see that she did begin to regain her health. That was my only reward. She maintained the sullen attitude she had taken whenever she was in my company, despite the fact that now I was trying to support her choice. Not for a moment did she treat me in any loving way, or acknowledge my abiding love for her, or accept my explanation that I had opposed her "happiness," as she called it, only because I had misgivings of a serious sort. Even such slight cautions as echoed perhaps in that statement were construed as an insult to her own judgment, and she took umbrage. Nothing could rekindle the light in her eyes when she looked at me. Her lovely face began to seem almost ugly to me.

Fearing my letter might have gone astray, I wrote several more letters asking for M. Le Brun's consent for Julie to marry M. Nigris.

Because of the great distance between St. Petersburg and Paris, her father's reply was naturally a long time in arriving. In that interval she accused me of not having written the letters. Her suspicion hurt me cruelly.

As pleasantly as I could, I offered to write another letter which she herself might read in its entirety and take to the post directly, without giving it back to my hand. Even then I did not reclaim her trust. Instead her loyalty remained with those who wished to inspire just such mistrust in her, and they continually painted me as an ogre. Sometimes I wondered if she had no memory of our happy and trusting times together, or our adventures and pleasures together, or how frank and open we had been in sharing our thoughts and impressions.

One day she said with accusing, hurt eyes, "I carry your letters to the post, but I am certain that you write my father other letters that contradict what you have said in the letters you show me. That is how you maintain the appearance of being my friend, when in fact you oppose me."

I was so stunned by her suspicions that I could hardly speak.

For just a moment, I saw something like a flicker of remorse in her eyes, but she quickly turned away and left me alone in the room.

If for a minute I had thought that her marriage might lead to a good life for her, I would have apologized for my anxiety and strong misgivings, but nothing I saw gave me the slightest hope. That she could be so cruel and unimaginative as to my position left me dazzled with amazement. I could scarcely believe it was true: that she believed the poison about me that had been pumped into her ears. I tried to show no resentment to her, but my heart was much grieved every moment until her father's letter finally reached us, a letter in which he gave the legal consent necessary for the marriage.

I thought perhaps she would realize that *she* had been mistaken in her estimate of my honest support, but she maintained the same mien toward me. It was as though she had succeeded in spite of me rather than because of me. It was a sign of her lack of adult aptitude that she could not relent from the pose she had assumed; she had to remain inflexible and rigid to justify her cruelty to me in her own mind. It had been a vain hope on my part that when her father's letter should arrive, she might tender a small apology toward me. She did not show any sign of gratitude whatsoever. Those she so foolishly trusted as more wise than her mother had alienated her heart from considering me or my feelings at all. In her mind, I deserved no consideration, though surely she had seen my suffering in the disappointment of my hopes and desires for a marital condition that would increase, not decrease, the happiness of her life.

No time was lost from the moment of M. Le Brun's letter's arrival in St. Petersburg. The marriage was celebrated within a few days. I gave my daughter a handsome trousseau and jewels, just as though I were pleased with her choice; I gave her a bracelet with some very fine diamonds surrounding a miniature of her father. For a dowry, I placed with Livio the banker the money I had earned for the portraits I had completed while in St. Petersburg. I knew that I could replace the money by painting more portraits.

THE DAY AFTER JULIE'S MARRIAGE, I visited her. She received me calmly. I marveled to see no trace of excitement or of genuine happiness in her face. I went home very soberly, fearful that I had been all too correct in my prognosis concerning her marriage to M. Nigris. I knew that he had taken his pleasure with no concern for her feelings.

After they had a wedding trip, I saw her in her home again, in fifteen days.

Then I asked her, cheerfully, "You are, I hope, very happy, now that you are married?"

Her husband was in the same room, but his back was turned to us, and he was wearing a clumsy-looking fur coat. He had it on inside the house because he was quite ill with a very bad cold. We both knew he was oblivious to our conversation, and besides, we spoke in low tones.

With a cool glance at his back and no expression of joy whatsoever in her face, though she was too proud to show regret, she said quietly, "I do confess that his greatcoat is rather disenchanting. How could anyone be in love with such a figure?" She tapped her finger beside her pretty nose as though to imply that *his* nose was swollen, red, and disgusting.

I went home as quickly as I could, shaken, because I could feel my face turn to ash. I think she blamed me all the more because I had been right in trying to save her from just such a mistake as she had insisted on making.

SOON AFTER THE WEDDING, I received news that Julie had caught small-pox. I went to her bedside as fast as I could. Her face retained so much fluid that I was terrified she might die. Though I had never had smallpox, I did not contract it during my vigil. I stayed with her throughout the illness.

For days, I prayed on my knees beside her bed, not for her beauty or happiness but merely that she might live. Yet, I remembered Mlle Boquet's similar illness, and I insisted that Julie wear thick gloves so as not to scratch and scar her face. The agony of watching beside the sickbed of a child is beyond description. I do not know if it is made all the greater by having only one child, but I do know that the taste of the fear of death on the back of one's tongue is beyond compare in bitterness. I was able to contain my despair only by knowing its expression would create an atmosphere inappropriate to healing and hope. To be so far from home, at such a time! In Russia, God seemed less caring.

But my unceasing prayers were answered, and my Julie recovered fully. Her lovely face was not marked at all by the pox. My joy at her return to the world of the living, to my world, was checked because I still saw no love in her face. Nor even affection. Her expression toward me was hard. Dutifully, she did thank me for my care, but in a calm, uncaring way. At best, in times when we were together, she maintained a civil neutrality toward me. Sometimes when we were in the company of others, she smiled at me, but I think it was more so that they would not think ill of her than it was to gladden my heart.

Every day, when I first saw her, at a distance, my heart leapt with joy. I was always glad to see her, no matter how she might crush me, in a few moments, with a disdainful glance or through her tone of voice.

I believe she thought my early opposition had blighted her chances for the kind of marriage some young couples create for themselves. If it had been my fault, I would have been heartily sorry and begged her forgiveness, but my sense of justice kept me from assuming responsibility that lay at her doorstep. Now I wish I had knelt in the gutter, assumed whatever guilt she wished to place on my head, wept, and pleaded that she forgive and love me again, as she had once, when she was a child.

And yet . . . I do remember that I myself had been disappointed in my marriage; and my mother, as well, certainly had been mistaken in marrying my stepfather, but we did not blame others for our own mistaken choices. Looking back, I am sure that my mother, though she kept a good face for the sake of the household and especially for Étienne and me, her young children, must have found my father's unflagging interest in other ladies quite hard to bear. Nonetheless, she had savored our outings and times at home when we did, in fact, enjoy each other's company as a family.

I grieved for my daughter's choice, but I hoped that she would also find for herself what satisfaction she could in her marriage or in occupations she might cultivate and find pleasurable. To think, fifteen days after her wedding, I saw no sign of passion for her husband left in her.

Because my daughter was unhappy, all charm seemed to have disappeared forever from my own existence. My love of painting had been a constant in my life, married or not, and by this time in my life painting sustained me yet, in Russia. My mother had found consolation in God and in the passion of Christ and the beauty of the rituals of the church. In music. Where would my daughter find solace? If I could, I would have turned my heart wrong side out, like a purse, and given her all its loving contents.

I was not in good spirits, or even healthy ones. I was exhausted from nursing Julie through the smallpox and worrying about her well-being and her future. My presence in St. Petersburg seemed blighted. Knowing how travel had always refreshed me, I decided to go to Moscow despite the fact that the weather was near freezing and there were mountains to be crossed. To stay in the city of St. Petersburg was a torture I could not endure.

Before I left St. Petersburg, I received a letter of apology from Count Czernicheff. He wrote: "I confess that carried away by my high spirits, I accused you of a thousand wrongs and I dared to reproach you bitterly, yet your own conduct was admirable. Your tenderness toward your daughter served as an example to all mothers and it causes me to blush with embarrassment for having harbored and expressed shameful suspicions about you, which were my own formulation. I beg your forgiveness . . ."

How could I forgive him? He had helped to doom my daughter to a life far less happy than that she was worthy of. I hid my pain. I complained not at all, not even to my brother, Étienne, with whom I was in correspondence. Alas, he informed me from Paris our dear mother had died a natural death in the city. Natural—so much sorrow!

I hurried as rapidly as I dared to finish the large portrait of the Empress Maria, the wife of the new emperor, Paul, and I left for Moscow on October 15, 1800, a year for which I had hoped greater general happiness than in the preceding century, but I found only the most profound personal unhappiness.

I recall that in respect to weather October 15, though quite cold, was still too early for comfortable traveling. The Russian roads were not yet frozen solid. The logs that would have been stabilized by ice were untethered, and the surface of the road bobbed up and down; our wheels visited deep ruts and were half submerged in mud. I thought I would die of misery.

At the only inn along the road, the Novgorod Inn, which I had been assured would provide well for me, I was served food that I could hardly eat. I feared vomiting. In my room, I soon detected a horrible stench. When I inquired, I was told, "Madame, a man died in the room just beyond the glass door dividing this room from the next. He's still there, and that must be the cause of what Madame smells." Without further inquiry, I ordered the horses to be harnessed again to the carriage and for us to continue toward Moscow. For the second half of the journey, we traveled in dense fog, so there was constant danger of collision and no view. The pall over the countryside depressed my spirits even more. In my hand I carried only a crust of bread snatched up as I left the inn, and I had nothing else till we reached Moscow.

FAR AWAY AND LONG AGO was that October from this May in Louveciennes. If I walk over this slope, on the sunny, south-facing downside, there trumpet daffodils will be in bloom in the open areas, and perhaps some

bluebells and violets as well near the shady margins of the trees. The daffodils are hardy, robust, with a slight greenish cast to their golden yellow;
they appear year after year, and yet I am always afraid for them, these flowers unguarded in the great woods.

My own garden would be jealous if it knew I lavished some feelings on
these little wild things. Back there close to my home, protected by a rock
wall should the breezes blow too hard, the tulips in my garden are blooming (their bulbs having been imported from the Dutch): bright red, daz-
zling white, some purple. They are cups of color, and later I shall pick some
for the table for my dinner party tonight. Best are the multicolored, ruffled
ones, flamboyant as parrots, or the streaked Rembrandt ones, sedate in
shape but inventive with their darts and stripes of color. And fragrant lilac,
I'll mix some of that with the tulips, both white and purple panicles of lilac.

With only a little stiffness, I rise from my chair, not having taken up
the pencil. I am rested in body. I will conjure up other memories to refresh
my mind and spirit. Ahead, at a certain place I have designated this morning, I will find by prearrangement another chair, an easel, my papers, my
watercolors, and my brushes waiting for me. Ah, the warmth of the sun
feels good on my face. And these daffodils, I believe they have more of glorious gold and less of sickly green about their faces this spring.

Oh, the golden domes of Moscow, when I finally entered that place,
unlike any other city in Europe, more like drawings of Persian Isfahan.
Ah, the wide streets of Moscow, the superb palaces situated with whole
villages between the palaces, all within the city, and the enormous golden
crosses surmounting those myriad golden domes! My artist's eye falls on
the soft fur of a young rabbit crouching among the May apples of Louveciennes, and I, an old woman, think, *Never have I loved any human creature so
well as I loved Julie, my daughter.* And yet I could not save her, child so wise,
child so foolish. Nor, though I preserved our lives, was I able to ensure her
happiness.

When I returned to St. Petersburg, relations between Julie and me
remained the same, while the atmosphere at court had rapidly deteriorated

into its own reign of terror. Aristocrats disappeared or were sent to Siberia for no reason other than the unreasonable suspicions of the new czar. Because I frequented the same social circles, I trembled lest some remark of my own might be construed as a threat. Quietly and properly, I asked for and obtained permission to leave Russia. I did not dare express my fear to Julie, but I perceived her and her husband to be safe enough.

So great was my relief at escaping when my westbound carriage became stuck in mud for a whole day, I happily used the time and material at hand in a creative way—to fashion a little statue out of mud! My instinct for survival had once again served me well. During the final period of my stay in Russia, I was more terrified than I had been in France.

XI

VIGNETTES

Italy
(continued)

PORTRAIT

FROM THE GUILLOTINE, at least, I did save both myself and Julie. Her father, I am thankful to remember, had the wit to save himself. But I should have gone to Italy in any case, as so many French artists did, to study the great masters. That the Revolution forced him to divorce me as a disloyal émigré caused me no sorrow, for the marriage had long since ceased to hold sentimental value for me. It was a relief to become legally what I already was spiritually: an independent woman who defined herself as an artist and a mother.

I never felt so free or triumphant as when first our stagecoach rolled over the Beauvoisin Bridge, the political boundary of France, into Italy. But the landscape was not reassuring. The high peaks of Savoy overwhelmed us, for they towered into a thick dark gray cloud melding the disparate elements of stone and sky. I had not imagined a world so massive or darkly unified. We were terrified by the upreared earth and feared it could fall and crush us. Of course it maintained its posture. As our initial terror resolved itself, the steep brutality of the mountains began to inspire awe and admiration. What we were witnessing was a manifestation of the sublime. With my hand on little Julie's shoulder, I could feel her body modulate as her own fear turned into inspired wonder.

In Italy we were to discover not only immense mountains but also roaring cataracts, and when we rambled beside them the overwhelming force and movement of the water coursed through us. Once I hired donkeys and guides through the Apennines so that we might visit the Terni waterfall, which from a distance looked like a great white cloth hanging from a precipice. Even more spectacular was our visit to Mount Vesuvius, the great volcano. The earth itself twitched as we ascended the flanks of the sloping cone, and we were instructed of nature's power to destroy and of the unbelievable heat that lives within our earth. I said to Julie that it was no wonder the ancient Greeks and Romans associated some of their gods with the awesome sovereignty of nature.

Julie grew accustomed to the idea that the natural world was full of wild wonders. Since I felt safe, so did she. With equal confidence we entered a new social world where new friends, and old ones met again (many had fled the Revolution), extended to us consummate courtesy and treated Julie always as though she were a small adult, a little person whose strong feelings and thoughts and talents were to be respected. How adept and eager she was then with paint and brush, with charcoal, with the pastel crayon, but it was the quill, dipped in ink, that she loved to wield. I never told her I had named her for the heroine of Rousseau's novel *Julie, ou la nouvelle Héloïse,* but I did wish for her the virtues, advocated in those pages, of authenticity, self-knowledge, and autonomy, which I understand to be self-confidence.

I could not foresee that Julie's independence would become a kind of willfulness: to satisfy herself and to defy anyone who sought to guide her; she trusted her desires and wishes so strongly that they convinced her of their primacy.

"You have made me what I am," she once accused. "You kept me by your side and force-fed me your opinions as though I were a goose with feet nailed to the floor and grain funneled down my throat."

"I think not," was all I could say, but my brain was flooded with images of her face full of delight when we watched and heard the cataract roar. Or of her awe in viewing Michelangelo's paintings on the ceiling of the Sistine Chapel. "They aren't pictures," she said solemnly. "They are the truth." Throughout her young life, she formed her own opinions, and I most willingly confirmed her pronouncements and offered her my respect.

I am only trying to convince myself that I need not be ashamed of myself as a mother to my most precious child.

Of course I made mistakes. I do not dispute that fact. Sometimes I acknowledge the truth: if I had been a capable mother, my daughter would be happy and alive today.

PERHAPS IF HER IMAGINATION had not been so strong, Julie would not have imagined romance and believed in her fantasy concerning the nature of M. Nigris, a minor count, in whom there was nothing of either that high energy or generosity that are necessary if life is to realize its potential for glory. Here is the metaphor I might have used to instruct her: Does the landscape have a pleasant contour? That is not always the appropriate question. Do veins of silver and gold lie beneath the surface? Ask that.

My thoughts are all a-scramble.

Certainly I have failed to read the deep character of others. What men were they—my stepfather and my husband—to take without second thought all that I earned while begrudging me far less than a tithe. Of course they were taking what was their legal right according to the laws. But never mind, never mind. I have no need of such riches now. I have enough: my Louveciennes in spring and summer, and when the chill winds whistle through the wood, I have the velvet and fur of Paris, of my own snug rooms, of the opera and the concert hall, of the warmth to be found at the hearths of many friends. And while my stepfather and my husband spent my money, I learned how to paint better and better, and how to converse in society, and how to find pleasures in nature in small glittering moments. I knew I could rely on myself to provide. Sheerly because of my delight in my painting, I have had a rich life.

WHEN JULIE AND I WERE IN FLORENCE, my eyes feasted on artistic treasures like any glutton's on a groaning board. Not that on the rare occasion I did not secretly criticize the great masters, though little of that came tripping off my tongue when I dictated my remembrances to my nephew's pen: *Souvenirs*, we called the memoir. In my *Souvenirs* I wisely refrained from presuming to note any critical thoughts about their magnificent achievements.

And as for Raphael, now? How I rhapsodized over him in my memoir! There I fully entered into the way I felt about him when I was a young mother. Now I have had a sea change about his work, which only illustrates that the old are not so set in their ways as some would think. Now I believe his colors are too bold, too brash, almost unbelievable. Rather than representing nature faithfully, he chose to wave the banner of his own importance. He abandoned the truth of what his eyes surely told him for the puissance of his own hand. Though Raphael envied and tried to learn from Michelangelo's paintings, Raphael lacked the truth of Michelangelo.

Michelangelo did not even need color; his sculptures prove that. He understood form, which is the basis for all artistic achievement. People say some of his work is unfinished, but to my eye, even in those late sculptures, he had ideas to unveil about the relationship of rough and smooth. A work must contain its own tensions if it is to embody the dynamism that is the stuff of life.

Such observations and ideas about art took root during those days of new-won independence, in Florence, and I also developed an eagerness for science. Would the art of painting be possible were it not for the miracle of the human eye? For much of my life, I have taken my eyes for granted, but in Florence I met a man who had an understanding, anatomically speaking, of how the eye worked.

Naturally I was fascinated by his knowledge, which he generously made accessible to me and to others through creating wax models. As he spoke to me in a low and gentle voice, he explained how muscles are attached to the eyeball and how, like nearly invisible threads, these muscles cause the eye to rotate in its socket so that we might look up or down or to either side. This scientist had made a very large wax model as a tool for instruction about the structure of the human eye.

Even more miraculous to know: the pupil of the eye is in fact a hole, a little, perfectly circular nothingness that allows light to pass to the interior of the eye, where it falls upon a kind of screen and activates certain nerves that convey an image to the brain. (Surely I *am* my father's child, for did not D'Alembert dine at our table, and were not the encyclopedists chattering endlessly about not only anatomy but many new discoveries, ever amplifying our sense of wonder?)

Though anatomical optic structures made of wax are not in themselves beautiful, I told myself, as I walked back to my Florentine apartment from the laboratory of M. Fontana, I must not be squeamish but take science on its own terms. What I learned inspired at least as much awe in me as revulsion, and I thought of how God had managed to make mere flesh marvelously effective and capable. We are amazing machines! That night after the insight and new knowledge made accessible to me by M. Fontana's models, I spent a long time on my knees.

In this posture, I thanked God for developing such mechanisms within us, and I thanked him that he had created in us the desire to use the wonderful optic instruments, our eyes, and also our intricate hands, built of intertwining blood vessels and bones and tendons and nerves, which communicated with the eye and the brain in order to create all the beauties of art. I felt humble and grateful.

Some of this knowledge I shared the next morning over *petit déjeuner* with Julie, who responded rapturously, "I love my eyes, Maman"—and here she squeezed her eyes shut as she spoke, as though to assert her control over those amazing instruments—"but I love your eyes even more, and the way you look at me through the steam over your chocolate cup."

Never have I felt more happy. It seemed the perfect moment, that moment when we sat talking at table, our cups steaming, the flavor of warm chocolate still in our mouths: I had shared as quickly as possible what I learned with my child, who not only appreciated the wonder of the knowledge but also had her own thoughts, ones that bespoke our love.

Then she added, "But suppose, Maman, that I could not see, and I could never never see your eyes, when they shine at me." Then she proposed that she would go and write a story about a blind girl.

For a moment, a black horror came upon me: the idea that my girl might not see, might not ever paint, or love the art of others, or simply drink in nature's light. I swallowed down this terrible idea as quickly as I could, and I cheerfully told her a story about a blind girl in ancient days, in Pompeii, at the time of the deadly eruption of Vesuvius.

"So thick was the ash in the air that all were blinded by it, but this young maiden, having long ago learned to make her way through the streets without seeing, was unimpaired by the ash, and she led many others to safety."

"I shall write that story," Julie said, "and show how all those who had ignored her previously and thought her limited"—her speech slowed to follow her forming thought—"and less than themselves, now understood her value"—she suddenly plunged confidently ahead—"and her courage, and they all fell in love with her."

With an easy, graceful leap, my Julie had placed herself into the life of a legendary figure and into the frame of narrative.

Now, all meditative, daughterless as I walk among the chestnut trees of beloved Louveciennes, I might ask what necessity compelled Julie's imaginative leaping, and what realities or fears about herself and her world did she escape by passing so effortlessly into the realm of fiction?

Not having had enough of the realm of science, during our sojourn in Florence, I rose from my tête-à-tête with Julie to return to my scientific mentor M. Fontana. Considering his name, I thought of him as a fountain of knowledge.

M. Fontana's laboratory, or cabinet, contained the wax body of a nude woman. During my first visit I had been so fascinated by the larger-than-life model of the human eyeball that I had lavished all of my attention upon it. But on my second visit to M. Fontana's laboratory, I noticed the wax body of a woman, mostly covered. She lay in a reclined position and her body below the neckline was covered with a sheet; she seemed to be merely a representation of a woman with a pale face and flowing dark hair, and I took little notice of the figure, since it offered no new knowledge. I did note a pearl necklace, or a simulation of a pearl necklace, encircling her throat. Her eyes were closed as though she were sleeping. Perhaps because she was life-size, her presence was somehow vaguely disconcerting to me.

M. Fontana noticed my glances to that part of the room and mistakenly construed them to be a sign of my curiosity.

"Would Madame Le Brun like for me to lift the sheet?" he asked, already walking toward the wax woman.

Reflexively, my heart stoppered up my throat such that I could not speak, but since I followed him across the room like a good student, the anatomist naturally believed I wished to see whatever was beneath the sheet. The white sheet was almost the same deathly hue as her pallid cheeks and neck. His hand hesitated on the top of the sheet. I almost reached out my hand to arrest his, but my vanity about not being squeamish held me back.

Though I was not really of a scientific disposition, it seemed evident to me in that fleeting interval that either a woman or a man *could* perform scientific explorations; nothing but the customs of society prevented a woman from following such a career. Was not I a successful painter, the painter of royalty in fact, though I was female? I was playing a little with the idea of being a woman scientist *in potentia*.

When he removed the sheet from the woman's torso, I saw lying coiled in the open cavity of her body a replica of human intestines. My own stomach rose with such violent nausea that I covered my mouth, lest I vomit. The colors I saw, coral and pink, a yellowish tinge, white ligature material, a purplish red background, were the most repulsive I had ever conceived. Their arrangement, twisting around one another, corrugated and slimy looking, seemed as threatening as a large venomous snake. Also laid bare was what he pointed out with his finger and identified as her rather asymmetrical lungs, with a heart nestled between. I turned my eyes, my head, and my whole body away. He quietly replaced the cloth, without comment.

I do not remember what excuse I offered or what thanks I may have fabricated, but I hastened from the laboratory clutching my stomach. Once outside I wanted to hide, but I knew the image was inside my head, and I could never erase it. I closed my eyes, leaned my back against the wall of a building, and instructed myself to imagine something beautiful. Florence's sublime, seventeen-foot-tall *David* of Michelangelo came to mind, but no sooner did I envision the marble youth than my own mind removed the surface of the stone and there he was, skinless, the striated muscles in his bent arm and the tendons quite visible, and in hideous colors. Anatomic eyes set in their sockets looked out from David's face at the world. Worst of all I imagined his intestines, and the shaft of his manly part which became a skinned snake.

As quickly as I could, I hurried home, rushed past Julie and her governess, simply saying I was not well, and with all my clothes still on my body hurried into my bed, pulling the covers up to my neck and allowing my eyelids to slide down. From viewing the waxen woman of M. Fontana, I knew just how the curves of lashes on my cheeks might appear to an observer. In a deranged way, my fingers explored my neck as though to make sure I was wearing no pearl necklace. I cried, and I deplored the tears manufactured by my human body that oozed through their ducts down the sides of my face. Grotesquely the tears entered my ears, and I thought I was a mechanical doll or statue recycling its fluids, as a fountain might.

I imagined M. Fontana looking at me through his clear spectacles, and his face that had seemed keen and kind now seemed fiendish. Though my chest heaved with sobs, I let no sounds escape lest they fall on Julie's sensitive ears a few rooms away. I was in a feverish state of anxiety. Portraits I had painted came to my mind, not lovely flesh or beautiful countenances but the garish anatomy lying beneath these lovingly re-created appearances. Even my friend the queen, whom I had painted many times, was stripped of her beauty, and I was forced to picture her mortal underpinnings of blood vessels, muscles, and even bones.

And did I, as a painter, deal only in the superficial? I knew how stupid it was to paint clothing with no hint of the body that lay within, how untruthful and inept! But what of that next layer of reality? The rest of the body that lay beneath a radiant complexion? The body within the sheath of skin, the concealed, many-layered body of bones, fat, ropes of blood vessels, and binding tissues that comprise our form?

Each terrifying visualization racked me till I fell asleep from exhaustion. When I awoke, I was not refreshed. Instead, melancholy permeated every fiber of my being.

For two full days after, I suffered from what I had seen in M. Fontana's cabinet. It was as though I moved and lived within a life-size bag made of gray gauze. When I walked to my easel or looked at the pigments on my palette, I wanted to vomit, and I pictured the most vile colors and terrible odors spewing from my mouth and all my orifices. I turned away from my work and any evidence of the artistic work of others. I felt my life, my art, was woven of a concealing fabric of lies.

No one seemed to notice that I had given up smiling, that I uttered no exclamations of pleasure. I stayed away from Julie as much as I could, not wishing to infect her. I ate little. I remembered how the gruesome conditions in France, before my flight, had made it impossible for me to work, but then there had been a real and palpable danger to my life. What I had seen in M. Fontana's cabinet was merely the veil lifted from nature. He had revealed the reality of mortal anatomy. And its image was grotesque.

Framed by her long hair, her lids closed, reclining as though waiting, wearing her pearls, she had seemed romantic, as though she had just been with or was awaiting her husband or lover. But then the exposed viscera— nothing could be less erotic. Who could want to make love to a pan of guts packed tightly together?

And yet that is what we are, both women and men, along with other organs inside us the like of which we never see in our ordinary lives, on an ordinary day. No wonder the church forbade human dissection at one time. The reality was too awful. How could the spirit inhabit the biological human? Where was the room! Surely, if they beheld the human interior many people would lose faith and feel we were beyond redemption and had no place in eternity. Our organs were like those of the beasts: we were but muscle and fat, vessels and pouches.

How could the inside and the outside be so utterly different? I thanked God for wrapping this mortal coil, this jungle of meat and blood vessels, in skin and for fashioning our nostrils and ears and private orifices such that they afforded no peephole to the interior. Heretofore, I had regarded the skin as an aspect of beauty; its hues subtle, harmonious, and complex, and flesh was pleasant and various to the touch. With my eyes, I had touched the cheeks, foreheads, and chins of others appreciatively; I had re-created them—so lifelike—on canvas with paints and on paper with pastels. But now skin seemed but a cloak for the horror within.

On the third day of my depression, I determined I would take myself to M. Fontana. I would tell him of my troubles. I would seek his help in overcoming the shock I had experienced when he pulled away the sheet.

He received me kindly and remarked immediately that I looked as though I had been ill. Knowing that he was a perceptive and intelligent person, I had no trouble opening myself to him. I said that perhaps because I was an artist and because the world as apprehended by the eye was something to which I was especially sensitive, what I had seen modeled in wax within the abdomen had appeared to my imagination like evil incarnate, like a snake in the garden in all its monstrousness, and that I had been thrown into a debilitating depression, one that affected my ability to work and in fact had shaken my faith. In headlong confession, the phrases spewed from my mouth.

Finally, I said more quietly that I sought his help in how to relieve myself from what I had seen. I felt haunted, and my newly stimulated imagination stood between me and what I had believed in as the nature of the world I inhabited.

"I cannot look at anyone without seeing through their clothing and then through their very skin. People are like walking meat skinned by the butcher."

"Of course what you saw was only wax."

"Oh no," I said, objecting to the superficial nature of his reassurance. "When anyone looks at my portraits, they do not say, 'It is only paint.' They say, 'There she is!' Or, 'There he is, himself, before me.' There is truth in art, and truth represented in your models."

He invited me to sit down, and I did so, facing him, he in one simple, straight chair and I in its twin. He arranged himself in a leisurely way and seemed completely relaxed.

"To me," he answered calmly, stroking his beard, "the human interior is interesting. I think we are fearfully and wonderfully made. This feeling of wonder has an element of admiration in it, not disgust. I want to know, and I feel everyone should know, what anatomical models can teach us."

I glanced over his shoulder and was glad to see that now a sheet covered even the face of the wax woman. She was shrouded like a corpse. On its stand, the giant model of an eye looked at me steadily. That it was displayed thus, as a separate entity, and one made unrealistically large, made it far less threatening than the lifelike model of a whole person, of a woman.

"I know too much," I said. "I see too much. I hear too acutely. I tremble at the slightest noise. My sense of myself and of my world seems shattered. I am too weak to carry out my work, even to be a proper mother. A great misfortune has befallen me."

Suddenly he smiled at me and even reached out and touched my shoulder.

"What you are calling a misfortune and construe as weakness is really a superlative sensitivity. You are a great artist, Madame, because of your sensitivity to the world and to your own response to it. You have rare gifts. Your organs for seeing and hearing, even your nerves, are made of finer stuff than those of ordinary people."

"But I am miserable. I live in a fog of depression. Is there a cure?"

"A cure? But of course there is a cure." His face was all friendliness. He spoke in a hearty manner, completely self-confident. "Your gifts are like all gifts. If you do not use them, they will atrophy and disappear. If you wish to diminish the discomfort caused by your extreme sensitivity, then stop looking at art. Stop painting."

As though pulled upward by a slow-handed puppet master, I slowly rose from my chair. I felt my face, my whole body, flame with anger. I was burning with outrage. I averted my face. What he had just said horrified me many times more than mere human anatomy.

I—no longer to paint! I—no longer to be myself, an artist!

I found myself on the street, rushing to my studio, toward my easel and paints, to my life. To paint and to live were and are the same to me. Destroy my sensitivity! I had thanked Providence many times for my innate artistic nature and abilities, for the discerning power of my sight. What a fool I had been. As I rushed toward home, I looked into the face of everyone I met: I considered their foreheads, the shapes of their cheeks, how their hair was arranged, how the flesh tones modified around the mouth and the tint of the lips. All this I could see. All this I could paint, if I chose. All this, the appearance that has its own reality, I could celebrate. Betray my gifts? Never.

I HAD SURVIVED A CRISIS so serious that it might have been a matter of religious faith.

My afternoon with Julie was joyful. Before the market closed, she and I filled our baskets with vegetables and delighted in the color and shape of long green squash, the hairy tips of orange carrots and their ferny tops; the dimpled skin of an orange made us touch its rough round-ness, and a cabbage looked so pompous and pretty, I was tempted to put it on my head. After taking home our bounty, we went to the pri-vate, walled garden of a friend of mine, and there we delighted our noses by sticking them into roses, and we admired the dark indigo petals and golden centers of spiderwort. I showed Julie the furry stripe down the falls of iris blooms, and she pronounced it to be like a woolly worm. A chessboard had been left set up on a stone table in an alcove, and I taught her the names of the pieces and how they were allowed to move in their flat world, and asked her whether she preferred the light or the dark pieces, but she could not decide, and we laughed and made the black knight kiss the cheek of the white bishop. All afternoon I saw the world again in all its splendor.

After that fruitful and very happy afternoon, when we were eating supper, little Julie said, "When I look into your eyes, Maman, I know I am looking at an artist." She was mild and matter-of-fact in her manner, con-fiding. Almost absentmindedly, she seemed to have taken up where our conversation of a few days earlier had left off. Her gaze moved around the room resting lightly on various objects she was enjoying seeing. But I real-ized that she was her grandfather's very own grandchild. She had echoed the truth my father had bestowed on me when I myself was a child.

"Are my eyes different from ordinary eyes, my child?"

"Oh yes," she said, her own eyes shining with truth, as her gaze returned to me.

Instantly I memorized her expression, and I resolved to render it in a small portrait of my beloved daughter, as soon as I could.

That night I lay in my bed brimming with happiness. I found I was smiling, and I touched the smile with my fingertips because it seemed quite special. Almost a secret with myself. I almost wanted to raise a looking

glass over myself so I could see just how such a smile was shaped. I imagined again my daughter's affirming, joyful tone of voice. There seemed an
encapsulating completeness to my life. Who and what I was now, in Italy,
echoed who and what I had been as a child, in France.

As I drifted toward sleep I thought of my need to be recognized and
appreciated by those whom I hold most dear. My father . . . my daughter . . .

XII
NIGHTFALL

FOUNTAIN

I N THE LATE AFTERNOON, an unexpected rain fell on St. James and Belgravia Courts and Fountain Court and Floral Terrace and on Central Park and the new green-surfaced tennis courts on the north end of the park, but the rain played itself out before reaching the East End, or perhaps it was less warm there, the population being not so dense and the air more chilly than the atmosphere hovering over Old Louisville. People who had come early to Amici's restaurant on Ormsby and to the new café across from the expansive Treyton Oak Towers looked out the windows and were glad they had followed the promptings of their appetites for good food, for now they sat safe and dry, looking out.

Really quite a hard rain, with wind from the southwest, Jackson Jones observed as he watched the storm from the doorway of Ermin's bakery and deli. As Osada Hiroshi lingered over the black bean soup at Carly Rae's, he decided not to text or e-mail, but to write an old-fashioned letter to his son in Tokyo. He would use a piece of paper and some sort of pen.

Those having stopped in at Buck's sat admiring the array of white flowers on the bar—an abundance of lilies and chrysanthemums displayed in heavy, cut-glass pitchers and tall vases from Victorian days; they noticed too the vases full of white Star of Bethlehem, borne on long green stalks, some with interesting curves or kinks in their journey upward. Passing the bar, they came to tables with white cloths and pretty china plates such as their grandmothers might have collected. With menus in hand, they wondered whether to choose crispy fish or gnocchi or bourbon steak. In the unchanging, ever-fresh elegance of the interior, they could forget weather. Tradition was what Buck's was all about.

At 610 Magnolia, the upwardly mobile yuppies from downtown businesses with cocktails in hand, alert and fashionable, made quick chat and breathed in the aromas from the award-winning kitchen. Their voices rose and they sipped their blessed cocktails and relaxed. One had to lean in close (that was nice, too) to hear or be heard.

At home on her sunporch in the back of the house, Ryn was reading portions of Élisabeth Vigée-Le Brun's memoir, *Souvenirs,* in French (a lovely three-volume set, a Christmas gift from Nancy in Birmingham, so light and easy to hold each slender volume). Might some French phrase yield up a nuance of Élisabeth's character that she had missed? Of course it would.

Looking from the sunporch to the western sky, Ryn saw that the rain was beginning to abate and soon the sun would show itself again—the clouds were rolling eastward—before sunset blushed the sky. Sometimes there was a rainbow in the late afternoon, if the sun came out again after a rain, but you had to be looking east to see it. If she stood on her sheltered front porch, looking east through the columns, perhaps she'd see a rainbow arcing over Venus. She felt weary, alone, sentimental.

Once with Peter, when Humphrey was just a little boy, five or six, when they were traveling out west as a family, they had seen a double rainbow. She had thought surely, surely it was a good omen: that they would be happy as a family. It had been a good moment, but she could tell even then that Peter was displeased about how jubilant she was over the rainbows.

She was restless. The visit to Leslie's condo had roused rather than soothed her nerves; she'd made herself call the confab short so that Leslie could get on with reading *Portrait of the Artist as an Old Woman*. It had been good to be together in the condo with Leslie and Daisy, two friends who cared about her and always encouraged her. She lay her book facedown on the sofa.

If she wanted to see the autumnal reds and yellows glazed with rain, she needed to go now.

At the front door, before she set the security alarm (the repairman had come and gone), she checked her jeans pocket for her cell phone, in case Yves would call, then she hurried down the semicircular front steps—always a pleasure, this liminal space of transition between her inner and outer worlds.

Oh, she had *forgotten* to change her clothes! And what did such forgetting signify? At least some part of her was acknowledging both that he was probably not coming and that he'd not bothered to call. Ah well. It was only an acquaintance, anyway. No doubt she had jumped the gun in inviting him up from Montgomery. A hideous drive. But she had liked his mind, his savoir faire, the interesting disparity in their categories of thought and in the dissimilar ways their two minds moved.

In any case: no word. So he wasn't interested. But she was. Or had been.

Well, she would be interested, then, in everything else. The sheen of the leaves, for example. Even at a distance the rain-glazed yellows and russets of the three tulip poplars were glowing.

Crossing Magnolia (she looked carefully because drivers would be returning home from work now and likely in a hurry), she entered Central Park and walked through the triangle formed by the three poplars: another liminal portal, one that engendered a frisson of excitement, her favorite spot in the entire park. Here was the park, a different world; the trees made it seem enchanted.

The trunks of the tulip poplars were dark, drenched from the rain, but they had held their leaves, yellow and mottled brown. Yes, the rain had been driven from the southwest, for on the northeast side the trunks were completely dry. A long and broad dry stripe of gray passed all the way up the rain-black trunk and followed the big branches as well. The gray streak was as distinctive, though temporary, as the stripe down the back of a skunk. Looking for red, Ryn turned right toward the stand of dogwoods, but the leaves were disappointing. She had hoped for a luminous glowing red, but the rainwater had soaked them toward blighted black.

Well then, she would walk quickly, make a fast loop—so good for her health. Nearly seventy? But how well she walked! Quickly and full of energy. Effortlessly. She always took care to wear comfortable shoes, *sensible* shoes, a generation or two earlier than her own would have said. Her mother had been born in 1901.

Her mother's toes had been pressed together into a permanent triangle with a bunion on the side, due to the fashionable pointed toes of the twenties. But she never complained that her feet hurt. Oh, maybe she said, sometimes, *Let me get off my feet for a while.* Ryn wished her mother could have come with her to St. James Court, after Ryn's books became best sellers, but Lila had loved the little house in the Highlands anyway. Far from being one to complain, her mother had said her designated bedroom was the most beautiful bedroom she'd ever had.

Ryn did not want to think of the hard time that came later, when her mother had become so critical of little Humphrey that he wet his bed every night. Lila could not look at the child without criticizing him. Once she said, *I don't believe he's a real boy, Kathryn.* She had poked her finger into his small chubby arm and said, *So soft, like a pudding.* Humphrey's face had crumpled and he had cried out, *I am not a pudding!* After she took her mother to the nursing home, Humphrey stopped wetting the bed, on the very first night. But that did nothing to assuage Kathryn's sorrow at moving her mother to the nursing home—a sorrow worse than any of the divorces.

Here she was on the far side of the park, near the tennis courts. She wished the high Cyclone fences were covered with self-sufficient climbing roses; she had seen tennis courts like that in Birmingham. Suddenly the light shifted, and Ryn knew she had missed the sunset, which she liked to view from her west-facing sunroom. Yes, the sun was gone for today, though it was by no means dark. Still plenty of ambient gray light. Should she stop by Amici's for an Italian supper? The Florentine ravioli she liked so well? The red-checked tablecloths and the mural of Tuscany filling one wall? It was fun to eat there.

She'd brought no money with her. It would be depressing to backtrack to home—she was on the far side of the park now, next to the recently renovated tennis courts—and then traverse the park for a third time today. There would be a hint of something desperate about carrying out such an idea, or at least the suggestion of aimlessness. Go home to stay. That was the ticket. The park looked sodden now, and she was a bit chilly. She remembered the warmth of the newly printed manuscript last midnight through the sleeve of her sweater and smiled a little. Perhaps tonight she'd print a copy of the book for herself.

But she was not ready to go home. From the tennis courts she would explore the northwest quadrant of the park, the area beyond the pergola, on the downside of the rise toward Sixth Street where the most gigantic oaks held court. She liked it that three-dimensionally speaking, Central Park was an asymmetrical little hill, with a pergola along the crest, a gentle slope on the east, and then a steeper side sloping down toward the west. The sides of the long pergola were Doric columns of poured concrete, joined by wooden beams, thatched with thick wisteria vines. Daisy had overseen their planting.

In their brief conversation on the balcony, Daisy, not knowing Leslie well, had nonetheless asked her if she thought she might marry again sometime. So like Daisy, Ryn had thought, to bring into the open a question central to the psyche, even if it was a bit premature. Daisy asked the question not with idle curiosity but out of a desire to understand how Leslie planned to face life. After Leslie replied that statistics showed that 80 percent of women over fifty who divorced never had even a first date, then added, "But who cares? I'm happy here." Daisy asked Leslie what the statistic was for divorced men and learned, predictably enough, that 70 percent of men married someone significantly younger within a year.

Ryn had quickly and awkwardly interjected, "Age did not wither her," semi-quoting Shakespeare on Cleopatra.

Leslie had finished that conversation by remarking, "At least we've learned not to discount ourselves." Placing her hands behind herself, on the small of her slender back, Leslie took a breath and stretched tall. Her posture seemed self-contained, relaxed.

"I know you both have things to do," Daisy had continued to Leslie. "I just didn't want to miss the opportunity to say hello. Your apartment is lovely, Leslie." As she turned to leave the condo, Daisy added, "I'll invite you both to afternoon tea on Belgravia, one day soon."

WHAT LESLIE HAD SAID WAS TRUE. *Yes,* women had learned, were learning, not to discount themselves because of age. Most of the time Ryn loved her space; she felt curious and happy doing what she wanted to do when she wanted to do it. Wasn't it a relief not to be in the presence of a spouse who discounted her value in dozens of ways? How could a brain surgeon have envied the success of a writer?

She thought of Mrs. Dalloway and the woman she most admired, Lady Bexborough, opening a bazaar with the telegram in her hand saying that John, her favorite, had been killed in the war. Automatically, Ryn prayed for the safety of Humphrey. Was not an ardent wish almost the same as a prayer?

It was going to rain again.

LESLIE SIGHED AND LOOKED AROUND her condo: it was beautiful and beautifully located. The two marshmallow chairs seemed particularly satisfactory. No stable shape for the marshmallows, always comfortable, impressively perfect, without smudge or blemish. She was here. Her time was her own. She would play the cello when she wanted to. She would take a walk if she liked. She would read her friend's book and try to help her with it. She could write tales in honor of Bach, or not. Flexing her fingers, Leslie felt rich with the indeterminate nature of much of her time. Probably she had ten good years left ahead of her. Before first frost, she would plant tulip bulbs and daffodils in the concrete containers on her balcony, for spring color.

Lightning split the sky, then a crack of thunder, and a second torrential rain poured down.

Leslie would create happiness for herself—she swore it. No matter what happened next. But what was it Leslie had left unfinished in her jolly conversation with Ryn? There was a question Leslie hadn't asked. Not about a day being a metaphor for a life. Something else; unfinished. About Joyce or Woolf?

About how sometimes a literary artist felt compelled to write against the prejudices, or simply the mores, of his time. Melville against religious bigotry, Leslie should have mentioned that—how Ishmael had worshipped with Queequeg his little wooden idol. Certainly Twain, in *Huckleberry Finn;* how Huck bucked the institution of slavery: he would burn in hell before he betrayed his friend Jim, a slave. The rain had a determined edge to it now and was gusting into the balcony. Leslie closed the French doors.

What made for happiness for women? For anyone?

It was the institution of marriage Ryn should question, Leslie realized. Not just its bonds: its necessity, its desirability, its legitimacy in an evolving society.

FROM THE FAR SIDE OF THE PARK, Ryn, without umbrella, ran for her house through the long pergola. Its rafters and the wisteria vines strained and softened the deluge, she thought. It was exciting to run between the columns. She had not run for a long time, and it made her feel like a goddess, as though she could whiz through time and space, leap into mythology, a female Mercury.

Once outside the pergola, Ryn was immediately drenched and cold. Wind blew the rain through the trees in huge gusts, and from a distance the trio of tulip poplars bent and tossed, their yellow and gold leaves thrashing in the torrent. She would not run that way, but down the side of the park past the gnarled Tolkien trees.

Before crossing Magnolia, she waited impatiently at the curb for cars to pass—too slowly moving now—their wipers dashing the water from the windshields. Couldn't they see she was without protection in the storm, then pause long enough for her to cross? No. But here was a break in the procession.

She considered running up onto the porch of the Conrad-Caldwell historical mansion and waiting within its ornately carved arches (Richardsonian Romanesque), but if she stopped moving she would simply get colder, so she panted past, slowing to a fast walk with a hand clutching her side, as she had done as a child when she ran too fast for too long.

All down the grassy median of St. James Court the gaslights flared and wavered encouragingly inside their glass lanterns.

Ahead, Ryn saw the fountain waters caught up in the wind, distorted, lifted away from the receptive pool, and blown askew over the iron railing. Venus stood dark green and unperturbed, the color of a dark olive. Self-contained and single, she rose. A drenching meant nothing to her bronze skin. Wind caught the water spurting upward from the putti's conch shells and twirled it away into spume.

Underfoot, the sidewalk became slippery, and Ryn dreaded the idea of falling and lying unseen, broken, and unconscious at the base of one of the easement trees. Lightning zagged down the sky, and she thought of the old scar down one side of her cottonwood, and how it had once been struck. She thought of Captain Ahab with a zaggy mark down one cheek. She began to run again as fast as she dared, her shoes squishing water, till she reached the three steps, which were now hosting a minor waterfall, bridging down from her walkway to the public sidewalk.

She forced herself to progress more slowly. On the steps, water gushed around her walking shoes and poured down the walkway. From above—a defective gutter—water pounded the curved steps to her porch. She took particular care on the wet limestone porch steps, and even more caution crossing the water-glazed tiles of the porch floor. Here in her damp pocket was the faithful key.

All that was left was to insert it into the door keyhole, and then turn: inside. Immediately she stepped over the hardwood onto the rug. She silenced the security alarm, while the house echoed with thunder.

She took large, careful steps, trying not to drip water from her clothing over the foyer carpet or the polished hardwood leading through the living room. Her shoes squeaking, she passed between the piano and the clock to the bath. Once on the tiles, she began to shed her wet shoes and garments, intending to wrap in a robe she kept here for guests. While removing her shoes, she paused to listen. There was an unusual interior sound, no wind, but the noise of rushing and dripping water, as though the rain or the fountain had followed her inside.

Glancing up, she saw water flowing down the wall between the bath and the kitchen. Water? Inside? She grabbed a towel and quickly rubbed it over her head and down the arms of her corduroy shirt. Raining inside the house? Not stopping to remove her soaked socks, she thrust her feet into the rubber sandals beside the tub. At least she wouldn't squeeze out water with every step; their soles were dry.

In the kitchen, water gushed down around the chandelier and through cracks leading to the chandelier onto the Alabama table. From the kitchen cabinets, she grabbed pots, the cookie tray-pans, and the big rectangular Pyrex baking pans and tried to center them under the leaks. How could this be? The back bedroom was over the kitchen. Was the water coming through the third-floor deck into the second-floor back bedroom, through the floor or down the insides of walls, and emerging in the kitchen at its ceiling's low place, the chandelier?

When she ran upstairs, she felt compelled first to check the library at the front of the house, her computer and the books. Water was falling fast through the ceiling of the library, near the floor-to-ceiling bookcase, but her white desk, an island in the center of the room, was dry and safe. She darted into her bedroom, past the high, giant bed, into the adjacent bathroom for an armload of clean towels. Before mopping up the library oak floor, she must struggle to roll back the area rug and its pad. None of the floors in a house over a hundred years old was perfectly level and water had seeped under the rug, but the towels were thick and wonderfully absorbent, once applied. She hated to think of the trouble it would be to launder, dry, fold, and shelve them all again.

Into the hall. Stored in the basement, she recalled, was a large rubber tray she'd used once a year as insurance against floor damage when placed under the water reservoir for a Christmas tree, but before she ran all the way down to the basement, she looked up.

No! The ceiling of the second-floor hallway was oozing water, but she sped down the carpeted stairs back to the first floor, grateful for how speedy and bold she'd seemed to become. Hurrying through the foyer and the living room to the kitchen, she noted water still dripped rapidly, almost a stream, from around the chandelier and when it hit the vessels on the table, much of it was splattering out. She clattered down to the basement anyway to fetch the rubber tray for the library.

Hadn't she bought a second tray when she'd considered having an upstairs Christmas tree in the bay window? Yes, there they both were, standing upright, their navy blue labels still pasted against the white rubber. They had been manufactured to go under washing machines. She snatched up the wide trays, light as foam though cumbersome, and maneuvered their width around the tight angles of the cellar stairs. What a nightmare! And it was entirely up to her to do something about it, as best she could. But exciting, too.

She ran all the way back to the second floor, placed a tray under the library ceiling leak—how could it leak in the library with Janie's apartment on the third floor, directly above? And then to the back bedroom, with the second tray.

Worst of all. Above the bed and beyond, near the fireplace, the drywall ceiling was bloated with water and leaking vigorously. It was impossible to pull up the floor-size rug there, with the heavy bed standing on it, so she placed the second tray in the wettest place on top of the blue satin bedspread.

When the trays filled with water, she'd have to bail them out, for they couldn't be lifted without spilling, but they could hold a lot, wide and flat as they were, with nearly a two-inch lip. While she stood still, she heard tree limbs wrenched from their sockets. But where were Janie and Tide in this deluge? Were they outside or in? Surely he was trained to seek shelter, somebody's porch, if a storm blew up. Her whole house was leaking!

She heard what was surely the sound of a tree falling, or trees, and she ran past the bed to the window to look south. All in an instant, looking down the backyards, she saw a mature pine fall into another pine, and that second tall pine, next door, swoosh down toward her cottonwood, which caught the two trees in its arms, shuddered and stood. She gasped at the wonder of its strength. She never considered running away; the cottonwood had persevered. The fallen pine trees slanting over the house next door did not touch its roof. They rested, caught on the diagonal, on the thick limbs of the cottonwood. *Noble old tree,* she thought of her giant cottonwood. Her eyes filled with tears of joy; the giant cottonwood had saved her. Her house. The former neighbor had wanted to cut it down, but it had saved that house, too, from a crushing blow. Behind her, water splashed into the shallow tray she'd placed on the bed, and also onto the carpeted floor.

No more giant rubber trays, but that large pot she had bought when Humphrey wanted to boil crab legs? It had been stowed under the back stairs and she was off to fetch it.

When she returned, she saw that the waterfall through the back bedroom ceiling was now only an intermittent spurt. She could lift the carpet, prop it up with footstools, crawl under and dry the floor. She did these things, but she was getting tired.

She hurried to check the library tray; while it was holding water, just a fast leak from the ceiling now, she needed more towels to catch the splattering. She dried the library floor again and spread two big pool towels that had been on the bottom of the stack, waiting for next summer.

She must turn off the pool heater. Really, she hoped Yves wasn't coming. A total mess. He'd have no place to sleep with the leaks in both spare bedrooms. It was ridiculous to think of a whole swimming pool full of water, warm as a bath but receiving a cold October rain. She shook her head in disapproval: *too eager to please,* she had always been. Leaving the pool heater on was the kind of spendthrift behavior that could leave her bankrupt.

Sodden and weary, beginning to feel the cold again, she went downstairs and looked out the front windows at the fountain. The downpour was becoming an ordinary rain, abating. The fountain waters had resumed their shape: the circular skirt fell straight down from the chalice with only a slight ruffling or an occasional wind-shifted slant; the skyward plumes had resumed their arcs.

Bronze Venus was gleaming emerald; she seemed pleased to be so thoroughly wet. Impervious. Perhaps someday she would slip back into the waters of the sea from whence she came, and earthlings such as Ryn would have to find a new way to embody beauty.

AS THE RAIN STOPPED, night quickly descended, and the residents of St. James Court began to come outside to assess and discuss the damage. Gas lamps still flickered all down the sides of the two grassy lozenges. The floodlights under the waters of the wide pool came on. There were Keith and Todd, always ready to help out and to comfort, from the flats. Ryn could see a heavy limb that had fallen from one of the east-side sentinel oaks onto the top of a car. Through the leaded glass sidelights beside her front door, Ryn watched Sandy patrolling the sidewalk to see if she needed to send for equipment from the nursery she owned. There was Judith, with her little deaf dog caught up in her arms, surveying the sky and chatting with Marilyn.

Could anyone have had as many ceilings leaking as Ryn? Inventory time: downstairs, there was the kitchen and bathroom; on the second floor, the library, the hall, the back bedroom. The slate roof on the baronial house to the south? Rolla's red tile roof to the north? She hoped at least they were intact. Insurance? She knew she had the best insurance company in town, but what about her neighbors?

Some sort of container under each of the leaks now, she reassured herself. Should she check again, more thoroughly before she abandoned ship? And weren't the house lights out all down the row, across the Court? Before she could go outside to compare notes, her cell phone rang from within her damp pocket. She had forgotten about it. Thank goodness, it hadn't been ruined.

Janie's voice said she believed there must be a leak. (Janie! All right! Safe in her apartment.) Janie said she didn't hear any dripping, but her rug was wet to the bare foot. Ryn said she'd come right up the back stairs.

AS ALWAYS, JANIE GREETED Ryn cheerfully. "The wind was fierce," Janie said, "and Tide didn't like the thunder one bit. I could feel him shiver against my legs. He's okay now. I told him not to be afraid."

Tide looked up almost apologetically at Ryn and wagged his tail slowly in the dim room. Janie had forgotten to turn the light on for Ryn.

"I was out walking," Ryn said, "way over by the tennis court when the second storm came up. It's taken down a lot of trees." She heard Janie's radio playing classical music softly: WUOL. A pianist was racing up and down the keyboard with Chopin's "Winter Wind" étude.

"Appropriate music," Janie commented as though she were following the path of Ryn's thinking. "Let me get you some light." With perfect aim, she touched the light switch and turned it on. "Did I hear trees falling nearby, Ryn?" she asked tentatively.

"Two big pines in the backyard next door, to the south. Our cottonwood caught them. I guess they won't be after me to have it cut down now."

"Sweet," Janie said, and Tide looked vaguely pleased.

"The ceiling above you has stopped leaking now, but it's discolored. I can see a few drops still clinging up there. I'll put the area rug up over a chair to dry out. Shall I put a pan under the place in case it starts again in the night?"

"There's a roasting pan in the drawer under the oven."

"You won't forget and trip on it?"

"No, we'll check out exactly where it is. Have you heard from Yves?"

"If I were him, I'd check into a motel. It's probably stormed all the way along I-65."

"Maybe he left a message on your house phone."

After positioning the roaster pan, Ryn said she'd go down and compare notes with the neighbors. Janie thanked Ryn for coming up, said she was glad her refrigerator was still humming.

ALTHOUGH RYN FELT SKEPTICAL about a phone message from Yves, when she returned to her part of the house, she checked the house line. And yes, Yves had left a message during the afternoon, perhaps while she had been napping.

His not coming had nothing to do with the weather. He'd cut his hand while loading the car, he said. Had to have stitches. Had to wait in the emergency room. Ryn was sorry, but she also felt defeated and rather angry about his absence, her neglect of the phone. It was her own fault for not checking the house line. She'd prefer that the disappointment not have been deferred. Her cell phone chimed: Daisy, calling to see if she was all right.

"On the east side of St. James, all the power's off," Daisy explained. "I called Leslie and invited her down to have a glass of wine with Daniel and me. She's coming. Would you like to come down?"

As they spoke Ryn looked across the Court: dark as the river Styx over there. No, she said to Daisy, but thank you. She was glad Daisy had invited Leslie and glad Leslie had accepted. She imagined Daniel was probably starting a small fire in their fireplace. He was a master at creating coziness. Kind and thoughtful. Daisy's Rock of Gibraltar. Ryn paced around her house, checking again and again, admiring the makeshift measures she'd quickly taken. The ceilings were still leaking in three places on the second floor, especially under the third-floor deck and dripping down the wall in the downstairs bathroom under the second-floor deck. But she was containing it as best she could.

Something about the deck construction in those instances had probably allowed the leaking, she speculated. It could be corrected. But the house roof had leaked, too, into Janie's apartment, the library, and the hall; that wasn't a deck problem. Ryn felt despondent. The rain must have come from an unusual direction, with unusual force.

She would go downstairs and have a small glass of pinot noir, sit in the gray twirly chair in the living room. The visionary chair from which and in which she had visited spacious joy and contained peace.

But her clothes were damp. She needed to put on all dry things first. Her flesh was pebbly with goose bumps. In the bedroom she went straight to the maple chest of drawers; it had been in their home in Montgomery; she'd known it all her life. As she changed her clothes, she tried not to look at the empty expanse of king-size bed.

She entered the media room on the other side of the bathroom. No leaks there. She supposed Yves could have slept there, on the pullout sofa bed, but it wasn't really comfortable. The kind of bed you could offer an understanding, lithesome niece in a pinch, but not a heavy male guest.

She walked slowly down the main stairway. It was good not to rush. Ignoring the dripping chandelier, she stood at the kitchen counter and poured the pinot. Then she took refuge in the living room, dry and intact.

The pinot was good. She regarded the two women in the large blue painting over the piano. The dominant figure, a trapeze artist shaped like the rocker of a cradle, was flying through the air in the foreground. In mid-picture, another circus woman walked a tightrope, which had gone slack. She was anxiously looking around for help. With her strong legs ready, the trapeze artist would swoop down and catch her friend under her arms, hold on tight, and wing her to safety.

Ryn thought of how Élisabeth the painter had tried to persuade her friend, the companion of her teen years at the Louvre, to leave Paris. Had Ryn remembered to include in the novel the fact that the former Mlle Boquet and Joseph Vernet's daughter, who had enjoyed the soirée *à la grecque,* were executed by guillotine? They had given a small bridal reception for someone, the last day at Château de la Muette. They were arrested, tried, and executed for wasting the people's candles.

No. The end of Kathryn's novel was about a visit by Élisabeth's nieces to Louveciennes, when she was very old.

Élisabeth had come to love her nieces on both sides of her family, after the Revolution, when she finally returned to France. Julie, her daughter, returned with her no-count Russian count, had died in Paris. Sad. Suddenly Ryn realized she'd forgotten to include that scene in her novel! What a lapse!

There was her cell phone again.

It was Peter. He didn't often phone her. If it weren't Peter, she wouldn't have answered; she was exhausted; nerves stretched to the end. Day's end.

When Peter said something unintelligible into her ear, she barked, "I can't hear you," scarcely trying to mask her irritation. And then she said, "What?" because she couldn't believe what she'd heard.

"Humphrey's coming?" she repeated. "Where is he?"

"In the air," Peter answered.

Humphrey had told Peter over the phone, from Göteborg, that he would come home as a surprise, not to tell Kathryn.

"Then he thought he'd better give notice. You schedule your life so closely, he thought you might already be expecting somebody. He called me from the airplane, to phone you."

"No," Kathryn answered, excited. "Nobody's coming tonight."

"He'll land tonight at one in the morning, after midnight. He'll stay the night in New York. We can pick him up at noon tomorrow."

"I'm so happy!" she exclaimed. She pictured him seated inside the airplane speeding through the dark sky, high above the dark ocean. "Why is he coming?"

Peter mumbled, but she made out the answer. Her son was coming to celebrate with her—that she'd completed the first draft of her new novel.

In a daze, she disconnected the call, scarcely registering their polite good-byes.

Ryn sipped her wine and relaxed more deeply into the gray twirly chair. She wondered what wines, if any, Élisabeth liked to drink. Humphrey was coming home to celebrate his mother's new book. She would like to toast Élisabeth while she sat in this living room of her lovely, leaking house. And a toast to handsome Humphrey, the light of her life. She raised her glass. And a toast to her writing and to her friends as well. She'd finished the first draft of her novel; she could rest, choose to indulge a bit. Humphrey was flying home.

She rose from the twirly chair and walked to the front of the house again to look out through the dark at the fountain: same as ever; the spotlights had come on fully. Golden glamour. Nobody was about. She could see the wet streets reflecting light. The pavement encircling the fountain was littered with leaves, stuck down flat and dark. Here came a car. She heard the crack of a limb the driver had run over rather recklessly. The car continued crunching its way down the street, but it was slowing now between her and the fountain. It came to a stop, and the driver commenced to park in front of her house in a waiting space.

Even through the rain-bleared windshield, she saw that the driver was unmistakably Jerry.

PORTRAIT

J UST AS DUSK comes to Louveciennes, with a sliver of new moon
gleaming in the western sky, I see horses and coach turn into the large
U-shaped drive that holds out its welcoming arms from my house. Thudding of hooves and rattling of carriage—as merry a sound as bells on Noël.
There is Caroline's face at the window, bright and eager as Étienne's, at
fifteen, when he looked back over his shoulder at me about to go to his
classes, and I said, *Stop still, for just a moment. I must sketch you now, and later
an oil painting to capture you forever.* And he obliged, stopping in midstride,
changing nothing of his natural bright expression, for in those days we
were just that much at ease with each other. It is that way now with Caroline, his daughter. The horses and coach move forward on the curve of the
drive as steady as the hand of a clock.

Their coach rattles in the key of not heavily laden. Luggage is light
for spending only a night. Within the swaying carriage, their hearts are
as light as mine. I hope they have noticed the sickle moon, which always

seems hopeful and carefree to me. For me, my monthly time always came with the full moon, with complete regularity, and it was the same for Julie. I have known families of many women whose monthlies *all* came at the same time as though there were some magic signal commanding them all at once to prepare their bodies for the possibility of fertility.

"We await the arrival of the General" (as she called their monthlies), Antoinette's mother, the empress of Austria, always said to her daughters in Vienna, though my mother spoke of the Governor. Being so simpatico and the same age, the queen and I were that close: we could speak of anything from our domestic past together. She missed her many sisters (in fact she never saw them again once she left Austria, not even one, though her brothers came to visit), but here they come, my nieces, true friends, and true friends of each other as well, through me.

But not so many guests in the carriage as I had anticipated. There are three women: my nieces and a new, slight figure, small and dressed in silver. It always surprises me to see that my nieces are of middle age, for they seem as young and full of life as girls, but this bright-headed maiden, not more than twenty-five, is truly young. When I embrace her in greeting, she feels as slender as the new moon, and her hair is a pale gold, like wheat.

The slight young woman turns out to be a pupil of my niece Eugénie (herself a painter), and this fairy, Sophie, has begged her teacher to take her along to meet me when the expected other members of the party suddenly found that they were unable to make the trip. At least that is the explanation given when I say, "And the others?"

But I see my nieces exchange a slight glance at my question, a glance that suggests I may have become confused in my expectations and mixed up this projected visit with one that I remember or hope for! They would never voice their suspicion (don't all elderly people get a bit confused, or sometimes stop in the middle of a task as though frozen in time while they remember or imagine another time and place?), but both my nieces descend on me from each side so that I am caged in their embraces, and they each kiss a cheek, and exclaim how well I am looking.

I have worn a light green frock to suggest the spring, with a dark rose shawl, a color that always became me, and as a sort of turban, a striped scarf combining similar hues but with glints of silver and gold woven through it. Only a soft frizz of my gray-white hair peeks out.

When we step apart, we all three laugh, for each of us who are kin have dressed with some reference to spring by donning a shade of green. Caroline's skirt carries a bold blue-green stripe. I think she knows that I've lately acquired a taste for those two colors together, of grass and sky. Eugénie, though my niece only through my marriage to Le Brun, is indeed the artist of the two, and her outfit is more subtle: the fabric of her dress is composed of the tiny, four-petaled flowers the English call forget-me-not, and the blue of the so-small flowers and the green leaves almost melt away into a pale green background, so one asks if the overall effect is blue or green.

Little Mlle Moonbeam is shy at first, but when she walks into my home, she lets out a small gasp of pleasure. I smile. Of course my colors and the furniture unify for an effect bold, knowing, and unfailingly effective in its selection and arrangement, for after all I am known as a colorist. Then she goes to stand before my painting of Emma Hart, and I explain that she later became Lady Hamilton, and then the lover of the British Lord Nelson (I say this quite forthrightly, for it is a well-known fact), who died at Trafalgar during the Napoleonic conflicts.

The mention of Nelson's death somehow prompts my inexperienced visitor to bring up the subject of Gros, my friend, a fine painter who died. "His must have been a difficult loss," the very young woman says, not unsympathetically (but what can she know of a lifetime of losses), "as you had known him since he was a child."

"Yes," I replied quietly, "I painted him when he was a child of seven."

"Did he show talent then?" Eugénie asks. Her tone matches mine. She is pursuing this painful subject a little so as not to let Sylvie, dressed in silver, feel that she has committed a faux pas.

"As a child, he would bring objects together of various colors," I readily explain, "just to see how the colors complemented or modified one another." I speak in as lively a fashion as I can, but really my dear friend's self-inflicted death is still with me. It is still difficult if not impossible to think of dear Gros in any context without thinking of his violent end. I feel my mood darken, and perhaps the beginning of the wish that the vacancy in the carriage had not been given over to this young person despite her pleasing, sylphlike appearance.

Niece Caroline kindly redirects the conversation by asking me if I have made a watercolor during the day.

"Indeed I did," I reply, rising to take them to my studio, "and both of you, my dear nieces, will smile to see it, for in its color it too references the coming spring, and it matches well several of the hues we have chosen to wear for this *primavera*."

"All along the road," Sylvie exclaims, "the chestnuts were in flower. Perhaps in your travels to Italy you saw the Botticelli *Primavera*?"

"First I saw engravings of it. Spring is a poor subject for an engraving, I think, because everyone wants to relish the new and delicate tints we associate with that season. Spring is a matter of color. But yes, eventually I did see the painting itself, in Florence."

"Better an engraving," Caroline puts in cheerfully, "than to have no representation of it at all."

"Did you suspect, Mme Le Brun, that Gros would be a colorist?"

Persistent child! So unacquainted are you with grief that you cannot recognize its traces. "Only lately I was in the Sainte Geneviève," I say stoutly, "and quite overcome with the compelling vividness of his glorious work in the dome."

I determine to make a speech, knowing that such a conversational stance sometimes staunches the flow of questions. "When I returned to France, I was awestruck by what I saw in the work of Gros. In the second volume of my *Souvenirs*, I freely admit that I had not been entirely prescient about his talent, though I had loved him. He was a genius. I say it loud and clear, without qualification. Make no mistake. He had the kind of original-

ity that is necessary for the founding of an entire school of art, which he
did found. He and I, when he was mature, became *extremely* close friends,
honest in both our praise and criticism of one another's work. In public, he
spoke in an extraordinary, brusque way; but in private he freed his genius
with language, for he was an original in that regard as well." I take a breath
and plunge on.

"His speech was full of surprising metaphors that evoked powerful
images in abundance." As I speak, I guide the trio to my studio.

"My father," Caroline interjects (it delights me for anyone, especially
his daughter, to summon up the image of Étienne), "used to say about his
plays that the path to the universal was most certainly through the particular, but all great works, like a bridge, must place a foot on each shore, one
concrete and one abstract."

"Do you remember"—Eugénie Le Brun addresses me—"how your
husband used to shake with laughter at the wit of Étienne Vigée?"

"I do indeed," and I smile readily, for it has been my steady habit, even
after our marriage was a disappointment, always not only to agree but to
savor anything nice that can be said of my late former husband. And of
course I am especially eager to let no breach of any sort occur in the intimacy I feel through the person of Eugénie with the Le Brun branch of the
family. "But here is my little watercolor. I suppose it is not much—nothing
to show to posterity—but I cannot begin to describe to you the pleasure
I felt in executing it. I enjoyed even the sensation of natural light on the
back of my hand as I strove with my brush to suggest distant light in its
naturalness."

My little guest inserts herself like a sliver between my two nieces and
brings her nose quite close to my paper fastened to the board. She has a
keen little nose, pretty in its own way. Beyond her through the window,
the planet Venus has risen, and I think of a line of English poetry comparing this evening star to a diamond on the cheek of an Ethiope, though here
Venus shines less sharply against the brief gray that precedes true night. I
enjoyed my stays in England.

Eagerly Sylvie exclaims, "I believe those must be chestnut trees you have painted, for if I look closely I see you have suggested something of the panicle blossoms. Do chestnut trees live a long time?"

"I have seen one at Versailles," Caroline replies, "that was planted by the queen, Marie Antoinette herself, near the Petit Trianon. That would have been at the latest about 1787. As it is now 1841, we can testify it has prospered for at least half a century."

"Fifty years is not so long," I say with a smile. It is a genuine smile, for I am getting used to the fact that in Sylvie we have an enthusiast; she has not cultivated, nor has anyone cultivated in her, the art of exquisite manners. Perhaps that grows to be a lost art, that particular kind of conversation we practiced in the salons that could blend propriety with spontaneity, the result of which was a certain shade of sincerity. "Now see this color," I say as though giving a mock lecture to the artists present. "This blue has remnants of strong green and cobalt in it, but blended with a bit of gray. The gray adds thoughtfulness to the appreciation of nature."

"But there is nothing sad in the painting," Sylvie remarks. And she is correct.

"That is because the willow has a tincture of yellow or even gold in it because the willow wands turn golden before shading into green. For me there is never anything sad in nature, and I would not allow myself to represent it that way, for that would be false to my philosophy."

With a sparkle in her eye my brother's daughter says, "But darling aunt, do you not think it sad when the hawk swoops down on the pigeon?"

"Of course that is sad," I reply. "Let me see. What was I thinking? I wasn't thinking of animals at all. But of the mountains, the great crags that some find terrible, barren, wild, and ugly. I was thinking of how they have their own grandeur. They are sublime. But sublime is not the opposite of sad. I am a bit confused in my categories."

Eugénie comes to the rescue. "Yes, you are thinking of Burke and the way he contrasts the sublime with the beautiful."

"There you are! Thank you, my dear," I reply.

SOON, AFTER NIGHTFALL, we are feasting on rabbit, wild and savory, made civilized with sage and enhanced by mushrooms. When I remark to my maid about the mushrooms, she replies that they were brought over by a neighbor, a very old man, to the kitchen door, as a gift.

The service at table is provided in the old style, that is to say with the servers almost invisible and the plates coming and going as though by magic, except for a rare moment or two when the servers know exactly whose eye to engage to add the cozy human flavor: we are all in this life blended together.

As we eat and chat, I love them all, even the student Sylvie, and I am careful to end the after-dinner conversation before it is quite finished, for this ploy always implants the wish in guests to return again soon. I do it this way:

Sylvie asks me to tell about the famous party I gave *à la grecque,* not very long before the Revolution.

"Although my quarters for entertaining were small, the highest nobility attended my soirées. They had to crowd in and even sit on the bed sometimes, for invitations were much sought after," I begin.

"In those days, we usually met about nine in the evening. While politics were not discussed, literature was often the topic of conversation, as were music and the theater. Sometimes we played charades to amuse ourselves, or someone read some of his verses. About ten in the evening, we sat at table and ate.

"Oh, at my house, the suppers at my table were always simple, like this evening. Usually some fowl, fish, a vegetable, and a salad. All very light food, and not much of it. I was even known to invite so many people, fifteen or so, that sometimes there was not enough food, but it didn't matter in the least. We were that comfortable with one another. And none of us was starving. The time passed so pleasantly, all in a wink, and my guests did not begin to drift toward their homes till almost midnight. Evening was the only time I allowed myself to relax, as I painted all day, and then at night, knowing I had worked my best, I truly was pleased to enjoy fully the leisure I had earned."

"Do describe the Greek party," Caroline urges, though her father, my brother, had been one of those present, and she had surely heard it described a number of times.

So I speak of how the idea first presented itself and how the party later caused people to gossip, almost immediately, about my high mode of living and my spendthrift nature, a calumny that followed me even after I left France, all across Europe and even to Russia.

"Your father, dearest Caroline, my beloved brother, had come to my apartment early (M. Le Brun was still building the house in Rue du Gros-Chenet), and he suggested we dress in Greek costumes, eat food with Greek sauces, and listen to recitations about the Greek way of life.

"I also knew that M. de Vaudreuil, one of the most kind and charming, pleasant, and witty men in the world, was planning to arrive late with M. Boutin, and we would surprise them by appearing to be a company of Greeks from the past, amazingly present in Paris.

"And as they came in, we even sang Gluck's chorus 'Le dieu de Paphos et de Guide,' with M. de Cubières playing his lyre."

"Paphos," Sylvie interjects. "Did not Saint Paul visit the Greek isle of Paphos?"

"Indeed he did," Caroline replies. "But more important to the occasion that our dear hostess has described to us is the fact that Paphos was the mythical birthplace of Aphrodite, the goddess of love and beauty; Venus to the Romans."

"We enjoyed two vegetables and a honey cake with Corinthian raisins," I continue. "Our only extravagance was a bottle of very old, very fine Cyprus wine. It had been given to me as a present." For a moment I feel embarrassed that we in Louveciennes are now eating such straightforward, untheatrical fare.

"Well, now you have the tale, inside and out. M. Vaudreuil and M. Boutin were so pleased with the evening that they talked about it all the next day till Paris was buzzing. Several ladies from the court asked me to repeat the evening, but I declined to do so, for a variety of reasons. I'm afraid they may have been offended by my firmness in the matter. Word spread of our glorious event even to the king, and as the word was spread people began to exaggerate quite greatly the cost of the staging of such an authentic, delicious, and original surprise. People claimed it cost twenty thousand francs.

"Then I learned the king was displeased to hear of such extravagance, but very fortunately for me (for I wanted nothing to suggest I lacked judgment, being so close to all the royals and especially the queen; and certainly nothing that hinted I was being lavishly overpaid for my paintings) one of the people to whom the king made inquiry was the Marquis de Cubières, who had played his gilded guitar-lyre for our singing.

"Since he himself was a guest at the party, the marquis could quickly convince His Majesty that the rumor concerning the cost of the party (not its appeal and charm) was a scandalous exaggeration. But the truth did not quell the rumor.

"When I was in Rome, after 1789, I was asked if the Greek dinner had not cost *forty* thousand francs; in Vienna, still later, I heard directly from the Baronne Stroganoff, to my immense surprise, that without blinking an eye, I had lavished *sixty* thousand francs on my Greek supper. By the time I was preparing to paint the Empress Catherine the Great of Russia in St. Petersburg, the rumor had reached a figure of *eighty* thousand francs."

At the mention of increasing sums of money, all my listeners stir in their seats in an excited way.

"How much did it really cost?" young Sylvie allows herself to inquire.

"About *fifteen francs!*" I promptly reply, for I have already mentioned the sum in my *Souvenirs,* which apparently young Sylvie for all her expressed admiration of my life as an artist has not yet found time to read. I smile at her warmly.

"Not fifteen *thousand?*" Sylvie asks.

"A mere fifteen."

"With your words you have done more than paint a picture," Eugénie remarks. "You have animated a scene."

"Thank you, my dears," I say to them, "for letting an old woman relive one of the most enjoyable evenings I can remember. I know you must all be tired. Shall we retire and commence our conversation again in the morning?"

Everything has happened as I have planned; I know it has been a lovely evening, ending in such a way that no one is overly tired. As I rise from my chair, I fully experience the coziness of this very moment, of the warmth and love of my dear nieces and of the awestruck face of Eugénie's pupil.

Yes, I have shared a shining memory with her of times she will never be able to witness. Is it possible that such perfect pleasures existed? I smile at these three women again, one by one, enjoying the face, particularly the eyes, of each. I add them to the gallery of images I keep locked in what I pray is the inviolable library of memory which neither moth nor rust can corrupt. And I remember those lost in the Terror.

For my unique delight, I recall once more the expression of amazement and unbridled joy that crossed the face of the Comte de Vaudreuil, who always looked at me throughout those Versailles days (though he was the lover of the Duchesse de Polignac, who was the queen's best friend for a number of years) with pleasure and admiration.

And then I let go of the past; it evaporates. Most tenderly I kiss in turn the dear and real cheeks of these three faces here before me. This moment. This beloved house. This supper.

NOW MY THREE GUESTS are in their separate rooms, each alone, even as I am. I take off my shoes by myself, but I allow my maid to help me undress; she unfastens all those neat little covered buttons and their loops so tenderly, I can scarcely feel her fingers moving down my backbone.

Perhaps we all, my guests and I, are each imagining the others and remembering a moment of conversation, or repeating some remark we're glad to have made, or regret and would amend, if we could. With the removal of my garments, my balance wobbles a bit. I appreciate my steady maid's assistance in donning my nightgown. She has eyes brown as chestnuts, and she smiles at me.

Ah, bed is a pleasant place to be. Doesn't the world contract a bit when one is cozy in bed? *Bonsoir; merci beaucoup* to my maid, who blows out the candle.

BUT STILL I SEE, through the paired eyes of memory and imagination. I picture my guests in their assigned chambers, among the objects and furnishings I have provided, each with its charms and congruences, its ambience, matched to the character of the inhabitant.

By candlelight, I am sure my Caroline has noticed her room faces east. In the morning, my Caroline will like the early fresh light at her window, for it matches her own forthcoming liveliness.

And when Eugénie, my niece who paints, first walks into her room, she will savor the way the colors and textures honor and contain her. Ripeness is artificed here: muted burgundy on the walls and reddish brown in the furniture, a slice of orange tending toward gold for the wool cloth draped over a satin chair.

And Sylvie? For her a light youthfulness to every aspect of her surroundings. She will like the glimmers of silver (the base of the candlestick with a twisted rope edge, a silver frame around one of my little watercolors, the carved silver vase holding three ivory tulips and sprigs of square-stemmed mint). To think that nature can grow a perfectly square stem when she wishes! The vase has a nice bulge to it, a generous, fecund shape that pleases hopeful maidens. Sylvie herself, her graceful, slender curves: like the new moon when I first saw her.

My fingers enjoy the deep lace edge at the top of my sheet, and I pull it up under my chin. Ah, luxury! I like to think of my portraits as I fall asleep.

THEY ARE SCATTERED—France, Italy, Austria, Russia, Switzerland, Germany, England, perhaps the Americas.

The house has grown still. We four women—one young, two middle aged, one very old—are each abed in our chambers. Even the footsteps of the maids, their breath as they blow out the candle flames, and the shuffling sounds from the kitchen are unheard now.

In this silence, I will remember two self-portraits. One that I painted in Italy, while Julie was still a little girl. And one that I painted in Russia, when only the attraction of my work saved me from despair.

After our trip to Flanders, when I painted myself wearing a straw hat, in the daylight, stepping forward with such youth and confidence, holding my palette and brushes for the first time in a self-portrait, I painted the Duchesse de Polignac again. (Let me linger again in France, before the self-portraits of Italy and Russia.) I painted her in a way that possibly could have reminded a viewer of the portrait of myself, for she too is in a straw hat, decorated with flowers, but the bouquet on her hat is to one side.

The dress of the duchess has a ruffled décolletage similar to mine, as is the sash tied just beneath the bosom. The bows of each of our gowns are limp and floppy. A black lace shawl entwines our arms in both cases, and our hair is arranged in much the same fashion. Our expressions are quite different, mine being eager and happy, smiling slightly; the Duchesse de Polignac looks pensive rather than animated. While I am pictured outdoors, striding forward, she is in repose, with her elbow leaning on the top of a cabinet.

Of course the duchess could not carry a palette and brushes; in her hand I placed a rose, the symbol of beauty, as I often did when painting the queen, and the hat of the Duchesse de Polignac also has a plume as does the straw hat of the queen when I painted her (scandalously, as it turned out) in a similar simple dress.

Some viewers would see an implicit comparison, a likeness, between the queen and her most dear friend, though in the crises of the Revolution the duchess fled, leaving Antoinette alone; on the other hand, a friend less in favor, the Princesse de Lamballe, forfeited her freedom and eventually her life in order to befriend the imprisoned queen with her company.

I have always wondered if a certain someone who knew well both the Duchesse de Polignac and myself, and who frequently enjoyed our company, looking at that portrait of the Duchesse de Polignac, might not also think of me, as well as of the queen. Would not such a someone think that I, though lacking titles, am the one of the three who is most filled with life? For I did capture that vivacity—how fully I felt my own alive hopefulness as I painted, in my self-portrait of 1783, alone, under the hue of heaven, with my palette and brushes, stepping forward, toward you.

May not an old woman, waiting for sleep, give herself permission to indulge in a bit of smugness: that she has left a secret for history to discover? Of course, no one ever will. That secret of unexpressed attraction will die with me. I never knew even if the object of my affection was aware of how I felt. And I feel smug about that, too.

In the self-portrait of 1790, I stand in Rome, before a canvas, depicted this time in the very act of painting, not merely holding my tools. The old days of life in Paris before the Revolution are behind me. I am standing in a city which I, like any artist, longed to visit, but I am painting, from memory, Marie Antoinette, queen of my country from which I have fled.

There is sadness in my face, in 1790. I am not the attractive young artist striding forward with blue sky flung about me. Again, in my left hand, I hold the palette and a number of waiting brushes.

The most interesting thing in the painting is the hand that paints. The tip of my brush is at the very edge, straight and limiting, of the canvas, but that position almost suggests that art can go beyond its boundaries. A mille-measure more and the boundary between art and life would be bridged.

The colors in the self-portrait painted in Rome, but housed in Florence, are stark: I wear a black dress with a flowing red sash. My face is held between two horizontals: my fluffy white collar and a white turban of almost equal size. The flesh tones of my two hands and my face triangulate the focal points of the painting.

Even now I feel happy to think of the ingenious magic of this painting, for in it, the painting hand, holding the brush tip to the edge of the canvas, also casts a shadow. I cannot say how much it pleases me to have rendered this very lifelike shadow of my painting hand. I still look directly out, but my expression is one of reverie; it is as though I am looking at a different land, at my queen in France, and yet my hand casts a shadow in the here and now of that moment.

During the ten years that pass, I travel Europe. During this time Julie and I live at the court of Vienna, where I am most hospitably treated for the sake of the queen, and I am there when I learn of her execution in 1793, and of the king's that same year, some nine months before her brutal death. A pall of sorrow drops over all of us in Vienna, at court. Life is shrouded.

Because I am told that many congenial French aristocrats are to be found in Russia, I go there, to the court of Catherine the Great, who engages me to paint her. I begin that work, but it is never finished due to her death.

When the century turns to 1800, I am hopeful that the new century will be the stage for more peace and joy than the last one. For all human-kind. But it is ten years after my last self-portrait, an important ten years in the life of a woman who journeys from thirty-five to forty-five; my daugh-ter is now nineteen. I wear a tight sleeve around my throat, to bind it up, for my throat is no longer beautiful. I depict myself in the act of drawing the queen with white chalk.

Again, my dress is black. Again, as in the portrait I painted in Rome for the Uffizi, I contrast the black with a red scarf, but this time I have twisted the red scarf under my breasts and around my shoulders and tied it high in the middle of my back. (I do not use the sash to define my waist, which has thickened a bit.) I wear a turban of twisted fabrics, gold and sheer white, fascinating in themselves. Only a bit of my hair, short, curly, and graying, peeks from under the edge of the turban. To ornament myself I wear a heavy gold chain, braided like a plait of hair, around my neck. This time I am facing to my left, and in three-quarter view. This new pose for a self-portrait has animated the whole effort with a certain freshness. I remember that it was rather fun to use my oil paints to represent chalk marks on the canvas.

What I like particularly about this portrait that makes me prefer it to the similar one when I was in Italy is that in the Russian painting, I seem actually to be looking at my model. Much more authentically than before, when my face seemed dreamy, I have the keen, focused expression of an artist at work. And I have truly achieved moments of happiness. I am happy, curious, and content, knowing and interested, pleased and expectant, to be at my work. It is my consolation, for Julie has turned away from me. And I turn to my work. What else can I do? Adamantine, the barrier she places between us. I must find the courage to paint, to continue to value myself. I did. And I do.

And so it has continued with me all my life. In the Russian painting, I feel no need to stride toward the world in all my youth and beauty, as I did in 1783. Now, in the year that has turned the century to 1800, I give my attention fully to the act itself of painting, for in that lies my happiness.

But it is hard to believe that now it is more than forty years later that I am alive in 1841. The time, especially the last twenty years, seems but a blink. I scarcely know anyone as old as I am. But I can remember Voltaire in 1778, who lived then to be as old as I am now, and how the ancient man was chaired into a huge ceremony in his honor. I am in better health than he was near the end of his life.

So I have revisited my gallery of self-portraits; my bed has been my boat to the land of memory. I have left my oil paintings, my legacy. My nieces will do what they can for them. It is said that Voltaire left more than two thousand discrete examples of his writing, books and pamphlets. Probably they are a very complete record of his thinking. But my paintings perhaps give more nuances of spirit and feeling, and the medium of my art is directly visual. It makes one see, but the thoughts of my viewers remain their own.

Tomorrow night, if I am wakeful, I will give myself the pleasure of reviewing my paintings of the queen and her children, and the next night my great painting of Hubert Robert, with his palette and brushes, shall stand before me in all its triumphant detail, and then paintings of other particular friends and patrons—but I am too tired tonight. I am happy that I was able to paint my beloved mentor Joseph Vernet, in 1789, before I left Paris. And he too is painted with his palette and brushes so that history may know him as an artist.

I think that my self-portraits have a direct truthfulness to them, a connection between the outer appearance and the subject's inner working of thought and feeling and knowledge and life that is found less reliably in my portraits of others, except when I was painting other artists, such as Hubert Robert and Joseph Vernet, whose inner lives I *did* know, or other intimates whom I knew well, my brother, my mother, my daughter.

I will remember my portraits of my daughter. I painted her once as Flora, her garments streaming in the wind, for Zephyr was the mythical lover of Flora. But there is more pleasure for me in remembering her as she actually was in life, our adventures in Italy, than to recall the portraits. None of them was good enough.

Still I can taste the vinegar and salt in the sauce for the eel *à la grecque*. A bit of anchovy to please the Comte des Plaines? Still I can picture, forever unchanging, the surprise and delight of the face of the Comte de Vaudreuil. Completely enchanted, if only for the moment.

Sleep comes shod in velvet. I hear her dusky feet crossing the carpet toward my bed. I sigh. I am eager for the next bright day.

Long ago, after a controversial performance by actors from the Comédie-Française of Beaumarchais's *The Marriage of Figaro,* the Marquis de Montesquiou made out horoscopes for a group of us. He forecast that I would possess a long life and that because I was not a vain person, when I had lived that long life I would be well loved as an old woman. I knew intuitively that my horoscope would be true. Or at least partly true. I have lived long.

And am I lovable as an old woman? I cannot say. But I am a loving old woman—my nieces, many friends—and happy in my love of art. Painting was innate in me, and my love for it has increased rather than diminished over time. Fervently I hope, I pray, the divine passion for art will be with me until my death.

And now I believe I know something else that will be true, as pertains to my future and to my death. Do we not all have the power to create our own horoscopes? After just such a pleasant evening with friends as this one has been, but in my apartment in the Rue Saint-Lazare in Paris, in that still-enchanting city that has defined so much of my life, I will retire to my bedchamber. Yes, I believe I see the future. In the dark, I will lay myself down and, having lived a full day, fall happily into a sleep from which I shall not awake.

For tonight, my sail, bearing me to the land of sleep, will be a particular canvas: the portrait of myself outdoors, with blue sky behind me, wearing a straw hat, moving forward, palette and brushes in hand, inhabiting my vision.

If only I could hear my Julie's voice!

FOUNTAIN

WHEN JERRY PARKED his old car in front of her house, Ryn—for somehow she had told him her nickname when he and Humphrey were together and she had been desperate to trust Jerry because Humphrey was so young—watched Jerry, now older, still insolent in his movements, through the sidelights beside her front door. It was dark now, but as always the fountain area of St. James Court was illumined. Her hand was shaking. She could hardly settle the wineglass on the writing shelf of her mother's secretary. She opened the front door and positioned herself, each hand against the wide doorframe, and stood looking out waiting for Jerry to notice her. The ground and walkways were sodden with downed leaves. Humphrey was flying over the ocean.

There was no use trying to avoid the truth of Jerry's presence. Why not finish it now? He had walked in on Marie and her son. He knew Ryn still lived across from the fountain. He would probably come again if she avoided speaking with him tonight. Most of the lights in her house were blazing away. He would know she was inside, though he had not yet looked at the porch. Because the power was off, the east side of the Court, behind the golden fountain, was a long swath of blackness. The glow of the fountain outlined his dark shape as he got out and moved past the hood of his car. She would send him away. Humphrey was coming.

Remember, she told herself, he's just another human being. And remember, at one time she had been very friendly with him, for Humphrey's sake. Nonetheless, he looked sinister as he nonchalantly climbed the front steps and walked toward her. He was heavier, nothing of the boy left in him. The light coming through her open door and the porch light illumined all of him as he mounted the porch steps. His facial expressions did not register her presence. It was like watching a person in a film walking forward, straight on, with no recognition of the viewer.

When he stood just opposite he said through the screen door, "Hello, Ryn. Can I come in?" His voice was neutral, almost polite.

"Of course," she said. "How're you doing, Jerry?" She was trembling.

And he was inside. He carefully closed the screen behind him; she could not even hear the click of the latch engaging. Control displayed itself in his hands, in his strong shoulders.

"Where's Humphrey?" Now there was an insistence, if not an edge, to his query.

They were standing close together. She told herself they were both standing near the open door. She had her bearings; everything was orderly and quiet. Normal. He wouldn't know about the leaks. He didn't know Humphrey was flying home. Neither said anything for a moment.

His eyes circled the foyer once, then rested on her eyes. "Well?" he said.

"Sit down," she said. "Wouldn't you like to sit down?" The striped chairs and the love seat were really very close to the open front door. The chandelier above them seemed rather too bright. He glanced at the chandelier, its dozens of crystal pendants, some of them snaggletoothed replacements, and blinked.

They both sat. He'd dyed his hair red and gotten a perm. It was curly.

"Still got your fancy chairs," he said, stretching out his legs.

"Yes," she said. "Rose and green. I never imagined I'd like that combination till I saw these on Goss Avenue. Maybe it's the stripes. Maybe the stripes keep the colors in order, keep them from seeming . . . seeming . . ." She could not find the word.

"Too fussy," he supplied, and held her gaze, almost helpless, for a long time. Then he broke the spell. "Still writing books?"

"Sure. I like your hair, Jerry." She didn't. But she had sounded authentically normal. He couldn't tell she was lying. Always he'd craved compliments so much that he could never tell if they were truth or lies.

"Ever get a movie contract?"

"Not yet."

"So what's Humphrey up to?" His hands rested loosely on his thighs, but he seemed hyperalert.

"He's married now." Would that settle it? Wouldn't it, would it, wouldn't it, couldn't it end the dance?

"Man or woman?"

Ryn was startled. She wondered if the implication were true, that Humphrey had actually been or was bisexual. She wondered if she hoped so. Which mode would be easier? Startlingly, the face of Frieda, her college friend, flashed in her mind. Frieda straddling a windowsill, her expression mysterious and knowing, pleased. Winter hung in the snowy air, white crystals were falling. New York.

Jerry was waiting for her answer, and his face was beginning to pass from neutral to a collection of escalating emotions: a sneer, then suspicion and anger. She had left the front door standing open. Somebody passing on the sidewalk might see them both, sitting there in fancy chairs, looking civilized.

"A man," she said.

"God damn," he said. He reached out and with a single swipe knocked over the little cabriole-leg table between them. The table fell, almost silently; the clear glass bowl on the table bounced without breaking on the rug. It was heavy glass. Expensive, carved with octopi and sea horses, a gift from Leslie. The delicate table, lying on its side, looked stunned and helpless. Without value.

She stood up. "You have to leave now," she said. She was frightened, but she felt sure that was what she needed to say. She said it quietly.

"Yeah." He didn't move. "Give me his address first."

"You can't find them," she said. "They've moved far away, out of the country."

"Where to? I just want to write to him. See what's going on." Was his voice going unsteady? "Maybe leave things less raw between us." His voice had stuck in his throat. He swallowed hard, and his head swung to one side as he swallowed. "Where is he?"

"Greenland," she said. She was sorry to hear Jerry's grief; she was glad that Humphrey and Edmund had moved so far away, but . . . wouldn't she have joy at noon? Her son at home?

"I hope you don't think you can get away with lying."

Did she hear Janie and Tide coming down the second staircase? Would Janie have been able to hear the table fall over? Probably not. The rug was too thick. But Tide would have heard it; he might have felt it. Wasn't that Tide's toenails clicking down the bare second staircase? Maybe Tide had thrust his muzzle into Janie's hand, told her they needed to go downstairs.

"I said you need to leave. I'm telling you to leave." She raised her voice and stood up.

"I'll leave when I have the address. In Greenland or wherever the hell!" His voice was quite loud, clearly threatening. She was glad the heavy front door was standing open. It had started raining again. Maybe someone passing would hear, but no one was passing. The way the door was bent all the way back, with the outside facing in, seemed unnatural. The sperm whale door knocker that Humphrey had given her caught her eye. She looked away, lowered her voice. It was raining very hard again, beyond the porch. Rain like long harpoons.

Maybe Tide had told Janie, his muzzle in her hand, that they were needed downstairs, but not outside. First, the dog would just get Janie to go down the stairs; doggy business, she would think. But then, once on the first floor, he would indicate *not* outside. Not *that,* he would say. He would point himself at the kitchen door. A tiny whine. Telling her. Tide was a kind of animal angel. Yes, Tide did love her, at least for Janie's sake. Wouldn't he come down to help? *He's so smart.*

Suddenly she realized that she had mumbled aloud her admiring, pleading phrase. Almost blown her cover.

"What did you say?" Jerry asked. He, too, had risen.

"They just moved there." She remembered all Jerry's cruelty to Humphrey. She remembered the gun. "I'll have to go upstairs to get the address." She would create time for Janie and Tide, time to figure things out. Maybe Jerry would just go away if Janie and Tide showed up. "I don't know it off the top of my head. Their new address." Without waiting for his reply, she turned and started up the stairs. *Don't follow me,* she thought distinctly, with silent force.

After the turn in the steps, she glanced down. He was standing still, waiting in the foyer. Its four legs sticking out, the little table lay on its side on the carpet like a dead animal beside the road. Jerry was looking through the screen door at the rain, and she could hear the sweep of wind. She finished climbing the stairs.

Through the library, through the open arch into her bedroom. She opened the drawer to the printer, lifted out a sheet, and tore off a strip. Quickly she wrote down what seemed like a possible address for a city in Scandinavia, but she couldn't remember the name of a single city in Greenland, so she wrote down the name of a city in Finland she had once visited with Mark and a postal code that was a combination of numerals and capital letters.

At that moment, from below, Jerry shouted, triple forte, "Kathryn! Hurry up!"

With a spasm of fear, she dropped the pen. Then she opened the drawer and took out the snub-nosed Cobra. Her fingers shaking, she found bullets in the corner of the soft bag. She pushed bullets—mostly hollow nosed, *lethal*—into the chamber and turned the cylinder so that a loaded chamber was aligned with the barrel. Quickly, she slid her arms into the sleeves of a raincoat and put the gun in the right-hand pocket. She wouldn't use it, surely not. She believed that. But she would feel less afraid. She wanted to appear less afraid. He would not hurt her son.

In the library, when her ears filled with the sound of hard rain, Ryn realized she must have accidentally left a library window open all this time. She hadn't noticed earlier, diverted by the leaking ceiling. Yes, over there below the raised window in the library bay, the nice oak floor was wet, the little puddle was glimmering but that scarcely mattered. The whole house was leaking again; she could hear the rain coming through the ceilings and splattering into the trays and pans.

With her hands in front of her so she could watch them (they were shaking, palsied), she crossed the library—directly below, he would hear her steps—grasped the window, and lowered it with a bang. Everybody lowers a window hard when the rain's been coming in. Confined to outside, the rain sounded more normal. Yes, outside the house now. Under control. Not the whole interior universe filling with rain. She crossed the library back to her desk. Yes, with a warning bang—she had lowered the window and validated her detour.

She placed the strip of paper, like a little white flag, in her left hand so that it would be clearly visible and distracting and started down the stairs. She wanted to call out "Hold on," in a neutral way, but her larynx wouldn't engage. Familiar and warm against her right hand—already the cross-hatched handle of the gun was becoming friendly—the gun and her hand hid, concealed, up to her wrist in the slash pocket.

Trying to gather her wits and to quell her trembling, she took her time going down the steps. She wasn't going to have an accident, break her neck. Slowly, carefully, she released the gun and trailed her right hand on the oak handrail, so he could see both her hands. Grainy with dust trapped under the varnish, the handrail reminded her fingertips that it had never been as smooth or as polished as it should be. She had always criticized it, found it lacking. Sufficiently sturdy for balance, though. The weight of the gun in her pocket pulled the raincoat down on that side. She felt its weight swinging from her shoulder. But it was a small gun, with its truncated barrel. Compact. He wouldn't notice it in her pocket. *Never let anybody take the gun away from you.* Had she been advised that? Maybe she just knew it.

Maybe she'd been imagining it before, but now she was sure she could hear Janie and Tide descending the back stairs, beyond the wall, footsteps, dog toenails clicking down the servants' stairs, and she knew she'd left her kitchen door unlocked, near the bottom of their stairs. Unafraid, they moved more briskly than she and they would reach the first floor ahead of her, but their tempo was matter-of-fact, not excited or terrified. They would hesitate before opening her kitchen door. *Don't knock.*

Taking a long breath, Ryn resolved to spare them by doing whatever it was she was going to do quickly, before they traversed the kitchen, before they could pass the green table, cross the realm of blue and red, pass her mother's piano. She wouldn't let them get mixed up in what she had to do, but she mustn't hurry. At least Janie wouldn't see. Ryn wanted to aim for his head, his smirk, if she had to.

She believed she wouldn't need to shoot. Wasn't he ready to go now? But what if he came back tomorrow, when Humphrey was with her? What if he tracked Humphrey down, if she let Jerry leave? He'd done that before. Humphrey had run away, but Jerry had found him, sweet-talked him back. Before their final parting in Atlanta. That wouldn't happen now. Humphrey was a man now. He knew.

He had Edmund. Humphrey loved Edmund, thank God.

She couldn't hurry on the stairs, so shaky she was, old, old; her legs were like jelly. Really old and shaking now. He'd aged her ten years. And it made her angry. As she put her hand on the newel post at the turn, she wondered if Janie had an emergency attack command for Tide. He was a big dog. Ryn felt nauseous with anxiety.

At the bottom of the stairs, she said, "I don't feel too well."

"Having a chill?" he asked, gesturing at the raincoat.

"It's October," she said.

Jerry had moved deeper into the house. The little table was lying on the rug behind him now.

Like scratches, lines were all over his face. A fever blister on his lip, alone and palely loitering. Heavier. Of course she was shaking even though the paper was a dud. It carried no lethal message, would not take him to the realm of Humphrey and Edmund.

When she held out the paper with the address, her curled fingers looked a hundred years old and the skeleton visible inside. She had never seen such an old hand, a flag of death, of human fragility. She glanced at his eyes, made eye contact.

For the first time, his face was softening a little, surprised; he was registering her years.

She handed him the paper, and he studied it. "Greenland," he smirked, and turned his body a little, toward the door. Maybe he would just leave. She had always tried to believe the best about Jerry, about anyone of intelligence and occasional kindness.

She could hear Janie and Tide crossing the tiled kitchen, then the dog's toenails snicking on her parquet oak floor. Moving quietly, Janie and Tide were making their way past the kitchen table, stepping into the living room. A moment more and Jerry would be gone, but already from the living room, a low growl, more threatening than thunder, rumbled from Tide's throat, and he was picking up the pace; Janie's knee recklessly bumped the piano bench because they had started to hurry. Surely Jerry was hearing them, too. He turned fully back to Ryn with an expression of pure contempt.

The glance struck her like a blow to the face. Like a claw, his contempt snatched the skin off her face and the scales from her eyes. Humphrey had been at the mercy of this man. Why had she not been able to protect Humphrey, to keep him safe at home?

"Married, huh?" Jerry said. "Well, he can just shove it right up his rosy red rectum."

She cried out with pain, a high, weak protest, a keening like unprepared dying, and her hand and the gun came out of her pocket. Then the long streak of dog between them, lengthening and leaping, hurling his animal self into the man's chest and shoulders, his dog face shooting past the man's cheek, and Jerry falling backward onto the downed table, snapping off two legs, a moving scramble—

And Janie's shriek, penetrating everything, calling Tide back, and Jerry rising as quickly as he could from the wreckage, Kathryn pointing the gun at the man's face, and Janie's fingertips, light as spider legs, running down her sleeve and over her bare hand onto the gun.

"Don't shoot him," Janie said, her voice quiet and breathy. The room stilled and fell to silence. Standing beside Ryn, Janie said, "Never, ever come back here." Her voice was soft with tender wonder. It contained nothing of command. Where did Janie find that voice? Ryn was numb, yet she could move.

Her finger curled on the trigger, the gun in front of her, her hand in control, and she was sighting down the barrel, carefully. He turned his face in profile, unafraid, toward the door. He would leave now, but she knew she should not let him leave, unafraid and contemptuous. Because she mustn't allow him just to walk away, she took new aim and pulled the trigger.

Something like a scorch and the residue of an ax blow appeared beside his foot, a four-inch hole of blasted carpet and splintered oak. Now he was a-tremble. Now he had wetted and shat himself; now his face was crumpling into something infantile as she took much more careful aim, closer, precisely, and thought *Squeeze don't pull* and then the second shot, perhaps less deafening, a second shot she recognized as the everlasting echo of the first.

Not only the carpet blasted but also the very margin of his shoe. At the curve where his little toe might have lived, there was devastation, and the beginning of the flow of purple blood. Without looking back, Jerry rushed through the door, more noise than man, across the glazed porch, a swath of clothing hobbling. Then he was thumping down the rainy stairs.

Kathryn shrieked like a banshee, "I'm old and she's blind, but we'll kill you! We'll kill you, you devil. If you ever threaten me or mine again!"

Silence. Heaves of breath.

Tide whined and pressed against their legs. Janie heaved a deliberate breath, then exhaled slowly. She quietly asked, "Did you hit him?"

"With the second shot. I only grazed the side of his foot, winged his little toe."

"That's where I would have aimed, too," Janie said, "if I could see. You had to draw blood, Kathryn."

"Yes." But she couldn't think. She couldn't think why. Thinking was gone.

"He wouldn't learn otherwise." Janie's voice was sad, wondering.

Kathryn shuddered all over. She felt sick and weak, as though her brain had shaken loose and her nerves come untethered. Uncertainly she backed up to sit down on the stairs. Janie was feeling with her hand for structure, found the shape of things, and sat beside her on the carpeted step. Her hand searched for, then quickly squeezed, Ryn's hand.

"Do you think he'll go to the hospital?" Janie asked.

"I wouldn't think so. There's just a little blood on the carpet. He wouldn't want the police. He has a record."

Janie began to rub Tide, who shook his head as though his ears hurt. She told him he was a perfect boy, a good boy, that everything was all right now. He shook his ears like leather flaps. "You didn't hurt anybody," she said to the dog. "No, you didn't," and Ryn winced at the words. Now with both hands, Janie traveled Tide's body and his ears and caressed his head, all of him, reassuring him with her firm touch. Her slender fingers traced down his legs to massage his muscles and tendons. Finally he yawned, opening his mouth wide, showing all his strong white teeth, then glanced up at her face. For him, it was over.

Kathryn felt made of pumice, crudely carved. She answered mechanically when Janie asked where the gun was. "Beside me. On the stairs. Resting on the carpet." She glanced down at it: rather handsome, the snub-nosed revolver, its gunmetal gray against the wine-colored carpet. Then her eyes traveled to the broken table and the ravaged carpet. It could be rewoven, cleaned. The gunshots echoed in her mind, unbelievably loud. One. Two. And again. Once, twice. Her finger wanted to curl, no, to uncurl.

"You probably should unload, don't you think?" Janie said with that special tentativeness.

Kathryn didn't want to touch it. Not yet.

"So loud," Janie went on. "I'd forgotten how loud guns are. At the shooting range, we wore ear protection. These shots—they sounded like transformers blowing. People would have thought two transformers blew. Because of the storm."

"Yes. Like transformers." Something stirred and shifted in Ryn, rehinged itself. "Did you hear his car drive away?"

"Yes. Didn't you?"

"I can't remember."

"That's okay," Janie said. "We're all right." She put her hand on Ryn's knee and squeezed it. "We'll stay with you."

Ryn reached out and rested her hand on Tide's smooth head. She closed her eyes. What short hair, her fingertips remarked.

"Jerry won't come back," Janie said with complete conviction.

Ryn stood up: she would cross the room, she would close the front door. It surprised her how she was able just to get up, without thinking, automatically. Now she was stepping around the wounds in the carpet and floor. Her feet avoided the hole. There on the floor lay the strip of paper, the fictitious address. It looked crumpled. White for surrender. When she looked out at the street, she saw that Jerry's car was gone.

On the wet sidewalk in the drizzle, a child was walking along, unhurried, under an enormous black umbrella, walking south toward Belgravia. No raincoat; just the hem of a red-plaid skirt was visible, bobbing along under the adult-size umbrella. The way she walked was confident, purposeful.

When Ryn closed the door, locked the bolt, and turned, she registered her forgotten glass of pinot noir. As though nothing had happened, it still sat on the writing shelf of her mother's secretary desk. Next to the wineglass, the light caught two small, silver-framed photos: one of her mother and one of Humphrey, happy, by himself, in college.

JANIE AND TIDE STAYED with her for more than an hour, in the living room, and Ryn started the gas logs. They had tea together and some stale cookies. Once when a car passed, Tide lifted his head. The rain continued, and Ryn knew she would need to bail out the trays and empty the water-filled buckets after Janie and Tide went back upstairs.

Ryn remarked that she'd like for Janie to meet her friend Leslie, just recently moved in, across the Court. "She's down at Daisy's now. They're having wine together."

The fire feeling too hot for Tide now, he moved behind Janie's chair, the bulky gray chair, but Ryn wanted all the heat she could get. She put down a cushion and sat right in front of the fireplace, hugging her knees. Because she didn't know what to talk about, she told Janie about the circus painting over the piano, about the woman on the tightrope that had gone slack and the trapeze woman coming to help her.

"Did you think I would kill him?" Ryn asked. Yes, that was what Ryn wanted to know about herself, what she needed to ask.

In her special Janie voice, delicate as filigree, Janie answered—uncertain, nonjudgmental, suspended, honest—"I thought you might." Then Janie asked, "Shouldn't we talk more about it, Kathryn? Or something else?"

Ryn nodded, but they both fell silent. The gas flames, full of heat, made small lapping sounds.

"But you didn't kill him. You were distraught but you took careful aim."

"I could have. And I would have."

"I know that. But he left. You didn't have to."

"I fired the gun. I fired it twice. It was the real me who pulled the trigger. I knew what I was doing." Kathryn saw herself on the fantail of the ship. *One, two, three* she had unerringly exploded the clay pigeons against the blue sky.

AFTER A MOMENT RYN ASKED, "Do you ever dream about snow?"

Then she told Janie about a recent dream.

"Snow had fallen, *snow on snow,* as Christina Rossetti wrote in the Christmas hymn. At first I had an aerial view. Belgravia and St. James, and all the homes in Old Louisville, all the way to I-65. Around Central Park the Victorian houses were swaddled in snow a foot deep. All the walkways and streets were choked with fluffy white, and in my dream nobody had walked on it. Then I was watching from my porch, inside the columns, and I noticed an unbroken swoop of snow covered my front steps.

"A white horse came clomping down St. James pulling a white carriage, an open carriage. Inside, there was a bride swaddled in white fur, like something from another century or Siberia, or the future, straight from the imagination. She was by herself. They circled the fountain, and the carriage wheels left narrow black tracks in the snow.

"The water for the fountain had been left on, and the green statue of Venus was entirely encased in gleaming ice. I remember the slow, hollow sound, the clop-clop of the horse's hooves, but the sound was muffled, too, by the snow. The bride adjusted her fur stole; her hands were bare and red from the cold. Then the carriage finished the loop around the frozen fountain and headed north, back toward town."

Janie asked, "Has the fountain ever frozen that way?"

"Yes. It looked like that one year. Completely encased in ice. The wife of the man who takes care of it was very ill that year," Ryn explained, "and he forgot about the fountain."

They were both tired. Ryn had the pans and trays to empty. She wasn't nervous anymore, just worn out. She turned off the gas logs, and Janie and Tide started back upstairs.

"What's the name of his breed, again?" Ryn asked. Her memory seemed to refuse to absorb the strange word. But she wanted to think of him properly.

"Tide's a Vizsla, a Hungarian hunting dog."

PORTRAIT

S END FOR MY MOTHER," Julie said to her dark friend, Spanish or Italian, far from her own home, caring for Julie in Paris. The friend bathed
Julie's broad forehead with a hand smooth and cool as satin. Julie imagined her forehead had grown broad as a continent, broad as the steppes of
Russia, a forehead where fires burned, here and there, and caught the dry
grasses at their edges till the whole plain roared with flame.

From within a carriage, Julie's husband pointed at the sweep of grass
and said, "I will leave you here on the road if you do not obey me in all
things."

"The coachman would not allow you to do such a thing."

Beside her ear, Nigris, her husband, exhaled hard, a snort of disdain,
and she imagined his eyes peering at her through tall, lion-colored
grasses, and she tried again, speaking to him humbly, as though he might
care, as though perhaps he could understand. "How *can* I welcome you in
the bed when you offer no consideration or endearment during the day?"

He put his arm across her shoulders and though they both wore thick coats—for there was hoarfrost on the long, dry stalks of the steppe—she felt the tightening vise grip of his strength. Like a stubborn child, he refused to understand, no matter how pliant her question. He squeezed till she thought her breastbone would buckle inward. Detached, she watched the torture of her body, heard gasping. Then she remembered what she must say. "I'm sorry." Then quickly: "It is a sin to speak to you as I have. You must punish me tonight."

"How?"

"With the tongs, you must lift an ember from the fire . . ." She stopped. She licked her lips because they were too dry to form words.

"And place it where?" he prompted.

"I will roll over. On my bare shoulder. Like a brand. For a serf."

"No." He shook her, almost gently. "Are you actually trying to tease me?"

Then he compressed her till her tongue lolled out of her mouth and she struggled for breath. A cold linen napkin passed over her brow.

There now. There now. Julie? Did someone care about her? Long ago and far away?

Where will the tongs place the . . . his voice was dim. His question guttered and died. The wheels of the carriage turned and did not stop.

"Where is your mother?" the friend at her bedside—Isabella—asked.

"In England."

"We will find her," Isabella promised. A kind, strong voice promising, the way the open palm of a saint promises to produce a spot of blood at its center, if needed. A voice of smooth beauty, like the brow of Michelangelo's Virgin holding her dead son across her ample lap.

Your voice cradles me, Julie wanted to tell her friend. Isabella stood, and her skirt rustled. There was an urgency, but Julie wanted her friend to remain.

How can I support an engagement which will lead to a marriage that will never make you happy? her mother had asked. The question almost sounded sincere. Her mother's lips were parted, waiting. Her eyes were

moist with patient love, but when they brightened with hope, Julie knew
she must be firm. Her own way—she must have it, or her mother would
control her soul.

Isabella had already gone to summon a messenger, but Julie whispered
her message to the air. "Tell her I will forgive her."

"Bring a torch, Jeanette Isabella," Julie sang. A Christmas carol from
her youth. Her mother strumming the guitar and singing, *"Hush, hush,
beautiful is the mother; hush, hush, beautiful is the babe."* With three fingers
and her thumb, her mother plucked the complete chord up from the
strings. *Hush, hush.*

And days freezing and burning passed, but not many. Julie's fever
burned in her lungs, or the cold capped her head, but always her friend
touched her in the way she needed—with a hand warmed near a blaze
when she was cold; with a hand like a scoop of snow when she burned.

"This is the way of true friends," Julie managed to say, opening her
eyes to see the pure pity of the kind, dark face so like a Spanish Mother of
God. Her friend's gaze was there waiting to meet her own, wanting nothing for herself. Her friend, Isabella, did not understand what Julie meant to
convey, but Isabella nodded gravely and smiled a little. Yes, her friend had
understood. Because she understood everything.

What had happened between herself and her mother? She had loved
her mother so much, and then she hadn't. All she had wanted was to be
free of her. When she pushed her away, then she had to keep pushing her
away to justify what she had already done. Yes, Julie was young and it was
her right to smile on Nigris. There had been power in her smile. Her father
had understood, but he should not have kept so much of her mother's earnings. Her mother was determined not to care about that. And now Nigris
had it all, but she was free of him. She'd refused to travel with him; truly
reporting, she said she felt she was getting ill. He was glad to go back without her, and she was glad, too.

She sighed. Her mother liked to make something out of nothing. She
was good at it. A fabulous Greek party; everyone made beautiful with

drapery, borrowed Etruscan vases, real antiquity, lard and eels, and the little girl in the mirror, her mother fastening a final flower in her hair. Was she real? Was it she? Could Julie really cause that mirror child to raise her hand? To slowly turn her head?

Yes. There was her mother, seated close, with love in her eyes. From England. Finally. Older.

FOUNTAIN

WHILE RYN WAS FALLING ASLEEP that night, she thought of Virginia Woolf and also of the books she herself had written, about how she'd always advocated the preciousness of every life. Was it something she really believed? She had pulled the trigger. She had betrayed herself. She wondered what she could honestly write now. She wondered about everything.

Befriended by Janie, Ryn had been magically lucky, but she felt humiliated. She breathed deeply in, then out. And lucky, lucky, lucky. When she stretched out her arms on both sides, she could not reach the edges of the wide bed. It was like a chilly plain, an endless prairie. She had fired the gun; she could have gone on and on, firing it. She was capable of killing. She would not forget; she knew that much. She was grateful that Janie and Tide had come to help.

And what about Jerry?

She knew she was glad that he was alive, monstrous though he might have seemed. Was, in fact.

Glad that he still possessed his life? Glad she hadn't taken it. *Let him be.*

And couldn't she feel glad, too, in the world of her making? She had written the draft all the way to what she had thought was the end, *Portrait of the Artist as an Old Woman.* She could be proud of herself for that. Humphrey was proud of her. In the morning, she would add what she had just imagined, the scene she had forgotten to include; of course the death of Julie had had a place in Élisabeth's *Souvenirs.* In the morning she would reread the passage in French, the loss of Julie, as it had been recorded by her mother. Ryn would lie on the green sofa in the sunroom and easily hold the slender book, *Souvenirs de Madame Louise-Élisabeth Vigée-Le Brun, tome III,* in her hand, Nancy's gift.

Ryn didn't feel the least discouraged about forgetting to include an important scene: it was often that way in writing. Crucial things that had been left out eventually came to the surface, could still be included. Scenes rose up in you while you were driving a car, stopped at a red light. For no reason except that the psyche wanted them to exist, you suddenly saw things once repressed, heard incisive sentences. For a while after the putative finish, the imagination wouldn't stop working. She never tried to turn it off; she welcomed the new ideas.

Practicing the art of revision was the best part of the art of writing, for her. Then you had something, instead of nothing. But she was tired now and welcomed sleep.

THAT NIGHT, FOR THE FIRST TIME since he had moved out, Kathryn dreamed of Mark.

In her dream, he had let his hair grow long and curly, like the wig of Louis XIV in the painting at Versailles, but it was a contemporary dream, and she and Mark and his new wife—not the young nurse but another woman, still someone perhaps a decade younger than Kathryn—had gotten off a train, when Kathryn and Mark suddenly saw each other, surprised, in the crowded station.

He looked nice; for all its curly tumble, his hair was carefully groomed, with a part dividing the dome of his head into two hemispheres, but he seemed smaller. His wife's face was tanned and wrinkled as though she'd spent a lot of time in the sun, but her eyes were bright and intelligent, blue. His wife was a little shorter than Mark (they were both shorter than Kathryn would have expected), and the new wife moved quickly, like a girl with energy to please; her hair was shoulder length, caramel colored, and too girlish for her leathery face, but her eyes were self-assured.

Kathryn was surprised at how happy Mark looked. Enthusiastic. She read his face. He was living his life, starting over.

She felt happy, too, and smiled at them. Then she turned her face and her whole self away as she walked through the crowded terminal toward the door to the outside world—she was warm and confident—to begin again.

ACKNOWLEDGMENTS

I can never thank enough the people who are supporting my professional life as a writer: my agent, Joy Harris, and those at William Morrow/ HarperCollins: my editor Jennifer Brehl; publicist (for five books now) Sharyn Rosenblum; HarperCollins president and publisher of the General Books Group Michael Morrison; Morrow publisher Liate Stehlik; Morrow deputy publisher Lynn Grady; and Morrow senior marketing director Tavia Kowalchuk; as well as the entire team, including editorial assistants, copy editors, art designers, and the marketing and sales staff.

Looking back now at the nine books I've published, I also want to offer heartfelt thanks to other key people in my publishing life, including Marjorie Braman, Lisa Gallagher, Paul Bresnick, Michael Murphy, Marly Rusoff, Leslie Daniels, David Godine, Mark Polizzoti, Roger Weingarten, Martha Christina, and Jim Brady.

Writer friends/family who have read and generously commented at length and very helpfully on the various revisions of *The Fountain of St. James Court; or, Portrait of the Artist as an Old Woman* include Julie Brickman, Pam Cox, Lynn Greenberg, Nancy Jensen, John Sims Jeter, Robin Lippincott, Karen Mann, Nancy Brooks Moore, Eleanor Morse, Elaine Orr, Lucinda Dixon Sullivan, David Stewart, Deborah Stewart, and Katy

Yocom. I am grateful to each of you for bringing your expertise and encouragement to my work.

I also wish to thank friends old and new for their participation in the creative community that has buoyed me up: Eleanor Hutchens, Loretta Clark, Ralph Raby, Maureen Morehead, David Messer, Gerald Plain, Frank Richmond, David Sisk, Luke Wallin, Charles Entrekin, Frye Gaillard, Helena Kriel, Jody Lisberger, Daly Walker, Rob LaFreniere, Greg Ellis, Alan Naslund, John C. Morrison, Bernard Moore, Bill Campbell, Kay Callaghan, Nana Lampton, Pam Sexton, Kay Gill, Mary Rose Mattei, Elaine W. Hughes, Chervis Isom, Elizabeth Sulzby, Alice Gorman, Marilyn M. and James Rockefeller, Charles and Patricia Gaines, Phyllis and Jerry Rappaport, Suzette Henke and Jim Rooney, Annette Allen and Oz Wiggins, Kathleen and Terry Driskell, Rick and Corie Neumayer, Neela Vaswani and Holter Graham, and Kim and John Crum.

I am truly grateful for the support of University of Louisville president James Ramsey and provost Shirley Willihnganz, the late dean Blaine Hudson, and acting dean John Ferré, as well as my students and colleagues at U of L, where I have taught happily for nearly forty years; also that of Spalding University president Tori Murden McClure and provost Randy Strickland as well as former president Tom Oates who welcomed the creation of the M.F.A. in writing at Spalding some twelve years ago, and former president JoAnn Rooney; and to all the wonderful faculty and students of the brief-residency Spalding University Master of Fine Arts in Writing Program.

Most especially, I thank all the members of my family for their love and support: Flora, Ron, Lily, Ingrid, Hugo, Bubba, Charlotte, Amanda, Pete, Ella, Daniel, John, Derelene, Lisa, Gregg, Kristina, and Chase.

And for this book especially, I must thank all my friends and neighbors of St. James Court and Belgravia Court, who have done so much to maintain our special, diverse, and caring community in historic Old Louisville and to cause it to flourish. Meet you at the Fountain! Or at the St. James Art Fair, at the Holiday House Tour, at the Hidden Gardens Tour, in Central Park, during a stroll, or on some hospitable front porch!

—SENA JETER NASLUND